"I'm sorry I did not get there sooner."

"You saved my life. Don't apologize."

Rachael smiled, but it didn't reach her eyes. "The marriage would have been called off anyway, even if Tenney had not been so malevolent. I would never have been able to disrobe in front of him."

"A man worth his salt wouldn't care about the marks."

Devlin didn't care if the scars were hideous except for the part of them that hurt her.

"Thank you for your kind words."

"Honest ones."

"Delivered with kindness."

She reached to the lapel of his coat. "I must thank you. You are a rake on the outside, but a knight on the inside."

"I would say there is a lot of night, but not the kind you are thinking of. Do not place too much store in me. If Tenney loved you, he'd just be thankful you are alive."

He was.

The knowledge lodged in him with such strength his breath caught.

This would not do. She was not a woman for a rake and he had learned his lesson.

Author Note

The idea for the missive Rachael receives in this book originated after I read a letter written by a man who died in the 1800s. He was writing to his intended. They never wed. I really couldn't grasp the words at first, just as Rachael couldn't in this story.

I'm not certain about what happened to the woman who received the letter, but I'm convinced that the dissolution of the betrothal was the best thing that happened in her life. One source said she later married and had a large family.

Writing this book was an opportunity for me to imagine her happily-ever-after.

LIZ TYNER

—

A Cinderella for the Viscount

HARLEQUIN
HISTORICAL

HARLEQUIN®
HISTORICAL™

Recycling programs
for this product may
not exist in your area.

ISBN-13: 978-1-335-40722-1

A Cinderella for the Viscount

Copyright © 2021 by Elizabeth Tyner

This edition published by arrangement with Harlequin Books S.A.

For questions and comments about the quality of this book,
please contact us at CustomerService@Harlequin.com.

Harlequin Enterprises ULC
22 Adelaide St. West, 40th Floor
Toronto, Ontario M5H 4E3, Canada
www.Harlequin.com

Printed in U.S.A.

Liz Tyner lives with her husband on an Oklahoma acreage she imagines is similar to the ones in the children's book *Where the Wild Things Are*. Her lifestyle is a blend of old and new, and is sometimes comparable to the way people lived long ago. Liz is a member of various writing groups and has been writing since childhood. For more about her, visit liztyner.com.

Books by Liz Tyner

Harlequin Historical

The Notorious Countess
The Runaway Governess
The Wallflower Duchess
Redeeming the Roguish Rake
Saying I Do to the Scoundrel
To Win a Wallflower
It's Marriage or Ruin
Compromised into Marriage
A Cinderella for the Viscount

English Rogues and Grecian Goddesses

Safe in the Earl's Arms
A Captain and a Rogue
Forbidden to the Duke

Visit the Author Profile page
at Harlequin.com for more titles.

Chapter One

The night was a success, in spite of his beloved aunt's pianoforte song, which she'd composed just for the occasion. The supposedly short piece had been the opening music and had lasted just shy of one hour—or that was how long it had felt to Devlin.

Now the guests gathered for the La Boulanger. His mother always ended her events with a dance easier for tired feet.

Devlin stood at the edge of the room, knowing the wide circle of dancers would likely take up most of the area. He noticed Miss Albright standing at the other side. One woman he'd not partnered. She seemed content to stand behind everyone. Almost hiding near the curtains by the window.

Their eyes met as he caught her stifling a yawn and her cheeks coloured. He acknowledged her with a nod to say he understood and took no offence, before he glanced around the room so she would not feel singled out.

He should have spoken with her during the soirée, but he'd just not seen her earlier—which seemed impossible. Perhaps she'd arrived late. Or maybe she'd spent the evening wandering in the gardens.

Now she touched her necklace, pulled it to the side, then returned it to the position where it had originally rested at the top of an extremely demure bodice. She stared off into the distance, absently rubbing a ring, a bauble that overwhelmed her finger. Not what he would have chosen for her. Not what she would have selected for herself, he wagered.

He imagined she was thinking of a man now and whoever the man was—he wasn't in attendance. Possibly the one who'd given her the jewel.

Priscilla Tremaine twirled by Devlin, covering him in a cloud of perfume and interrupting his perusal of Miss Albright. Priscilla danced with her beau, Baron Bomford. The Baron took her hand as he stumbled, chuckled loudly and then almost tripped over his own boots. Priscilla laughed, her bosom quivering. Her partner paid more attention to Priscilla's chest than he did his feet.

Devlin put his glass on the table, his attention riveted on the couple as they finished their rotation around the room.

The dance needed to end sooner rather than later. Priscilla and the Baron were likely to embarrass themselves. Bomford was hearing a different song from the one the musicians played.

Then Bomford turned in the wrong direction and Priscilla reached out to correct him, shoving him into the steps. The Baron jumped a few feet to catch his balance, but stumbled, his arm splayed towards Miss Albright.

Miss Albright caught his sleeve, trying to keep him upright, but he took another step, reached with his free arm and grabbed a side table, pulling a scarf which covered the tabletop.

A lamp on the table wobbled, its flame flickering. Devlin couldn't hear the music or comprehend anything else in the room but the flame inside the glass globe, the oil and the dislodged fabric under the base.

Then the table stopped moving. Devlin's shoulders relaxed. The lamp rested completely immobile. Safe. The oil inside burning softly.

Everyone in the room watched Priscilla and her partner, including the musicians. The room echoed with silence.

The Baron noticed everyone had ceased talking. 'My apologishes.' He took a handkerchief from his pocket, mopped his brow, then took a reverse step, bumped into the table, reached out his arm and this time knocked the lamp askew. It rolled off the table and Miss Albright's skirts fluttered as she stepped aside.

Devlin saw all the flammable fabrics. The scarf from the table. The curtains. Miss Albright's skirt. The lit wick. All too close to Miss Albright.

He darted forward as the globe shattered, its glass collapsing into shards. The bowl of the lamp cracked, oil leaking into a puddle. Flames flickered at the wick, which would be easily extinguished with a stamp of his boot. Not yet igniting the oil.

Then Bomford turned, grabbing a glass from Lord Wilberton's hand. 'No,' Devlin shouted, lunging as he spoke. But it was too late. The Baron flung the alcohol in the glass on to the flames, splashing wide of the curtain, across the oil and over the wick, and sending the now-burning oil on to Miss Albright.

Devlin was already across the room when the liquid

splattered across the flame and reached Miss Albright's skirt, igniting the flicker into a flash.

He knew what was about to happen before the flame began to take the light silk that covered her body. In two strides he had ripped the curtain from the rod, tackled Miss Albright and threw himself forward. He thrust the heavy fabric around Miss Albright to extinguish the fire. He wound the material tightly, forcing her into the wall, suffocating the flames, and slid her down to the floor. One of her arms splayed out. The other wrapped around his neck and her fingers grasped a handful of his hair. He pressed the curtain even closer, using his body as a shield, ignoring the other guests, only minimally aware of the people behind him.

He found himself in an awkward position in a hushed room, one knee on the floor, his hands holding curtains firm around Miss Albright's skirts as she kept one hand clasped on his hair and her other hand reaching out to steady herself against the wall. The smell of burnt silk hit his nostrils and the side of his face pressed into an amazingly soft bit of femininity with a heartbeat close to his ear. He took in a breath and let the scent of her skin replace the singed cloth.

For an instant, he was frozen. He held too much in his arms, and emotion overtook him. He could feel life in his hands and the seconds before could have changed so much.

'Did you put her out?' His mother's voice rang in his other ear. He preferred listening to the racing heart, but he pulled away, Miss Albright still clutching his hair. Their gazes locked, a second that lingered, then she released him.

'The fire's gone.' He again tucked the curtain firmly

around her, took her hand and put it on the fabric to hold it in place, then helped her stand. He made sure the burned spots displaying an appealing bit of beribboned chemise were covered.

'Oh, my. My dear.' His mother brushed past Devlin and took charge of the accident. 'Are you hurt, Miss Albright?'

Devlin's eyes connected with Miss Albright's still-dazed ones.

'I'm fine. But I don't know...' she whispered, wincing. She touched the curtain, slim fingers trying to arrange the cloth into a skirt.

No one seemed to know what to do next.

His body took over again and he sidestepped around his mother and slipped an arm under Miss Albright's knees and slid his other at her back. He watched her eyes, making sure the pain on her face didn't increase, and lifted her with all the gentleness he could muster. She gasped and now her arm rested loosely around his shoulder. He heard a second gasp which might have been his mother's, or her mother's. 'I'll take her to the sofa in the library so you ladies can care for her and I'll have the physician summoned.'

His face rested against her tresses and the strands brushed his cheek. The smell of freshly laundered clothing overrode the scorched scent and she wore a soft flowery perfume.

'Are you injured?' He spoke no louder than a whisper as he wove through the stunned observers.

'Yes. I think...not much.' The now husky timbre of her voice reassured a pleasant spot in him.

He put the guests behind him and shortened his stride as he reached the library. 'If you have need of anything…' his lips touched her hair '…be sure to let me know. It will be taken care of.'

He tensed his body so he could lower her on to the sofa without jostling her more than necessary.

Two ball gowns fluttered around him and he knew the mothers were on either side.

'I'll reassure the guests.' He kept his eyes on the sofa while he straightened his cravat.

Miss Albright looked at him as her mother stepped up to her and his mother pushed at his chest to nudge him further from the room. He felt a second determined prod.

He left, his steps swift to return to the guests with a reassuring expression on his lips. But he could still feel her in his arms.

Devlin opened his eyes in the darkness and twisted his head on his pillow. He pressed at the support behind his head. Sleep was impossible.

Before she'd retired, his mother had whispered, averting her eyes, that their guest had a few small burns on her…leg.

So, they were to be having visitors for the next two days while his mother reassured herself that Miss Albright recovered nicely. It simply would not do for the girl to be jostled in a carriage.

He slung the covers from his body. Stood. Pulled on the trousers he'd tossed over a chair and the shirt he'd worn earlier, ignoring the waistcoat.

He needed a cigar and a splash of brandy. Or maybe more than a splash. He kept thinking about Miss Albright.

The rug cushioned his bare feet and he glanced down the deserted, meandering hall, feeling alone in the house.

Devlin navigated the hallways easily in the dark, running a fingertip along the wall for direction as he found the library.

The door stood open and he saw the flickering light. His heartbeats increased as he imagined Miss Albright sitting inside. He needed to reassure himself she was fine.

Disappointment plunged into him when he stepped into the room. Instead of Miss Albright, his cousin, Payton, sat on the sofa, reading a book, brandy in one hand and a swirl of smoke at his head.

'Can't sleep?' Devlin asked.

Payton stifled a cough and quickly pulled himself into a dignified pose. He placed the book on the table at his side, as if he didn't know who the novel belonged to.

'Bit of a cramp in my leg. Had to get comfortable.' He put his hand over the title of the story. 'Best toddle off to bed now. Thank you for inviting me to spend the night. B'lieve I shall.' He stood, stretched wide and grunted a manly groan.

Devlin reached for the cigar box, helping himself. 'You can't leave behind half a glass and half a cigar. Finish your reading and I'll try to amuse myself by annoying you. Mother will be so impressed you're reading the same stories she does.'

Payton examined the cover. 'I picked it up by mistake, thinking it was another of your father's books of pirate stories. Bloodthirsty men.' He mimicked a seafaring growl. 'Yes. Pirates. I'm sure I'll find one in it somewhere. Need to make certain I've not missed one.'

His cousin plopped down, took the book again and glanced over the top of it while he reached for the glass. 'Please stay. In case I catch on fire. But if I do happen to get myself aglow—do not graciously—' he stared at the ceiling '—lift me gallantly into your arms to rescue me.'

'I won't.'

Payton sniffed. 'I say, if Baron Bomford had managed to get a bit of a burn, you'd have let him walk to the physician.'

'Yes, but she has a much better shape than he does.'

'So does a sow.' Payton frowned. 'Everyone talked about her after you whisked her from the gathering. She has a beloved, so don't get any ideas that her gratitude would stretch far. If it weren't for her father being in trade, she's the type of woman that a mother wishes for her son to settle with.' His exaggerated half-cough, half-choke filled the room. 'I'll wager she has her embroidery needles named.'

Devlin lit a cigar, using the candle. 'You've got your decanters named.'

Payton gave a brief shrug. 'Makes it easier for the servants.'

'So, what does her father do?'

'Sells silver wares, mainly. Shiny trinkets, too. Jewellery. But Father says if you've seen one of the shops, you've seen them all.'

Devlin nodded. His mother had mentioned the family a few days before, but he'd not paid close attention. 'Thankfully Miss Albright seems relatively unscathed from the soirée.'

'Everyone counted the evening as a success. The ladies swooned.' His cousin's lip curled up at the side, his hand rose in a wave and his voice became high pitched. 'Did you see what big strong arms Devlin has? He can set my skirts on fire any time he wants.' He returned to the pages of the book again, shaking his head. 'Was blasted embarrassing to listen to all the babbling about you. Those ladies spoke improperly. I was shocked.'

'Jealous?' Devlin sat, then, with his foot, he hooked the upholstered footrest and moved it into place so he could prop his feet on the woven fabric.

Payton spoke under his breath. 'No. I've my hands full enough now.' Again, he stared over the top of the novel at Devlin. 'I don't have to let someone else start the flames for me. Once they get sight of me, they melt.'

'I'm sure.'

'I suppose you have been keeping her a secret be-cause you know that she'd never notice you if I am in the room.'

'I'd never met her before the soirée. Mrs Albright hap-pened to be at Hatchard's a fortnight before and Mother remembered her from a childhood friendship and invited the family. They're related to someone in the peerage whom Mother knows well. I can't remember who.'

Devlin grimaced. 'I hope Miss Albright doesn't now regret that fate put her mother on the same path as mine.' Then he reflected. 'Miss Albright must use some special pomade on her hair or something. She smelled rather like a jonquil.'

'Jonquils don't smell. Do they?'

'They do. The red ones.'

'Jonquils aren't red.'

'The pink ones, then. You know—' he waved his hand '—the ones with the little petals.'

'Primroses.'

'I don't know. A thistle bloom or something. Nice. Flowery.'

'You're thinking with your thistle.' Payton stared at the print. 'So, will you be going with us tomorrow, or

will you be staying here, alone, hoping for a miss to mistake you for your handsome younger cousin?'

Devlin paused. 'I don't have a handsome younger
cousin.'

'Sad. To be losing your sight at twenty-eight.' Payton
paused. 'So, are you going with us to Cosgrove's hunting
box? We'll all be stalking our prey—at the card table.'

'Yes. But I may be late joining you. I must reassure
myself our guest is doing well. She had a *most* attractive derrière. Damn—she smelled good, too. A perfect
female.'

He heard the stout snort and raised his head to Payton, but Payton stared at him, open-mouthed.

He heard a feminine voice and turned his head to
the doorway.

'I would not say those are the qualities of a perfect
woman, Viscount Montfort.' Miss Albright stood at the
entrance. Even in the dimness he could still see the last
of the lingering grimace on her face. He'd judged her
too delicate and too winsome to give such a healthy
blast of disapproval.

'Oh, Miss Al…bright.' He stood.

'Thank you for saving my life and sniffing my hair.'
She stayed in the doorway. 'It's rose-scented. I like
roses.'

'Roses are pleasant,' he said. 'Way better than jonquils.'

Payton stood as well, tossing down a healthy swig of
brandy, snuffing out his cigar, then giving a most elaborate bow to Miss Albright.

'Don't hurt him,' Payton spoke to the woman as she
walked into the room. 'It's not his fault he's daft. He's

never recovered from the thumping I gave him when he was ten and I was only eight. Almost did him in.'

He slipped to the doorway and, as he stood behind her, he raised his brows, gave an exaggerated wink, put one lone finger over his closed lips, grinned and went out, still carrying the romantic novel.

She limped into the room.

'Do we need to send for the physician again?' Devlin asked, not taking his gaze from her.

'Absolutely not. My *most attractive* derrière—thank you, I think—hurts. I cannot sleep. Your mother told me earlier to make myself at home and I could have a maid bring me something to read if I woke in the night. I did not wish to wake a maid. I presumed this was the library. And I could have sworn your mother said smoking was not allowed in this side of the house.' She fanned a hand in front of her face. 'I must have misheard.'

'It's only allowed in the wee hours of the night and only for a short duration. A rule my father instituted and only the males are aware of the concession. Generally.'

But he couldn't keep his mind off her injury. 'I hope you recover quickly.' He waved an arm to the side of the sofa Payton had just vacated. 'Would you prefer to—?'

'Stand.' She limped inside the room. 'But please sit.'

He took a step to reach for the pull, but caught himself before he asked if she would like a maid present. Her hair billowed about in the candlelight. The borrowed dressing gown she wore was much too large for her and appeared as if it might slip from her shoulders at any second. Her bare feet poked out from the hem. The maid could sleep. He put out his cigar. If Miss Albright needed anything, he would happily fetch it for her.

He took a candle and lit the one nearest the bookcase before returning the light to its place. 'And in case you're wondering, my hair smells of acorns. My cousin Payton's valet has been using it on him since he was born and Payton swears the mixture will keep the hair growing freely.'

He took two steps, stopping beside her, yet leaving a comfortable distance. 'See?'

She moved forward, touched the sleeve of his shirt and leaned in, sniffing. 'That's a different scent.'

He held himself proud. *Imported.*

'Did your cousin swear by it or swear at it?'

He studied the wide eyes which had a devilish glint. 'I do regret the accident, but it doesn't seem to have impaired you in any way. Particularly your sense of humour.'

'Other than a distinct inability to feel comfortable sitting.' She shrugged and smiled—the brightest one he'd seen from her. 'Or a distinct inability to feel comfortable anywhere.'

She glanced at an empty chair and he imagined he saw longing in her face. He could not sit down in her presence. It would be unthinkable.

'I have huge gratitude for you rescuing me,' she continued. 'But only a most proper kind. I do appreciate your help. And the pomade doesn't really smell bad. Just woodsy. Autumnal.'

'I regret the fire and wish it had been me instead of you, but to hold such a lovely lady was a boon for me.'

Her cheeks grew a little pink and she tucked her head, seeming embarrassed. 'You've had many boons in your life?'

'Only the necessary amount, I would say.' Then he frowned. 'But embracing you was something I will never forget.' He'd spoken the words easily enough. He'd just slipped into the light-hearted banter he might speak with friends he'd known for a long time. Perhaps it was because of the lateness, or the way she'd remained in his mind from the first moments before the fire until now.

The moment he'd rushed across the room, he'd felt his own life was threatened and it had seemed necessary to his survival to protect her. He supposed it must have been because she was in his home. A primitive response and one he was thankful for.

Then he appraised her, shoving all the nonsensical words he spoke so easily from his mind, even though with her they didn't seem meaningless. Miss Albright seemed to enter his senses more quickly and deeply than any of the acquaintances or friendships he'd had in the past.

Perhaps it was her seriousness, something he usually avoided. Only on her, it didn't appear critical or condescending or even truly serious, just thoughtful and aware.

'Though I would have preferred our meeting under better circumstances in safer surroundings.'

The words jabbed at him, almost like a lie might attack his conscience. It was true he would have done anything in his power to prevent the accident, but he felt a sliver of fear that if it hadn't happened, he might have foolishly missed the chance to speak with her.

'I won't forget it either,' she said. 'And I do thank you. I'm fortunate you were there.' She shuddered. 'It could have been so much worse. My parents are so relieved you reacted as you did. Father believes you saved my life. He said he'd just not been able to comprehend what was happening and then it was all over.'

'Let's forget about the evening and just remember this part of it. How could I not be intrigued by a woman who makes me think of—toasted roses?' He wanted to put her in a better humour and not only for her. For himself as well. When she smiled, it made everything else fade into oblivion but her face.

She grimaced. 'Your eyes followed Priscilla's every step.' She met his upraised brows and raised her own. 'Or perhaps it wasn't her steps you were watching.'

So, Miss Albright had observed him. 'Priscilla has lovely eyes.'

'She has very big, plump ones,' she said.

He nodded. 'Eyes are important features for a person to have.' He locked his gaze with hers. 'Your eyes are beautiful beyond measure.'

She bit her lip, studying him, her cheeks flushing again.

'You may take that as a sincere and respectful compliment, as it was meant so. All of my observations about you are meant as appreciation of your womanliness and not to impinge on your respectability.' He ended the words with a slight, respectful bow for emphasis. 'And perhaps some normal preening male jealousy. You did seem aware of someone else and I cannot imagine you not having a sweetheart.'

She interlaced her fingertips and let out another whoosh of air, this one a reflection of the awe in her eyes. 'Mr Ambrose Tenney. He is my beloved. The way that little lock of hair keeps tumbling over his eyebrow. He even has a dimple.' Touching her cheek, she breathed out. 'And his hands—so elegant. We are to be married.'

He held out his own hand, examining it while he turned it up and then reversed direction. 'You can't possibly expect me to believe you've accepted marriage based on this Tenney's hands.'

He stretched his arm, staring. 'Blast it. I will never be able to wed or even dare ask a woman to be my wife.'

She raised her brows. 'What?'

He reached her in direction, showing her. 'I will never be able to compete with Mr Tenney. I have been marred.' He wiggled the smallest digit. 'Little finger.'

She took his fingertips in her own and his body started warming. The room was dim—too dim to be proper and they had been through a considerable adventure. She made him feel stronger than he ever had before, yet he'd never felt so weak.

She bent over his hands, examining them. 'Yours are…adequate, even if the one is out of alignment with the rest of them.'

Her lips turned up. 'I'm jesting with you when I use the word adequate. You saved me. Right now, I find them capable and competent. The best in the world. And the crooked one is distinguished. One might say elegant. Definitely distinct enough to make others jealous.'

'I would not go that far.' Inside he beamed. Miss Albright could dispense flattery if she wished.

'My cousin and I were playing king of the castle and the encounter became frenzied. I pushed him off the hill and he planned to take me with him, and that was all he could grab. I wasn't going off the mound.'

'Maybe you should have relented. Lost the game to save pain.' She tapped the little finger.

His hands were not the part of his body her touch affected.

'In hindsight, I could have let him tug me to the bottom and landed on him. So, for his sake, perhaps it was for the best. I would have used him as a cushion,' he said. But he understood something else about himself in that instance. The pain hadn't really hurt and he'd wanted to win. He would have repeated the incident just as he had initially done it. A clear victory. His father claimed nothing else mattered in a battle but a decisive win.

She glanced up, running her fingers over his knuckles, the touch so light he wasn't sure he imagined it. 'His hands aren't the only thing I admire about Mr Tenney. He's a barrister and will make a name for himself. He is so ambitious. That is one of the things I like most about him. That he's constantly striving to become more successful. I should like you to meet him some day, Viscount Montfort.'

Everything she'd just said singed him. He had no desire to meet Tenney. 'Whatever you wish,' he said. 'Except my given name is Devlin Bryan and I'd prefer to think we know each other well enough for you to call me Devlin as my friends do.'

'It would be an honour.' Her face bloomed as if he'd just given her a bouquet. 'And I would be pleased if you would call me Rachael.'

Then she turned. Leaving. Bidding him goodnight. Limping to the doorway.

'Rachael.' His words stopped her. 'You did not select a book. Please stay longer. We've shared such an adventure that I feel I have known you for ever. A few moments more of your time would be a treasure—that is—if you aren't in pain.'

Chapter Two

Rachael stopped and turned to Devlin, a man who'd taken her in his arms when they'd both been reduced to instinctive beings. In those brief seconds, he'd changed from a stranger whom she'd converse with reservedly to someone with whom she could speak her mind.

He was half-dressed, of course, only wearing a shirt and trousers, but it was his family home and it was the middle of the night. And she was wearing a borrowed dressing gown with no corset or chemise under it, hoping the cloth would not touch her burned skin.

Their familiarity seemed shared and, by the ease in his face, he didn't want to leave any more than she did.

Their bond surprised her. He wanted her to feel comfortable in his home and she did, but perhaps only because he was in the room.

Nothing else mattered to her but that she distract herself from the small ache in her posterior—and when they talked, the pain all but disappeared.

She'd regretted refusing the laudanum after the first dose, but she hated the way it made her feel—more a cloud than a person—a wisp of who she was—and her mind seemed dislodged.

Devlin distracted her in a completely opposite way. She could keep her feet on the ground and her mind safely in the room.

'I don't feel like reading.' Rachael took careful steps back, yet remained outside the doorway. 'Instead, I'm a bit like a child who doesn't want to go to bed and who is too tired to sleep. And my you-know-what hurts like it's still on fire.'

If she'd returned to her bedroom, she would have had to try to sleep on her stomach and doubted she could even doze off.

He took two steps closer, but didn't cross the entrance to the library. 'Stay for a chat, then. I've never been accused of an over-abundance of maturity and I'll attempt to ease the pain with nonsense. I can summon up a great deal of nonsense on occasion. Buckets of it.'

He leaned forward, and said, 'In fact, I can't think of the word maturity ever being used in reference to me.' His brow furrowed. 'Blasted oversight on someone's part, I'd say. Wouldn't you agree?'

'That's a trick question to ask a guest.'

'So, you don't think that was an accidental oversight?' He beckoned her. 'Tell me the benefits of maturity. Those have never been explained to me in detail. Or in any convincing way.' He stepped back. 'I don't think you can.'

In one second, something flittered behind his gaze. A seriousness, immediately replaced by a carefree air, and a lopsided grin. She recognised the ruse. He was bent on distracting her, just as she'd wanted.

Suddenly, she felt cosseted. She didn't want to hurt,

though, and only by playing the game would the relief continue.

'I doubt I could. I doubt anyone could.' She angled her head in a challenging pose.

'Try.'

She walked towards him. 'Maturity. You either have it or you don't.'

He strode to the window, opened the curtains wide, propped his shoulder against the wall and regarded the night. 'Well, that's my excuse then.'

She stationed herself at the other side of the curtains and copied his pose. She was so tired of standing.

The jesting evaporated. 'I've always been mature,' she said. 'I was born so. If the governess did not watch my sister or me closely, I would make certain that neither of us got into any trouble. In fact, the woman would usually nap during the day and I would wake her if my sister needed something I could not take care of. My mother once reprimanded me for not playing.' She gave a quick glance to the ceiling. 'She said I must let the governess do her job. So, I did. Except on rare occasions when I knew I must step in.'

'I had a problem with my governess about play also.' He flattened a fold of the curtain aside. 'My governess fell asleep once, too. On the same day a poor mouse had met a disastrous fate in the stables. I took the mouse and tied a string on it and pulled it across her feet. She woke up, screeched and clouted me. I predicted she would keep silent as she'd smacked me.'

'Did you tell your parents?'

'No. I feared my father might take her side and I knew my mother would not appreciate the humour in my bringing a dead mouse into the house. So, I disposed of it just as the governess insisted.' He took the curtain between two fingers of his right hand and waved it back and forth. 'She didn't tell me specifically not to put it under her bedcovers. After all, she had clouted me.'

He dropped the curtain. 'I had to spend the whole next day fetching things for her, and returning them, and when I refused and went to Mother… Mother sent me to the governess, telling me that no mice were allowed in the house and boys who brought them in would be forever fetching handkerchiefs or having to listen to their governess sing. My governess sang a lot of songs that day, mostly ones she made up about boys who had to be good…had to be good…had to be good, and she had a voice that permeated the walls and stuck like a knife in the ear. The mouse was not worth it.'

'And if you had a child who did the same thing would you severely reprimand him and silently congratulate him? Or just laugh?'

He touched his chin with a knuckle on his left hand. 'I would be concerned if I had a son who did not do such things. Much like your mother who told you to play. A child must be a child. Then they must be punished and taught to act like an adult. It's the way of growth.'

'Why? If you can skip that level of immaturity?'

'Let us say that you received a double portion of adulthood at birth and I received none, and I have grown to the stage of acting as a man when I am with women, at social functions and when necessary. When I am with other men, I relax and revert to the way nature intended us to behave.'

'That is a shame.'

'Depends on your perspective.' He straightened. 'But I have the most enjoyment.'

'Perhaps not,' she challenged. 'Perhaps I get my personal reward from being responsible at all times.'

'Well, I fear that is something I may never know. But I do know how much enjoyment I get from being irresponsible.' The grin returned and her heart bounced closer to the sky. He was an effective painkiller. Better than laudanum, though, perhaps, not as safe.

She almost laughed. Perhaps all the medication hadn't worn off. She pulled herself back to earth.

'You get enjoyment to a degree from being irresponsible,' she said. 'Even you have boundaries. Everyone has limits. Some are just set further apart.'

'You are right,' he said. 'You're correct, as I hope you always are.' He held up a pinch. 'Your limits.' He widened his fingers. 'My limits.'

'Truly?' she asked.

'Let me believe it. I would hate to think I've put all the adventures of my youth behind me.'

'Well, you did jump into the flames earlier. I'm pleased you didn't have a sensible reaction then.'

'It was the only one possible, Miss Albright.' He stared at the darkened window. 'If I had left earlier...' He shuddered. 'I wanted to. My brothers had already left.'

She felt the need to reassure him she was fine. To remind him he had been there and had done the right thing for her.

Putting a hand on his forearm, she grasped it. 'Thank you.'

When she realised what she'd done, she froze, then whipped her hand away. His shirt was paper thin. Much thinner than it appeared in the candlelight. Warmth, fine hairs and masculinity had answered her touch. She curled her palm close to her stomach and covered it with her other hand. She had to say something to erase the fact she'd touched him. She'd not planned it. It was a mistake. Something had been different. He was different from Tenney. Whereas Tenney was a balm, Devlin ignited something inside her.

He didn't even seem aware, which somehow felt like a slap, and he returned to the window. Nothing flickered in his gaze. Instead, he gave her a brief bow. 'Let's not repeat it, but it was the finest point of my life, I think. And I had nothing to do with it. I didn't know what was going on until I stopped and there was a…' He cleared his throat. 'The smell of burnt roses was in my arms and I knew you were uncomfortable, and I had to get you to privacy.'

Letting the silence continue, she wandered to the shelf with novels, and selected the one nearest her, without paying attention to its title. She needed to break the mood.

The spine creaked when she opened the book and she held it, letting her eyes linger on the words she couldn't read in the dim light.

'It is so odd how the night turned out,' she said. 'Mother was happy to see the invitation from the Countess. I almost feel apologetic that I ended the event. I'm thankful you were here.'

He returned her honesty with some of his own. 'I didn't get an invitation. I received a note to keep my evening free and was given the time to show up in evening dress.'

'You are a good son to do that.'

'Easy enough. I had to be somewhere on earth tonight, so why not here? It makes my mother happy and she asks for so little that I'm pleased to respond to her summons. One night absent from the clubs is almost a relief. Though it was getting dull until—'

He touched the windowpane's edge, flicking aside something invisible to her. 'One moment and the world changes for ever, according to the old pontificators at the club, and they are right. Perhaps that is why I buy them drinks and listen to their claptrap.'

Now that she watched him more closely, it was almost as if she could absorb the caring and generosity behind his eyes, but she questioned if it was caused by the late hour, the situation, or if he just naturally had a face that pulled her attention closer. She examined him again. His face. It did welcome her. A gift he'd been given by his birth.

He stepped forward.

She shut the book, tucking it under her arm. He took her fingertips and awareness pulsed inside her. She assumed he was going to kiss her hand, and in the light, and the night, and their improper dress, it would have been so much more than just a touch of his lips. Perhaps he discerned it at the same time she did.

He stared at her fingertips and rubbed a thumb over them, sending calming shivers into her. The moment brought her peace. A feeling of safety and security.

'If we were judged by the beauty of our hands, we would all be put to shame by comparison to yours.' Her fingers slipped from his when he increased the distance.

'That is kind of you.' Her words were a whisper and she didn't think he even heard them.

'Goodnight, Rachael. I hope you think gently of me and understand that I'm happy on my path of foolishness and jests, and I hope you gain much from your responsible life.'

'Thank you.'

Then his face changed and she could observe nothing beyond the penetrating eyes focused on her.

'Forgive my impetuousness. I must leave. You are a betrothed woman and I am a rake. In this case, it is a combination which can't be mixed, much like silk and fire. I must remember that.'

'Surely a few words between us runs no risk of anything untoward.' She didn't want him to leave. But it was only because she wanted to be distracted. Only because the day had been eventful. Only because they were becoming friends.

'No risk with a few words,' he said. 'But I feel we could speak long hours into the night and, as tiredness encroached, you might forget your maturity and do something foolish. I tell you as a friend that I would be hoping so with all my being.' On those words, he left, his footsteps not making a sound.

Chapter Three

Rachael recovered alone in a small bedroom, painted with gentle hues of blue and with paintings of flowers. Every blossom in England had to be represented in the room and she wasn't sure she liked them as much as she had before. Now she was afraid that every time she saw a bloom, she would associate it with a burning sensation.

She propped herself on one crossed leg while she returned to her book.

Breakfast at the Earl's estate had been informal, which had relieved Rachael's mother immensely, and Rachael had been given the option of taking breakfast alone or joining the family. She'd reassured both her mother and the Countess that she was fine and chose to remain in her room.

That evening, someone rapped at the door. Rachael untucked her leg from under her and stood. 'Please come in,' she called out.

A maid entered, carrying two dresses, a small portmanteau and a paper in her hands. 'Your father returned home and sent these things to you.' The maid bustled around, arranging the clothing. 'And your mother and the Countess are taking tea and wanted to know if you might join them, but will understand if you don't wish to.'

'I think I will be fine here,' Rachael said.

Then, before leaving, the maid gave her the letter. 'Your father also sent this.'

Rachael took it, feeling a pleased flutter in her stomach when she saw Mr Tenney's handwriting. She'd never seen anyone who could make such beautiful flourishes. Her name had never flowed so elegantly as when Mr Tenney wrote it.

She'd waited all through his university years and, now that he was becoming established as a barrister, they were to be wed soon. The unfortunate death of his grandmother had postponed things, or they would have already married.

Rachael ran her fingertips over the letters of her name and it was as if she'd been at his side while he penned them.

Then she slipped open the seal. She read and the words didn't make sense to her. She read the words again, going slower, taking her time with each one.

She folded the paper, waited, then unfolded it and read again.

They were to be married.

Were to be married.

Her betrothed.

She scrutinised the letter again. Surely it was a mistake. It looked like his handwriting, but…

He said he still wanted to marry her. He said it plainly.

She folded the paper once more and then again, hands shaking, then she took the missive and shoved it under her pair of gloves that rested on the table.

He still wanted to wed her.

They were to be married.

She rushed to pull the letter free and read it again. Yes, he still wanted to marry her. But the letter didn't make sense. He said at the beginning of the page and again, near his signature, that he would marry her. Yet it was as if all the words in the middle had been written by someone else and obviously the man who'd written them had no regard for her whatsoever.

She touched her face. Never had anyone criticised her so much.

She studied it closer, trying to comprehend something that she didn't understand. Her mind was playing some kind of trick on her, surely.

The movement and tension in her caused her injury to ache again and now it spread throughout her body.

Someone knocked at the door. She shoved the letter under the gloves again.

'Yes?' she called out, turning.

'We just wanted to make sure you are still doing well.' Her mother walked in as she spoke, the Countess right behind her. 'We had a lovely day and wish that you could have walked with us in the gardens. I even sent a letter to your sister to let her know that she needn't leave her husband's side in her condition and that you are on the mend.'

Rachael flexed her fingers out of sight. She bit her bottom lip. 'I'm well. Much better. Ever so much. But I wish not to jostle myself too much.'

He mother stilled. 'I understand. Are you positive you're healing?'

Rachael nodded, but stopped when her chin quivered. 'The physician told me it would be tender. Might feel worse before recovering.' Rachael rubbed her forehead. 'I've just been moving. Made it flare up again.'

'You needn't be brave, dear,' the Countess said. 'I will send for the physician immediately.'

'No. No. I'm fine. I'm fine. Really.' Rachael heard her sniffle and tried to turn it into a cough. 'It's just been a trying day, without resting well last night. That's all it is. I didn't sleep much and that's what's bothering me.'

'Rachael Marie, are you sure?' her mother asked.

She tried to clear her head. The medicine had obviously affected her. It had caused some cruel mire in her brain that flared up at odd times. When she read the letter again, she would find her error. The words in the middle would match the rest of them as they should.

'I'm well on the way to recovery, Mother. Once I can sleep well, I'll be as good as new.'

Her mother and the Countess shared a glance and her mother scrutinised Rachael. 'I suppose. But you must promise to let me know if your burns aren't healing as they should.' Both of the older women frowned, studying her.

'I promise.' She put as much reinforcement into the words as she could.

'Well,' the Countess said, rushing her mother out, 'we'll send for the physician again. Just to be sure.'

Before Rachael could protest, they'd both left the room.

She walked to the gloves. Her teeth hurt from clenching them. She relaxed her jaw and reopened the letter.

The words were still brutal.

It had to be a mistake. A misunderstanding. Lack of sleep. Confusion in her caused by the lingering effects of the laudanum she'd taken last night. Something.

She stared at the page, seeing her dreams evaporate into tiny little wisps that disappeared long before the light of day, never to be viewed again.

Either Tenney had become addled or she had, and neither option was a happy one.

Mornings were only to be endured, Devlin believed, and if one woke late enough their duration was lessened greatly. But he'd awoken early, concerned about Rachael.

He stretched, shook himself awake and wondered if Rachael had left. His rooms were so removed from the main quarters that it was unlikely he would have heard her depart. Somehow, he knew she was still there and he attributed it to the fact that he didn't think she'd leave without telling him goodbye.

Yesterday, Miss Albright had kept to her room. That evening, he'd even spent some time with her mother, discussing foliage. Or rather, letting her discuss it. His mother had joined the conversation and she'd known he was no Capability Brown and wouldn't be designing any estate grounds, but Mrs Albright hadn't seemed to notice. He'd wager his last strand of hair that the Countess had noted and mentally commented on his presence.

Devlin had asked his cousin to linger one more day before leaving for the trip to the hunting box. His two younger brothers, Eldon and Oliver, were likely already there, and it would be a grand time for them to test out-witting each other with their banter.

He really should leave with Payton. Another long discussion of foliage and he'd likely sprout thorns. He already felt that he'd been planted at the house the last few days, yet he didn't want to uproot and leave. The imagined scent of roses lingered.

* * *

After he was confident breakfast was safely over, he stepped from his room and found his mother, stitching flowers on a blue ribbon and Mrs Albright sewing two pieces of cloth together, while they sat in front of the two windows. Gone was the camaraderie of the previous day.

Miss Albright? Something must be wrong. His words couldn't come fast enough. 'How is Miss Albright today?'

Her mother's shoulders lifted in a defeated shrug. 'Better, she says.'

His mother's lips thinned and then she added, 'You could tell last night that she was fretting. I sent for the physician and he spoke with her briefly, but he didn't think she was as co-operative as she could have been and he feared she isn't being honest about her injury. She claims she isn't in much pain, but her mother and I could both recognise it in her face. The physician said she will recover just fine, perhaps some scarring... But then he said my father would be fine and he died the next day.'

Devlin's equanimity shifted. 'The physician was called again?'

'Last night.' His mother studied her sewing, but the part of the ribbon she perused had no stitching on it. 'I insisted.'

Mrs Albright pushed the needle into the cloth and pulled the thread taut before speaking. 'She will recover. I am sure of it.'

'Perhaps she is well enough to take a small stroll?' he asked.

His mother and Mrs Albright took stock of each other before answering.

'I don't think so,' her mother said. 'This morning, we

both asked her if she would like to join us and she told us she is fine, but says she is not suitable company today. We have been debating over whether I should send for her father to speak with her.'

'She wishes to return home,' the Countess said. 'I could not countenance it as she would be further from the physician.'

Devlin walked to the bell and summoned a maid. 'I'll find out if she's hiding symptoms.' Then he strode out of the room.

He met the maid in the hallway. 'Ask Miss Albright if she might like to join me in the library.'

As he waited in the library, the maid returned. 'She feels she would not be good company today and gives her regrets.'

'Is she in pain?' he asked.

'She's composing a letter, but she can't do it sitting,' the maid whispered. 'She sent me for paper, pen and ink earlier.'

'Could you please bring some sweet wine to the library and return to Miss Albright and tell her that I cannot accept any regrets from her? She can either speak with me or I will summon two mothers and a physician to her room to enquire about her health.'

The maid nodded, dashed out, returned with a decanter of wine and two glasses for the library, then she darted out again.

Rachael swept into the library, arms crossed, dress wrinkled and eyes dark. 'You seemed to wish to talk with me.'

Devlin stopped himself mid-stride. He'd been about to grasp the pull and send for the physician. But he forced himself to remain immobile and appear relaxed. Rachael needed comfort and the physician wasn't doing enough. Or the mothers weren't doing enough. He must find out what kind of assistance she needed. He'd get her to tell him what the problem was.

What good was an ability to soothe people if he didn't use it.

He poured wine for her.

'I was concerned about your burns. This might ease some of the pain. Yes?' He reached out, holding the drink.

'That remains to be seen.' She took the glass, thanked him and swallowed the contents. 'Delicious. Thank you for your consideration. I appreciate it.' She put it on the tray beside the other glass, watching the bottle's contents as if it might roil up like a wave. 'I have an important letter to compose today. That is all.'

He noticed the way her tongue formed around the word *letter*.

'I'm sure it's important.'

'Very.' Another precisely bitten-out word.

He just raised his brows, letting the silence prod her to speak.

She released the glass and put fingertips to her cheek. 'I have been up half the night, two nights in a row now.' She twirled around, facing the opposite direction, her upper body tense, her shoulders high, the knot of hair on her head coming loose from her pins. 'The first night because of the burn and the second night because I have been thinking of what I must do next.'

Again, he waited, letting his silence ask the question.

'Something has happened.' She took out a few hair pins and jabbed them back into place. 'My curiosity is engaged, to put it mildly. I must compose a letter to Mr Tenney and it's a difficult one.'

She looked over her shoulder at him. The distress in her face caused him to step closer.

'Pardon?' he asked, surprised at the elation he felt that she might no longer be entranced with Tenney, making sure to keep it from his voice. She wasn't ill. In fact, he would say she was doing a sensible thing. No man should postpone a wedding to her.

She returned to her former stance, but this time, challenging him with her stare. 'We have had some sort of disagreement and I need to determine what caused it.'

She seemed to expect him to argue with her and he saw no reason to accommodate. 'This is a different perspective than you had earlier.'

'Two years we courted to establish we were suited. Four years more we have been betrothed. Six years.' She held her chin high. 'And now, for the first time, it seems we are not in agreement. I may break our betrothal.' She dusted her hands as if removing the slightest touch of him. 'I would not marry that toad if he were a prince, a king or an emperor. I am not sure that he doesn't have two sides to him.' She made a fist, holding it over her stomach. 'Both detestable.'

'Then you missed getting a bad husband. But...' His lips formed a straight line and he shook his head. 'Don't let it upset you. I'm afraid you will have many more chances for a bad husband.'

She growled, the same type of grumble he'd heard when she'd entered the library and he'd been discussing her. He wondered if she did that because she was fighting an internal war to keep herself quiet and not entirely winning.

It wasn't a fierce or ferocious grumble, but rather like a trapped kitten that attempted to be challenging, yet it made one want to rescue it.

'In that case, I will never marry. If all men are like him then it will be no great hardship to be a spinster. It will be a boon.'

'Do you think I am like Tenney?'

She stared him up and down. 'No. I believe you are honest about your inconstancy. Which is a good thing, in a bad form—or vice versa, but still preferable.'

'I believe you insulted me and I instigated it, but I'm not sure I really deserved it.' He furrowed his brow.

'My father is a good husband to my mother and I expect my marriage to Tenney to be similar.' She looked to the ceiling, and harrumphed, again reminding him of a small, lovable animal that needed rescuing.

She still expected to wed Tenney. Devlin's teeth ground together. Well, it was what it was. He would wish her the best.

'Apparently, a good husband is rare.' Her eyes fluttered. 'I ignored what could be deemed boring qualities in Tenney and considered them a sign of his ability to stay constant.'

Ah, he understood. Tenney had said or done something which ruffled her, but chances were it would blow over soon and result in a rash of forgiveness requests, pleading and after a plethora of promises would result in all things being right again—for a time.

The image irritated him. Soon she'd forgive Tenney and tumble into her imagined, happy love fog. Tenney had probably flirted with another and she'd discovered it.

'My father is a good husband to my mother also. My father once relocated to a different residence when I was younger which reduced the broken glass here, yet he returned within a few years. Faithful? Hardly.' One side of his lips rose in a grimace.

'That is a terrible thing to say about your own father.'

'It's the truth and everyone knows it.'

'Even your mother?'

'I would assume so, as I've heard her whisper it at an extremely high volume so the servants wouldn't hear. And then she's said a few dozen times that she wished Father's mistress would make him happy enough to keep him out of the house. She said the woman is abysmal in that regard.'

'Your mother is a gracious woman, but I'm not of that level of graciousness.' Her lip curled. 'Not even close.'

He widened his stance. 'I'm going to ask you a question and I would like you not to answer it aloud. Consider if you and Tenney married and then, a few years later, you found that those delayed trips he took included a visit to another woman's residence and you had two children, and he said, on bended knee, that he had erred and begged—begged—with tears in his eyes for you to forgive him…how could you not?'

She didn't answer.

'You would have a family to save by forgiving him. Peace in the household. A life that the two children wanted. So much and for little risk at that point. That horse had already left the stables. The husband is well and truly contrite and means the words, at least when he says them. Why not forgive and pretend to yourself that all is well?'

'So that is how men think?' She shook her head. 'That is pathetic.' She lowered her chin on the last word. 'Men are hideous creatures if that is true and Tenney…'

'After a while you either just pretend all is well, or just accept that all is not. Those are your only choices. Or you take a lover in return. You both keep the façade of a family and all is happy, but you go along your separate ways. The household is not destroyed. The world goes on. You meet on holidays and special occasions and perhaps you keep each other as friends. Good friends. Friends you can count on to be at funerals and weddings. Friends who are there at your roughest times. A marriage.'

'What a load of manure. Do you usually deliver it by the wagonload, or is this just one of those special occasions?'

Perhaps he was better off letting her growl.

'This time you are the one being immature and I'm the one with the maturity. You believe in little rainbows and happy magic.' He fluttered his fingers about as if spreading enchanted dust for all to view. 'I comprehend the world as it is.'

'I hope you never subject a poor woman to a proposal of marriage. You are assuredly taking my mind off the pain.' She pointed to her backside. 'It feels much better to hate someone in front of you, than being irritated at someone from a distance because you know they are hiding something in their letter.'

'I'm sorry that you're in pain.' Empathy laced his words. He lifted the wine and held it over her glass, waiting for her to give him the signal to pour.

She put her hand over the top. 'No. I want my head clear. I have not been able to form a satisfying written response to Mr Tenney.' She glared at the liquid.

He stood there, the container tipped to the side and the stopper in his left hand, and poured himself a drink.

'A clear head in a betrothal? Is that possible?' He'd expected his jest to bring lightness to her face, not increase the scowl.

The gaudy stone she'd worn on her left hand was missing. Ah, this must be a serious disagreement.

He closed the bottle and stared at the empty finger. 'That was a sizeable ring you wore. Almost bigger than your hand.' He spoke lightly, but her bad humour remained.

'It had once belonged to his favourite grandmother.'

'If it did, I'm sure she was glad to get rid of it.' He lifted the glass. 'It would have been unfair to have buried it with her.'

She touched the empty spot. 'It wasn't my favourite.'

'Are you planning to end the betrothal?'

'I'm not sure. Sometimes I wonder if there is someone better out there waiting for me.'

He studied her, gently shaking his head. 'In London?' He frowned. 'Sometimes, there isn't anyone better to pick from. Just other humans and I'm afraid that is the best choice we have.'

'Don't judge everyone by your standards.'

'It doesn't matter whose standards I use, if it all washes out the same.'

'Devlin, I think you have raised immaturity to a new height—or dropped it to a new low. Or both. You're filling up a chamber pot with it.'

He took a wide step, put the glass on the table, and gave her a bow. 'At your service.'

'You are annoying. I comprehended you a total charmer and full of sweet sentiments of no value whatsoever and now I find that you're not a charmer and you have no sweet sentiments.'

'Yes, I do. I just left them quiet as I expected you wanted that,' he said. 'I envisioned you could accept the truth.'

'You're twisting the argument around to make me feel bad. Do you not appreciate how rough these past two days have been for me?'

'Do you?' He stepped closer, moving near her like smoke held to the earth by the winds from above. 'Do you really? I view one of the most fortunate women in the world in front of me.'

She chose her words slowly. 'I suppose the fire…it could have been so much worse.'

'Thin silk, cotton and you packed into a corset so tight that you wouldn't have easily wriggled out of it. A room full of people, mostly filled to the gills with wine, brandy and powerful punch. All waiting for someone else to do something. No water at hand.'

She deflated, her shoulders and chin dropping, her voice lowering. 'It still hurts. All of it.'

'I'm sorry.' He touched her chin, raising it until her eyes met his. His voice softened. His gaze was full of empathy. 'What did that boor Tenney do to you that is so bad that it will take him crawling to you on bended knees and begging? Has he added another year to the length of the betrothal? Or sent you a letter intended for another?'

'Neither,' she said. 'I have no reason to discuss it. There has been a mistake and I don't know what to do.'

'Are you sure? Six years of your life is a long time to toss out, but to ruin the rest of it to make those six years seem like a good decision could be much worse.'

She tensed her muscles. 'I don't know what to do.

What to think. I don't know if I should be searching him out for an apology or vengeance.'

'If you decide on vengeance, marriage would be the perfect vehicle for that.'

'I would not throw myself under someone's carriage in order to cause it to turn over on them.' She put her hands on her hips.

'Ah.' He picked up his glass and took a sip, then gave her the smile that usually melted anger. 'You are mature.'

Instead of an answering lilt to her lips, she grumbled again.

He studied her. Whatever had happened must have been devastating, or he would have been able to coax her into better humour.

Or, she didn't perceive him the same way others did.

It became vital to soothe her.

He would.

Chapter Four

She stood in the centre of the room, staring at nothing. 'Four years. Four years.' She shook her head. 'And two years making sure beforehand. I should have questioned that if it took us that long, something was wrong.' She pressed her fingers against her forehead.

Devlin briefly touched her lowered arm. 'What did he say to you, Rachael? Did the sap tell you he has another sweetheart?'

'No. He said he still wishes for us to marry.' Which she couldn't fathom as he obviously found her reprehensible.

'And just what about this has convinced you it is a bad idea?'

Instantly, she felt soothed by his voice and his presence. 'He said it in the vilest way possible. The most hideously vile way.'

She turned to Devlin and he clasped her hand, the grip reassuring. She looked at their intertwined fingers and felt his strength. The letter she'd received didn't seem so bad now. It was almost as if it were sent to another woman. Another Rachael, but she didn't want to be that person.

'In the first line he says he still plans to marry me, and in the last line as well. It is all the *tender* endearments in the middle that I have trouble with.' The expression in his eyes made her able to continue.

'What endearments?'

She shook her head, thinking more objectively about the words. 'Not ones I had heard before. How he finds me hideously awkward. How he detests my family.' Her voice caught on the word *family*. He'd always said he liked her parents. 'The shape of my nose.' She put a shaking finger to the tip.

'I find nothing wrong with it.' Devlin's eyes narrowed and he studied her face, turning to give it a better perusal.

'He always said I had a beautiful profile and that was one of the first things he'd complimented me on. I do have a good nose,' she said. 'It's my mother's. Not my father's.'

Once, Tenney had spoken on and on about how fortunate she was to have a well-shaped nose and that he had hated his own. In fact, the words he'd used to describe himself when he spoke with her were the ones he'd written about her in the letter.

'I have had no complaints on my appearance in the past and I feel confident my straightforward sister or my cousins, who were generous with their opinions when we were children, would have informed me if it is peculiar. My cousins commented on everything from how I said apostrophe to how I held my spoon.'

He stepped closer. 'It is not too big. Not too small. Just the right size for sniffing flowers.'

'And then Mr Tenney went on to tell me detestable things about me, but then he was reassuring that he would marry me. He called me a not-endearing country miss and said he expected to get a tutor for me as the social graces I have are sadly non-existent.'

'What did he say about your ears?'

She gasped and covered her ears. 'Nothing. What? Are you going to tell me they are longish, or wide even for a baby elephant?'

He didn't answer immediately and she lowered her hands and perched on the chair.

Devlin shrugged. 'They're perfect ears. Perfect like your nose. He is obviously losing his senses. Or something.'

'He always told me I had been fortunate concerning the size of my ears and nose.'

'You are. And he is a perfect arse.' Devlin loosened the buttons on his coat and sat on the matching chair. 'Forgive my bad language and manners, Rachael. But I do believe you've been exposed to so much already and I hardly think you'll lose sleep over mine on your behalf.'

She shook her head, her knot of hair wobbling. 'I have already started a letter breaking off the engagement, but I could not finish it… Well…six letters. Maybe seven.' She frowned. 'I cannot compose just the right words. And then I read his letter again, and I'm not confident he wrote it. The other ones he's sent are all at home and my eyes blurred as I tried to remember exactly how he writes.'

Devlin put his elbow on the arm of the chair. 'A man should not treat his beloved so.' He rested his chin in his hand. 'Perhaps he wants you to call off the wedding.'

'What do you mean?'

'If you call the wedding off, he achieves the break without a care. If he calls it off, you are likely to be awarded some compensation if you want to seek it. Breach of promise. That sort of thing. Women can do that. Men are seen as cads who engaged a woman's affections, affections that she could have given elsewhere. Men are seen as abusing a woman's trust and hurting her chance for a future.'

'I could never marry him if this is how he tries to achieve his goals.' She held out a palm. 'If that is what he wanted, he could have asked me. Nicely. In person preferably, but if not, by letter. I would have agreed and let the matter drop. I would think he would know me that well.'

'He doesn't have the spine.'

She jerked her head his direction, surprised at the anger sizzling in her. She was almost more infuriated at Devlin than Tenney. She took Devlin's comment as a criticism of her choice.

She met his eyes and could tell he'd read her thoughts. But he didn't flinch or soften his words. Instead he smiled, as if that would make everything better.

'If he had said in the letter that he wished to discard you, would that not appear beyond the pale to a court should you decide to pursue it?' Devlin asked. 'They would empathise with a sniffling miss, with one lone tear running down her face, while her father reads the letter that destroyed his little innocent's life.'

'I could never...' she said, then paused. 'Unless it is because of the way he told me.'

'He judged the letter the swiftest, surest, cleanest break. For himself.'

'He is a barrister.'

'Then by all means, you should respond in a manner he's familiar with,' Devlin said.

'I want only to be honest.'

He lowered his chin and blinked away her words. 'Please write to him and tell him that you were at first astonished that he was feeling so low, but you understand that this is caused by the pressures he is under in order to provide a wonderful life for you and the children you hope to have. You anticipate the happy day when you're married. Your love is as strong as ever—no—stronger now you're aware of the worry seeping through in his words. A tutor is a grand idea and perhaps your family may stay with you after the marriage and take advantage of the tutor. Send him your love and tell him you have been knitting baby socks for the many little ones that will reside in the house you will share with him. You're hoping to take in many stray cats and dogs also.'

She tensed her neck. 'I wouldn't share a table with him. I wouldn't share a cup of tea with him, or a few words.' Rachael fidgeted. It just hurt too much to sit and when she rose, she waved him to remain seated.

'You know that. I know that. But, please, don't let him know that. You must play the cards you've been dealt and use them to your best advantage.' His words calmed her.

Devlin sprawled, staring at the ceiling overhead. 'Just this once, put yourself first. Take the cards and put a few in your reticule if you must. You can return to maturity later. But how many chances do you have to gamble on a losing hand and emerge the victor?'

'That is not the honest way to do things. One must be straightforward and sincere.'

'I agree, mostly. And sometimes you have to push back because if you say yes nine times and the tenth

you say no, then you are seen as an unbearable ogre…
because by the tenth time the spoiled, selfish person
is convinced it is their right that you always say yes to
them.'

'I didn't think he was like that. I wanted to spend my
life with him.'

'But you don't want to spend your life with this as the
most eventful memory. And one that leaves a bad taste
in your mouth. You want to stand proud, stand tough and
return it on a silver platter. You have no choice. Your
memories of this must fade easily…and it may take longer than a physical scar to heal if you do not stand up
for yourself. Graciously.'

She lightly touched the area across her bottom.
'Standing is about all I can do. It hurts. On the inside
and out.'

'Maturity. It'll do that to you.' He shook his shoulders. 'Ghastly affliction.'

'Have you managed to escape *all* the growing pains?'

His eyes never left hers and his nod was slight.
'Enough of them. Perhaps you were born old in the maturity of your decisions. But I was born old in the ability
to deflect pain with meaningless diversions.'

He wasn't jesting.

'Right now, I would trade you.' She said the first
words that entered her mind.

'Never.' His demeanour changed and his eyes levelled
at her. 'Maturity suits you well. You only need a splash
of irresponsibility. Not the whole container.'

After Tenney's slashing letter, the sentiment of his
compliment reached into the edges of her pain and
washed it from her. She studied Devlin and he took in
her perusal without a flinch.

'Thank you.' The words were spoken softly, but weren't a platitude.

The silence grew between them, but the distance melted. He was a true friend. And yet, he was different from others. He wouldn't judge her harshly if she told him her truths because his own were much more jagged than hers.

'There's nothing I would like better to do than to flop down on a comfortable chair and cry my eyes out,' Rachael whispered. 'In truth, I have been jilted, though I am left to do the actual calling off of the betrothal.'

Devlin rose to his feet. 'Tenney's a— You'll be construed the fickle one.'

She fought for control. 'A jilt. Inconstant.' Her throat throbbed. 'I've never done anything bad in my life and now I'll be speculated about.'

He stepped closer, then held out his hand, waiting.

She took a step, and then another, and his arms folded around her in a loose embrace, surrounding her with the scent of spice and life, and the warmth of compassion.

She rested her cheek against the wool of his coat and the pain eased, and for a second none of it mattered. Not even Tenney's treachery.

'I feel guilty. For being in your arms.'

'For being comforted?' his voice said in her ear. 'Nonsense. Utter rot. Total drivel for you to feel so. The man showed a false side of himself to you for six years. He should feel guilty, but I assure you he doesn't.'

'It's a mistake. Someone copied his handwriting, or something like that.' She breathed in the secure scent of Devlin.

'Do you really believe it?'

'I don't believe he could actually write such a letter to me.'

'You're seeing him through your eyes. All people don't react as you do.' He brushed a hand across her back and it was as if he'd erased so much pain.

'Someone else must have written the letter. The reason my mother planned her next event was to give us a chance to announce the date of our wedding.' She reassured herself Tenney wouldn't do such a thing, but now she didn't care as much. 'It's a cruel jest. Caused by someone who envied him. He often said people were jealous creatures and didn't want him to succeed.'

His nose rested just above her ear. 'Is that what you truly believe?'

'I don't know.'

'You're too trusting.'

'I prefer to give people... Not to assume the worst.'

'Perhaps you should be judicious in that. I'm holding you. I'm comforting you. But in some corner of my mind, I'm hoping you and Tenney are finished.'

'You're only being nice.'

'That's how it starts. With kindness. Wasn't Tenney compassionate to you? At least at first? Wasn't he?'

'Yes. I can't believe he said all those things to me. Someone told him a lie about me, or someone else wrote the letter.' Even as she spoke the words, she doubted them.

'Was it his handwriting? Did it sound like him when he was upset with someone?'

'Yes, but...'

'He's changed affections.'

She raised a hand, steadying it on his chest. His arms fell to his sides. She took a careful step in reverse. 'That was a cruel thing to say. And Mr Tenney is—was devoted to me.'

'Of course. He still carries you deep within his heart. And he loves your nose.'

That statement was delivered with such innocence and a smile. Fury filled her limbs and she instinctively balled her fists. 'Devlin. You could use just a drop of my maturity.'

All humour flew from his face and lines formed at his eyes. He studied her. 'You're taking me seriously.'

'Is that not what I'm supposed to do?' She puffed another breath through her nostrils.

'Of course.' Then he added, 'Are you going to listen to me or to a man who tells you he doesn't like your nose?'

'Neither.' She crossed her arms.

He brushed the top of her shoulder. 'Wise choice.' Then he spoke, softening his words to decrease their impact. 'I still believe it likely that he has changed affections.'

'Are you judging him by your friends?'

His eyes narrowed. 'It doesn't matter if I am, because I'm saying the truth. You really need to write him the letter telling him that your mother may reside with you after you're married. Perhaps a few cousins as well,' Devlin said. 'Write to him as if nothing was wrong in his missive. That way you're safe if he goes along smoothly. Or…' he shrugged '…you can do as few do. Use your head to think. Definitely don't set the wedding date. You do not want your reputation damaged. It's important to you.'

'This advice from a rake?'

His brows furrowed. 'You'd expect…what? Me to ask you to pray for him at Sunday services? No.' He crossed an arm across his midsection, rested an elbow on it, and touched his knuckles to his chin. 'I'd rather watch you take him out at the knees, observe him falling with his face in the mud and have you use his hinder parts to step on as a path to better things.'

'I couldn't.' But if Devlin encouraged her, perhaps she could. It wasn't the words he said, it was the way he put her feelings foremost in his discussion of her betrothal.

He walked to her. 'Is it because you are too good hearted, or is it because you don't have the courage?'

'I have the courage. I just know he could not do such a thing. On paper. He could not.'

A door opened and closed in the distance. He looked towards the sound and lowered his voice.

'Then give him the benefit of the doubt. Put that sapphire on your finger. Keep the contents of the letter quiet and give yourself some time to set the deck to your advantage. Everyone who knows you sees you as almost married and it can damage you to be seen as inconstant. There will be talk. You do not want to be hiding your head in shame or embarrassment. And you will have to be the one to call the wedding off eventually as he has no courage to do it. He is thinking of himself, which is no crime. You must think of yourself.'

One thing she hated was deceit. Hated it. 'I will not practise duplicity. I did nothing wrong.'

'No harm in that. Sometimes.'

The words hit her with a swifter jolt than the letter and his jaw hardened, but he didn't beg her forgiveness.

She anticipated an apology.

But he said nothing. She couldn't read anything in his face. Except perhaps pity, which incensed her. She firmed her lips and he reached for his glass and raised it to her, a silent challenge, but she wouldn't answer. Not to defend Tenney or criticise him.

Then, with a brief bow that somehow irked her more, he left the room.

Emptiness washed over her and suddenly she was angrier at Devlin than anyone else. How dare he try to tell her why Tenney responded as he did. He didn't even know him. She steadied herself by grasping the chair.

Blast it. She wished he'd stayed. That upset her even more. She wanted to fight with him. Which just proved how much Tenney was suited for her. They'd never fought. Never, ever. Not once had they disagreed. Not a single time.

She stood, winced, and bit the inside of her lip. They could all rot. Tenney and Devlin both.

But then she considered that, after six years of her life with Tenney, she'd never experienced the loneliness she felt when Devlin left the room.

She must be mistaken. She'd got her sentiments with Tenney confused and her weary brain had made her think she missed Devlin.

She touched her forehead. Why did it hurt as much when Devlin spoke harshly to her than when Tenney's words had tried to destroy her on paper?

Suddenly, she remembered Tenney telling her once that he would never be touched in a breach of promise action and she'd not really paid attention.

Now she wondered if Devlin had grasped what was going on much better than she did. She wanted to dart after him and ask him to explain, but she feared he already had. And, if she followed him, she would end up in his arms.

Chapter Five

'How is your burn?' her mother asked, after entering Rachael's room.

Rachael leaned against the wall, holding the letter from Mr Tenney in her hand. She turned the paper so that the writing wasn't visible.

'It's much better.'

'Well enough to manage the carriage?' she asked.

'I would rather walk home instead,' Rachael said, patting above the burn. 'I tried sitting and it was uncomfortable.'

'I admit, I'm enjoying the hospitality of the Earl and the Countess seems content to have us here. She says the servants are competent at handling much more than two agreeable guests. She is making some calls now and we are to ask for anything we wish. She is also going out to a dinner this evening, but suggests we make ourselves at home in her library, and she can also provide us with more stitching supplies, watercolours, or pianoforte.' Her mother chuckled. 'She also suggests it is unlikely that Devlin will be here, but advises if he is that we do not ask him to provide music as he is forbidden to touch the piano.'

'He is not proficient?'

'She said his music tutor suggested fencing and he was a natural at it.'

Her mother stepped sideways and peered at Rachael's hand. 'And what was in the letter my future son-in-law sent? I'm so pleased to be welcoming him into our family soon. It will be as if we finally have a son.'

Rachael straightened a crease on the paper. 'He's busy with work, apparently, and it is wearing on him.'

'But he still had time to write to you.'

Rachael nodded. 'I am thinking about answering his letter now.'

'Be sure to remind him how much I appreciate his missing a few hours of toil to attend our family soirée. It will be wonderful to have my sisters and your grandmothers here. It will be a lovely event and the perfect time to announce the date of your wedding.'

Rachael couldn't speak. She had been so anticipating Tenney's next visit, but now she had no wish to be near him. None at all. She turned to her mother. 'Mr Tenney and I are—' Then she took in a breath. 'Mr Tenney is—'

'Yes?' Her mother leaned towards her. 'Are the two of you going to announce the date at the party as you'd planned?'

She saw the question in her mother's eyes and knew how devoted her mother was to Tenney. She could not break the news to her right before the soirée. The questions her mother would be asked would override the family joy.

'I just must speak with him soon,' Rachael said, flipping the letter between two fingers.

Her mother moved a half-step forward. 'What date have you decided on?'

'I think that will be taken care of, but...' She could not bear the hope in her mother's eyes. 'The brush with death has caused me to spend a considerable quantity of time thinking about...my future.'

'I would not say it was a brush with death.' Her mother's eyes widened.

Relieved that her mother had not pursued the subject of marriage, Rachael didn't want her mother to mention Tenney again. 'I could have died, if not for Devlin. I was frozen. I didn't know what to do.'

Her mother shook her head. 'It was so fast. The fire just tumbled on to you and instantly the flames had taken most of your skirt. But Devlin—it seemed he knew what was going to happen before it did—and he'd grabbed you and pushed you against the wall and covered you to smother the flames. We all just stood watching, unbelieving.'

'I could have died,' Rachael murmured.

'Nonsense.'

'I almost went up in flames like a brandy-soaked plum pudding.'

'Let's not think about that.'

'I can't stop thinking about it.'

Tenney's letter had already been composed most likely. And if she had died, her mother would likely have received it and opened it. Or perhaps Rachael would have been recovering from an even more serious burn and her mother would have read Tenney's letter to her. That would have been a grand topping for the burnt pudding.

Tenney almost got out of the betrothal much easier than he expected.

Rachael blinked, the paper in her hand crumpling. 'Life is so short.'

'Yes. I'm pleased you're going to marry soon. I want you to have all of life's happiness and, once you're married, I'm inviting the grandchildren to spend more time with me so I will not feel so alone.' She stopped speaking long enough to give Rachael a hug and kiss her cheek. 'I don't hold my two grandchildren nearly often enough. I'm so relieved you'll be living in London once you're married.'

Rachael saw her mother's happiness bursting out. She could not tell her mother that the betrothal was likely to be over.

'Mother, I would not want to make a mistake and…' she couldn't very well say marry in haste '…do something I might regret.'

'I would not worry about that at this point. You are a sensible woman. You've always been mature beyond your years and used your head, as is evidenced by your choice of someone like Mr Tenney. Now you can follow your dreams. I feel you have been too serious your whole life. It's time for you to enjoy the results. It's time for you to become a wife. That is what you wish, isn't it?'

'I'm not entirely convinced.' She lowered her gaze, breathing out.

'You have been waiting six years? And you're not confident?'

She answered her mother, 'I shall dance at the soirée. With Tenney. And I am confident that I will make the right decision where he's concerned.'

And as she said those words, she knew deep in her heart that the betrothal was over. She'd read the letter one last time when she'd returned to her room after speaking with Devlin and no longer believed the missive had been a mistake. When she viewed it with the memory of Tenney saying he never worried about a breach of promise and imagined him penning it with that in his mind, it made sense.

She dreaded the thought of dancing with him.

Earlier that afternoon, when Devlin had held her in his arms and consoled her, her body had melted against him. Feelings she'd never experienced before had awoken, shocking her.

For six years Tenney had done little more than brush a fleeting kiss on her lips. She'd consigned it to his deep respect at the time and never questioned the lack of affection.

Her betrothal had been a sham and she'd believed in it.

She would never be so foolish again.

Rachael left her room and went in search of a maid. She clasped the paper in her hand.

Devlin stood at the door of the library. Her room was directly above the library. He could most probably hear her moving about.

'Is that a letter you've written in your grasp?' he asked.

'Yes.'

He bent so that he could read the name on the paper. *'"Mr Ambrose Tenney".'* Devlin's eyes took on a wicked, humorous glint. 'And how will Ambrose take this message?'

'I'm not concerned about it at this point, but I have reconsidered everything twice at least.' She lowered her hand and frowned. 'I think he and I have both been wrong. A misunderstanding could have caused this. Yet, that doesn't mean we are to be married. I don't even want to be friends with him.'

'It pleases me, Rachael, to hear you are investigating this.' He reached out and took her fingertips, barely grasping them. 'But you must be suspicious of anything he says if he is so unkind to you.'

'I'll take your words into consideration.'

'Just be aware it is easy for most males to be rakish. So, if I were to agree I speak flattery, but you truly do have a most adorable nose, if for no other reason than it is in the middle of your face and beneath two expressive eyes, and lips that would make a grown man swoon, then how could you doubt it? Even if it is total nonsense— which it isn't—I have taken the time to praise you. Obviously, I feel you are worthy of a compliment as I have proven it. My actions speak to you, even if my words are lightly given.'

'I am much impressed. You have this business of being a rake down to a science.'

He put his other hand beside his first, and rested it at her wrist, then, he raised her fingertips, stopping just short of a kiss against them. His breath warmed her. 'Rachael. Being a rake is a twenty-four-hours-a-day endeavour. One becomes accomplished at anything if one practises that much.' Then he brushed his cheek against her hand before releasing her. She suppressed any pleasant feelings caused by his touch. 'You are treacherous.'

He released her. 'No. That boor is treacherous. I am accomplished.'

'And that was rude.'

'But not to you. I can't be rude to you.'

'Do you ever extinguish the rake part of you and just be truthful?'

He shook his head. 'If you are born with big feet, do you cut off your toes to make them the size of everyone else's? If you have flower seeds, do you lock them in a box or do you plant them? If you are born with a chance to put happiness on faces, do you hide yourself into a room and be silent?'

He stepped back, stopping at the door. 'I must get on about my day. There are smile bouquets to deliver around town.'

Still at the threshold, he continued. 'And, if you will beg my sincerest pardon, then I must let you know that you are the one being unmannerly. Everything I have said about you is of the deepest truth. It may be delivered flippantly, but it is true. Whether you believe it or not is entirely up to you. You are exquisite and I don't say that lightly.'

Footsteps in the hallway silenced their words.

Payton strolled into view, his arms spread to grasp the doorframe, and leaned in. 'Ready to leave——?' He stopped when he saw Rachael and gave her a quick bow of his head. 'So pleased that you are doing fine today, Miss Albright. I wanted to let Devlin know I'm about to leave. A business meeting we should attend. Cosgrove's.' He turned to Devlin. 'You?'

'Go without me,' he said.

Payton spoke. 'Large sums at stake. You should come along.'

'Miss Albright is still suffering from the incident. I cannot leave her.'

Miss Albright's mouth opened, and she regarded Devlin. 'You must attend to your work.'

'I can always catch up later.'

Payton chortled. 'An opportunity wasted for ever. Don't let him mislead you, Miss Albright. Only one thing is more important than duty to Devlin and that is chivalry.' He made a fist and thumped his arm over his heart. 'The family honour demands that a lady's comfort comes first. Always.'

'Of course. Go on to your appointment.' Devlin studied his fingernails. 'Just don't let anyone cheat at cards.'

Payton clucked his tongue. 'You've given me such an idea. I could pilfer Alfred's marked cards, replace them with an exact set, but the spots indicating different cards.' He shut his eyes tight. 'Wouldn't that be the biggest tale of the century. Right after I took his money, I'll let him in on how I did it.'

'You'd get yourself challenged to a duel.'

Payton laughed. 'Why not? Even that could be fun, if done correctly.' He touched his chin. 'Can pillows be chosen as a weapon?' He nodded. 'The problem isn't with duelling—it is in the choice of weapons.'

'Well, if you're interested in a duel,' Rachael inserted, 'could you be so kind as to fight one over me? It would be grand if Mr Tenney thought, if only for an instant, that someone should be so infatuated with me that they might think I'm worthy of such attention.'

Devlin observed her.

'You want Devlin and me to fight a duel over you?' Payton beheld her as if the last bit of her brain had fluttered out of the window.

'It's not so farfetched,' Devlin commented. Payton didn't have to appear shocked at the suggestion of someone fighting a duel over Rachael.

'Of course.' Payton caught himself. He pointed a finger and waved it rapidly between himself and Devlin. 'I just don't feel like shooting anyone today, or ever. Or running anyone through with a sword, particularly someone I could win money from at a card game.'

'I have a fine pair of duelling pistols,' Devlin said. 'They've never been used and Grandfather purchased them new.'

Payton's eyes widened. 'You've lost your senses.'

Devlin shook his head. 'A lady's honour is at stake, Payton.'

Payton's mouth opened, and he didn't speak for a second, then he turned to Rachael. 'Miss Albright, if I have done the slightest thing to impugn your honour, I heartily retract it. I would wound myself before I would hurt you.'

'You've done nothing to offend me at all,' Rachael reassured him. 'I think you a fine person and a delight to know. In fact, you are raising my spirits.'

Indignation flared in Devlin. His cousin was raising her spirits?

'Then what is all this duelling business about?' Payton asked Devlin. 'You know how fond I am of my boots and it's hardly likely that I'd want to get blood on them or be buried in them.'

'What if I show up at the hunting box and act enraged that you have dared to speak unkind words to Miss Albright?' Devlin asked.

'No,' Payton said. 'Never would I speak distressfully to her. Never. No one would believe that of me.'

'We can apologise after we see how close we have come to shooting each other over her. The story would make its way around London.'

Rachael stood closer to Devlin to capture his attention. 'That is kind of you, Devlin. Exceedingly kind. But that's a considerable effort. It touches my heart.'

'A duel could be a theatrical performance everyone is in on,' Devlin suggested. 'Those pistols may never have been fired and could remain that way.'

'We're family,' Payton agreed. 'We can't fight—openly. And I rarely reflect on throttling you. Though now, I'm thinking, if I could be the victor, it might be a good plan.'

'You've both brightened my spirits considerably and made me understand how foolish revenge is. Besides, I would only allow a duel fought with pillows.' Rachael clasped her hands in front of herself. 'Please forget we ever spoke such nonsense. I hope you both go to that business endeavour and that you don't have marked cards.'

Payton removed an imaginary sword from a scabbard, swirled it in the air before tucking it at his side. 'Should you ever need a duel fought in your honour, you know you only have to ask Devlin and me. We will fight to the last feather in a pillow for you.'

Then he doffed an invisible hat, gave her a bow suitable for a room of royals and turned to his cousin. 'You sure you're not going?'

Devlin waved him on. 'There will always be another card game, but Miss Albright is a guest and I want to stay here in case she needs someone to duel with.'

'He is an excellent choice, Miss Albright.' Payton extended his fingers and gave a rotating wave in a half-circle. 'I must be off. All this talk of duelling has concerned me and I must distract myself with the solace and respectability of gambling.' He darted out of the door.

'You should go with him,' Rachael told Devlin.

'I meant what I said. I want to make sure you have this behind you.' And if Tenney had second thoughts and arrived to throw himself at her mercy, he wanted to be there.

He took stock of Rachael. He couldn't imagine her being so gullible as to take Tenney back. He believed she'd realised she didn't truly love him and it was a relief. He didn't want to think of her suffering any more than she already had.

But when he took stock of her, it dredged up the two hurts she'd just had. One physical and one mental. And yet her jaw was locked. She wasn't weeping and she didn't throw herself into his arms. He admired that in her.

She shook her head. 'There is no need. Really, now there isn't. You've shown me that, while it may take a few days to put this behind me, it doesn't matter. I am fortunate that this happened. Very. It may cause a tumble inside me, but I am thankful for it.'

'Did you truly not care that much for him?'

Rachael didn't answer at first. 'I did when he asked me to marry him. I believed I did, up until the words in the letter made sense to me. I had arranged my own marriage, thinking it would be a love match later. A marriage like my parents'.' She laughed without humour. 'I gambled more than your cousin will, I suppose, and bet on a losing hand. The cards were probably marked in front of my face and I didn't know it.'

She shook her head. 'I bet on a losing hand. Now I have to live with the loss and the consequences.'

Ire flashed through Devlin's body. Women were to be protected. Particularly good-hearted ones such as Rachael.

He would fight for Rachael's honour. And it would be with the same determination that he'd managed to stay on top of the hill to keep his territory.

Chapter Six

Rachael could tell she was on the mend.

The constant burning had dissipated and her steps didn't hurt any more. As long as she stepped slowly and cautiously, she felt no pain.

The carriage ride concerned her, but she wanted to get home, although she would miss Devlin.

He'd had some of his meals with them and been attentive and ever so proper. Her mother glowed under the attention Devlin showered on the ladies at mealtimes and he could make his own mother laugh at the slightest thing.

She'd been surprised at the difference when he was in the room. Everyone seemed happier and conversation flowed more lightly.

But she'd not talked privately with Devlin since they'd discussed her betrothal ending.

She heard booted footsteps. Her skirts swirled as she rose. Devlin walked into the doorway and the sunshine from the window highlighted him, making him stand out against the dark hallway and seem bigger.

Then she remembered him pulling her into his arms

and lifting her. It was as if she'd weighed no more than a porcelain doll and he'd carried her with the same care.

Now he stood in front of her and secretly she admired his strength. Not just in his body, but the power he took for granted that was given him by birth and the depths she suspected that were hidden under the surface, but no one detected because he humoured everyone so well.

She shook the recollections of him from her mind. He was no more than a friend, but a friend was what she needed most. And having him for an ally had eased the awareness that Tenney didn't want her.

Devlin counted her a comrade and that was more value than a betrothed who considered her a burden.

'I sent the letter.'

He raised a brow.

'I sent the letter to Ambrose.' Yes, she would call him Ambrose to herself when she wished. He had said it would be romantic to wait until their wedding night to call each other by first names and endearments. She stifled a gasp that she had agreed to such a thing.

Devlin watched her and she could tell he was aware of her gasp. 'So, you must care for him.'

She saw that he'd misinterpreted her action.

'Not any more. I told him we must discuss our feelings in person. My mother is having a soirée next week and I had expected to announce the date of my marriage. He was to be there and I told him he must attend. I don't think he planned to be present when he wrote the letter, but it is important to my mother, and Ambrose and I must have a chance to speak with each other.'

Devlin's jaw tightened, but then he relaxed and spoke in measured tones. 'Don't forget that you are to evaluate your interests first. Don't be soft-hearted.'

She put her head down, shaking it an infinitesimal amount. 'I keep thinking he would never be such a boor. Yet I know now our betrothal was a mistake. A man who cared anything for me would have broached the subject with me, instead of dumping all the blame at my—'

Devlin grunted.

She raised her eyes to his. She couldn't read his feelings and yet she could. She knew his opinion of Ambrose well.

'Would I be able to have an invitation?' he asked.

'My mother would be honoured to have you.' The weight of the event lifted from her heart as if carried by angel wings.

'*I* would be the one honoured to be in your presence.'

The statement created edgy happiness inside her and freed her from guarding her speech.

'I so dread the next meeting with him. I never want to be near him again. I read the letter yet once more after we spoke and I cannot find any explanation other than he hopes I will end the betrothal.' She needed him to grasp how she felt. 'I have not failed and, yet, I have.'

'How can you say that?'

'Either I waited needlessly for a man who did not truly care for me, or I inadvertently caused him to fall out of love.'

His eyes narrowed. 'Don't take the blame for all the ills in the world. No one is strong enough to bear the burden for every wrong and no one should have to.'

'I waited patiently.'

'You can't undo the past. You must go forward.'

'Spoken like a rake.'

'A rake who sleeps like a babe.'

'Because you have never lost your heart.'

He took her hand, touching the finger where the stone had rested, uniting them in a way she didn't think she'd ever connected with Ambrose.

'Did you lose your heart to him. Truly?' he asked.

'A little bit of it. But not the whole. Maybe half.' She shuddered. 'Not the best half.' She held up her little finger. 'About this much. One sneeze and it's gone.'

'It'll likely grow again, bigger and healthier than ever.'

'Not for him. Now I am more irritated at myself for waiting all these years than I am for anything else. I'm wondering if...' she hated to admit it '...if I did not push him to wed because I didn't want to marry him either. And why did I not see that? I don't know who to be angriest at. Him or myself.'

'I can answer that for you. Him.'

She pressed her lips firmly together.

'The sooner you get over the anger, the better off you'll be,' he said. 'But, please, before you toss Tenney from your life, let him believe you're not breaking the betrothal. If he thinks he's not getting what he wants, you'll be more likely to witness his true self and you'll be able to put him behind you so much faster.'

'I'd hoped it was all a misunderstanding, but now, even if it is, I can't go forward with a wedding.'

He clasped the fourth finger on her left hand. 'I would never wish for you to wed a person who doesn't cherish you. Sharing a home with a person who finds reason to disparage you is like having shoes with thorns in them. It doesn't matter how sturdy your shoe is, or how shiny, or how well-crafted it is, it's still going to be an uneasy stride.'

She raised a brow, her words light, but with an undercurrent of directness. 'Are you happy?'

Something passed behind his eyes. A barrier she'd never seen before, but then it faded.

'Happiness? All that matters is how I can put other people at ease. It is natural to me and I'm fortunate I inherited the ability. As the eldest child, I'm to be the protector of our family name. To smooth things over.'

'Are you happy?' she repeated, a challenge in her voice.

'I never think about whether I am or not. Happiness isn't part of my role in life. And today—' his fingertips traced her jawline, leaving a trail of awareness behind '—your happiness is what's most important to me.'

He retreated, the contact seeming to mean nothing to him. 'If you will ensure that I get an invitation, then I will attend the soirée. It is totally up to you.'

She watched him leave, his natural strength arousing the femininity in her and making her aware of the masculinity in him.

She would see that he got an invitation. If someone had to be cut from the guest list, it would be Tenney.

Rachael's mother had been ecstatic that the Viscount wanted to attend their soirée. In fact, she'd been overwhelmed that Devlin might wish to be there and immediately set about double checking everything for the night. Her father had claimed it the best idea he'd heard in a long time and extended the invitation to the Viscount's entire family.

She tried to carry on as if it were going to be the night she would reveal her wedding date. Every time her mother detected any hesitation, Rachael claimed it was because of the burns. In truth, the pain hardly ever returned, but she still had to be cautious about how she stepped and dancing sounded excruciating.

Dancing wasn't the only part of the evening which concerned her. She hoped she could trust Tenney not to cause any disruption—after all, she would be giving him what he wanted. If he reacted publicly with anything but composure, he could hurt his future prospects. And he would sense that he must act with decorum. At least, to everyone but her.

On the night of the celebration, right as a carriage arrived at the entrance of the house, Rachael asked her mother to forgo announcing the wedding plans to the guests. A look of concern flashed across the older woman's face, but Rachael quickly reassured her mother with a kiss to the cheek.

A few moments later, Devlin walked into the room, his mother on his arm. Payton with them. The first ones to arrive. While Payton spoke with Rachael's father, her mother greeted the Countess like a sister and, after some quick compliments, they immediately started talking about Rachael's injury, their children and footwear almost in the same breath.

Devlin gave her a slight shrug and a companionable look as if to say *Mothers.*

His dark frock coat had no special buttons. His white cravat had a simple tie this time instead of the more elaborate one he'd worn at his mother's event. He appeared taller in the dark evening dress with a plain neckcloth and she wondered if his tailor and valet knew the effect they were creating—she was convinced they did. The simpler dress suited him best.

He wandered to her side, ostensibly to admire the fireplace carvings.

'I'm dreading this,' she said.

'Best to get it over.' His attention appeared to be on the fireplace.

'Your father didn't arrive?' she asked.

A flicker of his eyes in her direction. 'No. He could not attend because Mother wanted to enjoy herself.'

She hesitated, questioning him with her expression, and accepting his acknowledging nod.

'I would also like to have a pleasant evening, but I suspect it will be impossible—' his gaze glanced to the entrance '—since that friend of yours, if he can find his backbone, may also be here.'

'I have mixed feelings. I am happy for a chance to get him out of my life, but I cannot ruin this night for my parents. And I would like…' She drew in a deep breath. 'I would like to just write him a letter and tell him it is over between us. Now I understand his cowardice.'

'You may understand. You accept that it is easier, but you are still willing to handle it face to face. That is the difference between an adult and an immature blob of human flesh that is little better than what might be scraped from the sole of a boot. Not, of course, that I specifically am talking about Tenney.'

He sounded irritated, but his smile was still in place and that heartened her. Then a troubling idea lodged itself in her mind. Was she jumping from one entanglement to another at a breakneck speed? A predicament that would end badly? She truly wasn't in Devlin's social world and she accepted that. She could never see herself as a leader in society and Devlin's whole family was natural to that role.

She examined Devlin's face. No, they were entering a friendship. Her spirits blossomed. A true, lasting friendship was so rare. That would be much safer than anything else.

How she hoped they would remain friends.

'When he arrives, just remember to hold your head high—if he appears… You are entrancing. A goddess in human form.' Devlin's voice rolled over her, and settled, nestling against her.

His words embraced her first and then concern crept in. She could not fall into a deeper crevasse upon leaping out of a shallow one.

'Next time,' she murmured. 'Leave off the goddess part and I might believe you.'

He laughed. 'It's true.' Brushing a hand at her shoulders, he aligned his face near hers. 'Remember, my job as a rake is not to lie, but to merely point out what others are noticing but not mentioning.'

She wrinkled her nose, and he copied her movement, adding a teasing grin. But a little tickle of excitement lodged inside her. Devlin bolstered her spirits so and, when she compared him to Tenney who had always wanted to maintain decorum at all costs, Tenney felt more like an anchor than a beloved.

Immediately afterwards, he noted more visitors arriving. Her aunt and uncle walked through the door and made their way to her mother.

'Do you think your Tenney will be brave enough to show up after he made a complete fool of himself?' he asked.

She heard the emphasis as he'd said Tenney, but her mind focused on the word *your* and her jaw tightened.

She didn't correct Devlin, but Tenney was no longer hers…if he had ever been.

No, she decided, he'd never been hers no matter how she had deluded herself.

She returned to the conversation. 'He should. In the note I sent him, I told him we must talk.' Frowning, she added, 'I wrote that we must have had a misunderstanding and I wished to clear it…and that my mother expects me to announce the date for our wedding tonight.' She pressed her lips into a line. 'It was a short missive. A paragraph when I've never written less than a page in the past.'

His voice rumbled low. 'I should have delivered it for you.'

That image formed in her mind and she was forced to laugh. 'I might have let you.'

Now that she'd spoken with Devlin, the nervousness didn't seem so overwhelming. She'd spent more time on her appearance than she'd ever spent on one night in her life. She feared her coiffure might tumble down if she changed direction too quickly. And she didn't dare to bend over or her bosom might escape as well. And, of course, dancing would be a struggle with the new shoes and her having to take care not to reawaken the injury.

'I expect to have a grand time.' She put bravado in her words and waved her arm as if she were an empress. Then her courage plunged.

'I'm a fraud,' she whispered to him. 'I saw the mirror and I didn't even look like myself.'

'Then there are two of you, both beautiful.'

She pondered on his response. It would have been so easy for him to fumble with an answer. Tenney would have. If Devlin had complimented the woman in the mirror, then he would have insulted the true person she was. And if he'd praised the true her, it would have been an insult to the care she'd taken on her appearance.

'You have a positive word for every situation.'

'Except one. Remember, a man who'll spout untruths about your nose will lie about anything. And I repeat, you have a stunning nose, equal to the absolute best in London.'

'Thank you,' she said. 'I would have left it behind out of consideration for Mr Tenney's feelings if I could have, but I decided that would attract too much notice.'

He gave a quick clasp of her hand, and he smiled. 'You will be fine tonight. You are in your home, surrounded by people who care for you.'

Mentally, Rachael repeated the words of the letter, then reminded herself her nose was fine. In fact, it was almost the only part of her that felt normal.

But even her eyes had appeared as though they belonged to someone else when she'd prepared for the evening. They'd been rimmed with a dark powder and appeared larger. Her lips had been stained.

She'd even borrowed a heart-shaped necklace from her mother—one much larger than she normally would have chosen—and wore it.

If men could go to battle wearing armour, she supposed she could go to a soirée wearing more jewels than usual.

She even wore several rings, including Tenney's, and her stomach had rebelled when she'd placed the jewel back on her finger. She wanted to have it returned to him.

She remembered her hesitation when she'd first seen the gemstone. She should have listened to her instincts.

When Tenney stepped into the room, it was as if a cold blast of air blew over the spot on the fourth finger of her left hand. She made a fist and her hand instantly warmed.

Chapter Seven

Devlin watched the event, keeping a view so he could be aware of each arrival. No one had attended yet who could have been Tenney.

Payton's hand appeared, seemingly out of nowhere. He seesawed his flat palm in front of Devlin's face. 'There are other people in the room besides your old flame.'

'You dolt,' Devlin retorted sharply.

'If you would have said it, I would have laughed.' Payton stood at Devlin's side. 'Mmm. She is rather fetching tonight. She can set me afire any time she wishes.'

'Stay away—' Devlin stopped. 'Perhaps you would care to dance with her? After her beloved arrives.'

'Of course.' Payton smirked. 'I could waltz with her for hours.'

'Mind your manners. But let her know she's endearing. Nicely.' Devlin's eyes narrowed even more. 'And you *will* answer to my boot if you are anything but the perfect gentleman.'

Payton chuckled. 'I see how it is.'

Devlin ignored Payton, his attention caught on the

man with the over-dressed hair who had just
through the door.

'There he is,' Devlin said, as the man's eyes searched
out Rachael. 'I would wager that is the peahen she is
betrothed to.'

'Actually, I've heard he's rather clever. Has plans to
step up the social ladder if the ingratiatingly annoying
way he once introduced himself to my father is any indication.'

'He's not as clever as he thinks he is.'

'None of us is,' Payton said. 'Including you. You're
still playing with fire.'

Devlin shot his cousin a glare, but couldn't keep his
attention from Rachael. She'd noticed Tenney and the
recognition caused her to tense, her steps wobbling. Tenney stared at her.

Irritation simmered inside Devlin.

Tenney didn't even acknowledge Rachael. Instead,
he headed straight for the refreshment table, a glare in
his eyes.

'Ask her to dance,' Devlin said to Payton. 'Now. Make
her laugh, even if you have to bribe her to do so.'

'An easy task. No bribe needed,' Payton said, just before he strode to Rachael.

Conversation flickered between them. Payton appeared wounded, made a prayer clasp and then...vic-
tory, just as the people gathered for the first set started
moving.

Watching them dance, Devlin wondered if Rachael
might transfer her affections to his cousin and he hoped
her wiser than that.

Payton's awareness of Rachael was merely a man's

responsiveness to an appealing woman. Much like an insect might be called to a pretty flower.

Devlin detached himself from the surroundings. As Payton charmed Rachael, he wondered if he did the same. That if, in the initial aftermath of the accident, he'd committed himself to seeing that she was safe and it had merely carried on. It was definitely not a hardship.

Anyone would like Rachael. She had a big heart and her beauty radiated from within.

Then his attention latched on to Tenney and Tenney gave him the barest acknowledgement.

Devlin wondered that Tenney didn't quake in his boots if the man could read his mind, but then Tenney was possibly the most obtuse man on the planet. He couldn't even appreciate what a devoted wife Rachael would make.

Rachael promenaded between them as the dancers twirled.

At the end, Payton guided her from the dancers and straight to Tenney. That was not part of the plan. Devlin gritted his teeth.

Payton flashed his cousin a smile as he walked from the two and Devlin held up a fist, his crooked little finger extended. Payton laughed, raised his eyebrows and sauntered on, knowing Devlin could do nothing to him at such an event.

Devlin reminded himself it was not of his affair, but then the weasel spoke to Rachael and Devlin couldn't remain distant. Two long strides and he was beside them. He couldn't understand why he disliked Tenney so much, except that his methods were abominable. One did not discard a person after six years with a letter, particularly

if there wasn't a continent between them. A sh[...]
riage ride was not a great hardship, surely.

Devlin took an extra second to observe Rachael after he stopped in front of them. 'Miss Albright. Mr Tenney.' He ended his words on an upbeat note. 'It is so fortunate to see you both.'

Then he frowned. 'Forgive my manners, Mr Tenney. I'm Viscount Montfort. And though it may seem we don't know each other, I do feel that I know you as well as I ever could. Miss Albright has told me so many things about you.'

'I didn't know you were acquainted.' The man's eyes, which did a good impression of a reptilian blink, took in Devlin. 'Kind of you to say.'

Tenney could do with an adjustment to his nose. It was much too long and pointed. How dare he criticise Rachael for something so insignificant. Well, on Tenney's face, it was significant. Blasted thing was pointed straight at Rachael.

Rachael should thank the heavens she was not marrying Tenney. And, she didn't even have to concern herself about doing worse.

A silence surrounded them and, for Rachael's sake, Devlin ended it.

'And you, Miss Albright—' Devlin paused at just the right moment, giving himself the appearance of catching a faux pas. His voice softened. 'I only do not ask you for this next dance because I know the two of you will want to dance. Much to my chagrin.' Those words took his strength and he was surprised his teeth didn't shatter.

One reel was ending and another dance would start soon.

'Please. Do not let me keep you from dancing.'

Tenney studied Rachael before he held out his arm. After a brief second, she took it.

That would give her time to compose herself and get used to seeing that toad. Besides, two betrothed people should waltz and it would be noted if they didn't.

And Rachael could see how fortunate she would be not to be dancing with Tenney for the rest of her life.

Devlin watched them together. Rachael stared at Tenney's neckcloth. Then Devlin caught Payton's glance and his nod towards Rachael. His cousin doffed an imaginary hat to Devlin and Devlin decided he'd best leave the party for a short while. He spoke to the guests, each greeting winding him closer to the door, and made his way outside as if he were only going to talk with someone else.

He didn't want to make Rachael more nervous by watching her.

He found his carriage, discerned one of the drivers had wandered somewhere and the other's snores rumbled as his head had almost dipped into the neck of the waistcoat he wore while he still held the ribbons.

Bits of murmured conversations fluttered his way as some guests arrived and some left. The sounds of the horses nickering to each other. The creak as a carriage wheel turned. The drivers talking among themselves while they waited on their masters to finish the night. A bit of a ribald tale sounded, followed by guffaws.

The story was humorous and, he supposed, by the slurring of the man's words, ale had improved the flavour of it.

Life went on, as routinely as it always did, sprinkling happy and sad, contentment and upheaval, and irritations and joys.

He wondered if Tenney migh... who wallowed best in a pool of m... of the ... alive except when surrounded by mi... able ...

Who knew? Who cared?

He walked over to the drivers of anothe... didn't even know who the vehicle belonged... ...iage. He ...'Like a cigar?' he asked.

One nodded and stepped to the ground. Th... ...her declined.

Devlin reached into an inside pocket of his frock coat, pulled out a cigar and gave it to the man. The man used the lantern hanging from the carriage to light it.

'Do you ever get tired of waiting for the night to end?' he asked the man.

The driver took a puff of the cigar. 'Not unless it's freezing cold. We have a few hours to take it easy. To peruse the stars. Jasper can fall asleep as soon as the carriage stops, and if he starts snoring, I wake him up out of pity for the horses. They can't rest with all the noise.'

Devlin didn't speak.

'Kinda nice to get a glance of the women's fripperies. The men acting bored by it all, but doubt they really are. Me, just sitting in my comfortable boots, getting to rest my legs. Share a drink with a few friends on occasion. Always a bottle somewhere about for a long night to go easier. This is my favourite part of my employment. A chance to attend a soirée and yet not dance or dress uncomfortable.'

The other one in the seat added his opinion. 'I like Mr Albright's soirées.'

The cigar ash flickered off as the man's head darted to his friend. Devlin expected if the light were better,

n the man smoking give his friend a
he would h
stern star⸜lin asked.
'Why

Silen Devlin wondered again.
'W
'It' e family,' the one with the cigar admitted, the
light end waving. 'Mrs Albright remembers us. Near
the d of the night, the housekeeper sends a maid out
w⸜n a bite to eat. Only time I ever had tarts with fripper-
⸜es on it was at a party she'd had. Those little sprinkles
of sweetness were almost too sweet, but they were good.'

'You hope never to leave early from here.' The one
in the box spoke. 'And sometimes, a maid brings out a
bottle of wine or two. She said the mistress of the house
is pleased for her to do it. Makes the night pass more
speedily.'

'Then there was the juggler,' the one with the cigar
added. 'I didn't know a man could toss such things
about. A few of the maids brought out torches and we
stood about and watched. A sight it was.'

'A juggler?' He'd never dreamed of the night's entertainment going out to give a performance for the staff.

'Mr Albright can have a temper if things don't go as
he wishes, but he's got a good heart,' the other man said.
'His temper is like a blustery storm that leaves calm. His
staff say it's a grand house to work in.'

'Just like my staff say?' Devlin asked. Devlin doubted
his staff had ever stepped outside and said a word to the
carriage drivers, but one never knew.

'Absolutely. Of course.' Both servants spoke in tan-
dem.

'Best house ever,' the one with the cigar added.

Devlin hid his humour, assured the men had no idea

who he was or which house was h...
ter. The man speaking was a rake in it didn't ma...
lin supposed. ...n way, Dev-

'What do the staff say of the life behin...
here?' ...sed doors

'Not a thing,' the one with the cigar answe... 'What
goes on inside a house is sacred to all.'

'I would well respect and appreciate that,' Devlin ...id,
valuing a good fabrication when he heard it. He wou...
wager the servants shared many tales, but tact was required in employment.

He waited. 'I wondered, if in this household, it is all
a façade?'

'Don't think so,' the man from the box said. 'Least
ways, don't think it could be.'

'It's safe to say…' The driver took a puff of the cigar
and let the smoke drift into the night. 'I would think it
is safe to say, from just casual observation, that Mr and
Mrs Albright are on the inside exactly as they are on
the outside. They likely never get snappish with their
carriage driver.'

The other one chuckled. 'Except if a horse near steps
on Mr Albright's boot and then knocks him down. I
expect a servant who let that happen might need a set
down.' Both men shared a glance and a chuckle.

'So, it exists. True happiness in marriage.'

The end of the cigar brightened and nodded along
with the speaker's words. 'But only in sparse quantities,
if the tales of the other houses are to be believed. It is as
if a happy bolt of lightning struck Mr and Mrs Albright
and their servants reap the rewards. Sad Mr Albright
might not be having many more events like this. It's said
he's been a bit slow in payin' some of the merchants.'

'Did th...ntment bolt strike any other household
in Lond... evlin asked after considering what the
man sai...

The... with the cigar laughed. 'Many of them have
good li... —happy lives—but a bigger amount are more
sad th... happy even with all the fripperies they can pur-
cha... Some of them must get enjoyment out of being
cr...s.'

The man then scratched his chest. 'Hard to tell who
has it the best, us on the outside or them on the inside.
That lightning bolt don't know the difference between
a man with a heavy purse and a man with no purse who
has food. Just seems to strike and miss at random.'

Devlin gave a light tap to the man's arm. 'Well, I'd
best return to this event.'

'And who be you?' the smoker asked.

Devlin paused. 'One that was struck by a confused
bolt of lightning, I'd say.'

The man chuckled. 'Was nice tongue-wagging with
you.'

Devlin had to return to the house, pleased he'd
stepped outside.

Mrs Albright likely knew exactly how the staff enjoyed the night. Devlin didn't know whether to be disappointed or impressed that the Albrights' exterior ran
deeper than the surface, or sad that he wasn't sure how
deep his own interior ran.

He had no gift for numbers like his father and Payton had. No deep love of politics. No true affection for
gambling. The only skill he had was to jest without making people angry. He could say what everyone else was
thinking, but say it in such a way as to remain friends
with everyone afterwards.

off for years now and I am ready to wed. And wh
compare you to others, I immediately discern how you,
a glorified merchant's daughter, have not blossomed into
your potential.'

She had once stood outside under the eaves on a
wintery day. Snow had been on the roof. Someone had
slammed a door and suddenly snow had slid from the
roof and coated her head in moisture. Tenney's words
covered her the same way.

They danced on and she knew how it would have
been for Wellington and Bonaparte to dance together
to a funeral dirge. Only they would have respected each
other so much more.

'I am so sorry you feel that way,' she said. 'I have
waited some years to marry you. It is as if we were already married in my parents' eyes. Now you think you
don't wish to marry me. Six years we have courted. I'm
irritated.'

Irritated in that she would have liked to have put him
under the snowdrift on an eave and slammed a door.
With him lying in the snow, face up. And with icicles
on the roof, melting.

He gave a one-shouldered shrug within the dance and
her words rolled off him much easier than the snow had
melted on her face.

'You could not have informed me of this earlier instead of telling me you were waiting until you could
afford a wife and family?'

'Husbands who don't wish to be married can be rough
on their wives.' He gave a long slow blink, much as a
duellist might cock the hammer on a gun. 'It is in your
best interest to call the wedding off.'

She suddenly remembered his joy when he'd told her

of his uncle settling a plump sum on him so he could purchase a house for them. The money had arrived for Tenney, but he had yet to find the perfect house that would suit them.

'Will you return the funds to your uncle?'

He batted the question into nonsense with a blink. 'It is too late. I've purchased a house. But you will not be living in it. I do not intend to share one window with you. It is not in your best interest to pursue a marriage with me. Unless you are a bigger imbecile than I think.'

He had a way with his statements just as Devlin did, but in his case, he made people's stomachs roil without effort.

Music wafted around them so peacefully, everything seemed as normal as it should and she imagined a few more, bigger, icicles on a roof.

He'd just given her one more reason for needing her to call off the wedding. His uncle would likely understand Ambrose keeping the house if she didn't wish to wed him, feeling empathy for his nephew.

She searched her mind for the proper set down for him, but none in her vocabulary suited.

'In truth, I will not take one penny from you, Mr Tenney—Ambrose. I am my father's heir and he will ensure that I am provided for. I just cannot tell my family at this time as they will be inquisitive. I must have time to absorb the news. It would not do to burst into tears at a question.'

'Nonsense,' Tenney said. 'It is a feeble excuse in that you wish to grapple with me and try to get a settlement price from me.'

'No. I will take nothing from you.'

'That will change,' Tenney said. 'Your father's jewellery business is going bankrupt. The shops are, at best, wavering. It is only a matter of time before the creditors take them. You misled me about your station in life. You plainly deceived me.'

'I did no such thing.' Rachael stopped moving, but he gave her a tug and pulled her along with him.

Rachael used all her strength to keep moving and could spare none to speak. Surely Tenney lied about her father. Her father had mentioned economising on occasion, but never with a sense of urgency. Then she recalled the memory of her father's tightened lips when her mother spoke of a dowry.

She caught a sparkle of smug assurance in Tenney's eyes as he studied her expression.

The music ended, and Tenney led her from the floor without another word.

'If you wish for the marriage to be called off, Mr Tenney, I will do so.' Her words were soft so that no one else could hear, but she could not keep the frost from them, and she had no ability to smile as Devlin did. 'Sooner. Not later. You merely had to request what you wished for. Tonight is not the night. My entire family is here and I cannot bear to have them all question or commiserate. The night my mother worked so hard for will be ruined. Even a countess is here and that is a first for Mother. This is an important night for her. I cannot spoil it.'

'That is your problem. I cannot take on a wife with no prospects and I refuse to let this betrothal continue. You will only use the length of it to punish me in a legal action. One second more is too long for this to continue. You will end it. And tonight.'

'No. I will not. If you continue the charade tonight,

I will send you a letter that plainly states I am calling the wedding off.'

'It is in your best interest.'

'Miss Albright.' A voice rumbled behind her, caressing in its tone. She turned, almost falling into Devlin.

'May I have the next dance?' He put out a hand to stop her from tumbling against him. 'And might I say, you have the loveliest nose I have ever seen.' He held out his arm.

Tenney gasped and she saw him reach for her, but she stepped aside.

She spoke to Devlin. 'And might I say, you have the best manners I have ever seen.'

'You deserve the best, Miss Albright.'

She let him lead her to the furthermost area from Tenney. 'I fear I haven't had that in the past.'

Devlin didn't speak. His jawline appeared to be made of granite and his eyes even harder.

'But can we please not dance? I would prefer to stand still.'

'I hope he chokes on his own stench. He has doused himself in some shaving soap that only vermin could survive, which explains how he is still upright.'

'It doesn't matter,' she said. 'None of it does now. It's over.'

'What a waste of an education. What a waste of a human. What a waste of a nose.'

'I'm not going to miss him as much as I conceived.' She shuddered. 'You were right. I will not miss him at all.' She put a palm to her forehead. 'I will only question my judgement.'

'He is nothing more than a shrivelled stinkhorn mushroom.'

'He is much worse than any toadstool.'

Devlin paused. 'I agree.'

'Tenney and I have been acquainted a long time and it can't have been easy for him. I will say a kind word for him in my prayers if I can think of any. Perhaps that he live a long and wintery life with many icicles to keep him warm, although no mushrooms survive the cold.'

'The stinkhorn does.'

Rachael stared at Devlin. She didn't think she'd ever seen a toadstool in the wintertime, but then, she didn't go out looking for them and she'd never heard of a stinkhorn mushroom before, but the name fit. He always wore an overabundant amount of scent.

'I assure you, Rachael. You are better off without him.'

'You're right.' She turned to him. 'I feel lighter. This has weighed on me the past few days.'

She considered what she would tell her parents the next morning and ask her mother to share it with a few close friends who weren't known for discretion.

'He's a fungus,' Devlin muttered.

She brightened. 'Thank you for understanding that it has been difficult for me. I feel so much better that you have been here tonight to bolster me up.'

Devlin stopped, repeating her words. 'Bolster you up?'

'Yes. You always know what to say to make me feel better about the end of the betrothal. Tomorrow I will tell Mother that tonight Mr Tenney and I both agreed we have grown apart. I cannot say we are still friends. I can't. But it must get about that I am no longer betrothed and that it was a decision on my part. He fears I'll attempt a breach of promise and I won't do that. He's also concerned his uncle will want the funds replaced for a house that Ambrose purchased.'

She suspected the dwelling had a lot to do with Ambrose's timing. With the residence, he would be better positioned to approach unmarried women.

'I'm surprised that he didn't trust me enough to have a conversation with me. I would never subject him to a breach of promise suit. An ice storm, perhaps.'

'That is solicitous of you,' he said as the next dance began and they stood near the musicians, but where they could watch everyone. 'I would be happy to bestow an ice storm upon him if I had the power. But really, does ice bother mushrooms or are they already trampled underfoot by women with discerning and beautifully shaped noses?'

'Perhaps only one nose per woman?' she asked, imagining a woman with three noses stomping a low-growing Tenney-faced weed into the ground. She laughed.

Tenney must have recognised the laugh because his face darted in her direction, before he gave a glare and left.

'You are making this much easier,' she said to Devlin.

'At your service. Any time you need to rid yourself of a defective sweetheart, find me.'

'Hopefully, never again. Never.'

The music commenced for another dance.

'Tomorrow I will tell my parents,' she said. 'Then Mother will tell my aunts and cousins. It will be easy to explain to her that after I saw him tonight, I felt no affection.'

The world had not ended. She would be a spinster, but she would develop a pastime. Something that made the world better, or at least, made her feel better.

She remembered Tenney's comment that her father's business was in financial distress. She hoped it was another of his imaginations. Surely it was. But if he believed her impoverished and no longer wished to marry her because of her lack of funds…

Devlin watched her, concern in his face, and that erased the feeling of being spurned.

'You have befriended me at the time I needed it most,' she said. 'Your cousin reports you are an exemplary friend who could soothe over a windstorm and turn it into dust. It's true.'

Devlin didn't answer.

She compared his jaw to Tenney's, which always seemed smooth and soft. Devlin had been dishevelled in the library, nearly sporting a beard, but on him, it only made him more endearing.

She noticed the crisp starch of freshly laundered clothing, a hint of another soft soap that he'd perhaps used on his hair and a gentle leather scent. The delicate fragrance around him only contrasted against his strength.

'I believe I would like to do something risqué,' she said.

His brows lifted and her chin went up.

'Yes.' She felt daring and imagined she could combine her maturity and the spinster. 'I believe I will have another glass of punch.'

'Dare you be so foolhardy?' he asked.

'You've not tasted the punch. It's more potent than the wine.'

'I would be honoured to dance with you, Rachael, and help you show your daring side to the world. Are you sure you would not consider it now that Tenney has left? A waltz?'

'Perhaps something more respectable?'

Humour flashed across his face.

'It is just because Mother informed the musicians they must keep the waltzes to a minimum and they will not play another one.'

'Then we will take our chances with whatever music they play.'

Ending the night by dancing with Devlin helped her consider herself precious instead of rejected. His ire somehow made her feel protected, more feminine and without the many defects Tenney had listed.

She caught her reflection in a mirror and examined her nose. Nothing was wrong with it. Tenney was a liar.

Devlin must have been watching her. 'It has not grown this evening. I promise I will let you know if it swells or takes flight. And if you should have three, I will kiss the tip of each one.'

Her eyes brightened. 'I would let you.'

Devlin's lips turned up with soft laughter and his head dipped just a touch in acknowledgement of the private bond between them and it was as if they had kissed.

For such a disastrous night, she was surprised at how much better she felt.

But then she noticed Tenney had returned and was watching them. He huffed and stalked out of the door. In that instant, she remembered how vengeful he could be.

Chapter Nine

With fashion plates spread before her and her mother standing at her shoulder, the time would never be better. She filled her lungs and the words burst out of her. 'Mr Tenney and I will not wed.'

Her mother's rings flashed as she clasped her hands. 'Oh.'

Rachael bit the inside of her lip.

'So that is why you became distressed after you received the post at the Countess's?' her mother asked.

'Yes. I don't want to even be near him again. It was almost a game I was playing…being in love.' She traced her fingertip over the costly ballgown she would never wear. 'I missed him when he left. I waited for each letter. I read them time and time again. I would have married him.'

'Are you positive it's over?'

'I posted a kind letter to him today calling it off. It is in my handwriting and he will have proof I will not consider a breach of promise suit.'

Mrs Albright threw up her hands. 'My daughter. She sends the man verification to reassure him after she waits for him for six—six—six and a half years.'

Rachael felt she was in the lull before the storm, but in this case it was after. Her mother hadn't reacted with dismay as she'd expected.

'Are you returning the ring?' her mother asked. 'Promise me you will do the right thing and return the... object.'

'Of course. I sent it to him with the letter this morning.' She shut her eyes. 'It never fitted properly on my finger. I kept studying it, wondering how his relative could have tolerated such an atrocity.'

'Your heart may have been telling you that the two of you weren't suited.'

Rachael stared at her mother. 'Would you want the stone?'

'No. The person who cut that rock could never work for your father. The flaw was sizeable. And the colour?' She shuddered. 'It proved your fondness for him that you liked it. Besides, he smelled rather like a bottle of medicine. Not the good medicine, either.'

'That I tolerated the flawed gemstone was the indication I cared for him.'

'Perhaps the first three years. I'd say you tolerated *him* after that. Love is a jewel in its own right. And in Tenney's case, a defective one.'

'With inferior metal.'

Her mother smiled. At that moment, Rachael accepted that her mother hadn't been fond of Tenney and was pleased to see him go. It had never entered Rachael's mind that her mother might be happy about a broken betrothal.

'Not to mention he liked the idea of having the shops,' Mrs Albright said. 'He did comment on the nice lodgings above it for the Grimsleys and wondered about the rent per annum. We are fortunate that the Grimsleys work for us. They are such dears.'

Inwardly, Rachael flinched. If Tenney had determined he was getting a thriving business, but then heard it wasn't…perhaps he had never cared for her at all. Perhaps, for six years, she'd been duped. And perhaps he knew what he was speaking of when he said that her father's finances were faulty.

Rachael refused to ask her mother if their finances weren't doing well. Besides, she wouldn't know. Only her father would. And Mr Grimsley, but likely he would consider it disloyal to speak with her about such a thing without her father's blessing.

'Does your father know that you are calling the betrothal off?'

'No. I'll tell him tonight. Will you tell the cousins?'

Her mother nodded. 'And I will inform them that is why you never set a date for the marriage. Deep inside, you knew he wasn't right for you.'

'That might not be honest.'

'Then I will tell them that we are just extremely fortunate that you did not set a date for the marriage. And I will say that I suspected many times he wasn't right for you. It will not be a lie.'

Rachael examined the ring on her forefinger. One of her grandmother's many gems she and her sister had inherited. It felt good to wear the heirloom. 'At first, I was disappointed and I'm still hurt, but it is for the best. I will be happy to be a shop owner's daughter.'

She remembered Tenney's words about her father's business, and how, of late, her father often seemed preoccupied.

She'd even heard him ask her mother about the cost

of the soirée and he'd chewed his lip after she answered, but he'd assured her that no price was too much for his family to be happy.

An overwhelming loneliness engulfed her. She turned her head so her mother couldn't perceive the tears in her eyes, but her mother wasn't fooled.

Her mother bent to hug Rachael. 'He's not worth crying over.'

'I know,' she said, but she wasn't sure if the words were true. It wasn't Mr Tenney she missed. But Devlin. She'd not anticipated that removing Ambrose from her life would take out Devlin as well.

Devlin sat at his breakfast table, sipped his tea and half-listened to the Baron go on about his latest love. He pretended to read the paper and only spoke at the longest pauses Bomford delivered. The ones after he recounted something particularly lovely about Priscilla. Devlin wished the Baron would sometimes think before he fell in love. If only for half an hour. Less even. The time it took to turn the page on a newspaper.

Bomford was deeply in love with Priscilla and recounting her qualities, both of them, ad infinitum.

'Do you think you are falling in love with her excess of bosom?' Devlin glanced over the top of the paper and asked. Just asked, then he noted, 'It's hard to miss her. She tends to flutter about and reminds me of a loud bird.'

A true statement. Terribly unkind and he felt a cad for saying the most offensive thing he could think of. A test of his ability not to anger. He wanted to be certain he was not deluding himself in believing he could soothe almost any statement. Yet, it was important for him to know if he did have a skill he'd not grasped and which he'd taken for granted.

But, by the equanimity on Bomford's face, Devlin could see no offence was taken. He wondered if he had a calming voice, an inflection of tone, or a skill of making an observation at the right moment that took the sting out of whatever words he might utter.

'She cannot alter her bosom.' Bomford smiled. 'And she is a swan in a pool of lesser birds. If few men with substance have been fascinated by her, then it is time one did. I am pleased you understand that. Poor woman. I must be more cautious with her, to have been troubled with so many ill-guided attentions.'

Devlin shrugged. He could speak the truth and no one even held him at fault. He'd heard the phrase *silver-tongued* before and it hadn't entered his mind that it could possibly apply to him, or that he had a rare ability to speak without offending.

He turned the page of the newspaper, then looked over the top again. 'Do you think you have been quick to fall in love? Perhaps not really thinking?'

The Baron gazed into the distance. 'Good on you to watch out for your old friend, Devlin. Yes. I have. Now I can reflect on it. I will discuss it with Priscilla and find out what she thinks. Perhaps she and I will be able to find solace in each other's arms. I may propose.'

Devlin returned to reading the paper. 'You're being rash.'

The Baron nodded. 'I suppose so. Both Priscilla and I have been alone for so long. It is time we both found happiness.'

The paper rustled as Devlin again turned the page.

Well, perhaps Bomford and Priscilla were well suited for each other. Yes, he decided, they were.

Payton walked in. He had a folded newspaper and he used it to tap Devlin on the shoulder.

'Oh. You've got a copy,' Payton noted. 'Surprised you're not angry. Just anticipated you might be.'

'What are you talking about?'

'The newsprint.' Then he noticed the paper Devlin read. 'Oh. Wrong one. You're reading *The Times*.' He shrugged. 'A wasted life, yours. This auspicious one has all the latest scandals.'

Devlin cleared his throat and glared at his cousin. 'You are an idler.'

Payton laughed. 'You're correct. I'm right there with you.'

Damn. Perhaps no one took him seriously.

Payton opened his paper. 'The night that Miss Albright danced with Tenney, it's said that a lot more was happening. It's said she only had eyes for a particular viscount,' Payton continued. 'Tenney was deeply distraught. I am not even mentioned and she spoke some time with me. Guess one's not important if one doesn't have a title.'

Devlin held out a hand for the paper and Payton released it.

He spoke to the Baron. 'It seems Miss Albright has spurned Mr Tenney's devoted attentions after a friend alerted him she is becoming loose with said affections. He discovered it to be true, according to this friend who is not named.' He touched his chest and his voice took on overblown innocence. 'Who suspected she could be... attached to anyone but this Tenney?'

Each word Devlin read seized him, strangling his

voice. He had to crumple the paper before he could speak. 'It is not true and you know it. It is a malicious lie.'

'I don't believe Miss Albright is the fickle shrew she is painted in the story, but the paper reports it is to Tenney's great relief that she has called off the betrothal. It seems she dragged it along only planning to keep him until he was well established and so her settlement in a breach of promise would be more. It's said she acted outrageously at an earlier night and her flagrant behaviour may have resulted in an altercation between two men, causing a fire.'

'Tripe.'

'How do you know?' Bomford's eyes narrowed. 'And who was she dallying with that caused the fire?'

Devlin leapt to his feet, scraping the chair over the floor. 'I was there that night. So were you. You blasted set her on fire.'

'Oh, *that* fire. No lasting harm done. Priscilla said I was heroic moving everyone aside and putting out the edges of the inferno. Appreciated your support, Dev.'

Devlin pointed to the paper. 'Read what is said about her. That cad wanted to break off. She is doing the noble thing. Making it easy for him. This is what she gets. Painted like a strumpet for the world to peruse, and faithless as well. He wants to destroy her.'

'How do you know Mr Tenney wanted to break off with her?' Payton asked.

'Because she told me,' Devlin said, whirling to frown at his cousin.

Bomford and Payton shared a quick glance and a grin.

'Ah,' the Baron said. 'The sparks are between Miss

Albright and Dev. I did detect they couldn't take their eyes off each other.'

Damn. He could grab them both by the neck and bounce their heads together and they would not be angry with him or see what was in front of them. Rachael was being destroyed and only he could see the tragedy.

'Unusual for you to get so upset over a woman,' Payton said. 'And you never did make it to the lodge when she was recovering at your house.'

'He didn't, did he? Devlin is our mystery viscount.' The Baron chuckled. 'I will have to tell Priscilla.'

Devlin glared at them for a second. 'You're both wrong. But even if you were both right, it doesn't matter. The mushroom of a man is not worthy of her.'

Devlin stalked out of the room. He intended to go straight to Tenney and demand that he set the record straight.

Outside the door, he stopped.

He didn't know where Tenney lived.

But he did know where Rachael lived. He would have to find her and get the stinkhorn's address.

Devlin strode through the doorway, and passed the servant who'd led him to the sitting room where she and her mother sat.

'May I speak with your daughter alone?' Devlin asked, holding up the crumpled newsprint. He noticed that some of the ink had stained his hands. Fitting.

Her mother gave Rachael a questioning glance. 'But— I don't know if her father would approve.'

'I'm sure he wouldn't mind,' Devlin said. 'I want to discuss Mr Tenney with her. She needs to know what a…questionable *mushroom* he is. The poisonous kind.'

'Tenney? A mushroom?' Her mother rose, but remained in place, studying the situation. 'I would think him more a snail.'

'I would like to speak with Rachael. Alone, if you will approve?' He'd not meant to call her by her first name, but the word was already out of his mouth.

He expected her mother to argue, but instead, she beamed. 'Well, in that case, I will leave you two. Do take care.'

She bustled out.

'What is wrong with you?' Rachael asked. 'Now Mother likely thinks you are the reason for the betrothal to end.'

'You can tell her the truth later.' He paced across the room and then returned to his original position.

'Tenney is—he is unconscionable. He has spoken about you to the newspaper.'

Her mouth opened, but she didn't speak. 'And I sent him the nicest letter after Mother's soirée calling off the betrothal.'

He paced three steps. 'That was blasted considerate of you. I'd like to send him to an undertaker. Better yet, a body snatcher.' He held the paper out. 'Read this.'

She hesitated, then took the paper. She braced herself before she straightened it. She didn't even want his name mentioned in her presence and, from Devlin's manner, she wasn't going to like what she read.

She held the print and at first it was as incomprehensible as the letter from Tenney. She read through twice, the second time studying each sentence before she accepted the words in front of her.

She collapsed into the chair, clenching the paper. She

didn't want to believe it. Just like she hadn't wanted the letter to be true.

'You've done absolutely nothing to deserve this. Nothing. You did exactly as he wanted. You dissolved the betrothal. Yet he painted you as a conniving woman who used him to further yourself.'

'How did—? Even if he hated me, I can't believe he would do this. I presumed he cared for my parents. They welcomed him into our home. This will be so painful for them.' She held the paper in front of her. 'They'll be so upset. And he had to have initiated this. He had to have.'

'This is a bigger blow than just a slap to the face. It can hurt your father's business if people connect you to the ventures and question your integrity.'

'No one can doubt the value of the items we sell. The silver goods are marked carefully and the tariffs paid.'

'Oh, they can. Even if they merely question your honesty, it cannot benefit and can only damage your family.'

Her body deflated. It felt as if her future had been pulled from her, leaving nothing behind but an empty woman who must always pretend everything was glorious.

Devlin seized the paper from her hands and tossed it to the floor. He lifted her to her feet, with all the care of lifting the most prized artwork in the world. 'I will not challenge him to a duel. I will grab him by the scruff of the neck and take him to the newspaper offices and demand that he tell the truth. He cannot do this to you.'

She took Devlin's sleeves. 'It will do no good. It will only make the matter worse.' She shook her head. 'Besides, think of our mothers. Yours and mine. Anything you do will only make the scandal bigger and will embarrass them.'

'I want his words to blow up in his face.'

'You can't fight with Tenney. It will not help my reputation. Imagine the tongues wagging. *Well, we know the paper was right about why* she *broke things off.*'

'The letter you have,' Devlin said. 'It's in his handwriting. It shows the truth of him. No man worth his spit would do something like that. Let me have it. I will show it around at the club and before long all the wives and sweethearts will know. A version of it will likely end up being in the newspaper.'

She put her cupped fingers over her nose. 'No. I cannot. Don't defend me. It could go so wrong. I will be the centre of attention. All eyes will be on me—and on my face.'

'Then let me handle it quietly. I will pound him small enough to fit into a snuffbox if he doesn't tell the truth.'

'It's my fault as well.' She turned, eyes hidden. 'He changed. I've examined his letters, particularly the last ones, and I can see it now.'

His jaw dropped. 'You were rereading letters from him?'

'Yes. It's been on my mind. Why he did that. Why he could not discuss it with me first. But now I can accept what I missed. Because I did not yearn for him and miss him when we weren't together, it didn't seem odd to me that he was the same. Perhaps he felt he could not broach the subject with me.'

'You are making excuses for him. I want to throttle him and you want to ignore his disloyalty.' He shook his head, as if slinging poison from his mind. 'You have to tell your side. Or let me tell it for you. If anyone can smooth this over and make you come out smelling like flowers in springtime, I can.'

'I can't. I can't let you solve this for me. It's too new. Too painful. I'm humiliated.'

Devlin couldn't understand her logic. How could she feel humiliated? How? She had done nothing wrong.

She had to let him take care of this.

He had a weapon—his easy-going smile—and it would work wonders for her. His experience with being a rake would stand her in good stead. He could stir up so much support for her with a soft word dropped here, a question there.

Damn. With just a smile and a raised eyebrow at the right places, he could probably drag Tenney through more mud than the man had ever seen.

Rachael didn't grasp the situation. She had the proof in black and white of Tenney's perfidy, yet she didn't accept it. She was too gentle-hearted.

A statuette caught his eye, a butterfly, suspended glass baubles reflecting the sunlight of the window.

'You do not understand that you're supposed to be a butterfly,' he said.

Her eyes narrowed. 'Butterfly?'

'Yes. You're the beauty of the world. To be protected. Cherished. Adored. To nurture in return.'

'No. I have feet and arms instead of wings. I am created to work.'

'Isn't it much more pleasant to be an object of veneration?' he asked, wondering, and thinking it would bring her all the joy she would ever need.

Light he'd not seen before shone on her face. 'I will work.'

He waited, returning his perusal to the glass baubles. Letting the silence in the room grow.

'I want— What I really want—is— Late in the night while I was reading the letters over and over, my father noticed I was awake and was concerned. I confided that I wasn't to marry. I explained that I had changed my mind. He was crushed. I cried when I saw that and I begged him to let me have more to do with the jewellery he sells to take my mind from the fact that I'm never to wed. At first he refused, then he told me the truth of the finances. He said there may be nothing left there for me.'

'You need to consider that. A husband's funds can save you.'

'I may remain a spinster.' Her chin went high. 'I see nothing wrong with that.'

'Neither do I. It was a statement.'

'Didn't sound nice.' She glared at him, her voice tense. 'You don't think I'm capable of handling business matters and I should marry so I won't starve.' She shook her head. 'And you are the one who told me that a match with a disparaging person would be like wearing good shoes with thorns in them.'

Her irritation shocked him, and he couldn't speak. He'd meant nothing unpleasant by his comment, only having concern for her future, and she was upset.

He studied her. Yes, even her eyes were a little pinched. Those beautiful, expressive eyes that he could gaze into for hours.

Instantly, he stopped the direction of his imaginings. He was thinking like a heartsore spinster himself. He coughed, pulling himself into reality.

'It was meant as a sincere, respectful comment. The business might fail. You will have no way of supporting yourself if it does. If you marry, a husband's assistance can be vital.'

now, that isn't in my future. A silver and jewelry shop in London is. The small structure which sells goods in Manchester and has rooms above it. And two ventures in Bath and I want to make the best of them.'

'Then aid your father within the constraints of society. You cannot afford to let your name be tarnished in the paper. You cannot. Don't sit by and watch the business dwindle into nothing.'

He walked over and picked up the fashion-plate magazine. 'If you are not going to flutter about and pursue a courtship, then you'll have to take on more work. You'll have to be an ambassador for your family endeavours. My father attends events and, often as not, during the night a word or two of business is discussed that he acts on later. Perhaps a question is asked or a new idea is presented and the others give their opinions on it.'

'That doesn't sound like a relaxing night.'

'It is, to them. They are with friends, discussing what can go right and what can go wrong and why things work the way they do. I suppose it is much like mothers might enjoy discussing their children. The men are discussing their workday babies. The way they spend their daytime hours.'

For a moment, he'd forgotten who he was and when he remembered the ease returned to his face. He held a hand out, planning to touch her arm in a reassuring caress. He stopped just before he held her.

Devil take it, she must have the sort of charm he had, only hers worked on him, pulling him to her. Wrapping him up in her eyes and causing him to forget everything but comforting and being close to her.

He had to remain in control of himself. He couldn't let two alluring eyes, a perfect nose and luscious lips distract him. He was not a youth glancing at an attractive woman, yet he was unable to distance himself from an awareness of her.

'Let's sit,' he said and, instead of an embrace, he guided her to the sofa and sat beside her. As he sat beside her, a feeling of peace invaded him. He wondered if Rachael somehow did for him what he did for others.

His mind fastened on the image of her in his arms. It would not be the same as holding any of the fragile butterflies. Deep within, he knew he missed something vital by not clasping her, but she was too injured. He could not take advantage of her when she was in pain. He would not use someone's heart to manipulate them.

He wanted to comfort her, but holding her would only be diverting her from her problem. It wouldn't be benefiting her at all. It might be damaging.

He directed all his attention on what she needed.

'What is your plan?' he asked.

'I am to have a business. Jewellery would not have been my first choice, but it is what is in front of me. I am to take care of myself. I don't wish to spend my days getting my hair pulled and twisted and filled with so much hair dressing that my scalp is sore when it is being washed out, while my father is worrying about how he will afford the maid for me.'

'You know that life is a game,' he said. 'That's what it must be to have some happiness.'

Happiness. Deep in the pit of his stomach, a nagging feeling reminded him he might not comprehend his own feelings, but only how to create solace for others. A touch of anger replaced the doubt and then he shoved it aside, knowing he must soothe Rachael.

He opened the periodical to a page and randomly

glanced through it, a smile on his lips. 'This is a military catalogue for women.'

She let a whisper of breath flow through her teeth before speaking. 'You are a rake. It is a game to you. To me it has to be more. I must gather all my wits and duck my head and work as hard as I can. My security will depend on it. I can't spend my parents' limited resources on frivolities.'

'It's more than that.'

'It's more? Dances and drinking and gambling? You have the most fortunate life of all. To be the heir.'

'It is my role. I am happy that it suits me well. I represent my family, although it is not seen that way. If my father makes a misstep, and he has on many occasions— he doesn't get on well with my mother—sometimes word gets about that he has a new sweetheart and then I am there to make a bit of laughter. *It's the way of the Bryan family. For centuries*, I say at the club. I laugh it off. I might shake my head, but I make light of it.'

'It's terribly wrong of your father and you shouldn't jest it away.'

'I can't make it go away. But I can make light of it. When I see my mother, I twirl her around and tell her she is the best mother in the world. That we are indeed blessed to have her. She glows with happiness and I tell her tall tales to make her laugh. I am the rakish, wayward ambassador for my family. I duel in jests, dancing, gambling and whatever else that will make the world lighter.' He rose, lifted the magazine again, frowned at the cover and then held it up to her. 'And you must be the same. With soirée dresses. With smiles.'

She shook her head.

He tossed the periodical to the table, letting it slap

the wood. 'You have a man of affairs to handle the business of the day. You need to increase the customers. Let the man of affairs work with the numbers. You send the people to him.'

'I can understand numbers,' she said. 'Eventually. I will get a tutor if need be. I want to absorb what goes on behind the curtain. Why some endeavours fail and others succeed.'

He felt he was trying to tell her that very thing, but she had to believe it also. 'Calculate the true figures, Rachael. Mr Tenney just made a jab at your profits. I'm sure he was only wanting to protect his own reputation and finances. He didn't give a jot about yours.'

She must understand how precarious her financial future was. She mustn't be forced to marry someone because the roof was leaking, the larders were empty and her mother was hungry.

'In society, right now Tenney will not turn the other cheek and wish you well. He now holds a grudge against you. It is the way of people like him. Rise above. Rise above so you can drop the contents of a chamber pot on his head. A chamber pot filled with coins. When the night is long and you are tired of the dancing, remember Tenney and keep moving.'

She stood. 'Society doesn't fit me. They don't want me.'

'Build a bridge into it one smile at a time.'

'I don't feel like smiling.'

'Do it anyway. It's comforting to others. I seem to be able to say what I think and people don't hold it against me. In fact, it seems as though I can say rather straightforward comments and get praise because I have no animosity in my voice. It's my haphazard observation, not criticism. And presented as a jest we're all in on.'

'You flash a smile and people forgive you.'

'A smile can get a person far. I'm proof of that, I believe,' he said. 'It is a useful tool. I've used it many times.'

'Do you?'

'Absolutely. I build on success. The lessons…who would want lessons to learn more? I would rather learn from the people around me and discover what life has taught them. They are my studies.'

'You must have been a terrible student to your tutors.'

'No. They loved me. I wanted to do well so I asked questions and left the studies alone. I told them I might need their knowledge in my estate management some day and they tried to make the way easier for me.'

'Why not both the books and the tutors?'

'Would you say to a songbird perhaps don't spend so much time making the world happier with your music, But endeavour to wake up people in the morning like the cockerel does? And then would you ask the cockerel to sing for us so that he may be a better chicken?'

'You are adept at speaking nonsense.' Her upper lip tightened.

'You must control yourself, Rachael, and not try to be so obviously sensible. Life does not always make sense to the kind-hearted. In fact, the opposite may be true.'

She looked at the ceiling and then at him. 'I will try to be more nonsensical around you.'

'Yes. If you must think, please do so early in the day. Get it over with quickly so you can enjoy the remaining hours better. The people at the dances don't want you to show them how intelligent you are, they want you to listen to them. That is the secret. Ask them the questions to get the answers they want to share.'

Without his awareness, they had moved closer and closer, and now they were inches apart, connected and separated by the tensions that smouldered within.

He'd never stood so close to a woman and felt so much without them touching.

For the second time in an hour, he lost his ability to speak.

'I'm not good at deception,' she said.

His mindfulness returned. The distance between them increased. 'It's not deception. It's survival.'

She didn't respond, standing as firm as a statue and eyes as unfeeling.

He wanted to change the statue. To soften it. To bring it to life in a way it had never been before.

But it was not his role to take.

'You must be among the people who will be helpful and you must persuade them you're worthy,' he said. 'Life is like mirrors reflecting our outsides, not holding our insides up for everyone else to witness. People envision us through their own eyes and hardships.'

With a flutter of her lashes, she batted his statement from her. 'Words from someone at the top of the heap.'

'But it's a heap. And it can be climbed. Surely you have a drop of adventurous spirit inside you. You'd better if you're devising a plan of taking on a business endeavour.'

'You're proposing more than a drop.'

'You must don your armour. Your livelihood might depend on it. And your parents need you to be strong.'

'I don't have the funds to compete with earls' and bankers' families. To appear at the gatherings over and over and mingle with them. And I am strong.' Her voice faltered.

'Strong enough to help your parents?'

She flinched.

He couldn't summon a smile. It was as if he watched two people he did not know.

'I don't want to dance the night away,' she said. 'I want to be serious. To be myself. I want to learn from Mr Grimsley. Besides, I can't receive the invitations to go among society's notables.'

'You should trust me on this. I can help with the invites.'

'Perhaps.' One clipped word with not quite two syllables.

With the frost lingering in the air, he bowed and took his leave.

But he left a part of himself behind in the room with Rachael. It was a part that he could not see, or feel, but he knew something was missing inside him that hadn't been missing when he arrived.

They would likely never see each other again, except from a distance.

Chapter Ten

'Your mother told me Montfort is here.' Her father hurried into the room. He examined the space and discovered she was alone. He checked again, making sure he'd not missed seeing Devlin hiding behind a curtain or in a corner.

'Yes. He just left.' She picked up the newspaper, noticing the stiff creases. The places Devlin's hand had smeared the un-ironed ink. No matter, it would make excellent fodder for the fire.

'What's that?' her father asked, diverted.

'The Viscount wanted me to read the society pages,' she said.

'I heard.' His chest puffed. 'What did he think of it? Of the broken betrothal? The rumours?'

'He was dismayed.'

'Oh.' Her father's lips moved again, but no sound emerged.

'Dismayed,' he finally repeated. 'Well, your happiness is more important than anything else.' He moved into the hallway, shoulders slumped, seeming to forget they were having a conversation.

His footsteps plodded in the hallway. Rushed whispers. Her mother's voice. Consoling her father.

She opened the paper again and the words hadn't changed.

Yes, she had financial needs to keep her mind from this. For today.

She gathered her skirts in her hand and hurried out of the room and down the stairs.

Outside, she rushed to the street and saw the carriage, already trundling away.

She waved the paper wide and then flung it towards the carriage, scattering the pages into the air.

The wheels slowed.

She stood alone, watching each revolution as the cab springs squeaked while the driver slowed, then navigated a sharp turn.

Papers were strewn around her feet. She scooped them up and held them, waiting for the vehicle to return.

Devlin jumped from the carriage. 'Oh, did I forget that?' He smiled. 'I really was giving that rubbish to you.'

She scrunched it into a smaller wad. 'I'm making no promises. But I'll try. If you'll help me.' Wind blew a lock of hair across her face and she brushed it aside.

He was silent, but this time he knew it was because happiness was trying to flourish in his heart. The part of himself that he'd left behind had returned and filled him stronger than ever.

Rachael needed him and that made him whole.

'The Countess will produce invitations for you,' he said.

'That would be kind.'

He took the crumpled mess from her hands. 'You've got a smudge of ink. By your ear.'

'I almost always get newsprint on my face. It's a skill I have.' She brushed it, missing.

He nodded to the vehicle. 'Let me put this aside and we'll talk about the skills you'll need to navigate the finest ducal ball.'

He tossed the print into the interior of the vehicle and closed the door. They stood, the body of the carriage shielding them from most eyes.

'The smudge is still there.' He questioned with his brows, she nodded and remained immobile, while he brushed the speck at her ear. Bolts of warmth caused her to feel like a different person.

He stilled. 'You're perfect now.'

'I don't have a lot of gowns to wear for gatherings and festivities among exalted peers. You have to spend a great sum on many dresses. Mrs Grimsley's daughter makes all my clothing, except for the clothing for balls. I don't know if she is skilled enough for them.'

'You must not concentrate on what you can't do at an event, or in life, because the world is full of those things. You must ponder on what you can do. You must work on the bridge to build that will get you in the direction you want to go. The shortest path and the easiest path are already overfilled by others.'

She put a hand at her throat. 'That's what you say to help me? Encouraging me?'

He nodded. 'You will do what feels impossible to you. Humans do the near unobtainable all the time. Every single day someone is out there making strides. Some-one who ignores the struggle and focuses on the goal, who is willing to play the game with what he has and not what everyone else has.'

'I'm not skilled at the easy conversations people have in gatherings.'

'Again, you're looking for excuses. You don't need to walk into the room once and have everyone amazed that such a wondrous person has deemed to attend their night. At a soirée, you would merely have to convince them of your honesty, your integrity and let them admire the jewellery.'

He tapped her wrist. 'If you've a bracelet that goes with the dress, you must wear it and be seen. You are not to be *just* a shopkeeper's daughter. You bring every bit of your genuineness into the room when you walk in. And you are to make everyone envious of the woman who can drape herself in jewels and have no unease about the cost. They won't notice the dress. They'll only notice the loveliness. Are you aware of the expense of jewels?'

'Yes, but I can wear a new bauble once and it goes back to Grimsley the next day. To me, even the most expensive ones wear just the same as the glass ones.'

She held up her empty wrist. 'Once I took a bracelet covered in sapphires from Father's cases and it was too big for me, but I wore it around the house for the day until he saw it. I feared he would collapse. He said I had more on my wrist than the roof over our heads.'

'I like your wrist without adornment, but this is not about you. It's business. You can transform yourself with the gentle artillery, the battle plan and reinforcements if needed.'

'You make it sound like a war.'

'That's marriage. This is tactics.'

'Marriage shouldn't be a war. I didn't expect mine

to Mr Tenney to be such a thing.' Sadness choked her words.

'I assure you, only your gracious spirit could have made it a happy home. He would have been the ruler and expected you to stay safely under his thumb.'

'I wouldn't have believed you a fortnight ago. But I most likely would have done as he wished and never noticed it. I wanted to be a good wife. I wanted a happy household. I wanted…a marriage like my mother and father have.'

She wanted a marriage like her parents'? He suspected it was the same as hoping for the lightning strike the coachmen had mentioned.

Yet, he didn't have the temperament to tell her that. Nor did he wish to tell her that he'd almost stepped into a marriage similar to what she would have had with Tenney. He supposed that was why it had been so important to help her. Why it was still *so* vital to him to assist her.

He resumed his natural persuasiveness. 'It is a competitive field on the marriage mart. You must be careful not to make enemies there. A jealous woman will not buy your jewellery.'

'I shall be careful,' she said. 'I will not dance with any males I believe are searching for a wife. Only the older and happily married would I accept and rarely those. I will have a sprained foot, a broken slipper.' She paused. 'Or a pained knee.' She touched over her behind and patted the air. 'This part of my knee still pains me, but I can sit now.'

'I'm sorry I did not get there sooner.'

'You saved my life. Don't apologise.'

She smiled, but it didn't reach her eyes. 'The marriage would have been called off anyway, even if Tenney had not been so malevolent. I would never have been able to disrobe in front of him.'

'A man worth his salt wouldn't care about the marks.'

He didn't care if the scars were hideous except for the part of them that hurt her. 'Personally, I have never concerned myself about whether a woman might have a blemish on her…derrière. I don't know of a man who has.'

In fact, a man might enjoy spending a night caressing it when it healed. Might think it a treasured part of a woman he cared about.

'Well, my leg is raw as well. Mother says it will heal further, but it is difficult to believe.'

He held up his bent little finger. 'How much do you care about this?'

'Not at all. I'm sorry you were hurt, but it is nothing.'

'That is the same way I feel about your…wound.'

'Thank you for your kind words.'

'Honest ones.'

'Delivered with kindness.'

She reached to the lapel of his coat. 'I must thank you. You are a rake on the outside, but a knight on the inside.'

'I would say there is a lot of night, but not the kind you are thinking of. Do not place too much store in me. If Tenney loved you, he'd just be thankful you are alive.'

He was.

The knowledge lodged in him with such strength his breath caught.

This would not do. She was not a woman for a rake and he had learned his lesson.

He knew he could make his friends notice her, but he didn't want them to. She deserved a happier home than his acquaintances could provide for her. They weren't worthy of this gem.

But he hated her placing her future at the whims of people selecting wares for their home.

'Hunting one husband might be easier than roping in many of them and their wives to buy trinkets for their houses,' he said.

She shook her head. 'No. I deluded myself with a betrothal. Thinking back, I didn't like the feeling anyway. The weakness of my mind that came from being around that person. I don't want to feel like that ever again.' She frowned. 'But I rather like living well. I know the love of money is an evil thing and I don't wish for a romance with it, but it will keep me comfortable.'

He put his hand over hers and held it close to his heart. He liked having her near, it reassured him she was safe, secure. 'A romance is not always a bad thing, should it not go too far,' he said.

With that, he took her head in his hand as their foreheads touched. Their breaths mingled, lighting a belief in him that love wasn't only possible, it was inevitable.

Her lips parted and she said the only thing that could have dampened his ardour.

'Have you been in love?'

'Yes. It didn't last.' Words short. Clipped.

He gave her the barest wink and the softest smile. 'I will see that you have invites soon. And tomorrow, I will get my friends to tell the truth of the disagreement between you and the mushroom.' Then he escorted her to her house's entrance and returned to his carriage, leaving.

Chapter Eleven

The next morning, Rachael slipped out of the house with her maid who'd arranged for a hackney to take them to the newspaper office. Tenney had once told her how things could get accomplished. She'd disagreed with him at the time, but now she considered his solution.

Devlin was going to get his friends to help her spread the truth, but she'd lain awake long into the night thinking of how she could help herself.

Her mind had kept wandering to Devlin and how she'd felt, standing with him by the carriage. They'd been close in those moments. United. Then she'd asked about love and the fantasy of unity had evaporated, gone into the air as if it had never been.

Once at the building, Rachael went inside. 'Could I speak to the person who wrote this particular article?'

The maid held out the paper.

An unshaven man walked to the servant, lids drooping over his reddened eyes, and a wearied set to his mouth.

He coughed, studying the words. 'I did. 'Cause I write every word in that paper. Even the ones I don't like.'

'It's about my life,' she said. She couldn't see compassion behind those tired eyelids. 'And it's speculations. Untrue ones.'

He grabbed the paper, lids dropping further, taking his time while he read, then tossed the print aside when he finished. 'Show me the proof that it's lies. You can't. I print observations and suggest they could be true, or not.'

'If you could be so kind as to print an announcement that it has been a mutual decision, and Tenney and I have agreed to go our separate ways, I would much appreciate it.' She did her impression of a most prim and proper miss. The person she really was.

'That does not sell papers. No one cares. Give me something that does sell papers. Even if I did print a piece written exactly as you wished, it's not going to matter to anyone now. People like to read the worst whether they believe it or not. And, of course, they do.'

'You would be doing the right thing.'

'I don't print prayer books.'

She had to keep her goal in mind.

'It would mean so much to me.' She motioned to the maid. The servant wedged herself around Rachael and held open a box so the man could see inside.

Guilt trickled into her, but she pushed it away. She wasn't asking him to tell lies. But to be more honest.

'If you would print something to ease this for me— and it truly was an error in print, a malicious tale—then I will send my maid by with this gift for the lady in your life. You win in two ways, by doing the right thing and having a trinket for your wife.'

She lowered her jaw. 'Bread and butter tastes wonderful, but jewels last longer.'

Then she turned to leave.

Either it would work, or it wouldn't, and no sense in belabouring it.

'Don't be in such a hurry to leave,' the man called, stopping her. 'Sometimes I like doing the right thing. Let me have a peep at that charm again.'

She stopped. 'When I read the new story.'

'What story?' He chewed his lip.

She fanned her face with her glove. 'My scars concerned me. I didn't know how bad they'd be. And I didn't want to inflict them on Mr Tenney.'

'Scars?' His demeanour brightened. 'Scars, on a lovely person such as yourself, might sell papers.' He examined her, face pinched. 'But ain't nobody going to be convinced you've a blemish.'

'My leg.' She closed her eyes hard, then opened them, gathering strength. 'I was burned. Everyone knows. And truly now, it would be no lie to say I never wanted Ambrose to observe the injury. At the time, it all happened so fast I didn't think of it. But...' she shook her head '...now that I do reflect—no.'

'That should sell papers. True love...' He crossed his eyes for a half-beat on the word 'love', then his voice faded to a breathy drama. 'Blighted by a noble sacrifice. A damsel saving her intended, as she martyrs herself for her sweeting.'

'More or less.' Then she strolled to her hackney, her heart pounding in her chest. The maid gave a low whistle of approval.

'Don't forget my trinket,' he called out.

'My maid will deliver it when I see the newsprint.'

* * *

Rachael waited inside the front door. Her maid had taken a sealed letter to Devlin's house and delivered it directly to him.

Her house was dark except for the lamps Rachael used for light to read.

Three taps. Pause. Four taps. Pause. Then five taps.

She half held her breath when she opened the door. The lamplight reflected off his smile. He was little more than shadows, but she could fill in each facet as if he stood in sunlight.

Her heart thudded. He reminded her of an oasis, something to dream about in the wee hours of the night and every memory of him to be recalled before she slept. She added this sight to her images of him.

Internally, she shook herself. She could not be on that path. She'd not even fully escaped the last disastrous attachment.

'I can't believe you went to the newspaper office,' he said.

'I was being practical.' She raised her chin, even though she could hardly believe she had done it either. 'And I'm not always good with conversing in crowds, but I gathered my courage and found someone who might speak for me.'

'I told three of my friends the truth of the matter regarding the first story.' He clasped her hand. 'They were sworn to secrecy. Lord Bart was there, a fourth—I neglected to get a promise from him. It wasn't an accident. He's most likely to tell tales.'

His eyes dropped to her hand in his, as if he'd only just realised he was holding it, but he continued speaking. 'I told them I didn't know the true details of the scars, but I did remind them that I had summoned the physician. And that I had been involved when the accident occurred. My mother feels partially responsible and hopes to launch you in society. And that is true. She does.'

He lifted their clasped hands, and briefly brushed his knuckles against her cheek. A shaft of feelings moved through her body to her feet, immobilising her.

Heartbeats passed before she could speak again. 'That is kind of her to do so.'

'It is nothing but the truth. Mother has a weakness for broken betrothals. My parents were having a spirited conversation one evening and it appeared that my father had been attached to another woman and neglected to tell Mother that he had a second sweetheart when he asked Mother to wed. Old news, but still fresh enough in Mother's mind to bring out the protective spirit. She suggested that you get invited to more events in town. She thinks it was her idea and I never argue with her. Between her and my father, we are acquainted with most of London. Do not be surprised if she calls on you tomorrow.'

'Your mother is a dear woman and you inherited her caring.'

He examined her, his devil-may-care appeal rising to the surface. 'You might be a natural at this charm if you practise it a little more. It works on me. And with that said, if I might offer a suggestion...' He squeezed her hand.

'As you have offered several in the past, no harm in one more.'

'Walk head high. Act as if you were born in every room you are in. Carry yourself as a princess. Pick a woman who you admire and pretend you are her,' he said. 'No one can observe inside you to your doubts. No one can peer beyond the façade you present. When you forget and make a faux pas…' He shrugged. 'Do as she would do. Let it flutter into nothingness. Don't dwell on it. It never happened. Just imagine how someone you admire would act.'

'The Duchess of Pendleton. She is perfection itself.'

'The Duchess?' He seemed startled by her remark.

'Yes. My mother and I have seen her when she is out and about. She carries herself so well.'

She touched her hair. 'I understand what you mean, but that is not so simple. I'm not confident travelling in such esteemed circles. They've all been friends since the cradle and I barely know them. I'm lost when they all talk about an event that I know nothing of and I feel adrift. It has to be obvious.'

'My mother's maid can create the illusion of sophistication for you.'

Her eyes widened.

'Yes,' he whispered. 'The maid knows a few tricks with smudging things. I've seen it.'

'Smudging?'

'Yes. Around the eyes. Mother will be moping around like she has lost her best friend, then she'll get ready for an event and you would never guess how morose she had been only hours earlier.'

'You aren't serious?'

'It's not that you need any artifice to be beautiful. But you wish to glide into society with the most prominent people in town and you want to stand out, not only as if you were invited, but as if it is a birthright that won't be denied.'

'That is a frightening idea. That my future is determined by my confidence. My outward appearance.' She steeled herself.

'With people talking about the broken betrothal and it so soon after the injury, interest could be concentrated on you. This is a perfect time for you to shine.'

She touched her throat.

'Carry yourself proudly.' He took her shoulders.

'I do not want to pretend to be anyone. Mr Tenney's speech always speeded up when he spoke of the Duchess of Pendleton, although it took him twice as long to say her name as it should have.' It would have been a lie to say he drooled. At least a visible drool and he'd only seen her from a distance.

'She has the art of being the Duchess perfected to a science,' Devlin said. 'Perfect the skill of being a new Rachael Albright.'

Being a new Rachael didn't sound so bad. She wasn't happy with the old one.

'Have confidence in yourself.'

Everyone could tell she lacked self-assurance? Oh, that didn't make her feel better.

'Remember, you have two parts. An inside and an outside. Men tend to forget anything but the outside of a person,' he said. 'I suspect you tend to only think of the inside. This is not the time to even consider that part of you. Don't wear your doubts openly. No one can see past the façade.'

She touched a hand over her stomach. A façade? She wasn't a puppet.

He took her fingers and removed them from her mid-section. 'Don't be so dismayed.'

'How can I not?' Nothing seemed right with her.

'You will do fine.'

She let out a breath. 'At my last event, my betrothal ended and at the one before that, I could have lost my life.'

'When you put it like that…' He gently put his hands on her wrists and pulled her closer. 'Please do not be offended if I keep my distance from you.'

She freed her hands and jabbed a teasing nudge at his chest. 'Perhaps that would be best for both of us.'

As he stumbled into the wall, he caught her waist and took her with him. Then their eyes caught, stilling her with intensity. 'In truth, there is nothing wrong with the real Rachael.' The whisper of his voice caressed her. 'Everything about her feels right, sounds right and is right.'

He kept her close and she never ever wanted to separate from the clasp. Her skirts pressed against him and the power in his legs kept her upright, and his arms merely framed her, holding her in place, suspending her by the awareness in his gaze.

'But that is my impression.' His words caressed her skin. 'You must feel the same way and you don't. If you pretend you are someone else, you will believe in the things you do and not criticise yourself that your choices aren't right. They'll be her choices and you'll feel they're correct.'

'Are you this confident, or is it a ruse you play as well?'

His assuredness shone through. 'I'm happy with the dance of life, the game, the partners and all the rest, and I want you to be the same. I want you to have the self-assurance that will sweep you into a room and you'll be at home there…in whatever room you enter.'

She wanted to tell him she wasn't that person, but in his arms she felt a strength she didn't know existed in her.

She rested against him, feeling the energy of life combining them. Their bodies aligned and she'd never felt closer to anyone.

His mind tensed because his body was beginning to separate from his brain and only have an awareness of the femininity against him.

He should step away. Instead he savoured the soft scent of her and the pleasures she created. The way his blood surged more swiftly through his limbs and how nowhere else would be better than being where he was.

He let the wisps of her hair feather his face, but then he retreated, confronted with the innocence of her eyes, velvety, and with lashes that could sweep his feet from under him and swirl them into a bedroom.

He beheld her innocence and suspected how much grief Tenney had caused her, and he could not further something that would be unfair to her.

Anger at Tenney, frustration with her innocence and his demand within himself to do the right thing for her flickered to life inside him. He distanced himself even more. 'You'll find something that works for you and it will get easier.'

Then he took the key from the wall and put it in her hand. 'Lock up behind me and expect an invitation, courtesy of my mother's machinations, to arrive tomorrow.' He leaned closer, whispering, 'It was lost in the post and found just this afternoon. And there will be more. The social Season will be starting in earnest as people return from the countryside. So have your dancing slippers at the ready and be sure to thank my mother for her wondrous idea to bring you into the pomp of the social world.'

'I suspect it is the son's machinations that I am to thank.'

He opened the door, lingering longer. 'Do not forget, you are the scarred phoenix, rising from a broken betrothal, to some day become a woman who has her life in her own hands and will comprehend what it is like to control a successful endeavour as well.'

'It will be easier with you there.'

'I wouldn't normally attend and I don't want to draw more attention to the suggestion that I am the cause of your broken betrothal. I'd already agreed to be at my uncle's house that day and I'll be too late arriving home.'

He saw the hesitation in her eyes. He paused, still clasping the wood.

He wanted her to know he wasn't deserting her. That it was truly best for her not to appear attached so soon after Tenney. 'You will have everyone at your feet.'

In the night, standing in front of the light, she appeared a waif, lost, with luminous eyes and lovely lips. And he fell at her feet.

He clasped her waist again and the warmth of her skin melded into his. The planning dissolved—all he saw was Rachael and he could feel her breaths.

The kiss was brief, but he felt it searing through him, changing too much, too quickly. He stepped away, quickly, ending the intensity. Ending their connection.

He pulled his assurance back into himself. 'You'll be the most important person there.'

With that, he brushed a hand over her shoulder, a re-assuring pat, and he left.

He'd not realised how dark the night was and how cold it had turned.

Chapter Twelve

Two evenings later, Rachael tested her balance on her shoes. She hoped she didn't topple from her heels.

She leaned towards the mirror and studied the face that peered at her. This was definitely her best. Better than her best. But was it enough?

Her hair had never taken so long to be arranged, but it was swept up so naturally that she would have guessed it had tumbled into place on its own if she'd not been the one waiting for it to be finished. Some of the curls had been purchased, but they blended so well with her own locks that no one would detect the difference.

It had taken most of the day to become the person in the mirror. The stranger. A confident woman. Not just the woman with the burned derrière and the one who'd spent much of her life waiting for a marriage that would never happen.

She feared she hadn't chosen the correct jewels. She'd picked them because she felt hidden behind them and now she doubted she'd made the right decision. The necklace felt foreign against her skin and dangled against the bodice of her dress. The sapphires were lovely, but they overpowered her.

She straightened. The dress was a plain blue silk, one that was a favourite, but she wasn't sure it was elegant enough.

Her burns suddenly ached because she'd been so tense and even her body didn't feel like hers.

A different person stared at her from the mirror. One who blinked when she did and shifted when she did.

She brushed her cheek, then felt a tremble in her fingers.

She tried to get her hand to be still, thankful she would be wearing gloves if someone asked her to dance. Hopefully no one would scrutinise her closely and see the shaking.

But if they did...

And who would partner her?

She didn't know the people holding the event and she likely didn't know any of the men her age. No one would request a dance. She gulped in air.

In the past, she'd only danced a few dances with anyone other than Tenney and it hadn't bothered her in the least to be a wallflower. She'd used Tenney as an invisible partner. A beau who couldn't be there. Not dancing had appeared a natural choice, but now she wondered if she'd hidden behind him.

Devlin expected the impossible. He just didn't see it because he'd been born with so much at his fingertips. People separated, giving him room to join their ranks when he arrived in a room, and it had been so natural no one around him noticed. He had no idea that she only frequented the edges of that same group.

She wouldn't be able to increase her father's business.

She would be a hindrance to it. No one would respect her and everyone would speak of her broken betrothal. She wouldn't be a scarred phoenix. She'd be a burned goose.

Rachael studied the face gazing at her from the mirror.

She leaned down, putting both hands on the dressing table, stilling them by pressing against the wood. Then she picked up her gloves, pulled one on, pressed the fabric in place at her fingers, and repeated the process with her other one.

She couldn't do it. She would ruin what remained of the goodwill her family had. Her lack of social graces could cause people to dismiss the shop because they belonged to that *awkward woman's* family.

Searching out her mother, she found her leaving her room.

'Goodness, you're beautiful,' her mother gasped. 'I almost didn't recognise you.'

Rachael felt her last vestiges of faith in herself plummet.

'Your father is making sure the carriage is ready for us,' her mother said. 'I can't believe we have been invited to this event. Those days we spent with the Countess...' She let out a breath. 'I never imaged our lives could change so in such a short time.'

Rachael nodded. 'We have a slipper in the door of the best society, Mother.'

'It is a tenuous grasp at best.'

'True.' She touched her mother's arm, capturing her attention. Her mother would be a better ambassador than she would.

'I don't feel well, Mother. Please let it be known that I couldn't attend due to a megrim. My head feels like it could start pounding and I'm sure the drive there will make it worse, plus the music will not do me any favours.'

'Rachael—' Her mother gasped. 'This is a chance for you to meet other men now that your betrothal is over.'

'But I can't go. Something is wrong.' She held out her hand and showed her mother the trembling. 'I can't risk being out and about when I feel so unsettled.'

'Then none of us will go. If you're really ill, I don't want you left alone.'

'Nonsense. Of course you can attend. You must. This is a chance for you and Father to be among society. Please, pass along my sincerest regrets to everyone.'

'I'm not sure…' Her mother studied Rachael.

'You accepted the invitation and you cannot, cannot, let the Countess down because she wanted you to be there. Please.'

It wasn't the Countess Rachael feared letting down. It was her family. And Devlin. She could never be the person he wished her to be. It would be better to let him find out now than for her to begin a charade that would only end in defeat.

She hoped he could understand.

His plan for her to belong in society was overreaching. She was a shopkeeper's daughter and could not find common ground with a duke's daughter, or a woman who had had tea with the Regent's mother.

Devlin had been born in that world and he didn't understand the invisible barriers. Money sometimes erased the walls, but she didn't have that any more. This wasn't a game. It was a losing battle and she was no Wellington.

Chapter Thirteen

Devlin stopped by his mother's sitting room after his late breakfast. She sat by the window, her reading glasses low on her nose, and her teacup in one hand and a pencil in the other.

Devlin greeted her and walked around to peer over her shoulder at a list of instructions for the housekeeper.

'She wasn't there last night.' His mother put down the cup. 'Oh, my, the tea is cold. Terrible error of me to let it sit so long. But, no, Miss Albright was not in attendance.'

He'd not considered himself so transparent.

He held himself perfectly still. Well, that was the way of things. Rachael was her own person. If she did not want his interference, so be it.

He gave the tiniest nod of acknowledgement to his mother's words. But inside, he felt as if she'd been a sweetheart and he'd been at the event, and she'd chosen to stay home rather than to see him.

'Mrs Albright confided that she suspected the dissolution of her daughter's acquaintance with Mr Tenney had put her out of sorts for dancing.'

'Should have made her want to dance.'

'I suppose.' His mother turned, staring at him from over her spectacles. She took another sip of her tea. 'Just don't cause more grief for her.'

Grief? The only one he would like to cause problems for was the man she'd fancied.

She rested her cup in its saucer, a light whisper of china against china sounding in the silent room. 'It's not that I dislike her or would be upset if you were to court her. I just don't see you pursuing such a gentle sort. She's not used to the world around us. And people can be cruel. You can only promote someone so much and then it is up to them. Besides, you should know… I've heard rumours that the businesses owned by her father are not—are looking a little drab.'

'She needs this.'

'If she doesn't want to flounce about in society, you should accept that. Not everyone is happy spending an hour dressing, an hour getting her hair fixed, a carriage ride when trussed so tightly you can't breathe, then dancing with men you can hardly tolerate when they're sober, much less when wobbly from a strong punch. Punch, the drink. Not the action.' She made a fist with the pencil enclosed in it and jabbed the air.

'You make it sound like an ordeal to be in society.'

'No.' She rotated to write another word on her list. 'I enjoy it, but not everyone does. And I don't know that she would. Don't try to make her into a female version of yourself. We all return to our true characters.'

'She must become more visible.'

She didn't raise her head from her writing. 'If she embarrasses herself, it won't further her. And the poor girl doesn't seem to have a knack for being at ease.'

'She can learn.'

'Yes.' His mother let out a sigh. 'And I can learn to cook. Don't hold your breath. You'd be much better off eating one of my stunning flower arrangements than any macarons I might make.'

'Your florals do look good enough to eat,' he said, his mind still on Rachael as he bent to kiss his mother's cheek.

'I agree.' She gave his shoulder an absent-minded pat, her attention returning to the paper. 'I'll manage it so that she gets a few more invitations, but she's going to have to put her heart into it and her mother will have to respond with at least a few invites to tea soon, or it's all going to be a waste of time.'

He stepped to the door.

'I expected you to be gone today,' she said. 'How did your trip with your father and his brother go?'

'Uncle Ted's in better health. He sends his love. Or at least half of it. He said he doesn't want to steal you from Father.'

'Did he say that in front of your father?'

'Of course. Father didn't think it clever.'

'You're more like Ted than your father. You favour the Earl in appearance, but you inherited a brain from somewhere and I can't think it was from your father. It had to be his brother.'

'Could it have been from you?' He stopped at the threshold. 'You told me that the Hinshaw estates were for sale for a pittance because the Duke needed funds to invest in his shipyard immediately.'

She returned to her list, lifted her cup again and pushed her glasses higher on her nose. 'Had to wait a while to sell it, but we made a tidy profit, didn't we?

Ruffled your father's feathers.' Her chuckle was low. 'Loved it.'

Devlin remembered those days. He was surprised he'd not walked around with his hair standing straight out in fear. He'd taken a risk by using the strength of his future inheritance to secure the loan.

It had been frightening to invest everything his mother truly had that was her own, but she'd insisted, and then he'd had to locate the rest of the purchase price.

'Until then, your father deemed you a youth and couldn't get past those days when he was never questioned, just followed.' She flicked a fingernail over the paper. 'By both of us.'

His father had been angry and hadn't recovered quickly. Yet as he got over the irritation, he'd treated them both more respectfully. Devlin's parents' relationship even improved.

'We made a considerable profit.' He'd not cared particularly about the profit, but just that he'd not indebted himself for the future.

Movement in the room ceased except for his mother's face. 'It was a strike for independence, not just for yours, but for mine as well. Your father took it better than I judged he would.'

'We didn't make anything on the next one.'

'We broke even. A good learning experience for us. So, it was a success. And now your father trusts you and you've worked tremendously in that devil-may-care *I'm-just-enjoying-myself-and-what-property-are-you-hoping-to-sell?* way you have about you.' She focused her attention on her list again and mumbled, 'I created a monster.'

Devlin's stare jerked to her.

'Not you, my son. Myself.' Her eyes sparkled in laughter and she waved him out of the room.

Striding into the hallway, he accepted that his father had needed him, although none of them had seen it at the time. His father had trusted people too easily. His mother didn't.

Rachael's family business could increase. She'd have to take risks, but it was a bigger danger never to take them. He didn't want her to have to depend on a marriage to increase her status. He'd seen the pride in his mother's face when they'd sold the Hinshaw estates and made a profit and he'd had to talk her out of some of the bigger gambles she'd planned afterwards. She'd heeded each word he'd said and addressed them as if they'd been generated from her own perceptions.

His mother and father made a formidable pair.

Leaving the room, he pushed the images of a joined family aside, planning to find some friends with nothing more important than to plan a card game or have a spot of revelry.

He went outside and moved quickly to get beneath the canopied trees, his energy increased by the cooler day. At the nearby mews, he greeted the stable master, took the saddle before the man could reach it and saddled his horse, then he led it by the ribbons into the street and jumped astride.

In moments, he was riding along the street, which emitted a peaceful family presence. Houses surrounded him on both sides, silent reminders of caring groups. He could imagine a loving family behind each door. His imagination dismissed the possibility that unhappiness resided in any home. For the day, he was surrounded by caring families secure in their world.

He'd hated to be in his house when he was a child and both parents were in residence and were arguing. He loved them both apart, but couldn't stand either of them when they were together and were picking at each other.

He wondered if that was how he'd learned his ease around people, by trying to cajole his parents' anger or hurt into contentment. Or from watching his mother switch from being furious at his father to welcoming her guests with everything swept from view as if she'd had the most glorious day ever.

That was how he'd always presumed marriages to be. Two people joined together who could put on a happy face when they were around others, but who jousted for control in private.

Some of the fury he'd dissipated over the years must have hidden inside him. Now he felt a slow simmer of irritation at Rachael which surprised him. He was never angry. He didn't like anything which took from his joie de vivre. He didn't have a right to be upset with her. True, he'd offered advice and arranged to get her an invite, and she'd not attended.

A favour had been ignored. That was reason for irritation, he supposed.

The clubs would be a much better way to spend the remainder of the day than thinking about Rachael's future and the way she'd just tossed his advice to the wind. But his horse didn't want to go to the clubs.

It kept turning in the direction of Rachael's house.

And who was he to argue with a beast?

Three taps. Pause. Four taps. Pause. Then five taps. Finally, a butler answered the door.

'Tell Miss Albright the Viscount is here for her.'

The man hesitated and Devlin stepped inside. 'Now, please.' Devlin ended the request with a small bow that took the butler by surprise. 'Thank you,' Devlin added, as if Rachael were already on her way.

'Of course,' the servant answered and left to do as Devlin asked.

He'd just entered a man's house and convinced a servant to do his bidding, and he wasn't certain the butler even questioned it after the first momentary falter of surprise. A butler was trained to do as requested. A viscount was trained to request.

In a few minutes, the man returned, and led Devlin to a sitting room.

Rachael stood behind the sofa, waiting, almost mouse-like, as if she might skitter to some dark place of solitude. She watched her hand trace the pattern on the upholstery. Except for the intense scrutiny she gave to a fabric she must have seen thousands of times, he would have assumed by her expression that she didn't know he was in the room.

Relief overtook him, but his annoyance didn't evaporate. It seemed almost fuelled by the sight of her and the unfamiliar irritation warred with the relaxed poise imbedded in him. He felt jostled by his own body.

He absorbed the pale blue of her dress, the tousled hair piled on her head, the slender arm outstretched, and another, stronger surge of exasperation flooded into him. How could that daft Tenney not note how far above him she was and not get down on his knees and beg her to forgive him for even thinking himself worthy of her.

'How did you like the soirée?' he asked, his voice sounding like someone else's. Someone he didn't recognise. Or, perhaps he did. His father.

'You know well that I didn't go.'

'Yes.' He stepped to the front of the sofa, at war with himself over the need to be closer to her and yet keep a barrier between them.

'My mother once hired a companion for herself and part of the woman's job was to teach Father proper speech. I kept remembering it and fearing I'd say the words as he sometimes does.'

'To every newly born babe the world is a trial. Not every new adventure is easy.'

'It's easier for you. For them.' Her perfect chin jutted and her eyes sparked anger, and he absorbed it like a plant moving to the sunshine.

'For the others at the dance it is something they have been a part of since they were children.' The ire in her face softened and her words matched. 'They know each other and they visit with friends there. I am a newcomer to that part of society.'

Instantly, her softness pulled him closer and he couldn't keep the sofa between them, but walked around. She reached out for him, clasping his hand.

His mind crashed in all different directions at once, remembering how he'd rushed to save her, unaware of his steps or his life or surroundings, only moving for her safety. He'd had no choice to make, or even a decision. It had just happened.

And now she held him immobile and nowhere else would he have wanted to be.

'Society fits me like a well-made glove,' he said. 'But there is no secret handshake. No hidden password to get you into that world. You have to get there on your wits. You fight with a smile, an open heart and a strong backbone. You're not doing this for today. You're doing it for ten years from now.'

'It's much harder for me.'

'Doesn't matter. Every time you take a first step there is always someone who it was easier for. Someone it was harder for. Always.' Then he lowered his voice. 'Do you want to marry someone like Tenney? Or do you want to regard him with pride years from now and say to him without even speaking when you pass by him, *I could have been yours,* then give a little twist and walk on?'

Again, she calculated his expression. 'I didn't think you so vindictive.' Her hand slipped from his. She grasped his arm, lowered her voice and shifted so close he could scent vanilla surrounding her.

He'd not expected a wholesome fragrance to affect him so.

'I was too scared. I could not do it. I was shaking. I could not stop trembling. I could not force myself.'

'Tell yourself, starting now, that it is nothing but a little group of strangers who do not eat babies for breakfast. They are people. Like yourself. Humans. Humans you aren't at war with. The snipers only have words and they can be dulled with time and effort.'

'I cannot do it.'

'If you say that, then it's true.' He secured her shoulders, but in reality, she held him captive.

'Think of it, Rachael. Women marry. They give birth. All more risk than a simple dance.'

She turned her head. 'That doesn't make it less real. I don't know why I was so scared. It makes little sense. But I was. Real fear. After my parents left the house, I started shivering.'

'Then we will fight through it. The events aren't frightening. In fact, they get boring as the night lingers.'

She touched his arm. 'If I try again, will you be there with me?'

It was as if she imbued him with power, just from the light pressure on his sleeve.

'Of course.' He could have battled armoured dragons on the strength she gave him.

She melted into his arms and he couldn't risk hurting her, either by retreating or by pursuing. He brushed a hand up her back, feeling the layers of clothing and slight ridges of her backbone making a trail for him to trace. She was so frail compared to him. No wonder she'd been concerned. Softer than velvet, more lush than any green forest.

Immediately his mind travelled to a mossy bank and her lying beside him, observing the heavens, alone in the world of nature, primitive and free.

He shook the images clear. He couldn't let his imagination go there. All the purity of their encounter faded, replaced by his body's burning need. He stepped aside.

Confusion fluttered across her face, but he immediately erased it by taking a wisp of her hair between two fingers and tucking it behind her ear. But he couldn't free himself of the image of the two of them lying beside each other.

'I don't fit there,' she said, the pain in her voice corralling his thoughts. 'I know it. They know it. I'm an outsider.'

'Yes. You are.' But she wasn't to him. When he'd first taken her in his arms and carried her to the sofa, he'd somehow become her defender. A man who'd let himself be slain rather than let her be hurt.

'It will likely take years for you to become entrenched,' he added, forcing his mind to consider the facts in front of him. 'Years. But you still can wear those jewels and show everyone the wares your father sells. It doesn't matter if you aren't acknowledged at first. You'll be accepted in time.'

He spoke the truth because he intended to become her shield against the world. He just couldn't become more involved in her life. He couldn't let the weakness she inspired in him rule him. He couldn't remember the softness of her skin or the fragile woman who needed him. Or be aware that her life would change for ever and the fear inside him that if he wasn't in her life, she would face the world alone.

He paused.

The women in his past, none had needed him.

Perhaps they'd needed a dance partner, or someone to ease their loneliness or someone who'd merely listen to their heartbreak.

But none had needed him.

He didn't want to ruin something dear.

He'd heard men who'd been foxed tell the stories of the one true love of their lives and how they'd spoiled everything by treating her like every other woman they'd ever met.

He wanted Rachael to be the love of his life.

The one whose name remained just under the surface while he jested and made light of the world. The reason he was born.

'I want us to be friends,' he said, hoping he could live up to the word. Hoping he could find it within himself not to mar her trust in him, not to destroy the innocent faith in her eyes. 'For a long time.'

'We are,' she said. 'Friends.'

He wondered if the path to his own ache had already begun and he glimpsed into the wide eyes and knew that it had, and he didn't care.

He would suffer later, in the long hours of the night when he couldn't chase her from his memory. He would yearn for her and he would only have her in his dreams, and he would dread sleeping because when he awoke, he would know they were friends. And one put friends first.

'I'll be there for you,' he added, giving her a carefree smile. 'My mother will be having an event to welcome a few of her friends returning to London. You will be assured of an invitation, and, alas...' he gave her a rakish wink '... I am a dutiful son who must attend his mother's most important events.'

With that, he allowed himself the softest kiss, suitable for a sleeping babe, and slipped out of the door.

Standing against the wood he'd just pulled closed behind him, he gathered his resources, yet he lingered, reluctant to put more distance between them.

He must never touch her again.

It stirred memories of his past innocence. Something he'd left behind after he'd met a woman who said she loved him beyond all else. A woman he still spoke with on friendly terms, but one who meant absolutely nothing to him.

Rachael. He breathed the sound of her name.

Chapter Fourteen

Rachael lifted the perfume, putting a drop on her wrists and letting the aroma of springtime waft in the air. Devlin remained in her mind, much like the fragrance, settling softly. Not something she was really aware of, yet, still, in a quiet moment, recollections of him were easily summoned.

She'd chosen the fragrance that morning because it reminded her of the scent after the shears had been used to cut the grass at the edge of the gardens and always gave her the feeling of new beginnings. Much like Devlin did.

You did not often get chances to start afresh. She hadn't planned to get the opportunity, nor had she wanted it at first, but she hoped to make the best of it. She'd taken her favourite dancing dress with her when she'd been to select the jewellery. It had taken her two hours of trying different pieces and listening to her mother's comments and even seeking her father's opinion.

At the door, she returned to the mirror, clenched her teeth, raised both fists in a pugilistic pose and then went down to collect her mother.

Her hands were shaking when she sat in the coach

and her mother must have noticed. 'Dear, you're lovelier than ever. I've never been prouder of you. You've left that man behind and you're moving on to a new world. I know you'd rather hide in your room, but you aren't.'

Her father turned to her mother. 'What'd you say that for? Rachael's fine.'

'Yes, she is,' her mother agreed and spoke about the houses they were passing, rattling on as if they were all that could concern any of them.

For the first time, Rachael recognised the bravado in her mother's voice. The little quiver at the end of some of the sentences.

Rachael gathered her resources.

Her family needed her to be strong. This wasn't only about *her* courage.

Devlin stood near the piano, talking with guests when she arrived. He was in command of the group around him. She could tell by the upturned faces and the attention he garnered. He wasn't standing in the centre, but off to the side, yet he drew the people closer. Payton and the others burst into laughter. Devlin gave a nod, acknowledging the humour in what he said, but on the upsweep of his chin, his eyes caught hers and, at that second, everything else faded when his chin dipped and his eyes showed an awareness of her.

Then his attention returned to the crowd around him.

Devlin's eyes crinkled at the sides and he raised a glass, tilting it to his cousin. She heard Devlin say he was thankful the arrow that Payton shot through a closed window hit no one, but all the glass shards had been a devil to find.

Rachael knew that the story was about Payton, but every woman in the room heard and saw Devlin.

He had a way with a grin that somehow said he knew more than he told. His smile invited everyone to the soirée of life.

Rachael bit the inside of her lip.

She turned, but then she paused and glimpsed at Devlin. What harm did it do to gaze at art, as long as it was left alone and not touched? He was exactly how she would have designed a sculpture if she could have.

He made his way around the room, greeting most of the people and seeming to talk with everyone.

But the moment he stopped beside her and her mother, Rachael's heart warmed. This was no casual greeting, but more of a gentle commander's presence to bolster his troops.

Devlin and her mother chatted. Rachael observed the older woman relaxing into Devlin's words.

He only gave the briefest of glances to Rachael, but in that second their eyes met, a smile flashed from within him and the pleasant jolt of it lodged in her midsection. He didn't even need to speak specifically to her, but he'd reassured her.

Then he mentioned how glad he was that they both were enjoying themselves and excused himself to greet a friend. The temporary halt in his progress before he stepped away, little more than a flicker of extra recognition, fluttered over Rachael and nestled inside her, a warming hug with nothing more than eyes meeting.

Even after he left, the confidence he gave her remained. She wanted to challenge herself and stand alone in the room.

She turned to her mother and excused herself to visit

the refreshment table. A tiny woman with white hair, and a feather almost as long as her cane, stood waving an oversized fan.

She'd heard of the Duchess of Highwood. A truly evil woman, if the comments were to be believed. Rachael shored up her confidence, ignoring the rising sound of conversation in the room, covered only by scattered bouts of laughter.

She challenged herself to speak to the woman.

'Isn't the pineapple lovely?' Rachael indicated the centre of the table.

'What?' The lady's brow furrowed and she stared at Rachael's lips.

'Pineapple. Isn't it grand?'

Wrinkles formed deeper around the lady's lips and she spoke loudly enough that the people at the end of the room could hear. 'I've not tried the apple wine. Would you fetch me a glass?'

Rachael nodded, unsure of what to do next. But then she saw a footman with a decanter of undetermined flavour and motioned to him. In seconds, he'd poured the Duchess a glass.

The woman sipped, then took another and another. 'I can't taste the apple,' the woman near shouted. 'But I like it.'

Rachael walked to the nearest wallflowers. They greeted her as if poison had just dripped into their midst.

Her mouth became dry. She stood with them for a cold moment, but left before her teeth started chattering. She retrieved a refreshment, thankful for something to hold.

She perused the room. Devlin was in the midst of another group where everyone was at ease.

Every cluster appeared so caught up in their own conversation that she didn't dare progress closer to them and appear nothing more than a hanger-on.

Her mother was at the edge of another group of women. She returned to her mother's side, thankful she had a place to find some respite from attempts to be accepted.

Happiness wreathed her mother's face and she seemed completely oblivious to the fact that few more than the Countess spoke with them.

They were going to starve.

Where was a burning candle when you needed it? That event had been a rousing success compared to this evening.

Again, she felt the ache from the burn. And a softer twinge of loss, one from Devlin not being nearer.

Her mother left after saying she wanted to speak with Rachael's father, then Rachael saw the Duchess of Highwood moving her way.

Rachael refused to retreat to the ladies' retiring room.

'Are you not the young woman who was scarred so terribly?' The Duchess raised a brow. 'With the flames reaching the ceiling and everyone screaming? They've done a wonderful job of repainting the walls. And so quickly.'

'I don't remember it that way,' Rachael said. 'But everything happened so fast I was only aware of what was right in front of me.'

'Terrible that you had such a calamity so near the wedding and that you wouldn't be able to consummate the vows, but then one must think to the future. How bad are the scars?' The woman spoke loud enough that the group beside her had stopped chatting and listened.

The Duchess examined Rachael's skin. 'You can hardly detect the ones on your face.'

'Yes. It's fortuitous.' She pursed her lips. *Her ability to consummate the marriage had come into question.* She'd not meant the tales to go that far.

'Your Grace.' Devlin appeared at Rachael's side. 'I would so relish a dance with you. Is this one taken?'

'It is now,' the Duchess said, stepping forward to drape an arm around Devlin and to pull herself so close that her breast squashed into him. Hopefully she would not be bruised the next day, but it wouldn't be for lack of trying.

He smiled down at her. 'I'm honoured.'

'As you should be,' the Duchess answered, a robust cackle at the end of her words.

Devlin led the Duchess to the floor so they would be in place when the dance commenced.

'They don't make them like that any more,' one of the other ladies murmured. They all chuckled. Rachael didn't know for sure if they spoke of the Duchess or Devlin and she was fairly certain it was true on both counts.

The ground didn't open up and swallow her, and she seemed to have become invisible, so she retreated to a corner and sipped her second glass of wine, occasionally holding it with both hands when she noticed them shaking.

Even her stomach trembled, but when she watched Devlin's ease, and ability to speak to the Duchess, she calmed.

That was how it was done, she realised. This war wasn't to be fought with a sword, but with a smile. A smile for everyone.

Today, she only had to focus on baby steps, or, in the case of the wine in her hand, baby sips.

Then the Duchess's words bounced in her mind.

Except, blast it, the whole world now presumed she couldn't consummate a marriage.

While the others continued the celebration, she took a third glass of wine, but didn't even sip it, content to warm the glass with her hands while trying to remain inconspicuous beside the curtains.

She recalled the Duchess's comments. Her reputation would be fairly locked in place if everyone assumed her unable to make love.

But Devlin would know otherwise and that would put her most chaste plans to the test. He could easily make her forget all the cautions she'd lived her life following.

Devlin appeared briefly at her mother's side and Rachael watched the charm in his eyes, and the persuasion on his face. She didn't have to hear the words. He seemed to be whispering softly, then her mother glanced at Rachael and frowned.

Devlin focused only on her mother, and she saw the encouraging nod. He stepped to the side and blocked the line of view between them.

Rachael knew she was being discussed, intensely.

The conversation lingered a bit longer and then Devlin left. Her mother glanced at Rachael as if she'd never seen her before and wasn't really seeing her then, but watching a future unfold. A bleak future.

He stopped at the Albrights' door. Three taps. Pause. Four taps. Pause. Then five taps.

He heard the key turn in the lock. The door opened.

Stepping inside, he longed to reach out and hold her,

imagining their bodies swaying together in a simple, sensual dance in the faded light, but he'd promised her mother that he'd only be there for a few quick, respectable moments. He'd given the assurance freely at the time and would do so again for the chance to see Rachael, but he wished it hadn't been required.

Rachael hadn't changed her clothing, but her hair escaped from her knot, as if she'd loosened it after she arrived home. He didn't think she wore shoes either because she'd lost the height she'd had earlier. She'd turned herself into a little bird ready to close her eyes and nestle into a fluff of feathers. The perfect woman to come home to. *Come home to?* he mused. *Stay home with.*

He was starting to think like…

Like someone he didn't know. But someone he might like to become if it were possible.

He stepped into the tiny space as she shut the door, their fingers brushing, reminding himself that he must take care. 'I cannot stay long. I am taking too much risk with your reputation as it is just by visiting you.'

'I've already had a little notoriety. I don't like people noticing me.'

'Try to accept it. Some people love it.'

'The other guests tonight suspected I was there because your mother feels responsible for the accident. I'm thankful for that assumption because it's a positive one.'

'She does want to help you.' He couldn't help himself. He reached out, clasping her arm, giving her reassurance that all was well. 'But you survived tonight admirably.'

'Well enough. I stopped shaking and feeling so nervous, but I don't think trying to be society's darling is an easy task. I couldn't eat all day and was starved when I got home.' She waved an arm to the platter on the small table. Crumbs of bread remained.

'Everyone was taking stock of you,' he said. 'It is natural when a new member joins a group.'

'Yes.' She firmed her jaw. 'Rather like a performing bear. Is her heart broken? Is she defective?'

He hated her pursuing that direction. 'You're not a theatre act. You're a woman making the best of the hand she's been dealt.'

'I don't want to lose everything. I don't want my parents to lose all they've worked for their whole lives.' She stared at the key as if it had the answer. 'I want to return the favour they gave me by being such caring people. I want to have the strength to do right by them.'

'You do. Strength is merely determination to put your feet in the direction you want to go and not focus on anything else but moving your body into place for the actions you want to happen.'

She groaned. 'You make it sound simple, but it isn't. My innocence has been embellished. As soon as Father left earshot, Mother said someone she'd just met consoled her on having a daughter who could never wed and empathised with the scarring. Mother said she was speechless and I explained to her what the Duchess of Highwood had said to me. The tales have grown with each repeating, apparently.'

'That isn't fair to you.'

'After I considered it, I gained courage. If I'm to be above reproach, then it might be best if I'm seen as a woman who has been dealt misfortune. A little sympathy might open the way for me.'

She examined the key in her hand. 'You were there. The burn. Surely you saw my derrière, just a bit.'

'No.'

'You didn't?'

'I saw flames and you.'

'Afterwards.' She put the key on the hook.

'I noticed a beribboned chemise, and scorched fabric, and that you fitted in my arms nicely and you weren't moaning in pain, so I took that to be a good omen.'

He'd not really taken stock of what she'd felt like when he held her, but now his mind filled in the blanks. Not with imagined scars, but the feel of Rachael. The wonderment of her.

'I know it is to my benefit that some rumours circulate,' she said. 'But I am almost completely recovered.'

He didn't need to be thinking of her as completely recovered.

'I expect some scarring, but not tremendous ones. I've considered them. I can accept the damage to myself and be thankful I survived. You've helped me accept that the blemishes are just that.'

She inhaled, putting the force of her emotions into it. 'Thank you so much for all you've done for me.'

Falling into his arms, she clasped him in a hug. 'Thank you.' The words whispered against his chest caused his body to react as if she'd touched the whole of him.

She pressed so close that he forbade himself the slightest movement, because any waver would bring him against her.

She burrowed against him and he remained immobile.

He gave her a brief pat, then took her shoulders and gently stepped away. The slight distance he'd added between them made him feel deserted.

'It will heal.' Who cared about the scarring? She was alive and he needed to leave so he could stop thinking about how alive they were and how wonderful it would be to be alone with her in a forest with a moss-covered bed. Or any quiet place where they would not be disturbed. He imagined himself able to watch her for hours, much like da Vinci would have looked at one of the women he painted.

'You know, I'd considered the dark before. If I am to wed some day, my husband will never even have to view my derrière' She lowered her arms and let out a relieved breath.

'*That*—' he'd not known his voice could go so high '—is what you are still worrying about?'

'Yes,' her voice peeped out. 'I had decided no one would ever court me now. Because of my accident. My blemish.'

'Rachael, you can put that idea so far from your head that you need never consider it again. I assure you, from the depths of my soul, that even a man who doesn't care a jot for you will never concern himself with a scar on your derrière.'

He might even like it. Worship it. Dream of it.

'Truly?' she asked.

He had to convey the reason for his reluctance. 'I can't touch you because I can't *just* touch you. I can't. I can't treat you like Tenney did. I can't mislead you and then go on about my way when I wish.'

Again, he wanted to pull her closer, but he dared not.

He paused, surprised at the direction his imagination had taken.

She was a friend, not just someone he wanted to save. Someone he wanted to be with. He'd not really considered marriage, other than as a necessity for heirs. But marriage could be a solution. For both of them.

He had to keep talking—to distract himself with conversation. 'Can you manage another event in a few days?'

She groaned. 'It's easy to say that I will, but I can hardly stand the questions and assumptions about me.'

'If you must imagine yourself as a trained bear, then imagine the scraps of questions tossed your way are morsels. Tests of mettle. Or stinging insects you can bat into oblivion with a thrust of your mighty paw.'

'Mighty paw?' She held up her hand. 'It's not. But continue with the plans,' she said. 'I don't want the feeling that I had such a miserable night for no good reason. If I stop now, it was nothing but a waste of effort.' She recalled the moments. 'I couldn't even have a conversation with the wallflowers. I was so afraid they'd ask a question I didn't want to answer.'

'Those questions. The ones you dislike, switch the words, and repeat them aloud when they're asked. Give your mind a chance to muster. You'll give a better answer. You don't have to respond immediately with half an idea. But you can't be offended. You have to give people the benefit of the doubt even when none is deserved.'

'I don't even want a friendship. I just want the evening to end.'

He shook his head. 'You should get something pleasant from the encounter. The foremost thing about conversation during social events is to turn the talk to the other person. Things they're proud of. Don't ask curious questions, but caring ones about their life. You will make bonds of friendship with the kind-hearted people. And with the vipers, you can't let their distance bother you. They will come to you later if they want, or they never will. Don't fret about it.'

'The bonds feel strangling. They make me think of escaping the room.' She half twirled again and he caught her, taking her in his clasp and holding her just as he would a little bird. She felt as fragile as any fledgling, but he'd seen the strength in her and he wished for her to remain close.

'Shush those defeating fabrications. Instead of a captive bear, then imagine you are game being hunted, but you also have an empty belly, sharp teeth and luscious claws.' He pulled up her hand, drawing her fingertips along his cheek, feeling empowered by her as much as he hoped he gave her support. 'These delicate fingernails are not where your claws are. They are in your head, resting, sheathed—a bite disguised as a purr. Your strength is in learning to use your wits and yet not skewer anyone.' He pulled in a breath. 'It is the intimate joust of human conversation and competition.'

'The only reason I had someone to talk with besides Mother was because the Duchess was concerned about the scars on my face.' She spoke into his shoulder, not wanting to observe his pity.

'You've no scars on your face.'

'Please tell the Duchess, but I doubt you can convince her of something so ludicrous.'

He took her shoulders and turned her to the mirror behind her. 'Tell me the truth of what you see. You've a perfect face. None would fit you better.'

She squinted. 'Perhaps in this darkness.'

'Underneath the brightest sun. You would outshine it.' He couldn't understand why she couldn't see herself as he saw her. If she did, she would have the confidence she needed.

She rotated, slowly, facing him, or perhaps he was

so aware of her movements that his mind had captured every nuance of her actions, slowing them.

She stayed in the reach of his arms, studying him in the dimness.

She must be on her tiptoes…her mouth was gliding so close. Or perhaps his lips had moved nearer to hers. He wanted to taste the perfection that she couldn't believe, but which he could feel hovering about her, a caress of beauty that he wanted to touch, hold and savour.

She grasped his lapels and his hands naturally caught her waist. He had no choice. Rachael might topple on to him if he didn't. Arousal thrummed in him and he gave in to the sensation of his body bursting to life.

She touched his shoulder and stilled, except for her eyes.

She didn't take her hand away.

Falling into a kiss was easier than telling her goodbye. His lips brushed hers. Liquid. Warm. The edge of a crevasse. A ledge he would happily jump off of to be with her and he must not think such a thing.

He mustn't.

But he did.

He cupped her head and she pulled herself closer. Just as he was dropping into desire that could consume him, he stopped, reminding himself of the promise to her mother.

She took his wrist and held his palm to cup her face.

His thumb brushed her lips. 'I shouldn't return here.'

'You have to. I need you to further my survival in the world of society and of business. I get scared.'

Tentative lips touched his and he remained completely immobile. He attempted to be the perfect gentleman. He didn't kiss her, yet he could taste the sweetness and savour the bloom of rosebud lips.

She retreated, puzzlement in her eyes and a bit of hurt.

He couldn't bear for her to think he rejected her. He pulled her to him.

Their lips met, warm on warm and heat on heat beneath their moisture and the explosion of sensations. He clasped her, holding her upright and using the strength from the kiss to keep her in his arms.

Lips tasting of honey, a body fanning his desires with the vibrancy of thousands of bees' wings.

He couldn't stop her and wouldn't. The kiss lengthened and grew into a second and a third and mounted to a fourth.

He wanted to be alone with her. Somewhere no one could interrupt.

Then he held her tightly and stepped to the wall behind him, feeling the waves of desire pushing at him, a pulsing crush against his body, yet he did not let it influence him. He didn't know if sweat broke out on his brow, or if it was all on the inside of him, yearning to be released.

When he saw the longing in her face, he shut his eyes. It was the only way he could control himself.

Looking at her, he took his feelings, the situation and perhaps even the moon into his power. He needed that much strength to keep the moment chaste.

He couldn't release her, or she would be burrowed against him.

This wasn't right for her. He couldn't ruin their friendship. She was too innocent to understand. She'd courted a man who didn't want her to call him by his first name.

He took her face in his hands and the world stilled

while he gave her a brief kiss on her lips, the springtime flavours of her infusing him with longings stronger than he'd felt before.

Forcing himself to do the right thing, he looked into her darkened eyes. Words of love rose to the forefront of his mind, startling him with their intensity.

He could not offer her meaningless phrases and he didn't know the truth of them or if they were words generated to please her. He wanted nothing more in the world than to reassure and comfort her, but not at her expense.

'I must leave. It's late.' He remembered his last words to her mother. 'I reassured your mother that I would only stay for a few private words.'

'But I don't want you to leave.'

She was freshness and lightness and summertime, and he was far too jaded to be involved with a woman of such perfection.

He'd leave the sublimeness of caressing her to the husband she would some day wed. Just as long as it wasn't that dolt Tenney. She would be best not to associate with Devlin's friends either. None of them was worthy of her.

He imagined again her lying on that mossy bank.

Devlin would skewer Tenney if he tried to lead her on a path of lies again.

He would make sure to be careful after the next event she attended and he would not visit her afterwards. And how invisible was his carriage parked on the street? He must leave.

He had to leave and stay away, because next time, leaving her would require more strength. It would require more strength than ten men had.

He was only one man. 'I should be going home.'

She put a hand at his cravat, pulled the loop and slipped it into a firm knot. 'Think of me when you untie that tonight.'

'I assure you. I will.'

She shut her eyes and leaned against the door after she'd locked it, and wished he'd not asked her mother if he could visit, but had asked her instead. Rachael wouldn't have extracted any promise from him.

Her mother's lecture had lasted longer than Devlin's visit and had consisted of a hundred or so warnings all delivered in an ambiguous, meandering speech, but she'd ended by waving her hand in the air as she left, with the final admonishment of Rachael not repeating the same mistake twice.

Rachael had no intention of it.

With Devlin, she preferred to make new mistakes.

That knowledge troubled her, because she had been able to put Tenney behind her so easily. Devlin's presence had instantly banished Ambrose's significance in her mind. The Viscount was potent to her senses in a way Tenney had never been and she wasn't certain anyone else would be.

She would have to guard her emotions where he was concerned. For survival. She had escaped a mire so easily, but with him a romance wouldn't be easily forgotten. It would never been forgotten and she wasn't sure she was in his league.

She tried to remember seeing him out at an event and perhaps she had. In fact, she was sure of it. He'd had a woman at his side and all she'd seen was his profile, and it had captured her imagination. She'd not known who he was. No one had told her his name. But thinking back, she was certain it had been him. He'd been the forbidden fruit with a devilish attraction and she'd closed her mind to it.

Put it far, far from her memory so she wouldn't be tempted to think of man who brought sunlight into the eyes of onlookers.

A man who attracted the attentions of all the unmarried ladies who would cluster in his sight so that he might notice them.

She'd not planned to be one of those women. Known there was no future in it and only wanted a man who was constant.

Obviously, she couldn't trust herself where choosing someone to care for her was a concern. She would be better off remaining unmarried and settling on business. Far safer than attaching herself to, and believing in, someone who couldn't be constant.

Chapter Fifteen

Rachael waited in the back room while her father spoke with Grimsley. She pretended to be examining the necklaces, but in reality, her awareness remained on the men.

Grimsley ran a hand over his cropped silvery hair while explaining to her father that he planned to visit a silversmith who'd trained in France, hoping for some new designs, but her father was reluctant. Grimsley conversed longer about what had sold and what wares they needed for replacement, and her father's feet kept slanting closer to the door.

She stared across the silent street. Two people perused a window across the way, but no one seemed particularly interested in her father's wares. No one had even been inside while her father and Grimsley communicated.

'Do you mind if I stay behind?' she asked her father. 'I'd like to spend the morning with the Grimsleys.'

Her father tapped his silver-tipped walking stick on the floor. 'But I've plans... You can only examine the wares so long.'

He tapped his cane again. 'I know I said you could help, but it's much too complicated for you. And I don't want you disrupting Grimsley's day. Besides, people might mistake you for staff.'

'I'll mostly stay in the old apprentice's room where the ledgers and fixtures are stored. Something to take my mind from the broken betrothal,' she said, throwing that out so her father could latch on to it.

'Well, if you put it that way, I can understand. But you must promise to stay out of Grimsley's way.'

'I will,' she agreed, dashing a kiss on his cheek and nudging him out. She didn't want to give him a chance to change his mind.

Grimsley reminded her of a merry elf, but he was losing the twinkle in his eyes. He slipped the ledger her father had studied under the counter. 'Are you sure you want to linger, Miss Albright?'

'I heard you tell my father what had sold the last week and I decided to discover if I could understand what people like. Why they purchase what they do and how many sales you have in a month.'

'It's not a pleasant way to spend a day, especially for a young woman such as yourself. Rather tedious, I'd expect.' He thumbed away a speck of dust on the counter.

'It might not be.'

'Well, the details can be rather cumbersome.'

'I want to learn for myself.' She crossed her arms and met his gaze. 'After all, I might take over from my father some day and I want something here to take over.'

'You…um…think there might be problems?' he asked. His face sobered, losing its elfin quality. 'And you're still interested?'

'More so.'

'Don't you think you should leave this to me and your father? You should be protected from doing this work. It's not right for a woman to have to worry about business matters when she has a household to manage.'

'I may never have my own family. If I need to, I will hire a good housekeeper. I'm sure you've heard that Tenney and I are not going to marry.'

'I did. It concerned me.'

That jolted Rachael.

He heaved in a breath and his shoulders sagged. 'It's not all a pretty sight, I'm afraid to say.'

'Then we'd best get started.'

He gave a brief nod and brought out the ledger, tucking it under his arm. 'I'll get my daughter to watch the front and she can call me if a customer comes in and the bell rings while we're busy.'

After fetching his daughter, Grimsley took Rachael to the storage room and retrieved another ledger. Once he opened the book and began speaking, his words tumbled out faster and faster.

She didn't ask questions, but just listened, absorbing.

Then his speech took on a normal pace and he sighed when he turned the last page.

'I don't understand how you get these calculations,' she admitted.

'You can learn,' he said. 'I've seen it proven with my wife and daughter. My wife has known me all my life and when I started learning arithmetic, we would talk about it. She caught on as well as I did.' His cheeks expanded. 'Better in some cases.'

Rachael examined him. 'Your wife can understand these numbers?'

'Of course. It's not hard once you understand the mathematicals. Do you know the multiplication tables?'

'Mother didn't think they'd be necessary.'

'Once you learn them, the figures will all start making sense to you. I've a book I'll share and you'll just need to study it. My wife learned them. It makes it easier for her to keep records for the household.'

'I'm sure it's easier than making conversation with people I don't know.'

'That's part of being responsible for selling the wares also. It's all easier after you practise enough. The hard part seems to be getting the customers to stop here.'

'Practise,' Rachael repeated and relived the unpleasantness of past soirées before shoving them from her recollections. If she could learn mathematicals, like Mr Grimsley's wife, then she could manage a dance.

She understood that her father's belief that business knowledge was beyond her hadn't stopped her, nor had Grimsley's initial reluctance, yet people she didn't know in ballrooms smothered her courage if she didn't fight to keep strong.

She assessed why. Her father and Grimsley might doubt her, but they wouldn't disparage her with whispers. Strangers could easily reject her. She would have to silence her own doubts in herself to be able to deal with—and ignore—the opinions of others. The fear inside herself.

It was her own insecurities keeping her conquered… nothing else.

Chapter Sixteen

Rachael put aside the book from Grimsley and selected the one on her bedside table that she'd taken from the shelf in the sitting room. She ran her fingers over the worn cover. She liked this volume much better than the one she'd chosen when she was with the Viscount. That one had been about pirates and she'd not liked the brutal tales at all. She'd only chosen it because it was close at hand.

But this tome was different.

Her grandfather had penned his name inside the front cover. Her father's name was directly under that. Her grandfather had died when she was too young to remember him, but as she read the book, it was as if she'd begun to understand his thoughts. As if she could imagine him underlining the page and speaking the words to her.

Her father had told her that his father had said it was a disgrace to disrespect books by writing in them, but this was one he'd planned to pass on to his grandson and that it had guided his life. If it ever got into the wrong hands, he wanted it known that it was his book.

Her grandfather had taken the inheritance from his father and purchased wares, and he'd worked hard, rented several other buildings and the family's fortunes had increased. Her mother had claimed her father-in-law was a taskmaster who never seemed to stop working. In fact, she muttered that he'd been furious when Rachael's father had wanted to marry her and he had another potential bride in mind for his son…the daughter of a man who imported teas.

She read the title again. She doubted Devlin would ever consider reading such a book, but he could likely talk someone who'd studied it into telling him the best parts of it.

Rachael retrieved her pen and ink.

Underneath her father's looping handwriting, she wrote her name. The rest of the page was blank. Just like her life had been. She flipped through the pages. *But not any more.*

Thinking of Tenney didn't force her into the world to meet people, but the encouragement of people around her did.

She couldn't motivate herself based on revenge.

But imagining her grandfather giving her advice from beyond the grave inspired her. She'd searched through the pages, trying to read each scored section once and then twice. Messages that her grandfather had planned to pass to a grandson, but now she studied them.

She put the book away to prepare for the night's event. A business endeavour in fine clothing. A duel not to the death, but to the life of a venture.

When her hair was in place, her lips stained and everything about her appearance double-checked, she dismissed her maid.

Fluffing out her sleeves, she contrasted the feel of the garment to that of her day dresses.

Her sleeves were scratchy against her shoulders because buckram underneath made them flounce out. The scratchiness made her feel that her dress was armour-strong and she carried it well.

When she looked in the mirror, she could at least recognise herself more easily than she had before.

She touched the glass. She had to get to know this woman.

The dress, one she'd never worn before, hardly stood out.

The plan was that she could wear something she was comfortable in and its basic design would accentuate many different styles of jewellery.

She swirled, testing the dangling emerald and pearl earrings as they bounced against her jawline.

She wondered if butterflies ever longed to be a caterpillar again and decided they must. To grow wings and be buffeted about by the winds would be more taxing than squirming about attaching to stems and the underside of leaves. But butterflies were made to land on the flowers and fly into the blue above.

Again, she pulled at the top of her sleeves, arranging them to their full puffiness. She'd liked being hidden, but it wouldn't bring the results she needed.

When she walked into the soirée, the uneasiness in her stomach was the only thing about her that didn't feel perfect.

She clamped her teeth together, gave herself strict instructions to smile, not to catch on fire and to live until the end of the night. If she completed those three tasks, she would consider the event a success.

The bauble on her wrist sparkled, a woman decked in stones instead of munitions. She smiled. She must not even take a sip of wine. Well, she decided, one more and pretended being at ease, only letting the drink moisten her lips. The bracelet slid from her wrist almost to her elbow, and she lowered her glass slowly, enjoying the reverse glide of smooth metal against her skin.

Then she touched the necklace and interlaced her fingers through the chain before dropping the warmed links.

So much better than chainmail to wear into this battle.

She saw another wallflower. She would introduce herself to the woman and then find another person to meet. It didn't matter if the woman liked or disliked her. This wasn't about making friends. It was about survival. About battle.

And being able to conduct herself at a soirée successfully. Which she could do. She saw Devlin. She would prove it. And she could demonstrate it to him. She would flutter around like a butterfly without an attachment to any one flower. She would introduce herself to the wallflowers and older women and any woman who stood alone. She would dance with her father and with Payton, and she would practise being at ease.

She reduced her aspirations. She stood still to avoid spilling her wine.

Devlin looked so confident, relaxed and laughing, and so were the people around him. She envied his composure and then he glanced around the room, saw her and, with just the smallest nod, welcomed her.

She wanted Devlin to be proud of the strides she'd made, because he had helped her. Encouraged her.

She didn't mind being a wallflower any more because Devlin understood her true purpose. She was there to showcase her jewellery and again she lifted a drink to her mouth, pretended to sip, and let the bracelet slide. She had to admit, most of the ladies had more elegant dresses, but few could match her in gemstones.

The night meandered on and, during a lull between the dances, she felt a presence at her side and knew without turning that it was Devlin.

'I barely untied my cravat in time to attend,' the rich baritone teased, causing sparkles of pleasure.

'I'm happy I didn't tie it in two knots then.'

'You seem more relaxed,' he said.

'An act.'

'Acting is not all bad. Payton and I both became fascinated with the stage once. Not so much the plays, but the actresses. When they spoke of their trade, I realised that some of them were in a performance at all times they were with me. Perhaps in their lives. I accepted it as a ritual of society that is necessary for us all. That's why I tell you to do it at the soirées.'

'It's tiresome. Pretending to be happy when you weren't born to flutter about.'

'You were never born a creature to stay hidden.'

'Perhaps that is why it didn't happen. Perhaps the accident was fortunate all the way around. It saved me from Tenney.' Their eyes locked. 'And you from mindless chatter. It gave you a project. Me.'

He raised his glass slightly in her direction. 'A gamble with the same odds Payton accepts at the gaming table. An assured win.'

* * *

Devlin watched the guests, aware that the woman his father had once courted was in attendance.

He'd been surprised that his father had fancied her. Her gown was dull and made her look older than her years and she had woebegone jowls. Not at all the spitfire his mother could be.

'A woman my father once courted is here tonight. He led her to believe they were going to marry, but didn't propose. He decided he'd made a mistake and asked my mother to wed that week. He married within days.'

He'd heard the ever so polite but still vitriolic mentions when his mother spoke of it to his father. She'd not been aware he'd been courting the other woman and found out within days after their wedding. The former sweetheart had called on his mother to offer felicitations.

He'd not known about it until he'd heard his father laughing with a few friends about the error of his ways and the explosion the Countess had unleashed on him when he'd returned home. The insouciance had startled Devlin. 'My uncle told me about it when I asked him. I'd heard Father's side and I didn't want to ask Mother.'

His uncle had said the bungled proposal was merely a ripple in the pond of the Earl's indiscretions.

'Father has had many mistresses, but only one wife.'

'Spare me the nobility of that one,' she said. 'I now detest your father.'

'So did Mother for most of my childhood. But they seem to have reached an agreement of sorts. They never have hot-tempered discussions now. He's mellowed. And I rarely have a cross word with Father either. We have mostly left our own angry shouting matches by the wayside.'

'You're his son. That's the way it should be.'

'A title bestowed by birth.'

'You should value those titles.'

'Some come with estates. Some don't. I'm far better off to look at them as they are than to try to wish them into what they're not. And I don't.'

'That's cold, when it's family.'

'Depends on how you comprehend it.'

'How do you find me?'

'Your betrothed treated you badly and I want you to show everyone that he was a dolt.'

'Are you trying to absolve your father's indiscretions when you assist me? Or are you atoning for the women who expected more than a friendship from you?'

'Or a third suggestion. You fascinate me.' He gauged her reactions to his words. 'But we both could be playing with fire.' His gaze locked on her. 'And you know how it burns.'

Music started. He asked her with a flick of his brows if she wanted to dance and she held out her elbow for him to lead her forward.

She spoke as they waited for the dancers to line up. 'Fire makes swords stronger.'

'You escaped it once. I wouldn't want you to be hurt a second time.'

The dance started, bringing them closer. She spoke. 'But artillery is usually iron, or steel—metal stronger than flesh and bone.'

'Not yours.' He gave her the elaborate bow the dance required and as they raised their hands to touch, he led her in a circle. 'If you only ever listen to one bit of advice in your life, then listen to this one. You shouldn't play with fire when your heart is involved. It's not a gamble, it's a jump from a place of safety into an abyss.'

Rachael was no longer aware of the others at the dance. Devlin took so much space in her mind that it couldn't comprehend anyone or anything else at that moment.

'I commend you for the warning,' she said. 'But I expect you to know that people rarely heed cautions.'

'I'm not interested in how other people react. Only you.'

'What's one more gamble?' she asked. 'When I am undertaking a struggle to learn the multiplication tables.'

'I would hope I rate higher than that.'

'You do.'

He waited until they were at the end of the line and kept his voice low. 'Might I call on you again? As I did last time? The same time? Tomorrow night?'

'Yes,' she answered softly.

They parted in the steps and when they were at the end of the line again, he spoke. 'Did you notice that the Duchess of Pendleton is here? The woman you mentioned when you were thinking of someone to emulate?'

'Yes. I noticed. She is an inspiration. You cannot miss her.'

Then he glanced at the Duchess, unsmiling. 'I knew her when she was just plain Meg.'

When the dance ended, Devlin deposited her near some of the other couples he knew and managed to get her included in the conversation before he left.

* * *

Rachael didn't say a word, but followed her mother up the stairs after they'd arrived home. Her father had taken a detour by the kitchen.

At the top of the stairs, the older woman turned and interlaced her arm through Rachael's. 'I saw you dancing with Devlin. I trust you to be sensible. If he is anything like his father, he isn't at all reliable. Do take care with your reputation.'

'I know. I know the risk I take.' They stopped in the hallway and Rachael pulled away from her mother.

'Then why do you take it?'

'He may have saved my life once.'

'A nice thank-you letter to his mother would suffice. I took care of that for you.'

'And he's giving me support as I put Mr Tenney behind me and he's helping me feel comfortable among the *ton* so I can be an ambassador for Father's undertakings.'

'I've never regretted marrying your father.' Her mother reached to Rachael, combing an errant lock behind her daughter's ear. 'But if I had wed differently, you might have had a stronger place in society.'

'I'm completely happy with the way things have worked out.' Except perhaps she might have liked to have been in Devlin's social world. Someone he'd known all of his life and might consider like he'd—he'd thought of plain Meg.

Her mother put her hands in a prayer-like clasp and touched her forefinger against her lips. 'Are you sure?'

'I'm reading Grandfather's book.' That was true. And the life she was destined for. The life she promised herself she would have.

'You should not be reading that. It is not for women. Besides, your grandfather didn't approve of me and the man noted I was too high-born for his son. Perhaps that is why I can't discourage you with Devlin. You belong in that world, Rachael, even if you don't know it.'

'If Grandfather had lived longer, been as wise as everyone says, and known you better, he would have thought you perfect.'

'I'm not sure.'

'I have a duty to continue his legacy.'

'Your duty is to follow in my footsteps. To have children and to be a mother. What could be more important than that?'

She didn't want to tell her mother that providing for her parents could be foremost in her mind. 'I will always have your example in my heart.'

'Then surely you don't want to spend one second thinking about the drudgery that Grimsley handles?'

'I do. Our largest sales are to people who live in the best houses, but I think we can get many smaller ones by also creating a welcoming place for people of middling fortunes.'

Her mother grimaced. 'You sound like your grandfather. I used to hate when he would visit and all he would want to do is talk with his son about the shops. Your father put up with it out of duty.'

'I wish I had known my grandfather.'

Her mother put a hand on Rachael's shoulder. 'He rather liked his own way. Much like the rest of us. Even you. That may have been why you accepted Tenney. He didn't disturb your life.'

'I seriously considered Mr Tenney and concluded he wanted the same goals for us that I had. So, I erred tremendously. I tried to do everything exactly right and did as I believe I was destined. And that ended in a heap of nothing.'

'He thinks you were scarred by the accident. I've heard the rumours. I have tried to quash that, but everyone believes I am merely defending my daughter.'

'Oh, please, let them believe that.' It would keep others from speculating on her family's finances.

'I would like to have discovered that Tenney would have placed me above everything else in life...at *least* before marriage,' Rachael continued. 'I have been fortunate to discover how shallow he is.'

'But now you're acquainted with the Viscount. He may not be any more substantial than Mr Tenney.'

'He's far more aware than Tenney. He sees me as a person. Not a wife.'

The room was silent.

Her mother answered slowly, 'A wife is such a bad thing?'

'I didn't mean it that way. I only meant I waited years expecting marriage. I don't want to fall into a mire a second time. I like the Viscount. He is a friend.'

'If he just wants companionship, he should get a puppy. But do as you wish.' She shook her head. 'You will anyway, I suspect. Again, you are like your grandfather. My husband's family concluded I would beggar him and my family perceived him beneath me. But we loved each other and have had so much happiness. So, I can't tell you what to think. If either your father or I had taken our parents' advice, we would never have married.'

'Don't worry.' She put her arms around her mother's shoulders and drew her close for a second.

Her mother patted Rachael's elbow.

'I know the risks,' Rachael said.

'I hope you tread carefully and know I will always be here for you. I like the Viscount much better than Mr Tenney and not only because he saved your life. But I fear he is not as insincere as he lets on and that, perhaps, is what worries me. Perhaps he is deep enough to make you love him, but not deep enough to return the feelings as you deserve.'

'Would you think less of me if I told you that I wish to be selfish? If a man can leave his feelings behind, then I should be able to also.'

'You aren't like that.'

She paused. 'I want our family to be a financial success more than ever before. That is what I want more than anything. That will give me purpose and make me proud to be a spinster.'

'Don't use him to get more business for your father.'

'Devlin is agreeable to it. We may meet at some point to discuss it.'

'Rachael.' Her mother gasped the word.

'I like him, Mother, and he is straightforward with me and I am honest with him. Perhaps we are two of a kind.'

'Now I will not sleep a wink.'

'You can sleep peacefully.'

'Plubbt…' her mother gasped. A garble. 'I'm not that forgetful. I know what it is like to be young.' She turned, her face hidden. 'But I understand.'

'Don't worry.'

Her mother dotted a handkerchief to her forehead. 'I'll worry. His father has a chipped tooth.'

Chapter Seventeen

The next night Rachael crept down the stairs, holding a lamp and a plate of biscuits, and a pencil and paper were tucked into the book under her arm. She'd left her book of Byron's poetry behind.

She unpacked her bounty and sat by the entryway in the overstuffed chair, prepared for a night of reading.

The butler heard her and appeared, giving her one of those *I know what you're about* glances and she tried to answer with a *so do I*, but it had more of a waver in it. 'I will be fine.'

He hesitated.

'I expect to inherit this home some day,' she said. He left.

Rachael lifted *The Complete English Tradesman,* but couldn't concentrate on it.

She hoped she knew what she was doing. For the past two days she had studied ledgers and multiplications and cosmetics. The new understanding of the ledgers had jarred her and she needed comfort and couldn't find it in a pot of lip stain.

She needed to feel Devlin's strength and assuredness

that everything would work out. And it might not. If her father lost everything, she and her mother would as well. Then she would have to marry for money and whoever she married would always wonder if she'd have chosen him if her fortunes hadn't changed.

The business had to succeed.

She considered whether she would have liked to have lived in a way that the words *mad, bad and dangerous to know* could have applied to her, even if they were exaggerated, and decided she wouldn't.

She was reserved, restrained and asleep before nine.

But it was well past nine.

She'd eaten one and a half biscuits and read part of a chapter when she heard the pattern of raps.

A knock sounded and echoed in the empty entryway. She paused. It would change the course of her life for ever if she didn't move. It would be the safest thing. And she could endeavour to get invitations through her mother's relatives.

But then it was as if her heart had stopped beating.

She leapt to her feet and opened the door. He stood there, a dark shadow with an emotionless face that told her more than if he had smiled.

Her pulse pounded and her mind raced so fast everything else slowed by comparison. Her body responded to him, every feeling heightened—from the tips of her toes to her fingers to her breathing.

His eyes—the ones she thought lacked emotion—didn't.

He stood, strong enough to hold the ribbons of two horses going opposite directions and keep them steady, a man whose body had been naturally created for strength, and who was so used to it that it couldn't be imagined any other way. She could have spent all her life imagining a man built to perfection and her mind would never have been able to conjure Devlin.

His face was recently shaven, as if he'd known that the morning one wouldn't last throughout the night.

She closed the door behind him.

Her composure faltered and she retreated into her manners. She reached for the plate. 'Have a biscuit,' she said.

He picked up the lemon one she'd half eaten. 'I take it you didn't like this one?'

'Yes. No.' She heard herself and ducked her head.

He popped it in his mouth, chewed once, then swallowed. 'Thank you.'

'Mother mentioned that your father has a chipped tooth and I should remember it.'

'She was warning you about my family's trials,' he said. 'Rumour has it that a man had the audacity to throw a teapot at an earl, chipping a tooth.'

'That's wrong.'

'Father said he shouldn't have been at the man's house, in the wife's room, having tea, with the husband gone for the night.'

'Tea.'

'Yes. Truly. Tea and biscuits.'

'That must have been tense.'

'Father said it is not to be repeated. He was thankful the tea had cooled and that they had not been polishing a broadsword.'

Silence lengthened between them and she wanted to end it.

She bit her lip. 'I wonder if the teapot was one produced for us. One should always check the marking on a teapot,' she said. 'One wouldn't want to throw one of inferior quality.'

'I doubt he paid any attention. He was more concerned with escaping with all his parts intact. I think it changed his perspective.'

'Then I'm pleased a teapot could help change someone's life.'

A silence drifted between them again and she touched his sleeve. 'Thank you for the efforts to make me more comfortable in society. I view it as an act with everyone in on the performance.'

He gave a nod of approval.

'Your mother guided me after you left,' she said. 'She chatted with a few people with whom she expected I might share a common interest and introduced me to Susanna Winston, whose betrothed had died. I embarrassed myself by replying that we cannot all be so fortunate.' Rachael shrugged. 'But after Susanna had spluttered somewhat, she then laughed. But she had loved him and had been devastated.'

'Lord Johnstone. What did you think of him? You spoke with him while I was there and danced a reel with him.'

'Yes. A forlorn lord who'd lost his wife and was just out of mourning.' A shoulder shrug. Words tossed aside with a flip of her hand, but he caught her fingers and she let them rest in his, amazed at how much warmth could flow between two people simply touching.

'He's not a bad sort.'

'He gulped away tears when he spoke of his lost wife, but then a peach tart distracted him.'

'That's Lord Johnstone. The one and only.' Their clasped fingers rested between them and he ran a fingertip over the knuckles of her hand. 'He would likely wed you if you pursued him and threw in a few confectioneries.'

'Contrary to what the world thinks, marriage is not my goal.' She contemplated. 'Which is good for me. Everyone thinks I'm attending to society because of the broken betrothal. Not because of the vagaries of business.'

'Spoken like someone with an eye to commerce.'

'Did you enjoy the evening?' She had to know. After he'd slipped away, she doubted he'd returned home. But that was his way of life. What she would expect of him. Not to spend his nights doing something that might be admirable, but something entertaining.

'A little long. A little dull after I left the party.' He looked at her as if to say *after he'd left her.* 'I'd promised to finally make good on my promise to Payton to join a few card games. Some drink. Light stakes.'

This time she didn't move closer to him, but she didn't have to. Only their hands were touching, but it felt as if they were one person.

He shrugged. 'Payton was there so I knew not to wager much. The odds are not in favour of anyone who bets against him. I mainly played to watch him win. An attempt at trying to work out how he does it.'

'You relish gambling?'

'No. I enjoy the camaraderie, but even that bores me sometimes. It appears I'm gracious when I'm winning and leave, but I'm not. I'm just doing what I wish and everyone assigns me good motives. I'm always assumed to have the best of intentions.

'It's true.' His face was towards her. 'The perfect society events usually fascinate me for the first hour or so, and after I've spoken with everyone I leave, ready to search out friends for more revelry. I enjoy them immensely at first, get bored, then I want to find something else. Often, of late…' he chuckled, an inward jab at himself '… I sometimes just long for my own bed and my own pillow.'

Perhaps he was more of a homebody than she expected. Not entirely the devil-may-care man he appeared. Or, perhaps, he just knew so well what to say.

'The first dance that I attended with you there… I can't think it bored you.'

'The night rather grabbed me by the throat.' He regarded the floor, shaking his head before giving her a gaze followed by a commanding glare. 'Don't do that again.'

'Once you've experienced it, it doesn't bear repeating.'

'It was a living nightmare. What if I hadn't been there? I was so grateful I'd promised Mother I'd stay until the end. I hadn't wanted to. But I knew it meant a lot to Mother, particularly as my brothers left earlier. The longest night of my life was in the seconds I ran across the room.'

'I didn't really comprehend what was going on.' It wasn't the longest night of her life. It was a second, a flash, the Viscount throwing his body against her and people staring. She'd really not understood what was happening, except she was in pain and everyone was aghast. A secret that she hoped to take to her grave was that she'd almost slapped him, except somewhere deep in her brain she'd had a realisation that he had just saved her.

'That night, later, I woke up, the enormity of what

had happened blasting into me. And the scent you wore. Even with the toasted silk around you, it was as if you smelled of a summer day's innocence.'

She held her wrist in his direction. 'The same perfume I'm wearing now.' Nothing special. 'I couldn't believe— and can't—after all that has happened—you were interested in what my hair smelled like. I could give you a bottle of the mixture.'

He took her hand in the same way he'd clasp a dandelion stem, not wanting to disperse the fluff. He lifted her closer, her arm rising, and he kissed the little hollow opposite her elbow.

She was off balance and only in place because of his strength.

'It would never be so enticing in a bottle. Never. Or never on another woman.' He took his time, rubbing his cheek along her skin, letting the bristles rub against her. She stilled. Savouring. Breathing. He had some power over her body that she'd never experienced before. When he'd rescued her, he'd changed the connection between them for ever. She understood now the legend of owing your life to the person who'd saved you.

It was not based in fact, but in the emotional realisation that the person had given you the opportunity to live another day.

'I didn't even know you, but within a few moments, I'd always known you,' he added, reflecting her unspoken words. 'Almost that we were a part of each other. I'd never been so close to a woman before in such a short time.'

She knew what he meant. Could see it. Just an honest statement from him filled with nothing but the truth. And she'd experienced the same connection with him.

'I'm grateful.' She filled her body with a breath, freeing her from the emotional hold he'd captured her with and she could have stepped further from him, but she didn't want to.

With a caress, he released her wrist. 'I remember that giant ring,' he said. 'You stared at it as if someone you cared about had given it to you. I envied the person who'd captured your attention so wholly and I couldn't ignore you. Probably why I realised you were in danger. My senses had heightened where you were concerned, almost blurring out anything not connected to you.'

He laughed softly. 'Later, I woke up thinking of you. Hoping you would be in the library. Disappointed at first you weren't. Then surprised by you and the relief I felt. On the inside, I could have wept for joy. You were basically unharmed and you were also mortal. Not a dream I had imagined. I'd begun to wonder if I had conjured the intensity I'd experienced around you.'

He released her hand and walked to the butler's entrance and even though the space grew between them, the expression on his face kept them close. 'It was as if I'd only been born for that act of putting out the fire. That's how I feel.'

'So, now, do you join a monastery, or will you drink to the sunrise every morning?'

A shrug. 'Neither.' He straightened his coat sleeve. 'When I schooled you on how to act, it seemed I was teaching you that the things I'd always been most comfortable with were little more than a charade at life. Without either of us intending it, you are changing my life as well.'

Then he raised his eyes to her and he smiled, a reflection of trust and admiration that could erase all the mistakes he'd ever made. 'When I held you in my arms, I could feel your heart beat. With my entire body. I could feel every nuance of your skin. I didn't know anyone could feel like silk and velvet and...'

She knew what he meant when he said he'd seen her across the room and she'd captured his attention in a way no one else had. He'd faded everything else in the world.

'Or perhaps I'm feeling the loneliness caused by all the years of thinking of myself first.'

Silence flowed like soft music and the flickering light danced around them.

'If you've spent your life thinking of yourself first, perhaps you need to get a dog.' She remembered what her mother had said. 'They're faithful. And they don't judge.'

And much safer for her if he chose something besides her to shower his attentions on.

'And you? Do you judge?'

'Yes.'

'Then I'm surprised you let me in.'

'I don't judge harshly. Not among friends.'

She moved to him. Soft. Easily. Unable to stop.

'You might reconsider that.' He touched her hair and leaned closer, his breath against her lips.

'I have lived my whole life without taking risks and they found me. I think I should take a few of my own choosing,' she said. 'I'd like to take a gamble with you.'

'That's something else you might wish to reconsider.'

Chapter Eighteen

He saw the moment she took his words as rejection and he felt the pain as a direct hit to his abdomen.

'Sweeting, no matter what happens, never feel rejected by me or anyone. If we do not choose to understand the beauty in you, it is our loss.'

'Easy words to say.'

He moved so close their lips almost touched and their breaths intermingled, unable to pull himself from her gaze and do the safe thing. Leave.

He remembered the partings he'd initiated in his past. He'd have preferred them not to feel necessary.

But he'd used his abilities of persuasion to soften the disappointment. And he'd given kind attentions as he'd distanced himself. The sweetness had melted their frowns and he'd discreetly made them aware they would soon have the chance to toss him a glare or a laugh in front of a new beau.

He didn't think Rachael could take a gentle goodbye easily. A few more years in society. A few more rakes to laugh with and maybe she would. But he didn't want her hurt. Abandoned. Or fighting a battle alone.

She should not be forced to make her way in the world without someone by her side. It wasn't fair to her. Even a husband like Lord Johnstone would be of benefit to her. He could entrench her in society.

He understood that he'd never had to scramble for a footing in society. Although, at boarding school, the boys had insisted he prove himself worthy of their camaraderie. He'd enjoyed the challenge.

The test of matching wits had been a game. Matching strength and agility had been easy for him as well.

Even the challenge of marriage hadn't always daunted him.

Rachael was someone he wanted as a friend for the rest of his life and her future husband might not accept them together so kindly if they'd had a liaison.

His words were low. 'You don't understand what you're risking. If things change between us, we will never be able to return to the innocence together we have now.'

'I have already lost a lot of my innocence.' She puffed out a breath of air that ruffled the wisp that had fallen in front of her eyes. 'I've learned the multiplication tables.'

His eyes narrowed. 'I don't think it is entirely the same.'

'I'm feeling stronger now than I've ever felt in my life, even though I've recently been—for all intents and purposes—jilted, injured and I've discovered my inheritance is little more than dust. I'm angry and it's no time for me to tread lightly. When I did exactly as expected the results were near disastrous. I should experience life, because living cocooned hasn't kept me from adversity.'

'But you could have many more trials. Particularly if you were to take unmanageable chances. We cannot continue to meet secretly. Too much is at risk. Your financial future cannot have secrecy or whispers attached to it. You have to be above reproach.'

'Yes. I will take care. But I've decided scars don't hurt as much as I'd expected. They're a part of living.'

The dark walls surrounding them didn't seem austere, but enveloping and secure.

'It feels like you're keeping a barrier between us. Like you're pushing me, trying to get me to leave.' Rachael wrapped her arms around his waist, resting her cheek on the crisp fabric of his coat.

'I shouldn't have visited tonight,' he said.

'I would have been disappointed if you hadn't.'

'I understand where our feelings are going, and it's a slippery path I don't want you to travel. Too much at stake.' He pulled her free so their gazes could lock.

'I'm willing to take it.'

'I'm not.'

'It's no hazard for you.'

'Yes. It is. I don't want to lose our friendship,' he said. 'And that you think this isn't a serious step for you concerns me. I cannot take advantage of naive innocence.'

Her fingers hid in the lapel on his coat. 'Things have happened to me recently which changed the direction of my life. Both of them could have had disastrous results. Marriage or death. This time, I would like to choose my direction. Not be a victim of what is going on around me.'

'You can't tell in advance what cards will be tossed last on the table.

'You're acting as if, because I am a virgin, I'm not capable of deciding things for myself. Perhaps I need to be a little more jaded. If I had been a little more worldly,

I might not have been happily, innocently, betrothed to a man who didn't want me to call him by his first name.'

'I don't want to be your method of revenge.'

She stilled, contemplating his words. 'I don't want revenge on him. If he deserves trouble, he'll take care of it himself.'

'I think he does by not marrying you.'

She appreciated the supportive words and crossed her arms around herself, letting her emotions tumble out. 'It's a rough world and I'll be better prepared if I'm stronger. I accepted things I shouldn't have in the past. I questioned nothing. The sun will never rise on another day like that for me. I'm going on my own path now and if it fails, it fails. I take responsibility for that.'

She unfolded her arms and stepped closer again. 'I can't stay innocent for ever. I can't remain in the nursery of my parents' home and watch the other children go out and play and taste life.'

'Yes. You can. If I have anything to do with it.'

'Innocence got me a suitor who couldn't get rid of me fast enough when he discovered I might not have the fortune he wanted.'

She studied him, trying to get beneath the distracting veneer and understand the person with the sincere smile which deflected so much. 'You want to brush me aside like Tenney did.'

He took one step from her. 'I don't want to brush you aside like I did with all the others, or like I have been.'

She stared beyond the distraction in front of her, forcing herself to respond. She made up her mind the direction she would choose and she'd deal with the consequences later. 'You said you've always remained on friendly terms with the women in your life.'

'But distant.' The word seeped into the room with quiet finality.

'You're trying to keep me from being close to you now.'

'Some would say it's impossible to be close to me. The smiling veneer only goes into another smiling veneer, and you can't find what isn't there.'

She walked to the mirror, touched the skin on her cheek and stared. 'The two men I have cared for do not wish for me to touch them.'

'That's a lie.' He stepped behind her. 'Tenney may not have wanted you to touch him—' his voice lowered to a gravelled whisper '—but I do. Since the first night I held you in my arms, I've wanted to hold you again.'

He hesitated. 'But we cannot continue to meet privately and expect it to remain secret. You would risk too much and I would risk nothing. It's not fair to you.'

He put his hand on her shoulders and his head dipped, resting against hers. The caress of his lips against her neck created a fiery yearning that pulled her against him.

Raising his head and staring into the mirror, he clasped her wrist and caught it up so that her hand touched his face. His eyes closed and he inhaled.

She turned, stepping into his arms. If strength had a scent, it surrounded her, wrapping her in a blanket bigger than any she'd ever find on a bed, clasping her with gentleness and swaddling her in wonder.

'I want you to make love to me,' she spoke softly, but sincerely. 'I know it's a risk, but my life seems full of hazards. And I would like to choose one of them.'

'Then let me show you my home.' The words whispered against her skin reached into her depths and transported her with the touch of his lips on hers.

* * *

'My rooms,' Devlin said to the driver and, within seconds, the horses dashed over the uneven road as if they had wings hovering them above it.

The carriage rolled to a stop not in front of the estate, but nearer the side, and Devlin released her hand to jump from the coach, rotating to hold out his arms for her.

He lifted her from the carriage and swept her around in a half-circle before she could put her feet on the ground and she tumbled into him. She extricated herself, looking up into the moonlight reflecting from his eyes.

He held out his arm and led her to a nondescript door far from the main entrance. The entryway had crossed swords on one wall and a case with a map and spyglass on the remaining side.

'It's the oldest part of the house. It's private.'

Inside, the air smelled differently from that the other side of the house. This was tantalisingly male. Leather. Ambergris. Wool. Burning oil from the lamp he'd lifted to shine the light to illuminate her steps.

He led her into a room filled with overstuffed chairs and a large painting of a horse standing at sunrise. A newspaper lay folded on one of the seats and a fireplace took up most of one wall.

He put the lamp on the table and his shadow reached well past the ceiling.

'This is my home, my true home. I wasn't given this suite until after I finished university. In fact, I never plan to relocate to the Earl's rooms should my father die. I suppose I could feel differently later. But I don't expect to. I could be a world apart from everyone else who resides here. I'm out of the family pathways, except for Payton's because he could find me on another continent.

Everyone knows they'd best not plan on sharing this area without my permission, and I don't give it.'

His desire for solitude surprised her and he seemed to want to set her at ease, and the effort welcomed her.

Clasping an arm around her waist, he said, 'You don't have to worry about anyone disturbing us. I've never brought anyone here before, but since we met in this house, I wanted you to visit my suite.'

He ran a hand up her back, drawing her close, and together they stood connected. She couldn't think of anything except his presence and her awareness of the private man.

Something told her that she was seeing inside him to a part he kept for himself and now wanted to share with her.

The kiss he gave her as she folded her arms around him swept her from the reality of the night into a dream fuelled by his lips.

He didn't move away as he released the pins from her hair and let the locks fall aside. A heated, moist breath. A whisper of phrases that sounded endearing, murmured in a language she didn't understand, and yet she grasped the lyrical words.

A moment when his darkened eyes took her in before he pulled her closer, their bodies pressing. Her breasts tingled from the length of him and his hardness urged her nearer.

He led her to a room that only had one shape she could make out in the darkness, a bed that overpowered the small room. He stepped to a dressing room at their side and shadows flickered as he set the lamp aside and grasped the top rung of a chair and slid it closer. She heard the easy slide of his boots and stockings being removed, but she watched the outline of the man, his movements illuminated by a single light that fixed her attention on his frame.

After he put his boots aside, in a fluid stretch, he rose. He should have been diminished in his bare feet, but instead he appeared assured, commanding and taller. He took up the doorway space and crossed over the threshold, returning to her.

A body designed by nature at her best. Perfection in every sinew and plane. Something he took for granted, yet her eyes could not.

He stood before her, and nothing seemed rushed, but as if the universe slept just for them and the night would last for ever.

In that second, she imagined the night unfolding and paused.

He immediately stopped, his hand on the tie of his shirt. 'We don't have to continue. We can cease at any moment you wish. I'll take you home now if that's what you'd like.'

'No. Not that.' She rested her head against his shoulder. 'It's the lamplight.'

'The light?'

'Yes. Please put it out.'

Immediately he doused the lamp, then he returned.

'I don't want you to see—' she whispered.

He waited.

'My scars. I don't want you to see. You must promise not to look.'

'I assure you. I assure you that they don't matter to me.'

'I—I don't want you to see them.'

He ran a finger along the side of her face, not stopping until he'd traced the seam of her lips. 'You're price-less. A treasure. And you should never doubt that. Are you certain that is the only reason you're hesitating?'

'It is. It is. The only reason.' She grasped his waist. 'It seems so very important to make love to you. To know that I'm desirable and the scars don't matter.'

He lowered his head so it rested against hers, his fingers tangled in her hair and holding them close. 'You can't feel that—that we must make love to prove something so nonsensical. You must not even consider that you are any less perfect now than on the day you were born. You aren't.'

She didn't speak.

'Listen to my voice. Hear the truth in it. The only person who has any right to have any discomfort about the marks is you, because you felt them and you experienced the pain that grew with them. But no one has any justification to think them any less than another wondrous part of you, like your starlight eyes, your lips that taste of preciousness, your hair sweeping silken against my face and arousing me with each strand brushing me. How can any true man not adore your skin? It is a miracle of womanliness.'

He used both hands to hold her head, his thumbs at her cheeks, and he placed a tender kiss on her lips.

'We cannot make love in an effort to make you feel more beautiful, Rachael. I would stop now if that were the reason. You must understand first that the scars are less to me than the smallest freckle you have. Only because they are a part of you are they of any consequence at all. You make them special—they do not diminish you.'

Warmth followed by the hint of night blended with the taste of him. 'Do you believe me?' he asked.

'I do.'

A swathe of his essence enveloped her and her knees almost gave way as his touch fell to her shoulders and then down her arms to encircle her, holding her. It was as if he'd swept the floor from beneath her feet, his arms holding her tightly enough to keep her standing.

Lips grazed her jawline, sending shivers throughout her body. She caught her breath, awash in the different textures of Devlin against her. The brush of his cheek, the texture of his hair, muscles flexing beneath the skin ignited her body.

He found her mouth again. He tasted of lemon and brandy, his lips open so that their tongues could touch and their breaths blend.

He backed away. She feared he'd changed his mind and she yearned for him in a way that was new to her.

Instead, he led her to the bed, sat and ran his hand down her length, the curve of her increasing the intensity of feelings. She'd never expected so much of his masculinity could be absorbed by her body, just from the brush of fingertips.

He pulled her on to his lap and held her with one arm while he removed her shoes and dropped them to the floor.

She felt like a porcelain doll, perfect, held secure and cherished. Moments she would appreciate for ever.

Burrowing her face against his skin, she breathed in, savouring the experience, prolonging the feel of their embrace.

He stood, taking her with him and helping her to her feet.

His lips cut off her ability to speak and she pressed her body nearer him, flattening into his shape, held as one against him. Instead of feeling a lesser person, she absorbed his strength, buoyed along with him surrounded by waves of yearning.

He slipped his tongue against her lips and passion grew, heating her with a longing that would have protected her from the coldest storm.

He touched her dress, releasing the hooks and slipping it from her shoulders, in one long, draping slide that teased her skin as the garment flowed from her body. In seconds, the corset fell to the floor.

She spread her fingers, letting them trail over his chest, relishing the textures.

Lifting her, he placed her on top of the bedcovers. He finished undressing, his trousers falling to the floor, and slid beside her, lips again touching. His movements created friction, teasing her nipples, sending molten lava sparks inside.

She wrapped her leg around him, pulling him close. His fingers tangled in the chemise and the fabric glided over her head, giving her a chance to gasp a breath before their lips touched again.

Caressing her breast, he moved gently back, yet she felt his member touching her, causing an insistent yearning she'd never felt before. Then he rocked against her, holding her hips closer, and then again and again he moved, until the intensity grew so that she couldn't contain it.

She released and as she did, he joined to her, moving inside, rocking together, slowing the intensity in his body, and he held her close, but instead of releasing, he pulled away. Then he lay beside her, her name a gasp on his lips, until he completed the moment.

While he held her close, she shut her eyes and rested

against him, sated in a way she'd not known existed, and she felt her lips curl into a satisfied smile.

She awoke. She'd had the most delicious dream. She stretched her arms wide and her fist bumped a body. A body nothing like her own except it had the necessary amount of appendages with one more.

'Devlin,' she gasped and saw a fortress of naked male, all bristly and furry and firm, propped against the pillows where he half sat.

Her memories of the night inundated her. 'I fell asleep. I've just been so busy. The parties at night. Learning during the day.'

She had thought about making love to him. She had thought about him leaving her. But she had never considered that she might wake up beside him.

He took the fingers of her left hand and brought them to his lips for a tender kiss, then pulled her into the curve of his arm. 'I could have easily woken you.'

'I was sleepy because I was up so late last night. There's so much to get right.'

'You have people to help you. Grimsley. Your father and mother. Me.'

'I know. But everything is so different. So many changes. Even tonight. It's as if I stepped into someone else's life, but not my own. As if I'm still acting a part. I didn't expect to feel that way. I expected to feel as if I was claiming my own future.'

'Acting?' The word snapped from his lips.

'Yes. I don't know how I should react. What I should say to you. I should tell you I love you, but I'm afraid to. I'm afraid that it might send you away from me. And what if I don't, then it might drive you away, or make you unhappy.'

Instantly, he pulled her close. 'This is not about us making each other happy. It's not. It's about caring. It's about sharing a part of ourselves. It's about not acting, but being ourselves. The true us. Without that, we have nothing. Do you regret tonight?'

'Not at all.' She didn't. How could she regret something that she couldn't even comprehend fully?

'Then don't worry about anything else. Not anything.' He ran a hand down the side of her body, soothing her. 'You don't have to concern yourself about what it felt like, or how you're supposed to react, but about being together.'

His words were meant to reassure her, she thought. But they didn't. They rumbled the earth underneath her even more. She'd somehow always considered that two people would immediately separate to their own rooms after making love. That it would be something she could reflect on when she was alone in her room.

Not. In. Devlin's bed.

'Are you sure you don't have regrets?' he asked again. The low rumble of his voice floated into the room.

She did as he'd told her to do and repeated the question. 'Regrets?' This time, she contemplated the question and herself. 'I don't.'

She just didn't want to make the mistake of becoming lost in a new world that she was unfamiliar with. Of making a new life that was someone else's.

No, she didn't regret being with him.

But she imagined herself forced into a marriage because she had to save her reputation and steeled herself to stay on her own path. She did not want either of them forced into a marriage. Whether he resented her or not, she would believe he did.

In one fluid movement, he pulled her to him again so that his lips could brush hers.

'I can't promise all that I will say will make you happy and I can't assure you I will always think before I speak. But you will be able to look at my face. You will have more to judge than ink on paper. You will have me in front of you. I will not hide behind paper. Will you promise me the same?' he asked. 'If you wish to end our friendship, say so now. To my face.'

'I don't. I know I don't.'

Her voice was the merest sound that could have reached his ears. Her words lingered in the air like a fireplace ember sparked from the rest and which lay there glowing on and on.

The last speck of the luxurious haze of romance evaporated and she saw herself plunging into another unsatisfying commitment.

Another chance at a humiliating dissolution of a future.

Then a clock chimed once, twice, three times. Then a fourth.

'Four?' She realised how long she'd been gone from her home and on the heels of that revelation others thundered into her brain, clearing the haze that had focused everything so that her mind had created a whirlwind with Devlin in the centre of it.

'Blast,' she said, rolling with the covers. 'I'm... It's...' She gaped at the window. 'I am not thinking clearly. This was a wonderful, beautiful between us and I wouldn't have missed it—but where are my clothes?'

She heard the covers rustle and he sat alert.

'As long as you're not having second thoughts.' His voice came through the darkness, reassuring in tone.

'I'm not. I have to get home. Now.' She jumped up from the bed, pulling the sheet with her, and wrestled her shift on. 'Double blast it backwards.' She switched it around without taking it over her head. She grabbed her corset and stepped into it. 'Help me.'

She moved to the side of the bed where he sat and turned away from him. She felt the tugs of her ties. In seconds he had her in the corset and she stepped into her dress, leaving the hooks undone as she reached for her stockings. 'I must get home now.' She couldn't fall into his arms.

As she slipped her stocking over her foot, she imagined the murmurs. If anyone heard of this, so soon after the broken betrothal, everyone would assume she was latching on to the Viscount to salve her pride. The very thing she feared when ending it with Tenney.

She gave up on getting the cotton perfect, letting a snarl of it remain at her heel.

'Rachael,' he soothed. 'It's not morning yet. You've time. The driver will wait. He'll drop us not far from the house and I'll escort you inside. We'll be dark shadows walking in the night, like a stableman and his beloved. No one will know tonight. We need to discuss this.'

A discussion. She didn't have time for a discussion.

'The maid is to wake me at six.' She slipped on one shoe.

'Six?'

'Of course. But I fell asleep. Where is my other shoe?'

'Rachael.' He rose from the bed. 'Nothing is going to change in the next few hours. You've time to leave. But why would you have a maid wake you so early?'

'My shoe? Did you see it? Never mind.' She didn't want to answer.

He bent over and picked up the shoe and handed it to her.

'How do I get out?' she asked, slipping it on.

'Once I'm dressed I will get you safely home.' He pulled up his trousers. 'It will look better if I'm not walking along the street naked.'

She handed him his shirt. His being naked would not be a bad sight, but it would certainly not keep the encounter secret.

'Thank you.' He took it, slipped it under his arm and twirled her around to do her hooks.

When he finished, he hugged her tight. 'What's wrong?'

Instantly, she stopped moving. The tone of his voice tore at her heart. He didn't understand. He couldn't, because she didn't.

She turned, cupping the bristly jaw in her hands. 'I'm overwhelmed. So much has changed in the past few days. The past few moments. I have to have some time to catch up with what is going on in my life.'

Clasping her fingers, he said. 'As long as you don't regret it.'

'No. Not at all. Yesterday, I asked my maid to wake me early. I didn't think about…this.' Six o'clock would give her time to prepare before the tutor arrived. Those multiplications were challenging. Then the tutor would be gone by the time her father woke. Her father slept later and she didn't want to risk him seeing her struggle and forbidding her to take the lessons. He'd told her before that education was difficult and his family would not have to struggle. 'I'm having…lessons.'

'Lessons?'

'I never really did as a child. Except the ones in sewing and music and dancing. Now I'm having the ones about numbers and sums. Mr Grimsley arranged for his wife and her brother to help me and I am trying to learn as quickly as possible. There is more to business than I ever imagined.'

He stilled, nodding, and she sensed respect, and maybe admiration, in his gaze.

Someone else might not understand how much the Grimsleys did for her family. She imagined Mr Grimsley being let go. Mrs Grimsley without a home.

If word got out that she'd been with Devlin...

She could almost hear one of the women saying that she wished she'd caught on fire instead of Rachael, followed by giggles.

With imagined laughter ringing in her ears, Rachael ignored the wadded stocking in the bottom of her slipper and tried to act as if she'd merely requested a carriage. 'I must go.'

Chapter Nineteen

Devlin sat in the vehicle. Rachael perched alert, unsure if she could touch him without making the situation worse.

He took her hand and she relaxed inside, awash in the closeness.

'You're too far away,' he said.

Something tugged at her heart. She put her other hand over the top of his, switching, so she could lean into his arm on the seat.

True, she'd needed his support, but she didn't want to lose their friendship. To become a part of him so much that he couldn't even see her.

Always she would remain the woman he'd rescued. The woman he'd saved again and then again.

She was so aware of the man beside her. Aware of the way he made her heart warm and her body burn and melt with desire. He'd changed her and touched her in a way no one ever had.

'You saved me from the fire and have encouraged me to navigate in society,' she said. 'I'm grateful. But my gratitude, and your undertaking to assist me, created a friendship between us and maybe we're mistaking it for something more.'

Yes, she would always be the woman he'd trained to handle conversation. Perhaps he felt connected—even without realising it, because he'd saved her life and tasked himself with making her comfortable in society.

The carriage wheels lurched after hitting a rut, a movement echoing the feelings tumbling along inside her.

She put her hand over his knuckles, amazed at the raw strength she felt contained in him. 'Our moments together meant everything to me. Something I'll always cherish. You'll always be in my memory, but I don't think you or I could be happy rushing into something,' she said.

Her blood thundered in her ears and emphasised the quiet walls of the carriage, and she shifted from being with him to being alone.

Her hand still rested on his knuckles, but now she could feel distance seeping between them.

Rachael heard a whispered curse. A masculine chuckle followed. 'I've said that before.' He turned his face to the world outside the window.

She'd said the words, yet they'd made her feel rejected and a little broken. And alone.

She couldn't speak for the emotions inside her that she couldn't understand.

The coach rolled closer to her house and he didn't alert the driver to stop until they'd passed it and turned the corner.

He was perfection, lifting her from the carriage as if he'd spent a lifetime training for the moment. Perhaps he had.

Then he rushed her home through the darkness, his touch never leaving her as he held the small of her back.

Outside the door, he stood in the shadows, brushing a kiss over her cheek, asking her if she was well.

She nodded, though she felt it a lie.

'What will you be doing later?' he asked. 'After the lessons. When you have time to yourself?'

She grasped his hand and he rested his forehead against hers.

'I will likely be studying metals,' she said. 'I've told Grimsley to expect me.'

They stood, lingering.

Now, her greatest fear unfurled in her mind. The re-alisation settled.

She had been jilted by a man she didn't particularly care about. Devlin was different. She didn't want to tie her heart to him and find herself telling him she loved him, and hear the words come back to her that she'd said to him that night. Words about how much the person meant to you but, really, less than they'd expected and only a fragment more than anyone else.

'But it's not necessary to check on me,' she said. 'I'll be fine.' As long as she didn't fall in love with Devlin and stumble off the ends of the earth.

And yet, forcing herself to move one step inside the door seemed herculean. Impossible.

He helped her, opening the door and letting his hand slide from her. One kiss and he was gone.

The butler stood in the shadows with a lone candle, holding it for her 'Miss Rachael. I heard a carriage roll past and thought it might be you, and you'd need a light.'

Out of habit, she thanked him, took the candle and walked up the stairway.

She heard the rasp of the key in the lock and she paused at the top of the stairs. The butler had locked the door and, without another word, retreated to his quarters.

She sat the candle down on the floor and knelt to sit, her feet resting on the treads below.

The butler's kindness to her had reinforced the fact that he, and every servant in her house, depended on her family, just as the Grimsleys did. If her father's business failed, so many other people would be affected.

It wasn't just about the soirées she wouldn't be invited to, the dresses she would not be able to purchase and the trinkets that wouldn't appear.

Many people depended on her father and she'd seen the accounting books and understood enough of the numbers, and the hope in Mr Grimsley's eyes.

Now she knew why he'd not brushed her aside with an admonishment that this was best left to men.

She was his last hope, and his wife's last hope, and her family's.

She just wished to be held in Devlin's arms and to be reassured that all was well. But nothing felt well any more. Nothing had felt safe since she'd spoken those words to Devlin. Words she meant, but had sounded hollow when Devlin laughed.

They had to sell some costly pieces soon. Grimsley had only taken half the pay he'd been promised for the last year. He told her that her father had been generous, practically overpaying him, and he and his wife had needed so little, but the winter had been cold, requiring more to heat than usual, and a window had been broken, and he'd named so many little things he'd had to purchase but which had added up. Her father didn't know that.

Grimsley had had tears in his eyes when he'd told her that her father was the best man he'd ever worked for.

Devlin would never understand what it had meant to witness Grimsley's face. The feeling of pride she felt when someone believed in her abilities.

Hannah Humphrey had managed a print shop and Rachael remembered walking by the window and seeing all the pictures. It had been grand, she thought, and her father had expressed amazement that a woman could do such a thing and sadness that Mrs Humphrey hadn't married and been able to let a man take those trials from her.

It hadn't seemed like a trial for Rachael, but an interesting life and much more fascinating than her father's ownings of mostly pots, and silver buckles and kettles. Even the jewellery hadn't fascinated her much.

Yet now her viewpoint had changed.

Likely no one would even consider her as having failed…as they would have if she'd been a man. She had no risk in that area as she wasn't expected to succeed or even try. But she would always know.

She knew she couldn't do it. Alone.

She squared her jaw. She'd survived the Duchess of Highwood. And while she might not be able to learn the business fast enough, she had an army she could muster to contribute. Her father. Her mother. Grimsley. The former apprentice. Her grandfather's book. Together, they would make a force.

She jumped up and ran to her room, hoping for a chance to read over the studies before Mrs Grimsley's brother arrived.

But with the book in front of her, all she could think about was Devlin and the feel of being in his arms.

* * *

Devlin left the carriage in a deft lunge, avoiding the steps while the vehicle stopped at the ornate main entrance as he'd requested. He gave a quiet goodnight to the driver and suggested he sleep the morning away.

He waited as his conveyance rolled into the street, letting his mind catch up to his body, leaving the solitude even more pronounced.

The night air had perfection in it, enhanced by the scent of a flowering bush in a nearby garden, or perhaps his own. He didn't know.

He didn't know what kind of plants grew in his garden and wondered if he was missing out on something.

In the distance, he heard a dog's muffled whine which ended on a whimper, the poor soul sounding tortured. He questioned if the noise was an unusual occurrence, or if every night the animal barked just to hear himself.

Stars glowed overhead. Just as they always did on clear nights, he supposed. And they didn't care if he saw them or not. They did as they wished.

But he knew that dark early mornings didn't usually feel like this one. They weren't so clear. So pristine. Wholesome. Alone.

He heard her words again. *Cherish... Memory... Rushing into something...*

He'd not realised how clichéd the phrases were. They'd been convenient in the past. But now they mocked him.

He contemplated his life while staring up at the heavens.

Even with the disastrous discussion with Rachael, he preferred the feel of the solemn night over the murky ones caused by too much revelry. The world he was created to be in. The celebrations of life. The laughter of others. Rachael's world called to him as well.

The thought that had reverberated in his mind as she'd lain sleeping beside him had been how he'd wanted to see inside the world of other families when he'd talked to the drivers that night.

He'd wondered if Rachael's parents were truly happy, or had created an illusion for their family. The coachmen had convinced him it was real.

He huffed. To merely create that appearance of happiness was a feat. One his own family hadn't mastered easily.

One thing was an unknown factor in such an endeavour. The man he saw in the mirror. How could he ask Rachael into his world when he could not promise her happiness in it?

He didn't want to grow old some day and see Rachael despairing. And he certainly never wanted her to entertain the idea that she would have been better off with Tenney.

He knew more about the social world and she knew more about a quiet home life and had the example of her parents' marriage to examine. Just as he'd guided her in society, he'd begun to wonder if she could teach him about family.

He remembered the feeling when Payton had retorted that she'd probably had her embroidery needles named and his instinctive realisation that if she'd been born into higher society she would have already passed through his life.

Devlin had thought it all for her benefit, but now he saw how leading her into society had furthered his opportunity to pursue her. He'd not considered his own motives before.

Just as it always did, his mind seemed to be thinking without letting him in on the fact. He was grateful it was on his side.

Shaking his musings into the recesses where they would not trouble him, he strode into the house, past a doorway perfectly adorned by flowering vines.

He lived on one side of the house. His father lived on one floor and his mother another, and his brothers were spaced so everyone could take different paths and rarely run across each other.

A well-ordered family.

The butler greeted him, voice groggy from sleep, the servant pretending he'd been awake all along. The overstuffed chair at the base of the stairs had probably heard more snores than the man's bed.

Devlin didn't know why Tomlinson had stayed at his post so late. He wagered the one man knew more about the family's lives than either his father, his mother or he knew.

Yet it could have been dedication that led to such knowledge. He wanted to find out.

He accepted the offer of a lamp to light the way to his suite, his excuse for entering the main doorway.

'Does the Earl tell you to wait up until we are all home?' he asked.

The butler stood straight. 'No... Not now...'

Devlin waited.

'When you were younger. Now I await your brothers.'

'You stay up to see that Eldon and Oliver are home? Why?' They were old enough to manage themselves, particularly when they were together.

'The Earl. He asked me to.'

'They're with Payton and they might not even arrive home until daybreak. Our cousin will make sure they have no funds left to lose to him. Their allowances should go directly to him. Go to bed instead of waiting.'

'I would, but your father may…'

One foot on the bottom tread, he stilled. 'Is Father home?' When the words left his mouth, he realised how often he'd asked them. How often he'd entered through the main entrance after his night out…to get the lamp the butler had for him…to ask if his father was home. Then, later, to ask if his younger brothers were home.

'Yes.' The butler's words brightened. 'He is.'

He took the steps two at a time, then stopped again. The butler hadn't left the post. 'Why does Father ask you to wait for my brothers?'

'You'd have to ask him.'

Devlin reversed directions and strode into the second lamplight. He smiled at the butler. 'What would your guess be?'

The butler spoke just as Devlin knew he would. Everyone trusted that smile and he supposed they should as it wasn't false, just useful.

'His children. He just wants to be reassured they are still returning home. That they are managing well.'

Devlin remained, knowing his presence, his relaxed question and his quietness prodded the man to continue. What good was a gift of encouraging people to talk if you didn't use it?

'Some day you'll be doing the same to your children,' the butler added. 'On occasion, at night, the Earl wanders down the stairs and asks who is here.'

'He could ask the next morning and he usually leaves

his carriage for my brothers. The driver can let him know what transpired.' A ruse Devlin had known his father used to keep up with him when he was younger.

'But I suspect he resumes his sleep easier if everyone is at home. Or if he just hears word that all is well. It seems to soothe him and he rarely returns a second time in the same night. He's said that if I'm not here, he knows everyone who is supposed to be home is in bed.'

'Ah, we must have disturbed your night so many times…'

Tomlinson answered with brief nods and a smile. 'I'm fortunate that I don't need much sleep.'

'I'll hire someone to assist you so you don't have to stay awake so often.'

The butler put his head down. 'Your father already did and I let the young man help with my other duties. But I couldn't let him take this one. Not often anyway.' His words softened and he glanced up. 'I feel better knowing everyone is safe.'

Devlin thanked the man, an inadequate gesture, but heartfelt, and continued up the stairs. He heard the butler settle into the easy chair. Another member of his family that he'd not realised existed.

He took the long hallway to his rooms.

Who knew? They'd been a family going their own directions his whole life, or so he'd thought.

A tradition he'd not really wanted to follow, but he'd not seen any reason to marry and risk adding another person who might clutter the peace it had taken them so long to obtain.

He laughed in the silent hallway as he thought of his father. Perhaps his family wasn't as disconnected as he thought.

He remembered the thousands of times his father had told him to keep an eye on his brothers and watch out for them, then recited a litany of mistakes the boys could make.

His feet stilled and his mind whirled, racing over the nights of his youth.

He realised that part of the reciting of the mistakes his younger brothers could make was most likely for his benefit and he'd never suspected.

Likely his father had done something similar to his siblings. His brother had once complained to him that they were tired of hearing of Devlin's missteps from their father and he wished he'd not been the youngest because their father constantly warned him not to do this or that because it hadn't been well for Devlin. His brother had complained that Devlin had all the adventures and all the fun and they were being punished for it.

Devlin shook his head.

He'd thought himself watched carefully because, as his father reminded him so many times, he was the oldest, the heir, and he had to set a good example.

Changing direction, he went to his father's rooms and knocked the same pattern he'd tapped on Rachael's door.

He let himself in and his father jolted awake. 'What's wrong?'

'Tonight, I heard words I'd said before coming from someone else's lips and it wasn't a proud occasion.'

His father slumped back and reached out to fluff his pillow into the shape he wanted for his head. 'If we were held accountable for every utterance…' He slapped his pillow. 'What words?'

'The words where you say how much someone means

to you, but really they don't mean as much as they'd prefer.'

'To that woman you saved from the fire?'

'Yes.' That his father knew of Rachael didn't surprise him as it would have only moments earlier.

He snorted, slapped the pillow again and mumbled, 'Woman must not have a thought in her head.'

'Perhaps she has considerably functional ones.'

'Surely not.'

'I don't know whether I'm relieved or my pride has been hurt. Or sad. Or what.' He had been surprised at the reactions he'd felt when she'd spoken and wanted to rush out. He'd been incredulous. After all, they were so new to each other.

Next, he'd been engulfed by wave after wave of loss.

With the women trying to catch his attentions, when the friendships ran their course, he'd usually ended them or they'd naturally faded away.

The loss still surrounded him and seemed to be laughing at him in the darkness, calling him a fool.

Somehow, his conscience teased him that he valued her more for leaving quickly than he would have if she'd lingered.

He could not imagine what direction his brain was taking when it hinted he valued a woman more because she didn't want to be with him.

His father pushed the covers to the side, put his feet into his slippers and stood, his nightshirt to his knees. He donned his robe. 'Sounds like a wise woman.'

Devlin didn't think he'd ever seen his father in a nightshirt without a dressing gown, but then he'd never entered his father's room in the middle of the night.

His father snapped his fingers. 'There's a hundred

women who'd say yes to you if you asked them tomorrow. Easily a hundred.'

'Not a thousand?' Devlin asked and his father stopped moving and peered around the room as if he'd not seen it before.

'I wouldn't go that far.' He glanced at Devlin and recovered his poise. 'Well, perhaps I overestimated. Ten. Eleven on a good day…'

He took off his dressing gown before he'd even tied it and threw it to the bedpost. 'Women fall easily at your feet. Just like they did at mine when I was younger. It becomes about the conquest. Not the woman.' He returned to his spot between the covers and picked at them, placing them just so. 'They're all so perfect. Perfect. At first, anyway. It has to be about the conquest because when you get to know them better, they're all irritating. They're all blemished. Just like us. Your mother is the best of the lot.'

Instantly, Devlin reacted, his voice light. 'I searched throughout all London until I was certain I'd found the only woman who'd not be interested.'

His father chuckled. 'That's what I expected you did. Don't worry, son, the next one will be daft enough to please you. You've practically been tripping over agreeable ones your whole life.'

'It was time I met one who's particular.' Devlin noted how easily the smile came to his own lips. How easy to find words that would diffuse his father's irritation.

His father deliberated on Devlin. 'Is that all you woke me up for?'

'I came in to tell you that and that you're tolerable.'

'You're tolerable, too, son. Now that you're older. Sometimes better than tolerable. Sometimes not.'

'Sometimes you're better than tolerable also.'

His father burrowed into the bed, rolled over and pulled the covers high. 'Now go to sleep. And don't darken my bedroom door again unless you need fatherly advice.' He laughed. 'I'll be glad to give you hours of it.'

'You probably won't chance upon me here again, then,' Devlin said and walked over to tap his father on the foot that was hidden in the covers. 'Sleep well.'

'Same to you.'

Devlin left, taking the lamp.

His father's words might have had some truth in them.

He tried to think of anyone he'd ever been unable to convince to do as he wished and his mind flickered to Rachael.

As a viscount, with a fortune at his fingertips and an amiable attitude, people found it easier to accommodate him than not. He really asked so little of anyone. Truly asked nothing of them in most instances.

He'd also fallen into the same trap of the people around him. He'd fallen for his own easiness.

He walked the hallway to his rooms just as he had so many nights before.

He was little different from the barrister. Rachael, as a secret merchant, had her own thoughts and he'd not expected that. He'd expected her to put everything aside to turn her attention to him.

He'd expected Rachael to refuse to make love until he'd proposed. Perhaps even obtained a Special Licence. He'd truly expected that. That he'd been prepared for.

Inside his sitting room, he didn't stop until he reached his bedside and put the lamp on the table.

He felt in his waistcoat pocket and took out the small

parcel not purchased from her father's building. He'd not wanted her to know he had it for her.

Unwrapping it, he extricated the trinket. He'd had the choice to go either to ornate or to the plain. He'd seen the gaudy stone Tenney had given her and known that simple would be best.

Turning the gold band with a ruby stone in his fingers, he imagined it on Rachael.

He'd not presumed she would even think of any financial concerns after they'd made love. His laughter at himself sounded hollow in the room.

He'd not planned on a secret merchant for a wife. He'd known that his skilled man of affairs could take on the particulars of the business and evaluate each on merit, giving Albright a say in minor decisions. Rachael would be relieved—at least she had been in his imagination.

Now he wondered if he'd been thinking like society and not taking her dreams into consideration. It was more than just her dreams he needed to understand. It was her willingness to educate herself in the endeavour and accept challenges.

He smiled. He couldn't help himself. Rachael was willing to take on the strategies needed to succeed, even though she was afraid. She had a warrior's heart hidden inside.

The ring reminded him of the folly of his thoughts and he slipped it on his little finger, then took it off. Rachael had a trove of trinkets at her fingertips and more than likely a discerning eye for only the best of jewellery.

He had no knowledge of baubles, but he did have an understanding of what made true beauty, and he hoped that he hadn't directed Rachael to destroy the true loveliness that was inside her in an attempt for her to become accepted by society.

But he didn't know the real woman, or perhaps he did, and that was why he'd considered her for a wife.

He'd encouraged her to concentrate on her father's business and she'd taken his advice.

He'd not thought how it could change his life.

The old Rachael would have wed him. The new one that he'd influenced her to be had reservations about a commitment.

The old Rachael would have been easy to please. A keepsake that would have satisfied her of his devotion and care. She would have liked the little trinket and been satisfied.

This Rachael expected more.

Perhaps she wanted the impossible, but he wasn't sure exactly what that was. He didn't know if she was aware either.

The jewel he held was just a token. It didn't prove anything. He walked to the window, opened it and thought about tossing it outside. It would be the second ring he'd disposed of that way. But he couldn't. Not this one. It was the one he'd selected for Rachael.

Then he shut the window and twisted the latch one sharp turn. The latch broke, scraping his fingers.

He held the cold, broken metal in his fist, but the window was locked, and he couldn't toss it out.

He sat on his bed and examined the ring. Examined his life and what he wanted for his future.

Then he slipped the circle on his smallest finger.

Chapter Twenty

Devlin travelled to Rachael's house at near teatime. When the butler told him Rachael wasn't at home, the information hit him like a jab to the stomach. He spoke before thinking. 'Are you telling the truth?'

The man moved a half-step away in reaction.

Devlin remembered his manners. 'My apologies,' he said. 'I didn't mean that to sound harsh. I was just disappointed, and I thought…she might truly be home and not wish to see me.'

The butler smiled, eyes knowing, then spoke. 'She really isn't.'

Instantly, he realised where she was, gave the servant a nod of thanks and went on a search for her.

When Devlin arrived at the building, Mr Grimsley and a patron stood at the counter, discussing the ornate possibilities for necklaces.

As the man finally paused his conversation to examine another bauble placed in front of him, Grimsley asked Devlin if he would mind waiting, or, if he wished, Grimsley would summon his wife to assist.

Devlin ignored the words. 'I thought you might have another person nearby this afternoon. I am here to speak with…that person.'

'Ah, yes,' Grimsley said and directed him to a curtain. Beyond that Devlin saw a plank door, which hung askew in the frame, causing a thin triangular gap at the top of it.

He rapped and the door creaked open. Her face peeked around the edge and she smiled.

Relief flooded his body.

She stepped back, took his arm and pulled him inside. 'No one knows I'm here but the shopkeepers and my parents.'

He swept in and put an arm around her waist, pulling her close as he shut the door. 'No one knows I'm here either, so obviously we're somewhere else.'

For a second longer than necessary, he held her close, reassuring himself that she still welcomed him as a friend, then he immediately pushed himself away as his body started to long for her.

He turned, examining the room, distracting himself from the realisation that she was so close.

A desk sat in the centre. A stack of ragged volumes sat on each side of her chair, which was missing a slat.

Rachael didn't need to be in such surroundings and she didn't have to be. All he could think of was that she preferred this over him, yet she seemed unaware of his displeasure, which didn't surprise him. It had been unusual for her butler to notice the anger and Devlin's dismay had faded once he saw her.

He pushed aside the strange emotion of jealousy and let himself be impressed. She was working like an apprentice to learn the trade and no part of it seemed too lowly for her. This would be the person he wanted beside him in a battle.

* * *

'I expected to find you surrounded by jewels, not dust, ledgers and fixtures.'

'Jewels at night, mathematicals in the morning and this in the afternoon.' She swept her arm out to encompass the room, as if she were some sort of sorceress and the surroundings would suddenly turn golden. Instead of gold, the dust only gleamed more.

He saw the tiredness under her eyes and a pang of regret hit him. Not regret that he'd been with her. He'd never feel that. But the knowledge that instead of relieving her burdens, he'd added to them by keeping her awake longer.

But he would not apologise for their lovemaking.

She put a slip of paper in the book on the desk, marking her place, and closed the cover. 'This was the apprentice's old room. He wanted to become a silversmith instead and Father let him leave. Now, we order goods from him. Mr Grimsley said a new apprentice isn't needed now and we can order almost any metal item a customer wants. We are expanding to have more gold wares and we'll make more from them.'

'If someone wanted flatware designed, for instance?' He should leave, but he didn't want to go and he didn't want to abandon her.

'Mr Grimsley would be able to sketch what you described until he had a picture of it to send to be made. That is an easy task. If it weren't for what you said, about being more visible, I would probably discontinue the jewellery altogether. We make little overall from the baubles, but I'm hoping to change that.'

She paused and he held out his hand. She joined him, her skin delicate against his and filling him with fresh desire.

Even standing surrounded by drabness, she glittered. The excitement in her eyes transferred to him and she took a step and ended up in his arms again.

For a brief moment he held her and savoured every pulse of her closeness. He'd not known the simple solace that could be found in such innocence and that holding Rachael could make him feel a different person. Perhaps that was some of what she'd felt in the night. He hoped, in encouraging her, he'd made her feel her own strength. Her own resilience that hid beneath the surface and would always bring her rising up like a phoenix.

Then, he heard Grimsley's voice. She'd heard it as well. She drew away and shook her head, lips pressed together.

She found a small box, opened it, and slipped another oversized ring on her finger. He couldn't understand her taste in jewellery. Again, it was large on her finger. Then she held her hand flat and flicked the side of the metal with her finger and the bauble opened, the top sliding away.

'It's for headache powders.' She spoke softly.

'I didn't know you had headaches.' Their whispers kept them close.

'I don't usually. But I sent the silversmiths drawings of poison rings. I asked if they could reproduce it. And I've told them if they have any fresh ideas, to please let me know.' She flashed the ring. 'I found this one. I didn't know we had it. This one is rather ghastly, but I'm hoping for smaller designs, mostly using paste stones so it will not be an investment for the customer, but a novelty. Beautiful rings, however, that would stand alone on their own merit. My plan is that unusual items may bring customers in and then the other wares will tempt them while they're here.'

He took her fingers, drawing her near, impressed with her delicate hands.

'I don't plan to have many for view because I want the women to have the option of having something no one else has seen.' She reached out and when she touched his chest, it was as if they'd embraced.

He could no longer study the ring and he didn't care, reassured to be near her again. 'You think ladies will be interested in something so macabre?'

She nodded, clasping him, causing him to feel that he surrounded her as snugly as the ring fitted on her finger.

'It's like having a surprise within a jewel,' she said.

The words would have fitted her as well.

'Something different and I am planning to have a simple matching necklace and earrings to sell with it. I want them to be as unique as possible, so the ladies will have something to show and compare with their friends. If it goes well, I may offer bracelets which can hold a note, or a drawing or lock of hair from a loved one. I have two already on order.'

He could feel her excitement and the rush of enthusiasm she had for the project, and it matched his own feelings for her.

'It will also give me something to talk about when I am with others if I have one noticeable trinket. Meeting new people will be easier. I've instructed Grimsley that the silversmiths must use the finest craftsmanship and if the container jewels sell well, we will be able to use gold.'

'What if someone really uses one of the rings for poison?'

'Well, I would assume they can use one of the spoons I sell for the same thing. And they hold three or four times as much. And a silver teapot could be used for poison.'

'And as a weapon. Remember Father's chipped tooth.'

She put her fingertips to her lips. 'It would be fun to design a teapot with a dagger in the lid, I suppose, but again I don't want anyone to be serious about using the wares destructively.'

She closed the remaining ledger that had been open. 'We are planning other unique items. I saw a walking stick with a spyglass as a handle and have ordered one. I asked Grimsley to draw a horse's head on a cane to suggest a man might have a walking stick with his favourite animal's likeness at the handle. If we sell one-of-a-kind items people can talk about with their friends...well, the uniqueness may cause people to speak favourably about all our wares.'

'I had no idea you would take this so seriously so quickly. And have good plans a man of affairs might not even imagine. I'm looking forward to how your suggestions will improve the business.'

'It is like a puzzle to see what will work and I think it's fascinating. Grimsley has some ideas and we've made several lists, trying to work out the costs of each idea and the possible profits. We're also trying to plan large, impactful items that might catch a customer's eye. Grimsley said they might notice the bigger item and carry that affection to a smaller thing closer to the amount they can spend. It is like having one wine for sale for an enormous cost, then having many lower-priced wines that don't seem as extravagant next to the one. And all equally matched in taste.'

She turned, picking up a huge silver urn, running her fingers over the metal. 'This has been here since Mr Grimsley started. It hasn't sold and it might be best hidden under a bed. We thought we could send it to the former apprentice and have many smaller items made from the silver. In fact—' She pulled out another piece of paper. 'Mr Grimsley prepared a list of things we can use to turn into sales with little expense. He believes it will help us while we increase patronage.'

Devlin was almost jealous of the urn and of the affection she had developed for the business. He didn't want to be relegated to the background of her life. He wanted to be beside her, experiencing successes and failures with her.

He twirled her around, wanting to capture her attention. 'What future plans do you have in the social world?'

'Tomorrow Mother and I are to take tea with the Duchess. I hope she is not overly caustic.'

Caustic.

'Highwood?' He raised a brow in question and Rachael agreed.

'Unlikely. To her there is no such thing. Just pretend it is a sleight of hand with words and it means nothing more. Which is the best way to approach it,' he said,

He paused, then continued, 'I remember recently, the strangest thing happened to me. I was out and about in the early hours of the morning returning a woman home. And even though her words seemed to say otherwise, I suspected she might wish to meet me again. Was I right?'

'Yes. That is, if I was the woman you were returning home. If not, then I think she would likely wish to never, ever be near you again.'

'Do we remain friends then?' The words almost hurt him to ask. In the past, when someone became a friend after lovemaking, it meant they were about to travel different directions.

'I hope always.'

'So, Rachael, if I were to visit tonight, would you open the door for me?'

'You must promise to be careful not to be seen.'

'I will. But few things can remain secret for ever. If romances are kept private, and unacknowledged in the light of day, they are respected as such when only two people are involved.'

'So, everyone will become aware if we continue to meet?'

'Yes. We are all animals with instincts. And people sense when something changes in actions between two people. As much as we might try to continue to act as we always have, it's nearly impossible to do so.'

'If we continue on, do you think everyone will notice?'

'Just the ones who matter to us and the ones that like to spread rumours. So, yes, except for a rare few. You have made another step forward into society. To be recognised enough that other people are concerned about your actions.'

'Mother thinks I am working here so you and I will have a place to meet.'

'You can never let society know that you are toiling and expect to be welcomed at the finest houses. It could destroy your efforts and do the opposite of what you wish. It would be better for you to take the ledgers to your home.'

'I will be careful,' she said. 'But I need Grimsley's

help and I need to school myself on as much of the merchandise and transactions as I can. I need to be able to understand what the notes in the ledgers refer to.'

'You aren't planning to give this up? If the business turns around and Grimsley can handle it?'

She shook her head.

He thought of the impact that could make on her life. On his life and he chose his direction.

'I want to call on you at your home and I believe it should be in the day, and at the front door. I think it is important to you. To both of us. I will be at your house tomorrow afternoon if that will suit you.'

A romance would have to stand the light of day if it were to proceed.

Indecision raced across her face. He saw her thoughts plainly. She would be risking another chance of her private life being discussed publicly.

'I will just stop in briefly, if that's what you wish. I considered your suggestion that I get a dog and one was whining near my house last night. I sent my staff to search it out in the morning and now we have found the right pet for me. I want to introduce the two of you.'

'You want to introduce me to your dog?'

Then, just before he left, the words that had been settling in his brain and absorbing him fell from his lips. 'Yes. I thought if we were to marry, you'd best meet the newest member of my family. There's no one else for me but you.'

Her eyes widened and he deemed she would have taken rejection easier.

'It's just an idea for you to tumble around in your thoughts. Not a question, you understand. Just a consideration.'

'For both of us?' Her expression hadn't softened.

'I would wait for six years for you,' he said. 'But you do not have to wait for me.'

He walked to the urn and ran his fingers over the cool silver. 'Before, I thought I loved someone and when she rejected me, I looked around me and decided love wasn't worth it. It wasn't needed. It didn't matter. I would always be surrounded by people I could make happy with a smile and jest. And then I believed myself complete. I don't want to be complete any more—can't be—unless you are at my side.'

He held the urn so he could see his reflection in it. 'I have to become the man who can make you happy in marriage.'

Chapter Twenty-One

The butler let Devlin into the sitting room and left to fetch Rachael. At his side stood, or wobbled, his new pet. He reached down to pat his head and was rewarded with a whine and a distinctly dog scent.

'The butler said you have brought a friend with you?' She looked at his feet.

A half-growl or half-sputter greeted her.

She gasped. 'That's your dog?'

He viewed the bulldog with half of one ear missing and a rather droopy eye. The dog limped two steps, knees stiff, and gave Rachael a puzzled glance.

'Yes. He's worn, but not entirely worn out,' he said.

'Is he injured?' She put her knuckles to her chin.

This wasn't the praise he expected to be heaped upon him for his commitment. But he inspected the beast. He liked Scamp.

'My stableman found him limping near my house. The dog needs a lot of care. I had to carry him from my carriage. He's not the steadiest of dogs, but he can rush when food is prepared.'

'He's definitely not a puppy.'

'No. I thought an older dog would be prudent, particularly as he didn't have a home. But then I saw that he's not in as good a condition as you'd expect. It is hard for him to navigate the stairs. I think he gets confused halfway and forgets which direction he planned. He needs someone to carry him. The butler has enlisted a stable boy to help. The stable boy is pleased with his new duties. He sees this as an advancement.'

He reached down and rubbed the dog's head. 'He's a bit dotty, I think.'

'You could have had a puppy.'

'Perhaps later. But after I saw Scamp, then it seemed unlikely anyone else would want him. I didn't want someone to think him more a problem than a pet. They could select a puppy and where would that leave Scamp?'

'Does he do any tricks?'

'Just walking and barking.' He looked at her. 'And those are not always easy for him, but you cannot discount barking. It's much better than whining.'

'You have taken on a commitment to him. And you chose an animal that is in advanced years and you have added staff to care for him.'

'I thought you'd be pleased.' He scratched Scamp under his chins and the dog grumbled again. 'That's his most pleasant noise.'

'You have a companion that hardly demands anything of you at all. Just staff.' She laughed.

He frowned. 'Scamp is a good dog. I knew instantly that he was right for me.' He reached down again, patting the dog. 'He's got a hint of a rattle in his bark and I suppose his bite isn't that trustworthy. He's lost his teeth.'

'Can he see?' She bent closer.

'Seems to.'

'That's fortunate.'

Silence grew between them and he reached down, picking up Scamp.

'He's unwieldy,' she said.

'Yes. He hates to walk. Even if you don't consider Scamp much of a pet, I do.'

'It is good that you took him in.'

'He needed a home at the same time you'd suggested I needed a pet. I thought it a happy accident.'

Rachael's mother walked into the room. 'I thought I heard a dog bark.' She scrutinised Scamp. 'And I did. Poor thing. How old is he?' she asked.

'I'm not certain.'

'Have you had him long?'

'Not at all.'

'You took in an elderly dog. How noble.' Mrs Albright clapped her hands together. 'A kind gesture. Devlin, your generous spirit amazes me. I'm so thankful that we've had the privilege to know your family.'

With those words, she left.

Devlin shot Rachael a glance, telling her wordlessly that her mother understood.

But it didn't matter to her. Her mother was kind and all the things a mother should be, but she'd been married to a man who truly understood commitment to a family, though he didn't understand anything about business.

Devlin knew more than he let on about the intricacies of making money, but less about creating a true family.

She'd thought him getting a pet might bring them closer, as he learned to care for it and she shared his joy in the new closeness he'd discover, but now she saw that it demonstrated the truth of a relationship to him.

What she saw as commitment, he saw as a need for additional staff.

A wife would be an extra person in the house, mostly cared for by the servants. A family member needed to supply needed family members. Again, mostly cared for by the servants.

She couldn't step into such a role.

'Are you thinking of obtaining a wife in a similar fashion?' she asked, her jaw tight. 'Perhaps one a little older than all the rest and whom your servants will care for?'

'No. I like Scamp.' He cared for Scamp even though he was drooling on his hand. That ought to prove something.

'Maybe she will expect more than to be liked. I would. And she might expect to love you. I would expect to do that with my husband. And if I did, I would not want it to distance us.'

'I'm sure it would not.'

'Are you?'

'Yes.'

'I was in love with Meg once, or so I thought,' he said. 'Truly.'

'Are you still in love with her?'

'No. My first romance and the one I would never repeat. I planned to marry her with all a young man's fervour. I rarely even kissed her. She was too precious. I expected to surprise her on her birthday with a proposal. But the day before that, I received a note. Oddly, within days of the Duke's wife dying, Meg found she didn't love me. She hoped I understood.' He raised a brow. 'I did. Eventually.'

'Are you sure you don't still have feelings for her?'

'Within a year, I knew I'd been in love with love. Not her. I found out she was fascinated with the peerage. When the Duke's wife had died suddenly, within a few days, she offered him her condolences but had to wait until his mourning was over to make it permanent. When I discovered that, I was thankful my father was an earl.'

'But she seems so happy and perfect.'

'I'm sure she's happy and she's perfect for the Duke.'

Scamp growled. Devlin agreed. 'Well, I'd best be getting Scamp home, I don't think he can handle much more excitement today.'

'Will you be returning later tonight?' She heard the longing in her voice and cursed herself for it. She planned to spend the evening studying ledgers, but she would be home before dark.

His eyes took her in. 'Would you like that?'

'Of course.' She stepped closer to him. The dog growled again, forgetting he didn't have teeth.

'Quiet, Scamp,' he commanded and, with one additional yap of displeasure, the dog obeyed.

Devlin put Scamp on the floor and closed the distance between Rachael and himself, removing her from the dog's line of vision.

He lowered his voice, smiled and tried the charm that had worked so many times to get him what he wanted. 'But not if you're certain that you don't wish to wed. I think I'm going to wait until I get a ring on my finger.' He held his head high.

He already had a ring on his finger.

Scamp barked.

'You dog,' she said.

He blinked. 'Were you talking to me?' He lifted

Scamp. 'I hope you were because my pet doesn't like to be called names.'

She didn't answer.

He turned sideways, holding Scamp's head so he wouldn't nip at her, and dropped a kiss on her lips before leaving. 'I'm sure you were.'

The simple kiss ignited desire within her, but in moments he was gone.

The emptiness that followed, plunging deep, shocked her.

Suddenly, she felt more abandoned and smaller and less strong than she could remember ever being before.

She wanted to accept Devlin's proposal. She did. But she couldn't. What if she did and later he changed towards her as Tenney had done? Her feelings were so much stronger for Devlin in just a few days and seemed stronger every time she saw him.

Instantly, she ignored those feelings, reminding herself that he was walking out of her life.

Devlin might have given her the courage, but it was she who'd scrambled forward, grabbing purchase where she could.

She headed for the stairs.

'I apologise,' she called after them.

Devlin stopped and turned, the ever-present smile in his eyes.

'Then perhaps I will call on you again before too long.'

'Perhaps. Perhaps tonight if you wish.'

'Yes.'

Scamp growled.

Apparently, he'd not accepted her apology as easily as Devlin had.

'I'll see you then,' Devlin said. 'Scamp is hoping you don't wait until the last minute to decide.'

Then he stopped moving.

'I want you to think about whether you like me because of who I am, or because I can make people happy so easily. I know you don't want to change your path and I understand that. But I don't want us to marry if you don't wish to try to make me happy. I've spent my life putting smiles on other peoples' faces and smoothing things over for them. I don't want to wed unless it is someone who considers me worthy of the same treatment.'

Chapter Twenty-Two

Rachael felt as if someone had raked a cold, sharp diamond over her skin. She raised her eyes from the bracelet she'd just tried on and listened, returning the other jewels they'd received that day to the bag.

Her name. She heard her name spoken from beyond the door. Her first name. And it was Tenney's voice. He'd always called her Miss Albright. Never Rachael. His voice rose.

Ambrose was just beyond the curtain. She could smell his soap.

She stood, still clasping the bag, and walked to the door, pulling it open. The curtain fluttered against her as she forced her way through it and into the now-tainted air.

Rachael appraised him objectively before he discerned she'd entered the room. Overall, he had a genteel handsomeness. A dimple in one cheek when he smiled might have been the key to that. But he was bland. Exceptionally blank, as if he had toiled at it and it had been more fruitful than usual.

In fact, she could not understand how she'd ever found him fascinating.

'I know she's here,' Tenney said, his voice slithering into the air.

'I can't say, sir,' Grimsley said. 'If you'll give me the candlestick, I'll return it to the shelf and you can leave.'

'Not until after—'

Grimsley's eyes had flickered to her and his arm rose in a halting motion, waving her not to step forward.

'Can I help you?' she asked, her voice stumbling. 'Mr Tenney?' This didn't seem like the same man she'd sat for hours and hours with.

He whirled around and Grimsley used the distraction to retrieve the candlestick from Tenney's grasp.

Still clutching the bag in one hand, she reached her other hand out to Tenney in greeting.

Tenney started as if he felt the same brush of cold diamond that had chilled her. Then he grasped her hand, the wintery contact jarring her. She'd not expected any reaction to him.

He brought her fingers near his lips and kissed the air before releasing her.

She let her hand fall, absently brushing the folds of her skirt, wanting to free herself of the feel of him.

They had touched so little when they had been betrothed and she now understood why. It meant nothing to either of them.

'Rachael. So good that we meet again.' He sniffed. 'I'd heard rumours that you'd been seen here and I thought you might be in your father's little diversions... with the help.'

'Mr Grimsley is my father's man of affairs and extremely experienced.'

'So.' He shot a quick glance at Grimsley. 'He is responsible for your father's losses.'

'No. The shops are doing well and it isn't any of your concern.'

'I'm sure. You always had a good eye for beauty,' Tenney said. 'When we went on those carriage rides and visited Somerset House, the curator thought you a natural at selecting the best pieces.'

'He was kind,' she said. 'It was no chore to admire the paintings.' She indicated the wares around her. 'And when I am here, I feel I'm in an art display that my own family has collected.'

She took off the bracelet and handed it to Grimsley. 'I think this will suit me. Can you ask Abernathy to design a matching necklace?'

'Let me see it,' Tenney said.

She did as he requested, making sure their hands didn't touch a second time.

'It is stunning.' He took the bauble and held it to the light, examining it, one eye squinted. 'I like it.'

'Are you sure you wouldn't like a different one?' she asked.

'No. This one is perfect for her.' He handed it to the shopkeeper with a flourish. 'Wrap it up for me.'

'It is a perfect gem,' she agreed. 'But we have a large selection.' A large selection that hadn't been on her arm first. 'Today we received three from one of my best suppliers, Mr Abernathy.'

She opened the bag and took out one with a small pearl which was half circled by three diamonds and let him examine it. Then next was a sapphire sparkling against its gold filigree band. She also took out one with rubies set in the silver circle—the stones reminded her of blazing coals.

He studied the bracelet, frowning.

She didn't want Tenney's new beloved to be wearing a piece she'd worn first. It didn't bother her except she wouldn't have wanted to be given a jewel such as that.

Tenney smiled, returning the bracelets. 'I like the other best. The first one. It's not as fine as my betrothal ring you returned, but...'

'Your family heirloom gave me an idea for some new additions to our selections.'

His brows flicked up in acknowledgement.

She returned the bag to Grimsley. He gave her the tiniest shrug, put the bag aside, then reached in his pocket and took out a cloth to wipe the candlestick before putting it on the shelf.

Her feelings truly weren't there for Tenney and she would thank him for the rest of her life for writing the letter that ended their friendship.

She was a better person for it and it hadn't even left a scar.

And the scars she did have were only on the surface and a surface that was mostly out of the way and, for the time being, she was thankful for it. The path to her new life had begun that night.

'Since the pastime is doing so well, I'm sure you won't mind gifting me the bracelet,' Tenney interrupted her thoughts.

His eyes told her she had heard correctly. 'I don't think so.'

'You know, Rachael, I have a lot of friends in society. It will not do well to have questions stirred about your past. About your life. About your future. The comments about you breaking our betrothal are just now fading.'

'Truly?'

'Yes.'

'No. That's not what I meant when I said *truly*. Truly, you are going to sink so low?' She blinked and he was still there and still had the same reptilian stare.

That stare worked on her like a snake strike and she reacted instinctively, but she didn't dodge. Instead, she planted her feet. 'Do your worst. But it will not be unnoticed. Because of you, I've become acquainted with the editor of the newspaper. He recently printed that I was a sparkling gem at Countess of Merriweather's ball. And I'm soon to be attending an event where I will see the Duchess of Highwood. We have recently shared a quiet conversation. I'm sure she would not mind sparing more time to chat with me. And she isn't known for verbal discretion.'

She paused, lowering her voice to a purr. 'I would step softly, Ambrose. The people I have tea with are the people you might like to work for. And if you tell lies about me, I will tell truths about you.'

He waved an arm, stepping back. 'You can keep the rubbish. There are better merchants in town.'

He stalked out, the bell above the door clattering as he left.

Grimsley walked to her, the candlestick back in his hand, staring after Tenney. 'Say the word, Miss Rachael, and I will go after him and give him a knock on the head.'

'I wouldn't want to inflict that on the merchandise.'

Grimsley spoke under his breath.

'I believe I will order that ring we discussed when I arrived,' she told Grimsley.

'The one for poison powders?' Grimsley watched

where Ambrose Tenney walked beyond the window. 'I can have it filled for you.'

'No. It's not for him. The gimmel one.'

Chapter Twenty-Three

He directed his carriage to halt one house further from Rachael's. The moonlight was bright and he didn't want to take more chances.

He'd been tempted to stop the vehicle closer to Rachael's home and have a shorter distance to walk, arriving quicker, but instead, he asked the carriage driver to find the darkest shadows and wait there.

It was odd how doing something secretively and not getting noticed could increase a person's belief that they could never get caught.

And if they were seen together, and Rachael's reputation was hurt, it would be a loss for everyone. He would never know if she felt forced into a marriage to save her reputation and the shops. Or, if rumour got out that they were together and the business suffered, he would blame himself for her financial disaster.

As he approached the house, fabric fluttered in place at an upper-storey window. He supposed he would be waiting for Rachael to join him. Instead, the front door opened, Rachael ran out and a male voice told her to take care.

She ran to him and he lingered, drinking in the vision of seeing a sprite in the moonlight. Relief overflowed inside him that they would be together again.

He clasped her, giving a swirl and spinning her around before he allowed himself the joy of bringing her into his arms and holding her along the length of him, for one brief sweet, torturous moment before letting her go.

'Who spoke to you as you were leaving?' he asked, putting an arm around her to bring her close and make it less likely she would be recognised while he hurried her away.

'The butler.'

'The face at the upper storey?' Her feet pattered along beside him and he slowed his steps to make it easier for her to keep pace.

'Oh, that was likely my mother,' she said. 'They are all concerned for me.'

'They *all* know you are meeting me?' He slowed again in an attempt to discern her face.

'All except...well, my father may know as well, but be keeping it a secret from me. My mother said she must trust that I know what I am doing.'

He marvelled at the cocoon of closeness she had around her and pulled her near for a brief hug, reassuring himself that she was, for a moment, with him.

The carriage rolled towards them. When it stopped, he reached to open the door and, with both hands at her waist, lifted her in a swirl of skirts. He kept his elbow out to protect her from the door. 'Lower your head,' he said and she disappeared inside the doorway.

With one boot on the metal step, he pulled himself

into the vehicle, turned back and captured the door, closing them in.

He stopped, just to breathe in the flowery, womanly scent that was Rachael and feel the contentment of knowing they would have a few hours together.

He put fingertips to her cheek and let them dance along her jawline, her contours resonating in his body.

Their kiss was liquid emotion, tasting of things innocent and sweet, yet pulsing with desire.

Rachael moved up the stairs with Devlin, pleased that it wasn't a moonlit night, but in his room, Devlin stilled before adjusting the lamp. 'Out, or, as I would prefer, left on?'

She couldn't answer.

'I want you to feel comfortable. But I also want you to be proud of your beauty.'

'On.'

What if Devlin flinched at her scar?

He moved back to her and rotated her body, undoing the hooks of her gown and slipping the cloth upwards. The silk slid over her shoulders, but the sensation didn't calm her.

'You have nothing to fear,' he said. 'Nothing.'

He slid the fabric free, then untied her corset and dropped it, holding out his hand so that she could keep her balance as she stepped from it.

The chemise that had been pressed against her body fell loosely as she moved and he drew her against his chest, the thin layer of her chemise doing nothing to diffuse the feelings he stirred.

His arms encased her, surrounding her with the feeling of the most security she'd ever known in her life. She felt fragile and yet unbreakable.

His moist lips against her skin erased every pain she'd ever felt and she turned, capturing him in a kiss.

Next, he stepped aside enough to remove his trousers. With a delicate touch, he slid the chemise over her head.

His hardness pressed against her stomach, and he slid his hands down her back, stopping to grasp her waist and pull her closer.

Summoning her courage, she took his hand from her waist and guided it over the scar, holding it firm, making sure he didn't press too hard.

She needn't have concerned herself.

His fingers trailed softly over the uneven skin and he traced the marred area, sending shivers into her that touched her core. 'If it were not for the discomfort to you, not worth a fuss. You're made even more unique. They show you are a survivor.'

'That is kind of you to say.'

His lips rested in the crook of her neck, the honesty of his words reverberating inside her. 'I'm not being kind at all. Just truthful.'

Then he stepped back, guiding her with him, and lowered himself on to the bed, keeping her above him.

'Your scar only increases your perfection and beauty. It makes you all the stronger.'

'You saved me.'

'If I had known, I would have prevented the accident, because I ache at the thought of you suffering. I would happily bear the pain myself, rather than it be inflicted on you.'

He kissed her, guiding her on top of him, uniting with her and leading her into a path of passion and discovery.

* * *

When their lovemaking was completed, he slid from the bed.

An expanse of male chest was in front of her. He was completely unselfconscious and that gave her pause.

She'd not imagined herself ever to be so relaxed in front of him, but then his eyes raked over her, with the sheet around her, and caused a heat to soar inside her and a tingling in her breasts, freeing her from self-consciousness.

Perhaps she could.

'Does the burn still hurt?' he asked, while donning his trousers. He sat to slip on his boots before returning to his feet.

She shrugged. 'Some. Nothing bad. I'm careful not to wear a corset too tight.'

He donned his shirt and then his waistcoat. 'Are you going to lie there all night?' he asked. 'I'd expected you to be jumping from the bed and rushing me to get you home. Like last time.'

She pulled the sheet with her and sat. 'I didn't schedule anything for early in the morning.'

'Thoughtful of you.' The words were drawled into the room.

'It is vital to me. To change the direction of the shop. To keep my grandfather's hard work going as he would have wanted it,' she said.

'Because it's important to you, it's important to me.'

She'd not expected him to say that. 'I didn't think you liked it.'

'I would rather it not concern you. I would rather your life have no more worry than what colour ribbon might improve a bonnet and let someone else handle all the rest of it. But I wouldn't like my life to only be what style my next hat will be and I suppose you feel the same way.'

'I do. Plus, I don't trust my feelings. I saw Ambrose today and that frightened me anew. I came within a hair's breadth of an unsatisfactory marriage.' She could not admit to him how pathetic she now found Tenney. She'd been so wrong. So wrong.

'I'm not Tenney. Don't hang on to his memory to push me from you. If you wish to end our connection, I understand, but don't use him as an excuse. Don't compare me to him. We're not the same person.'

Aligning at the bed, he lifted her hand to his lips. He placed a kiss in her palm and then closed her fist over it. He grasped her wrist lightly and moved it so that her hand touched over her heart.

'I'll lace up your corset when I return,' he said. 'And then we'll get you home safely and quietly.'

'What are you going to do?'

'I'm going to alert the carriage driver to be ready.'

He walked out of the door and she realised a marriage proposal would have been a much better end to lovemaking than having a carriage readied.

Chapter Twenty-Four

The next day, Rachael was summoned to the sitting room. Devlin stood as she rose. His cravat was black and his eyes intense.

'He ran away.'

'Who?'

'My dog.'

'Scamp?' she asked. 'He could barely walk.'

'I know. He had to be determined just to get down the stairs.'

'How did he get out?'

'The butler opened the door to go out and Scamp charged into the street. The stable boy tried to stop him and Scamp tripped him and drooled on him. I had to give the stable boy another promotion quickly or he might have run away as well.'

'Scamp could actually run?'

'Yes. At least out of my front door. I can't imagine him able to get much further. The butler thinks the dog had a flicker of lucidity and he remembered where he belonged. That's what we hope for anyway.'

'How can you be distraught? You just got him and

you chose him because of his age. You gave him two happy days or so.'

'Yes. I know. But I feel rather betrayed. As if he didn't choose to be with me.'

'He remembered where he lived and wanted to find his true family.'

'He had excellent staff at my home.'

'A home isn't judged by the number of servants.'

'Don't make light of it.' Devlin stared at her. 'This was a test for me. A chance to test how well I might get on with something other than family. I'd given him a good house and meals, and spent time with him.'

'Perhaps you could get another pet?'

'None would need me as much as Scamp. I liked that dog.'

'You couldn't have been that fond of Scamp.'

'I was fond enough. I was proving that I could be—a dog owner.'

'Maybe you should have started with a bird.'

The glare he gave her would have shocked his friends because they wouldn't have believed him capable of appearing so cross. She burst out laughing. 'He just remembered where his owner was and wanted to go home.'

Devlin levelled a glance at her. 'When Scamp was in my life for just a short while and I was drawn to him, I wondered why. At first, I thought he needed me. He wasn't impressed by me which gave me pause. He treated me the same as he would have an underservant.'

The words remained in the air between them and gently evolved.

'You think that is why you are attracted to me. Because I'm not impressed by you?'

'Yes.'

'Oh.'

'Am I more to you than others?' he asked.

'Yes.'

'That I even considered that question does not bode well,' he said. 'If I don't feel it, then I wonder if you are capable of putting me first in your life, or if you will always find a reason to pursue something else before me.'

'Are you telling me that you don't wish to continue our friendship?'

'No, I'm asking you to make sure you want to. I'm asking you to put me above all others.'

For the first time since her accident, she anticipated going to the dance, expecting a perfect night.

She'd talked to Mr Grimsley earlier in the day and he'd been the happiest she'd ever seen him. He'd mentioned customers had arrived to examine the rings and that one customer had purchased a matching set of bracelets and a necklace. Then a betrothed woman had stopped at the shop with her mother because they were selecting items for the bride-to-be's new residence. Grimsley steered them away from particular specially designed rings.

The only disappointment was that Devlin wouldn't be at the event. He'd promised to spend the evening with his father.

When she arrived at the soirée, her first sight was the wallflower, Susanna, whom she'd met when they'd discussed the failure of both their betrothals. They stood at the refreshments when the music began for the opening dance.

'Your earrings tonight are lovely, but by far my favourite jewellery you've worn was the sapphires at the last soirée,' Susanna said. 'I told Mother how much I liked them and she said she will let me have a similar pair for my birthday. They were close to a match with my eye colour.'

Rachael studied Susanna's irises. 'I've seen jewels that are the exact colour you need. I know someone who could locate some and make earrings like the pair I had on. The stones themselves aren't as costly, but I think you would be happier with them because people will be more aware of your eyes.'

Susanna ducked her head. 'That's the feature people notice most about me, I'd be thrilled with jewellery to match.'

Then, as she raised her face her expression tensed when she saw someone behind Rachael.

'I hope she doesn't talk to me,' Susanna whispered and Rachael saw her glance at the Duchess of Highwood. 'She always makes me nervous.'

Almost before the words were out of her mouth, the Duchess noticed them and came their way. Susanna cringed, standing closer to Rachael.

'So sad you had to spend the last year in black, but I think you should have mourned an extra year to show you really cared,' the older woman said to Susanna. 'Attending parties is not the way to sufficiently exhibit your love.' She patted Susanna's arm. 'Fetch me a glass of wine.'

Susanna raised a gloved finger and a footman responded, and brought a tray by them.

They each took a glass.

'I told Lady Smith not to plan any waltz music tonight. At first I approved of it, but now I see how it could corrupt young ladies like yourselves, assuming you've not been corrupted already with those broken betroth-als.' She rotated her arm, almost colliding with Susanna.

Susanna retreated to avoid the Duchess's glass and stumbled on her skirt hem. Her drink wobbled and she lurched to catch it.

The liquid splashed towards the older woman's face.

The woman shrieked. Half the musicians stopped playing and all eyes turned her way, observing the wine dripping from the point of the Duchess's chin and run-ning in rivulets down her collarbone on to her décolleté.

The last instruments stilled.

In that second, Rachael recognised the silence. She'd heard it before.

Even though Susanna was still standing, her face had crumpled and her empty glass dangled from her fin-gertips.

'I am so sorry, Susanna.' Rachael's voice rang out and she couldn't have stopped it if she'd wanted to. 'So sorry. I didn't mean to bump your arm.' Then she al-most choked when she saw the Duchess's glare. 'Please forgive me.'

She moved Susanna aside, attempting to take the Duchess's arm, but the woman jerked it aside, sloshing her own drink and adding to the spill on her cleavage.

'Abomination. That's what this is. An abomination.'

For some reason, Rachael wanted to giggle when she saw the footman standing, open-mouthed, and his grip locked on his own tray. 'Handkerchiefs, please,' she in-structed him. 'And will someone assist Her Grace to the ladies' retiring room?'

Rachael took Susanna, her voice strong enough to carry to all the guests. 'I don't know how I could have been so clumsy, Susanna. Will you ever forgive me?'

'I will never forgive either of you,' the Duchess muttered. 'This dress is ruined.'

'I will direct that the bodice of your dress is replaced by the best seamstress in London. And, everyone…' she briefly viewed the others '…please check that all the lamps are strongly secured. We must all be thankful I have learned not to stand near them.'

A few muffled laughs answered her statement.

Rachael waved to the musicians. 'Could you please start the music again? And, everyone, please *forget* you ever saw this.'

'Awk!' the Duchess called from just beyond the room. 'I will demand that everyone remembers this.'

Rachael shrugged, then led Susanna to a man at the side. 'Are you hoping for a partner in the dance?' she asked him. He bowed to Susanna and led her to the row of dancers, and the music commenced.

Rachael blew a strand of her hair to the side of her face and followed after the Duchess.

'I will never forget this,' the lady of the house said, close behind Rachael. 'We all would have liked to have done that to the Duchess at some time or another. And I'll be sure to invite you the next time I plan something. You do tend to liven things up. Please stay. I'll attempt to calm the Duchess.'

An older man approached Rachael. 'May I have the next dance? I want to be near you to see what happens next.'

'Nothing, I hope,' Rachael said.

'Well, if it does, I want you standing by my brother. He's infuriating with his self-importance. It would be good to have him adjusted down a notch and you're the woman who could do it.'

* * *

When her father stopped to take her mother's arm, she knew he wanted to leave and she joined them.

Before they stepped into the carriage, she removed the feather in her mother's turban so it wouldn't be broken on the roof and gave the plume to her mother.

'Thank you, dear.' Her mother checked that the turban remained the same. 'I was watching. I know you didn't tap Susanna's arm. I'm proud of you.'

'I didn't choose to do that. I just had to.'

'Which makes it all the better,' her mother said. 'You're a woman who does what she has to. What she believes she has to do. And, really, that's what makes the difference.'

'It's a shame your grandfather didn't live long enough to know you. He'd be so proud,' her father added.

The words fluttered inside Rachael, adding a balm to an awkward evening.

'I didn't observe the Viscount in attendance...which surprised me,' her mother said. 'Was he expected?'

'He went to the country with his father and Payton to retrieve some horses. He said it was long overdue. He's returned, but I expect he was busy with his father.'

'Of course. Family is important.' She straightened the ostrich feather and put it flat across her lap. 'I can only thank him for what he has done for us... For you... You're not the same Rachael and I'm pleased that you seem so much more comfortable now than you did with Mr Tenney. Take care, though.'

'Father, might I take the carriage after we arrive home?'

She heard the sputters and even in the darkness she could see him puffing up into an explosive answer.

Her mother touched his hand. 'Your father doesn't

think it's a good idea. And, Dear One, that's not what I meant by taking care.'

'Before he left, Devlin mentioned he planned to propose when he returned and I would like to know if he was serious. I've been thinking about my answer.'

Her mother sputtered this time. 'D-Dear, you didn't pursue the question at the time. You had to think about it?'

'Are you daft?' her father shouted.

Immediately her mother pulled down the shades in the carriage, although Rachael didn't grasp how that would keep the discussion more private. The coachman had surely heard the shout and the horses had even been aware of discord as they'd picked up speed.

She patted the side of the carriage seat. She seemed to be testing people's vocal range more than usual.

'I could not marry him because he pitied me. Or because he needed an heir. He just said that we should get married and I could not risk another meaningless proposal.'

'Yes. You could.' Her father's voice hadn't lowered. His arms crossed. 'She gets these ideas from you.' He spoke to her mother.

'I was betrothed for a long time to Ambrose Tenney and I do not want history to repeat itself. I don't.'

'You could have suggested the Viscount obtain a Special Licence. You are too old to be waiting.'

'Father. I am past waiting. I'm not waiting on anyone now. And I don't want to be a pitied victim.'

'Dear.' Her mother reached out, one hand resting on Rachael's and one on her husband's. 'You are not a victim to anyone. You never were. Not even to Tenney. If you remember, when he courted you, you were completely happy to keep him at a distance and wait. A letter sufficed and you were content with that.'

Her mother sat deeper in the seat and crossed her arms. 'You never even saw the other men who tried to catch your attention in the meantime. But almost immediately, when you formed a friendship with Devlin, you were meeting privately.'

'They're meeting privately?' her father shouted again.

'Don't scare the horses and the people in the houses we're passing by don't need to be aware of our conversation,' her mother spoke gently.

'The Viscount is charming. And I do care for him. Apart from my family, he is the best friend I've ever had.'

'And you, my dear daughter, are lying to yourself if you think you're easily led,' her mother said. 'I have no qualms at all if you are to remain unwed. I am all for it if it is what you wish. But do not lie to yourself. You are no one's victim.'

Her father snorted again and repeated her mother's words. 'She's no one's victim.'

'What if I were to marry Devlin and he were to change affections?'

Her father grumbled, 'I would assume you wouldn't even ask for his carriage, but you would just take it and do as you wished. As you have with my London shop.'

She didn't speak.

'I saw the purchases,' he continued. 'Grimsley's suggestions didn't all come from him. He would never have had the courage to do that alone.'

'The former apprentice is so excited in the changes that are planned for the shop. He's offered his own suggestions that he would like us to try. We need to expand.'

'How can we expand?'

'We have the inventory in storage to be melted and reshaped. Grimsley's found another shop location and, if we take it, the agreement is that the rent on the new shop will be almost nothing for the first year. We're to take in an older journeyman at the new site and Abernathy will work closely with him. So, for one year, it is almost no risk at all, only profit, and we will add to the merchandise with items that we have created from old ones we already have. Nothing extravagant. You make the future profits when you create or buy the merchandise, not only when you sell.'

Her father spoke to her mother. 'Do you think the Viscount had any idea what he was taking on when he asked our timid little daughter for her hand in marriage?'

Before her mother could answer, Rachael inserted, 'He did not ask. He spoke of it as a given. As if it were already decided.'

'Blast.' Her father gave a slap to his forehead and gaped at his wife. 'You always said she would not listen if you told her what to do, but if you asked, she would break her fingers in helping.'

'Just like her father.'

Both parents' heads nodded in unison.

'Can I borrow the carriage?'

'Tomorrow,' her father said. 'I've never had much say in your life. But I do have control over the carriage driver's employment and you would not be able to get a hackney tonight. It would not hurt you to spend a night thinking about your strength and how you have made decisions these past years.'

'Do you think Devlin suggested marriage because he

sees you as less than you are?' her mother asked. 'Or because he wants a strong woman at his side?'

Her mother patted Rachael's knee. 'And even if he cannot put it into words, that's what he wants. That is what he tried to create in you when he encouraged you to go to the dances and become a part of his world. Our actions are truer than our words.'

Thunder rolled in the distance, muted by the walls of the carriage and the sounds of the horses' hooves.

'Wait until later in the morning to take the carriage,' her father said, 'since you are not dashing off to meet a future husband. I've already arranged for Grimsley to be collected and give me the fortnight's accounting of the shop. I want to review the plans the two of you have had. And I want to make sure there are no canes with swords in them ordered. I cannot believe you ordered so many of those *headache powder* rings. It takes courage to order such things.'

'Does it really?' her mother asked, her words for him, but her face towards Rachael. 'I would think there was little courage involved. In business, not all ventures succeed. Not all marriages. Even though Devlin's parents aren't a perfect couple, each has been rewarded from it. Vows are symbolic and the foundation of a marriage. They are glue, not sweetened fluff.'

'I know full well it is not a meringue.'

'Don't expect perfection. Marriage is a skill some people have—like business talents.'

'That is not romantic.'

'Perhaps not. Your father's and my marriage is a habit of courtesy and love that we fell into and with honesty and strength almost any two caring people can do it.

Unfortunately, you won't know if the strength is there beforehand. No one does. Just like profits in a shop.'

Her mother put her hand to her chin. 'I would say it is a lot like starting a business with a partner and you can only prepare as much as possible beforehand and hope that you know what you're doing.'

'You make it sound like too much of a risk for a sensible person.'

'Everything worth having is a risk.' Her mother patted Rachael's knee again. 'Even children. When the Countess and I met again after not seeing each other for all those years, I told her how long you'd been betrothed and that Tenney couldn't seem to pick one day out of three hundred and sixty-five. And she told me she had three sons, none of whom seemed to be aware that all the young women she'd been inviting to events might be more than just dance partners.'

'You were both matchmaking?' Rachael asked, surprised.

'Attempting. We left the actual decision up to the two of you. But, never doubt that it gets your ire up if someone *tells* you what to do. I've asked you to do things your whole life and so has your father. Other people are not so well trained as we are.'

Chapter Twenty-Five

That morning, Grimsley came to give her father the accounts for the business and her maid summoned her. Rachael was pacing the floor. She'd been ready to leave shortly after she'd woken and she'd woken early.

'Your father asked if you might attend the meeting with Mr Grimsley.' The maid rushed in, her cheeriness flooding the room.

Rachael straightened her skirt. She might have trained her parents well, but they had done the same with her, no matter what her mother said. She walked downstairs and listened to the men talk and she gave her opinions forthrightly.

After the meeting had concluded, Rachael rode with Grimsley and her mother as he was returned to the shop.

Instead of going to Devlin immediately, she went inside to inspect Grimsley's latest acquisitions as she'd agreed earlier that morning when speaking with her father.

'We've another arrival from Mr Abernathy.'

'I must see it,' she said. Abernathy was her favourite

craftsman. Metal was his canvas and the jewels were his oils.

'Six rings this time,' Grimsley said. 'He purchased the rubies at a small price and is happy that you said we would buy all he can provide if he passes the bargain on to us, and that he can make them as he pleases. And he was able to make a gimmel ring for you as you asked. With tiny rubies.'

He secured the bag, held it out and she picked out the treasures one by one until she saw the rubies. She pulled it into the light. She didn't know for sure what she would do with it when she requested it, but now she was certain.

'I believe I will keep this one.'

Grimsley's grin sparkled many times bigger than the small swirl of rubies. 'Excellent choice.'

She clasped the bands so that they pressed against her skin.

'Do you think we can do it? Make the shop a success?' she asked.

'For the first time in five years, I am anticipating the future. Mr Abernathy and I talked at length when he dropped off the jewels. We both have a new enthusiasm for our work. And he will ascertain that Miss Rachael gets his best designs.'

They both gave a nod before she walked into the dreary day, but the air had a crispness that pleased her more than if the sun had shone brightly.

She hurried to the carriage, her mother beside her.

Inside, she picked at the lace on the sleeve on her oldest, most favourite dress.

'Have a maid stitch that in place for you,' her mother said.

'This one is always being mended.'

'Perhaps you should get a new one.'

'I don't mind. This suits me.'

Rachael straightened the skirt, examining the faded flowers on the fabric. This was not the glorious gown she might wear to a soirée, cloaked in jewels from the shop.

This was the dress for home. For bookwork. Not the dancing dress—the one with the poufs of cloth and the best cloak.

She could be comfortable in both. Wearing the jewellery did not change who she was. Nor did she wear it to elevate herself. It was beauty and, as Devlin had pointed out about songbirds singing as they should, the same was true for everything. No one would ask flowers to please stop blooming as their petals were much too graceful for a sad day.

She could wear the flowing strands of armour, the baubles on her wrist as gauntlets and the rings as shields while she danced into the night and she could put everything neatly on the shelf when she returned home.

It wasn't about how she appeared to others, it was about who she was when she thought of herself and it was no disservice to imagine herself as a strong person, particularly as she had been so afraid at the first soirées.

No one had been her friend and she'd often been seen as an outsider, but it didn't matter. It only mattered how she saw herself and that she continually took steps to increase her internal promise of retaining the vision of who she wanted to be.

Mr Grimsley had told her that it was impossible to gauge what would sell and what wouldn't. Originally, he'd not felt it right to risk the success without her father's agreement. One had to take chances and her father had become unwilling to take those leaps of faith. As his failures had dwindled, so had his successes.

Devlin was worth the risk of failure and the risk of success.

She thought of the last few days.

He was more important to her than the jewellery shop. He made her heart glow as bright as rubies. As sparkling as a betrothal ring shared by lovers.

She didn't want to live without him and she didn't want to live apart from him if she had a choice in the matter.

Immediately upon opening the door, the butler's eyes darted around, searching for a chaperon, then her mother stepped into view behind her.

'We're here to speak with the Countess.'

'I will see if she is in.'

With the briefest amount of time, the butler returned and led her to the Countess's sitting room.

After tea, Devlin appeared in the hallway, but didn't move to join them. Giving a quick greeting, bow included, he waited, perfection on view, filling the doorway, the light from the window seeming to reflect from his smile and showcase the trim length of his legs.

He'd been created for light, laughter and her eyes.

'I hate to disappoint you, but she arrived to visit me,' the Countess said, rising. 'Her mother wished me to have a handkerchief she'd embroidered.'

'Perhaps Rachael would like to take a stroll in the garden,' he suggested.

The Countess stopped in front of her son. 'I suspect she might.' She brushed him aside. 'Now I want to show

Mrs Albright some of my stitchery and it is a shame I didn't bring a needle with me as you would move from the doorway much more quickly if I had.' She made a jabbing motion with her hand and he took one step aside.

It surprised Rachael to see the Countess jesting with her son and his mother gave him a sideways hug when she walked by him.

He took one step inside, waiting until their mothers left. 'My butler informed me you were here. I hope you came to see me.'

'Yes.' She rose and stood in front of him. The ruby ring still rested on her thumb. She took it off. 'I saw this and wanted to give it to you as a thank-you token for saving my life. Well, I wanted to give half of it to you.'

He took the ring and, with a deft movement, separated it. The two circles interlaced to make one and slipped apart to make two.

'When I went to the parties and you weren't there, they were devoid of music. You add to the simplest moments. The moments of quiet talking. The moments of dancing. All of them are better with you in them.'

'You need to know that I'm proud of the steps that you've made.'

'Father told me the shop has improved and he feels hopeful for the first time in years. I don't want to put it aside. I appreciate your offer of letting your man of affairs help me and I will ask for advice, but I want to continue my family's heritage. If I have children, I want the excitement of training them to follow in my steps, if they want, sons or daughters.'

'What better plan for them than to have a mother who loves them and wants to help them grow into the path they prefer? But I would also want them to have a strong family in their lives. A purpose for life itself.'

He took the ring and it fitted perfectly on his smallest finger. He returned the other half to her. 'I'll treasure it. Will you marry me so I can perform the custom of giving you the matching circle as a token of our love during our wedding ceremony?'

'I love you,' she said and threw her arms around him. 'Thank you for asking. Yes.'

He'd not even noticed that he'd held his breath while he waited for her answer, until she'd spoken.

This time, when he heard the word *love*, it was as if he'd been given a pair of wings that could take him anywhere.

He pulled her into his arms, the kiss blazing and nothing else mattering in the world.

Then he stepped back and slipped the ring from his other smallest finger. 'I have this for you, if you want it. I chose it for you, hoping you would some day be my wife. And if not, I would always have it as a memento of our time together.'

She reached up and clasped her fingers around his, their hands together, holding the jewel. And the devotion in his eyes pulled her closer and she knew she'd made the right decision and the one that would build her strength, her heart and her happiness.

Chapter Twenty-Six

The month following the wedding had been one of the most blissful of Rachael's life. She'd wanted a simple wedding. Vows spoken softly and a quiet wedding breakfast, but Devlin would have none of it.

He insisted that it would be best to show everyone that theirs was a true love match and that they'd discovered each other on the night of his mother's party, and it had been a quick path to what would be everlasting devotion.

The newspaper had even reported their happy news and claimed that the true reason for Rachael's broken betrothal was that once she and Devlin had met, he'd known that she was the spark in his life and she was the flame in his. The article made twenty-three flammable references.

Payton told her she should thank him as he had provided the story as he had been repeating it often enough.

Devlin said it didn't matter what was printed, all that concerned him was that they were together.

Both his parents were at the wedding breakfast and, even though they did not always get on well, their connection was obvious. In public, they thrived on being a couple and, in the privacy of their home, they thrived on verbally jousting with each other. It was a marriage that they had made their own, an imperfect one at times, but one that suited them both.

When she'd seen them together and saw their verbal jabs, Devlin confided to her that was how he'd developed the easy way he had and the ability to calm most situations. In part, his early life had trained him to soothe them and lighten the situation. But she had met his uncle and she saw the family charm that couldn't be kept below the surface. A twinkling eye, a mouth that always ended in a smile and all the gentlemanly courtesies anyone could ask for.

The biggest shock of the marriage hadn't been that Devlin sometimes wore spectacles when he deciphered the smallest writing regarding his father's properties, but that he found it so easy to shed the gaiety that he presented at parties and become silent when he was at home, comfortable with sitting beside her, poring over ledgers and writing instructions in the margins of them.

She'd asked him why he wrote in the volumes and he'd been puzzled, telling her he'd never paid any attention, but he'd done it as he thought of what he'd just seen and it helped give them a record for the future.

He and his father often shared breakfast, even if his father arrived late for it, and they always spoke of their properties and the course of action they should take to keep everything running smoothly.

His mother avoided the breakfast table, but Rachael had taken to eating with them and they'd listened to her questions about her plans for the shop as if it were their own venture, yet neither had insisted she take their advice which they offered freely.

Now she felt as comfortable in the house as if she'd been born there and no longer felt she had a tenuous slipper in society, but a well-placed one. She'd even looked through the fashion plates again and found the dress she'd thought much too costly and attention-grabbing for her. Devlin had told her she would look lovely in it and insisted she purchase it.

And for the tenth time, Grimsley had reassured her that sales had doubled and their profits were even doing better. In only a few days, the new undertaking would open and he and the apprentice were both working long days to get everything in order.

'I found Scamp,' Devlin said as she stepped into the bedchamber, swirling the silken dressing gown around her like veils, letting the sunlight from the window reflect off them. She let the fabric float to her sides.

'His owner was walking—well—creeping along with him and I stopped the carriage. He said he'd been visiting near my house one night and thought Scamp was asleep in his curricle, but when he'd returned Scamp had been gone. He was ever so relieved to see him again.'

'Aren't you happy that they were able to find each other? I would hate to think of keeping him when his owner had lost him.'

He nodded. 'It did please me. And I discovered that Scamp's true name was Gerald, which made me take in how little I truly knew him. But the owner said I was free to stop by his home at any time if I wanted to visit with Gerald.'

'That sounds lovely.'

'To everyone but Scamp. He growled at me. I think he was afraid I'd take him from his owner and he'd have to find his way home again.'

'Well, you proved with your devotion to a really frail-looking dog that you could be protective.'

'But didn't you already have an idea of that?'

'Yes, I did. When you saw what was going to happen before anyone else and you grasped me up in your arms and smothered out the flames. I hate to think what would have happened if we hadn't truly met that night.'

'I suspect it was meant to be that we would encounter each other at a time in our lives when we were receptive to finding a true commitment,' he said. 'Just like the fact that I may have seen Scamp many times over the past few years, yet I never noticed him until I heard his barking near my house one night. In fact, had I left him on the street a little longer, his owner might have found him. He said he searched for him well into the night and the next day. But then a few days later, he drove his carriage by my house, still searching, called out and Scamp…er… Gerald, bounded out and to the carriage.'

'Perhaps when we recognise something's worth, that's when we find it.' Then she held out her finger so he could see the lustre of the stone.

'I'm pleased you aren't wearing one of the poison containers,' he said, moving to her and holding up both her hands and giving an exaggerated inspection.

'I like the one you gave me best,' she said.

'You seem at ease when you are out, wearing them.'

'Yes.' She pulled her hands free and studied the jewel. 'I'm more comfortable now with the large ones that are noticed and pull the eye. With the smaller ones, I enjoy showing the craftsmen's skill and the artistry. Each item we have is like a little treasure to me now. Even the buckles for shoes.'

She slid against him and took off the small band on

her finger. 'This ring is of exceptional quality. The gold has been lightly mixed with other metals and still has a softness and a sheen that lets me know the value.'

She held it up. 'The engraving you added makes it even more precious. *You warm my heart.*'

'And my life. With you by my side, I can see myself better. I don't always like what I learn, but not everything that's true is easy to accept.'

He embraced her as she slipped the ring back on. 'I hope you like it and all the changes in us that it will bring with it.'

'I do. At first, being in society was a charade that I had to live, albeit a charming one. But now I don't feel the same. It's a part of me. I wear the jewellery like a cloak. A uniform. What I wear to go into the world and joust with others, or now even laugh with them. I am comfortable wearing it and at night, I'm comfortable taking it off.'

His lips brushed her ears and she heard the intensity in his words. 'I'm comfortable with your taking it off.' His voice became serious. 'The ornamentation doesn't matter to me at all. The person on the inside is who I married.'

'Mmm…' she said, relaxing against him. 'I do love you.'

'Before you said you loved me, I realised I didn't want to go anywhere but into your arms, your bed and hold you for the rest of my life. That one small word, which meant more than I ever expected, convinced me you would be the only one for me. For ever.'

* * * * *

If you enjoyed this story, why not check out these other great reads by Liz Tyner

"Hud," she said, a little breathless as understanding dawned on her. "But you…"

"Yeah?"

"You like women. A lot of women."

"You're going to hold it against me that I like women?"

He was just a breath away from reminding her that her precious Chuck apparently liked women, too, and by the way, Hud had never cheated on *anyone*. But he couldn't do it. He couldn't hurt her by throwing that in her face.

"No," she said, shaking her head, still obviously drunk and confused. "It's just…just…"

Now he hated himself for bringing this up at all. It wasn't the time or place. She couldn't make good decisions. He was an idiot.

"Never mind. Forget I said anything."

"Don't be mad," she said softly, reaching for his arm. "Please."

"I'm not mad."

"Promise?" she said, wiping at her cheeks.

To make his point, he pulled her into his arms. She snuggled into his chest, as she always did, and he squeezed tighter, as he always did. She snuggled to get comfort, and he squeezed to keep her in his arms.

It just never worked.

WELCOME TO WILDFIRE RIDGE!

Dear Reader,

Welcome to the third book in the Wildfire Ridge miniseries. Some of you may recognize our heroine, Joanne, from an earlier book, *Airman to the Rescue*. The moment my editor said, "Poor Joanne," about her character in *Airman*, I knew I would give her a happily-ever-after of her own...someday. Fast-forward three books later in this world, and I finally get to tell you the story of this incredibly strong single mother who's raising her son and running a bridal boutique. Does she sound like supermom? Okay, I get why you might think that, but she's far from perfect. And since blowing up her life at the age of sixteen, Joanne has rarely taken chances and has played it safe. Especially when it comes to love.

Enter Lieutenant Hudson "Hud" Decker. With a series name like Wildfire Ridge, you knew I'd have a firefighter hero, right? Hud and Joanne come with a bit of a combustible history. When their young first love burned out (I can't seem to stop with the fire metaphors), they managed to salvage their friendship. But when Joanne is jilted at the altar, Hud isn't going to just put her back together for someone else this time. Ironically, playboy Hud has never quite gotten over his first love and this may be just the right moment for a second chance. First, he'll have to convince Joanne he's worth taking the risk for a chance at forever this time, and it won't be easy.

I hope you enjoy.

Heatherly Bell

The Right Moment

—

Heatherly Bell

HARLEQUIN

SPECIAL
EDITION

Recycling programs
for this product may
not exist in your area.

ISBN-13: 978-1-335-89445-8

The Right Moment

Copyright © 2020 by Heatherly Bell

All rights reserved. No part of this book may be used or reproduced in
any manner whatsoever without written permission except in the case of
brief quotations embodied in critical articles and reviews.

This is a work of fiction. Names, characters, places and incidents
are either the product of the author's imagination or are used fictitiously.
Any resemblance to actual persons, living or dead, businesses,
companies, events or locales is entirely coincidental.

This edition published by arrangement with Harlequin Books S.A.

For questions and comments about the quality of this book,
please contact us at CustomerService@Harlequin.com.

Harlequin Enterprises ULC
22 Adelaide St. West, 40th Floor
Toronto, Ontario M5H 4E3, Canada
www.Harlequin.com

Printed in U.S.A.

Heatherly Bell tackled her first book in 2004 and now the characters that occupy her mind refuse to leave until she writes them a book. She loves all music but confines singing to the shower these days. Heatherly lives in Northern California with her family, including two beagles—one who can say hello and the other a princess who can feel a pea through several pillows.

Books by Heatherly Bell

Harlequin Special Edition

Wildfire Ridge

More than One Night
Reluctant Hometown Hero

Harlequin Superromance

Heroes of Fortune Valley

Breaking Emily's Rules
Airman to the Rescue
This Baby Business

Other titles by Heatherly Bell
are available in ebook format.

To the real Iris and K.R.

Chapter One

Her groom was late.

Joanne Brant peeked through the bridal tent the wedding coordinators had set up outdoors. From here, she'd walk with her best friend Hudson Decker down a rose-petal-covered path to the glass-enclosed gazebo in the middle of a meadow. Every touch, from her Vera Wang dress to the gardenia garlands decorating the outside of the gazebo to the string quartet now tuning was breathtaking. Beautiful.

Still no sign of Chuck.

She was nervous enough as it was. Where was he? They were supposed to get started soon. She worried a manicured fingernail between her teeth.

This didn't make sense. Chuck was always punctual, sometimes to a fault. Stomach churning, she wondered what could be the cause of the delay. Was he hurt? Caught in traffic? Accident?

It had better be a good excuse.

"What time is it?" Joanne asked Nora Higgins, her maid of honor and head seamstress at Joanne's bridal boutique. "I don't have my cell phone with me."

"Um." Nora glanced at hers. "It's one thirty."

"What? *One thirty*? He's half an hour late. How did I not realize that? We're half an hour late to start!"

This wasn't funny. When he finally showed up, she'd… She'd… Well, she'd marry him.

"I'm sure he's got a good reason," said Monique Brandt, Joanne's cousin, and another bridesmaid.

"Maybe traffic is bad." Eve Wiggins, Joanne's IT person, always went with logic.

But Chuck always accounted for traffic because he hated to speed even more than he hated to be late.

Hudson or "Hud," her best friend and the one who'd give her away in place of her late father, strode into the tent. He was six foot plus of hard body, and every time he walked into the bridal tent every one of her bridesmaids licked lips and tossed hair.

"What's happening?" His tone was clipped. Annoyed. It was no secret that he was not a fan of Chuck Ellis.

Right now, neither was Joanne. If he embarrassed

her by being much later, she might go on their honeymoon to the Bahamas alone. That would teach him.

"I need my cell phone," she said to anyone who would listen. "Where is it?"

"Yeah, maybe he's been texting you," Nora said.

"He should not be texting you," Hud said. "He should have his ass here. Now. That's what he should be doing."

"Maybe there's a problem, though," Joanne said, as always, making excuses for Chuck.

Emily Parker-McAllister, the event planner who ran weddings at Fortune Valley Family Ranch, walked in, a practiced smile on her face. "Looks like we're missing a groom. Do we need to delay much longer?"

"I'll check," Joanne said. "Who has my cell phone?"

It took far too many minutes to find her phone, set to vibrate and hidden under three different garment bags. She glanced down at it. Her phone had blown up with text messages from Chuck.

I'm sorry.

I can't do this.

Are you going to answer me?

I know I should have said something sooner.

And the last most devastating message of all:

I'm not coming.

Joanne dropped her phone and slumped on the closest chair, nearly falling over. She felt as if all the color had drained out of her face. This wasn't happening. It couldn't be. Not to her. After so much planning. The perfect dress. Perfect venue. She owned a bridal boutique. She was supposed to know weddings.

This didn't make any sense. Chuck had meant safety and security to Joanne for the past year. They were well suited to each other in many ways. Compatible. Chuck had claimed to want children with Joanne and was already saving for their future education.

He was reliable. Steady.

He'd made her feel secure and wanted never even once looking at another woman. This was so out of character for him. What could have possibly changed his mind?

"Is he hurt?" Nora said. "Has there been an accident?"

"What's wrong?" Hud demanded.

Oh, God. Too many questions. She couldn't speak. It seemed as though Hud's words were coming through a voice changer in slow motion. Her bridesmaids, eyes wide, jaws gaping, looked like caricatures of themselves. They knew something was horribly wrong. Maybe Joanne hadn't been the best person in the world during her thirty-two years on earth, but even she didn't deserve this. No one did. Unbearable humiliation and shame tore through her.

When she still hadn't answered anyone, Hud crouched low in front of her, right in her line of vision. His eyebrows were drawn together in confusion, or concern. "Jo…tell me."

"He's not hurt but…" She met Hud's green gaze, so kind, so worried. "He's…he's not coming."

Both Monique and Nora gasped.

"I'll be right back," Emily said, and left them.

"What do you *mean* he's not coming?" Hud asked.

Her best friend was the only one in the room who still didn't get it. When Joanne didn't elaborate, Hud searched for her phone and picked it up off the floor. Reading the messages, he then cursed loudly enough to make Eve, Monique and Nora move closer to Joanne and circle her, putting shaking hands on her shoulders. But Joanne wondered why *she* wasn't crying. Why she wasn't devastated. She simply felt… humiliated.

And in all honesty, a tiny bit numb. Make that more than a tiny bit. Shock, she assumed.

She'd had doubts too, these last two weeks, but those were normal. Right? They were called wedding day jitters for a reason. *Am I making a mistake? Do I really love him?*

All normal.

Joanne had told herself that the tiny spark between them would grow with more time. The important thing to her was that she had a fiancé with a rock steady plan for their future. And he was committed to her. Ha! What a joke.

"Where is he?" Hud said in a low menacing voice. "I'll go get him for you."

He would, too. If she'd wanted him to, Hud would find Chuck, hog-tie him and drag him to the ceremony. He'd proceed to threaten him to within an inch of his life if he tried to run again.

"You can't. He...doesn't want to...get married." The words came out slow and measured, as if she were trying them on for size. She was almost too shaken to speak.

"Then he shouldn't have asked you."

But Hud didn't know that she'd been the one to suggest marriage in the first place. She wanted to settle down. Her sixteen-year-old son, Hunter, nearly grown now, it was finally time for her life to begin. She wanted a life partner and didn't want to be alone anymore. She'd waited so long and sacrificed so much. Worked long hours putting herself through fashion design school while raising a child. She'd opened a successful bridal shop with seed money from her father and put in long hours.

Chuck had agreed that marriage was a good idea, too, and claimed he was ready. He'd given her the ring, handed it to her over breakfast one morning, certain she'd accept it since the whole thing had been her idea. There was never an actual proposal, almost a business agreement.

One he'd backed out of at the last minute.

Outside, a small commotion had started. Confused and annoyed voices. "I gave up a golf date for this," someone said. "Do we get the presents back? Because I'm not bringing another one if they try this again!"

She heard her son's voice, or was that his father's? They sounded so similar. Her mother would be heartbroken when she heard the news. She'd liked Chuck. Thought he was good for Joanne. Bad enough Dad had passed away before he could see Joanne married, but now this. Mom didn't take humiliation any better than Joanne did.

Emily walked inside the tent. "Everything's taken care of. We're letting everyone know that a small emergency has prevented the wedding from going through today. People are beginning to leave now. Your family will probably want to talk to you."

Yes. Her mother. *Hunter.* Oh God, she'd have to explain this to her son. She already embarrassed him enough just by breathing.

"I'm going to find Aunt Ramona and explain," Monique said, rubbing Joanne's shoulder. "Calm her down."

"Please," Joanne said, then turned to Emily. "I'm so sorry about this. Thank you for everything."

"We'll talk again soon." Emily excused herself.

And there would be plenty to talk about. Such as food for the reception that might rot before it could be consumed. A DJ who would insist on being paid regardless. The minister. A deposit they'd never get back.

Hud stopped pacing in front of Joanne. "What do you want me to do? I'll do anything."

"Get me out of here. I can't talk to anyone right now. Please…just take me home."

Like her groom, the tears didn't show up. Not later that day, nor later that night.

Hud had driven her home, she'd changed from her beautiful sweetheart collar Valentino dress—being the owner of a bridal boutique had its perks—and dropped on the bed wearing nothing but her underwear. Laying back, she laced hands behind her neck. She needed time to think. To be with her own private thoughts. She'd asked Hud to leave, but in his typical maddening style, he'd refused.

She could hear him downstairs, doing something in the kitchen, opening the door to someone. Talking to them while she lay in her bed staring up at the ceiling wondering why she'd ever thought marrying Chuck would be a good idea.

Had she really been that desperate to finally get

married? For another child? For a true partner, both in bed and in life?

She's upstairs. Yeah, I'll have her call you. Thanks for bringing all the food. Sure, we'll eat it all. Don't worry.

Then presumably on his phone:

Bastard...just need two minutes alone...no, I'm just kidding...sort of.

Joanne groaned. Sounded as though Emily might have brought the food from the reception so that at least it wouldn't completely go to waste. Great. Wonder if between all of her friends and family she could get rid of all the meat, scalloped potatoes, rolls and vegetables?

Later, she wasn't sure how much later, but the bedroom had darkened and long shadows filtered through her blinds. She'd just changed into shorts and a tee and sat back down on the bed with a pad of paper when Hud again opened her bedroom door.

"Jo."

She didn't answer and kept her back to him. Let him go away and leave her be. He was beginning to piss her off. She had a life to reconsider and re-plan in case anyone cared.

"Joanne," he commanded.

"Go away."

He knelt beside her bed and handed her something. Something cold, metallic and small. It seemed to be a phone.

"You need to answer Hunter's texts. He's at Matt's and freaked out. They both need to know exactly what happened."

Oh God. Hunter. He'd been scheduled to stay with his father, Matt, and his new wife, Sarah, at their home for a month this semester. The idea was to give her and Chuck time to adjust to married life after their honeymoon. Hunter had to be wondering what was going on. And Mom. It was a shock she wasn't at the front door banging it down. She assumed she had Monique to thank for that.

"And your mother," Hud continued. "If you don't call or text her, she's coming right over."

No. She didn't want Mom coming over now. She just wanted to be left alone, not that Hud would listen.

Hud stood in the doorway waiting, arms crossed over his wide chest, watching her carefully from under hooded eyes.

What was she supposed to tell her son? She was too ashamed to come out with the harsh truth. *I'm sorry. Chuck was a loser. But instead of me realizing that in time, I let him fool me. He simply told me what I wanted to hear. And I was too desperate to believe it.* Hunter didn't need to know all the details because he was still technically a child. A man child, her son, with dreams of becoming a Marine. Maybe she could text him, his preferred mode of communication, and she didn't have to *sound* upbeat. She just had to write happy and inspirational words. She'd never wanted to be a Hallmark card writer as badly as she did at this moment.

Hey, honey. Something happened to Chuck and he couldn't make it to the wedding so we canceled. Don't worry, everything is going to be okay.

Hunter: What? He's dead?

Joanne: No! All is okay. We'll talk soon. Have fun with your Dad.

Hunter: Still getting married later?

How was she supposed to answer that question? There was no point to lying. She told herself that he'd know sooner or later. All they'd need to do was mention it to one person in Fortune, where it would spread like their wildfires.

Joanne: I don't know. Maybe not. I need to think.

Hunter: You going to the Bahamas?

It hadn't even occurred to her to go. In the Bahamas she wouldn't know what to do by herself for two weeks. Granted, she'd be in a luxurious honeymoon suite, but still. She could hide out in the Bahamas or here. She chose her comfortable and familiar bed.

But what if she told everyone she was going to the Bahamas? They'd at least leave her alone for a while.

Joanne: You know what? Maybe I should!

Hunter: You should. I say go for it!

She finished texting with Hunter, with further assurances that if she went to the Bahamas (she was not) she'd have loads of fun. She'd surf (in her dreams), snorkel (please), and take plenty of selfies.

She glared at Hud. "Okay. Done. Happy?"

Exhausted by the effort, she threw the phone down. Hud gave her a "nice try" look and reminded her, "Your mother. Now."

"Really?"

"Monique told her everything but she wants to hear it from you." He glanced at his wristwatch. "And you have about ten minutes to do it or she'll be here. With food. And you have enough food downstairs to open up a restaurant."

"I need to think. Figure out what my next steps are. Hud, I'm the owner of a bridal boutique who just got jilted! Do I look like a person who can make a phone call right now?"

"You do."

"Damn it!" He wasn't going to let this go. Joanne

picked up her phone and dialed, steeling herself for the onslaught.

"Joanne! Oh, my darling. I'm sososo sorry," her mother started in on the waterworks without delay. "Chuck didn't show! You of all people don't deserve this."

"I'm okay."

"Of course you're not okay. Don't hide the pain, dear. Just deal with it, work through it. There are no shortcuts. You'll be better for it. What stage are you in?"

Joanne wrinkled her nose. "Stage?"

"Grief. There are seven stages of grief and you should be at stage one right now. Though I know you've always been such an overachiever. But don't rush it, honey."

Joanne wondered if stage one was anger because right now she could feel it bubbling up inside her.

Chuck was nothing but an ass who didn't have enough courage to face her. If he'd changed his mind, he could have told her before today.

But her mother always brought everything down to a self-improvement book to read, or a supplement to take. Perhaps a vitamin. Meditation. She wanted to help, but Joanne didn't think life was ever that simple. All the plans she'd had were gone. Plus, she was the owner of the only bridal shop in town and she'd been stood up at the altar.

Was there a supplement for that?

"I'll be right over with some of my chicken soup. Hud says you have too much food there now as it is, but nothing is better for a broken heart than my chicken soup. Remember I fed you this soup after you and Hud broke up? After Dad died? You know it's got my special ingredient. Love."

"That sounds…wonderful, but I'm going to be leaving for the Bahamas." Joanne cringed at the lie but if it got her mother to give her some time alone there was no harm done.

"Alone?" she screeched. "Honey, no! You'll just get depressed."

"Um, no, no. Not alone. I'm going with…with Hud."

Hud, who had been listening in the doorway quirked a brow, then slowly shut the door to her bedroom.

"You and Hud? That sounds like a wonderful idea. No one cheers you up like he can. He's absolutely the best medicine next to my chicken soup. Plus you'll be the envy of every woman who thinks you two are actually together."

Ha! Her and Hud together. No, that had happened many years ago and they'd been lucky simply to salvage their friendship from the disaster.

She wouldn't ever do anything to mess with that.

Chapter Two

Hud Decker had a choice.

Find Chuck Ellis, kill him and hide the body. It could be done. He had friends. Friends who owed him.

But who was he kidding? As the lieutenant running Firehouse 57, a murder charge wouldn't look so hot on the résumé. No. "Chuck E." wasn't worth it. He didn't deserve Joanne, never had, never would, and might have actually come to that realization himself. Good for him, then. Unfortunately, his timing couldn't have been worse. He'd embarrassed Jo in front of family and friends, which made Hud want to destroy him. But he couldn't. Wouldn't. Instead, he'd put Jo back together. Maybe, when she finished writing all her lists and making new plans, she'd realize this was all for the best. They'd laugh about idiot Chuck breaking up via text message like the coward that he was.

I would have shown up. She should have been mine.

No, that wasn't right. He didn't deserve her, either. Not after the damage he'd caused. He'd been lucky to enjoy her close friendship and had learned to accept over the years that it had to be enough.

Hud was still dressed in his tux, but had removed the jacket and cummerbund, rolled up the sleeves and lost the tie. When Emily and her entourage arrived with the platters upon platters of food, they'd stuffed everything they could into plastic bowls and into the refrigerator. The rest they'd arranged on the counters, on the kitchen table, dining table and even the family room. He'd never seen so much food in one place in his life and he worked in a firehouse with men who often ate like it was their last meal. Emily had suggested giving some to family and friends. Before she left, he offered her a platter.

He'd take food over to the station right now, only he didn't want to leave Jo until Nora and Eve arrived. They'd texted him that they were on their way. Apparently, Monique was already trying to book an earlier flight back to Colorado. He also had to get home to change out of his suit and pick up Rachel,

the dog he'd adopted from Paws n Pilots, a local rescue. Jo had wanted him to name her Coco, and Hud
had called her the ridiculous name for about a day.
Then he put his foot down. If he were going to provide a home for a cockapoo mix who was more poo-
dle than cocker, *he'd* get to name her. End of story.
And yes, he'd named her Rachel after his first celebrity crush, the character from the TV show *Friends*.

And if he was going to stay here much longer, he'd
need to get Rachel. If he left her alone for too long,
his furniture would pay dearly.

Needing something to do while he waited, he
packed up the food, using Tupperware and alumi-
num foil. He began to assign them. Three platters for
the fire station, one for the police station. One he'd
send up to Wildfire Ridge Outdoor Adventures, one
to Pimp Your Pet and another to Magnum Aviation.

Next, he called up friends and asked whether
they had dinner plans. First come, first served. They
started arriving an hour later, while Joanne continued to stay in her room. The last time he'd looked in
on her she'd dressed in shorts and a tank and was sitting on top of the covers probably writing one of her
lists. She loved her lists. Her order. He hoped "kill
Chuck and ask Hud to hide the body" was at the top
of this new list. That made sense to him.

What didn't make any sense was the weird tinge
of relief that had washed through him the moment
he realized that Chuck wasn't showing. The wedding

wouldn't happen. Guilt pulsed through him, making his gut burn. This was not something he should celebrate. He should be a better friend to Jo even if he'd never been one of Chuck's fans.

No, that had been Jo's mother and most of her girlfriends. They saw a man who billed himself as someone ready to commit, settle down, have a family. The women ate it up. Most of all Jo.

Hud told himself that what Chuck had done didn't have anything to do with him. Jo listened to him, but in the end, she made her own decisions. Like Chuck. And if Chuck was weak enough to allow Hud's dislike of him to play a role in all this, then he was even less of a man than Hud had realized.

If it had been him, he wouldn't have let an old boyfriend stop him from marrying Jo. Nothing could have stopped him.

Jett from Magnum Aviation and his wife showed up first. They were on a tight budget and were happy to take some of the food off his hands.

Hud called his good friend Ty Brody from the station and asked him to come pick up food for the guys. Together they loaded boxes of food into the backseat of his truck.

"Sorry about what happened."

By now, it would be all over their small town. *No wedding. Did you hear? The groom didn't show.*

"Jackass," both Hud and Ty said at once.

"And Jo? How's she doing?" Ty asked.

"I don't know. She's making a list."

"If the guy can't hack the pressures of wedding day, he'd run at the slightest hint of trouble. She's better off."

"Yeah. Try telling her that."

"This wasn't the way to do it, agreed. Hate to say it, though, but this could be your moment."

"For *what*?"

"You and Jo, together again."

"Ancient history."

Ty grinned and waggled his eyebrows. "Then how about a reboot?"

"She's probably going to hate all men for a while."

"Aw, crap. Probably right."

It wasn't that Hud hadn't ever pictured the 2.0 version. He couldn't even blame his mistakes on youth or an imperfect understanding of relationships. Because even back then, he'd somehow...just known.

And still blown it all to hell.

He'd had all the arrogance and conceit of a kid who'd just discovered the wonders of sex. It had made sense for them to see other people and he'd suggested that. Who met their soulmate at sixteen?

He'd tried to recover, tried to get her back, but by then it was too late. Their lives were changed by one careless impulse and placed on a trajectory that would keep them apart for years.

Hud handed Ty the keys to his house. "Bring me

Rachel, her food and a change of clothes? I'm staying until her girlfriends come by."

"What about her mom?" Ty asked. "Can't she come over?"

"Jo told her mom she was going on the honeymoon anyway. With me."

"Dude! Don't you wish."

"Think she wants some time alone before everyone starts pitying her. I mean, I get it."

"She knows *you* won't feel sorry for her." Ty nodded.

True enough. Hud would never feel sorry for Jo, though he did feel compassion for what she'd been through. But he'd always been tough on himself, his staff, family, friends, and of course, Jo. He saw no point in regretting what could not be changed. Time to toughen up. She'd have to get over this jerk and the sooner the better. He'd make it happen. Hud would make sure she didn't spend any more time on the loser than he was worth.

Maybe she'd come to understand on her own that being with Chuck in the first place had been a mistake. Deciding to marry him? Pure insanity. Hud didn't believe a lifetime commitment could be based purely on being practical and passing some kind of compatibility test the way Jo claimed she and Chuck had done. There had to be passion and connection, too. He hadn't seen a spark between them but then again maybe he wasn't the most impartial judge.

But he'd once accused Jo of not being in-love with Chuck. She'd protested. A little too harshly. Almost like she was trying to convince herself.

After Ty took off, Hud went inside and checked the time. Joanne would need to eat, so he heated some canned soup instead of the leftovers he didn't think she was ready to see and brought it upstairs with a glass of the sweet tea she loved.

She was still writing the damn list. She looked up when he came in. "What now?"

"Time to eat something." He set the bowl of soup on her nightstand.

"Okay," she said, and put the notepad down. "Ugh. You're such a pain."

"You know this. Why be surprised by it now?"

"I don't know why you don't just go home and let me be."

"Because you have to eat." He sat on the edge of her bed, forcing her to move.

She did, and her top shifted to reveal one smooth bare shoulder. One *shoulder*, in a bed, and he was already fantasizing.

Do not. Go. There.

"What do you have?" She sat up straighter.

"Soup." He reached for the bowl, offering it to her. "I'll force-feed you if I have to."

"In your dreams, buddy." She squinted at him, showing a little bit of the sass he loved.

"Don't make me."

She took the bowl. "Did my mother really come over here anyway?"

"Nope. This is canned and from your cupboard."

"What? No special ingredients?"

"Piss and vinegar."

"Ew, and you expect me to *eat* this?"

She took a spoonful. He was sure it was because she realized that he wasn't moving or going anywhere until she ate.

"Why did he do this to me?"

"Because he's an ass."

"No, I mean, really. Why not just tell me before the wedding day and save me some trouble? Not to mention the shame. Even if I've been through a lot worse than this, it's just not okay. You know I can't stand for people to pity me and that's what they're all doing."

He winced because he was somewhat involved in the "worse than this." "Not me." He nudged his chin to indicate she should take another spoonful.

Jo wrongly believed that when people pitied her, it meant somehow she was pitiful. Not true, but she had a little misfire in her brain where it came to this. In his mind, she deserved some sympathy and should accept that nobody was cruel enough not to feel sorry for what she'd been through.

"Of course, not you, but everyone else." She had another bite or two of soup, stared off into space and dropped the spoon. "What do I do? How do I get past this and save my business?"

His chest pinched uncomfortably and he glanced at the notepad which did indeed have a numbered list. "What does the list say?"

She nudged her chin at the list. "Go ahead. You know you want to."

He picked it up and read:

1. Figure out if I can return the wedding dress or look into other ways of selling it.
2. How much do I still owe on the dinner? Check statements.
3. Make a list of all expenses and demand he re-imburse me.
4. Get back to work immediately so everyone sees that this won't affect the business.
5. Call Mom.
6. Assess any other damage control.

The list went on, but Hud stopped reading there.

"I don't see 'ask Hud to help me get rid of Chuck and hide the body.' I'll do it. You know I will." He tried a smile.

"I know." She sighed and finished the rest of the soup, somehow, then handed it back to him and went back to her list. "Will you leave me alone?"

"For now. But Nora and Eve are on their way." He shut the door against her groan.

A few minutes later, Ty was at the door with a change of clothes for Hud, and Rachel at the end of a leash. In typical fashion, her butt wiggled at Mach speed, and she tried her best to climb him like a tree. She wore her pearl studded pink collar that Jo had insisted he buy from the *Pimp Your Pet store*.

He picked Her Highness up, waited for her to lick and slobber him, then carried her upstairs. "You've got a job to do, Rachel, and the last thing I need is any shit from you. It's been a bad day."

One thing he'd realized about Rachel early on: she should have been a therapy dog. At the station, she'd wrapped everyone around her paw in a couple of minutes. Even the old-timers, who swore they'd never own a "froufrou" dog like her. Once he'd been one of them. But Rachel was a good dog. She was smart and already knew how to roll over and play dead. Until he gave her the go-ahead she wouldn't move from her spot. It was uncanny.

"Someone's here to see you." Hud set Rachel down at the edge of the bed, where she instinctively sensed the need to be closer. She belly crawled to Jo until she was just inches from her face. She licked her nose.

"Oh, Coco," Jo said, because she was his biggest pain in the ass.

"Rachel," he ground out.

He shut the door, hoping Rachel would do her thing.

* * *

Cleaning always helped with thinking. That's how Joanne found herself on her hands and knees an hour later, scrubbing the kitchen floor tile. Coco sat nearby head cocked in mild interest.

"Don't give me that look, it's cheaper than therapy."

Hud had left Coco with her and gone off to take care of something on Wildfire Ridge, where he occasionally picked up a guide shift on his days off. He wouldn't be back until tomorrow.

Joanne scrubbed, putting her back into it. She pictured erasing Chuck out of her life. He'd stepped on this floor and gotten it dirty, the bastard. First, she imagined erasing his eyes. Then his nose. Lips and jawline next. Finally, when only his stupid chin was left, she wiped it away furiously.

She'd always hated his pointy chin.

The doorbell rang and Coco barked as if to announce danger was clearly looming on the other side.

"Calm down."

Joanne carried Coco into her bedroom, set her down and assured her all was well, then went to open the front door. She'd already been warned by Hud that Nora and Eve were on their way. That was good. They could discuss plans for the boutique. For a while now, she'd wanted Eve to make one of those pixel thingies for the boutique's Facebook page. Then start some ads. Maybe she should expand.

Well, not now that she had wedding bills to pay.
But soon. The Taylor wedding was coming up and
Joanne had worked hard to get their business. The
wedding of the year in Fortune, and Joanne had sold
four of her designs to them. Some of her best work.
All that remained was for them to choose one final
design and she and Nora would order the material
and start sewing.

So, at least her professional life was intact, even
if it had to be weird for the brides who had heard
about her wedding day fail. Still, she'd recover from
all this. She had to.

When Joanne opened the front door, Nora grabbed
her in a hug. "Oh, Joanne."

Ugh. "I'm okay. Really."

"How can you be?"

"It's a break-up. I've been through them before."

"But this is different." Eve said, walking inside.
"I brought cookies. Your favorite."

"You shouldn't have. I have a ton of food here, including desserts. Someone has to eat it." There had
to be twenty or more bottles of champagne, not to
mention the wedding cake.

The. Wedding. Cake.

She'd almost forgotten.

Her friends followed Joanne into the kitchen.

Opening up the refrigerator, she found dozens
of containers of food crowding every shelf. Hud's
doing. He was an organizer, a leader and someone

who always took charge. The three-tier cake had been boxed, labeled "cake" and placed in the refrigerator, which was exploding with plastic-wrapped platters of food.

"And Hud already gave a lot of this away." Joanne reached for a box. "Cake, anyone?"

Both Eve and Nora glanced at each other.

Nora shrugged. "Well, it would be crazy to turn cake down."

"And I'm not crazy," Eve said.

"I have to agree. We're very sane women here." Joanne sliced into the top layer with joy, tossing aside the plastic couple where they landed on the clean floor. That was the end of the plastic faux Joanne and Chuck Ellis. "I wasn't hungry earlier, but now I'm famished."

Two hours or so later, the cake was in pieces. Literally. Taking zero care to appearance, each one of them had used their own fork to cut into the cake any which way. Taking what they wanted in haphazard patterns. Leaving the rest.

"Who knew a cake could look so ugly?" Nora said.

"We went after it pretty hard." Joanne licked her fork.

Eve cleared her throat. "Joanne, we have to talk about it. *You* have to talk about it."

"She's right," Nora said. "Chuck left you. Aren't you even going to find out why?"

Joanne had considered it, to be fair. During all the hours today that she'd stared at the ceiling and worked on her lists of what to do next. She'd wondered. Should she ask him if she'd done anything wrong? Pushed too hard? Nagged too much about all his away baseball games?

But, no. Far from it. She'd encouraged him to pursue his dreams. Admired him, even, for never giving up on someday reaching the majors. All the time Chuck spent traveling meant that her life hadn't really changed all that much. The difference being that after marriage, he'd move in with her, and they'd start a family. He would give her more children. At thirty-two, some days it felt like she was running out of time.

She'd done nothing wrong, unless you wanted to count the decision to agree to marry him in the first place. It might have been a little…misguided.

"I don't care why," Joanne said. "No reason is good enough."

"Even I'm curious," Eve said, touching her chest. "I mean, who even does that?"

"Not a real man," Joanne said.

"A chicken shit," Nora said and they all laughed.

"I'll drink to that!" Eve said and raised a fake glass in salute.

Then Joanne remembered all of the champagne bottles in the fridge. "I can help with that!"

They drank the bubbly wine from flutes and after a while, Nora got deep. She was clearly drunk.

"You know whah I tink?"

"What?" Joanne said. She was lying on her back in the living room. All three of them were, the tops of their heads touching in a semi-circle.

"I think love is really, really…hard."

"Uh-huh," Eve said. "Preach it."

"Sooooo hard," Nora said.

"That's too bad," Eve said. "I don't think that's fair. It shouldn't be so hard."

"Guys are terrible, too. That's no help," Nora said.

"Not all guys," Joanne added.

"Word," Eve said, "Just…most. You know?"

"There are good guys. Like…um…whosit? Whatshisname?" Nora groaned. "Oh yeah. Um, lieutenant Hudson Decker."

"Yeah, but he's like…taken so you can't have him," Eve explained.

"Right." Nora nodded.

Joanne knew Nora was nodding because she felt her head bob up and down against hers. "Wait. Who has him?"

Two heads bobbed up and were right in Joanne's line of vision. She actually blinked it was so sudden.

"You," Nora said.

She shook her head. "Not me."

"Please don't tell me you haven't noticed how hot he is," Eve said, coughing. "Oh, please."

"I try hard not to notice, okay?"

It wasn't that she didn't realize Hud was the "classic" definition of handsome. That was part of the problem. Every woman noticed him, and he in turn, noticed them. Frequently.

He had sandy blonde hair, shimmering and intelligent green eyes that noticed the smallest thing, a smirk of a smile that tipped to one side when he was tired, and…well, she could go on. But again, she tried not to notice.

"That's too bad," Eve said with a deep sigh. "Because we can't date him, either. He's your ex."

"I wouldn't advise it," Joanne said. "Not unless you want to be tossed over for the latest model in a month or so."

It was one of the reasons Joanne had gravitated toward Chuck. He wasn't classically attractive and the farthest thing from a player. Not at all. But he was a coward. A liar. Not much better.

"Yeah, no thanks," Nora said. "I'm going to be thirty next year."

"I would take him," Eve said. "For one night."

"One night? That's all you want out of a man?" Joanne asked, incredulous.

"From Hud." She winked.

"Yeah," Nora said. "I bet he's good."

They both looked at her expectantly. Shocked, she sat up. "I don't know. We were teenagers!"

Eve stared, dumbfounded. "Never again, over the

years, not even once? You know when you were both lonely and between relationships. A little something-something? Never?"

"No!"

Why did everyone always ask her that?

Looks weren't everything. She had a list of qualities she wanted in a man. First and foremost was the ability to be monogamous.

And Hud had already proven himself incapable.

Chapter Three

The next day, Joanne woke up to something cold and wet on her toes. She lifted her head from the pillow to inspect.

Coco.

Oh, excuse her. *Rachel*. Which, by the way, was not a proper name for a dog, least of all a cockapoo who should clearly be named Coco. She closed her eyes again.

She'd been dreaming of warm sandy beaches. Mojitos by the pool. She wore one of the many two-piece swimsuits she'd bought for the honeymoon. A black-and-white polka-dot number that made her feel like a blonde Audrey Hepburn. The sun was toasty on

her legs and her eyes were shut against the bright-
ness of the day. Suddenly someone was pulling on
her leg. Playfully. She kicked, hoping whoever had
her foot would let go. They didn't.

"Jo," a deep and commanding male voice said.

Man, that voice. It gave her pleasant sexy shivers.
Desire poured through her. She opened her eyes to
check out this cabana guy or whoever was making
a pass at her while she slept on the beach and found
Hud staring at her. Oh. Wow. Source of sexy deep
voice. A sexy man. What were the odds?

Joanne shook her head. Re-direct! Re-direct!

Hud's forehead was creased in concern.

She stretched. There were layers of cotton in her
mouth. Strands of hair were stuck to her chin. She
appeared to have drooled a little bit. "W-what?"

Oh, for the love of God, she was on the floor. The
living room floor. She vaguely remembered eating
cake and drinking champagne. No wonder she felt
like death. All that sugar.

"Looks like you had some fun in here."

She followed his gaze to four empty champagne
bottles and what looked like a massacred cake. It had
three large knives stuck in what was left of the cake.

"Where are…?"

"I got Eve an Uber. Surprised you slept through
all her moaning and apologizing."

"What about Nora?"

Hud shrugged.

"Oh yeah, she's probably already at the shop." She groaned. "What time is it?"

"Two o'clock." He gave her a hand, and she rose, swaying a little bit.

When he caught her, his large warm hand touched bare skin and it was then that she noticed…she was wearing a short T-shirt that came to her waist and cotton panties. Nothing else.

She stared at him, at her panties, then back at him. "I was hot!"

"Clearly." He bit back a smile.

"Oh, no. Coco! Is she okay?"

"I just let her outside and she peed for several minutes."

"Good girl." Joanne bent to pick up the little ball of fluff she'd come to adore and gave her a snuggle. "I'm sorry I forgot about you."

Hud was still staring at Joanne. He was staring below the waist. "Stop staring."

"Sorry," he said, raising his head to meet her gaze. "Nothing I haven't seen before."

"I need a shower." She handed Rachel back to him. "Do you mind waiting until I'm done?"

"No problem."

In the shower, she allowed the hot water to pound her aching neck. She washed her hair. Then she rinsed and applied conditioner. Used her big-toothed comb to detangle. It was her ritual and required no thinking. She appreciated that. Right now she didn't want to think about much of anything, other than maybe plan where she'd bury Chuck's body. Method of death? Poison. Anything else would require more strength than she had at the moment. Or she could beat him into a coma with her words. Pointy sharp words which would tear into his flesh and punish him for taking so much of her time.

Her money.

Her pride.

She toweled off and went for all her beauty products, neatly lined up. Moisturizing cream to hold off the wrinkles that were creeping up on her. Hair products that gave her a bouncy and glossy shine. For who? She didn't care. How about for herself? She liked to look good. Her preparations were complete when she brushed and flossed her teeth like she did every morning and evening.

Boy, it almost felt like she hadn't had a bottle of champagne and half of a chocolate cake. She felt normal.

Dressing in her yoga pants and another long T-shirt, she went downstairs to apologize to Hud for being in her underwear and on the floor when he arrived. That was embarrassing. It wasn't even her best lingerie. They were the rabbits with pink bowties cotton panties. The ones she wore on laundry day. Ugh.

From her kitchen, she saw Hud's back as he faced the yard, head lowered, hands in his pockets.

Watching Rachel as she sniffed around every bush. Crouched to pee. Then sniffed another bush. Repeat. When she finally came to him, her tail wiggling, he bent to pick her up and tenderly held her. The image of this big man holding such a tiny creature in his hands softened her heart. Hud was gentle when he wanted to be. Loving, kind and funny when he wasn't being a pain in the butt.

He stepped inside, quirking a brow when he saw her standing in front of him, arms crossed. His head bent low to allow Rachel to lick his face he looked at her from underneath his eyelashes. "What?"

"You saw me in my panties."

"So?"

"What do you mean 'so'? I want to apologize for not being dressed."

"I barely noticed. But if it bothers you that much, you want to see me naked?" He undid the top button of his cargo pants.

"Don't do it." The thought was so titillating that she covered her eyes with the heels of her hands.

"Relax. I'm not that easy. Got to buy me dinner first. Or at least a beer."

When she brought her hands down, he was giving her his easy smile. The one that reminded her how many times he'd rescued her. Cheering her up after a bad date with a guy who seemed perfect until he announced he hated "snotty nosed" kids. All the other men who were shocked that she, who seemed like such a *smart* and educated woman, had a teenage son. Didn't that mean she'd been a teenage mother? Why, yes. Yes, it did. Hud had always been there to confess that men sucked. All of them. He'd remind her that she had a wonderful son, a thriving business and great friends. At one time that had been enough. She wasn't sure how all that had changed and when she got up on her high horse and thought she needed more.

He set Rachel down. "Jo, I've got some bad news."

"Oh God, no. More?"

"I saw your mom in town. She knows I'm not in the Bahamas with you."

She faced palmed.

"It's going to be okay."

"Hud," she whispered. "I don't know where to start fixing this mess."

He opened his arms wide. "C'mere."

She went into the arms of a man who, hands down, issued the greatest hugs. He was, at heart, a big teddy bear of a man though not many realized this fact. A long time ago she'd decided that if she ever found a man who gave out hugs like Hud's, she'd marry him in a second. When that never happened, she'd settled for Chuck. But this time the hug was different, as if he was holding back. Not squeezing as tightly as normal. Probably because he felt guilty about checking her out when she was half naked. On the other hand, if that were true, why did he smell her hair?

He pulled away abruptly. "Let me get you some lunch."

"You don't have to do that."

"It's no bother. You're having sliced meat and potatoes and vegetables. You're having that forever."

"The food." She sighed. "I don't want to eat food from the devil wedding."

"Might as well eat what we can today and throw the rest away."

"What happened to all that food?" She plopped down on a stool near the counter.

Hud informed her of how many friends, family members and local community services, like a homeless shelter and another for battered women had enjoyed the food for her reception. At least it hadn't gone to waste. A few minutes later she was seated in front of a mini banquet with all the food from her almost wedding to the son of Satan. Before her were sliced meats—the best Fortune Valley Family Ranch had to offer. Marinated tri-tip, top sirloin and New York strip, freshly baked rolls from The Drip, and scalloped potatoes.

"I was supposed to eat this food as a married woman. With my husband, the son of Satan."

"You could eat it now, with your best friend, the stud." He served her a plate and plopped it in front of her. "Eat. It's actually very good. Have the last laugh on him."

"I'm worried. What's going to happen to my bridal boutique now?"

"Why should anything happen?"

She dropped her fork in emphasis. "I'm a jilted bride."

"What? It's contagious?" He smirked.

"Don't laugh. Brides can be a funny bunch. I've seen all kinds over the years. Brides who will only marry on a double-digit day, brides who will only marry on months with a full moon. I'm getting back to work, now that my mother knows the truth. Not hiding out anymore."

"Good. That's a plan."

But Joanne wondered why she still hadn't cried. Shouldn't she cry or at least want to cry?

She was more upset over the humiliation of what Chuck had put her through. Of what her brides would think. Still, she'd loved him, right? Sure, it wasn't passionate or lusty love, but it was the sort of love that grew with time. Or so she'd thought. In some countries, she and Chuck would have been matched together due to common interests and goals. They were well suited to each other.

Hud bit into a roll with a bit of hostility. "Have you talked to him yet?"

"I've had no time to talk to him."

He shrugged. "You could have texted. Emailed. Carrier pigeon. I don't know."

"I don't want to talk to him. What is there to say?"

"How about 'Hey, asswipe, you owe me money.' Click, Send." He made a motion with his fingers.

"Do you think that's all I care about? The *money*? He humiliated me."

"He humiliated himself. Too much of a coward to face you. Breaking up via text on your wedding day gives new meaning to low-down dirty coward."

She didn't disagree. But not everyone could be Hudson Decker. Not everyone would run into a burning building. Some had a built-in sense of self-preservation. Then again, Hud had built his own defenses around his heart. That heart had never been fully open to anyone. It was the one risk he wouldn't seem to take.

That aversion to emotional risk had him breaking up with her after their only time together. Little explanation. It was over. Her sixteen-year-old self had raged in hurt and confusion. In classic teenage immaturity, she'd assumed Hud was "the one." Forever. Gave him her virginity and her heart. And then he'd abandoned her.

So he'd only wanted one thing, like most boys. She'd simply retaliated by going on a date with the most popular guy at school: Matt Conner. Her only motivation had been to make Hud jealous.

She'd accomplished that, but in a much more epic

way than she'd ever planned. Matt got her pregnant their first and only time. Still, she'd gotten Hunter out of it, so no regrets. Her son had been the one bright light in her life for years.

Matt had offered to marry her, of course, but she'd turned him down. She would have a child by a boy she didn't love but that didn't mean she had to marry him. Not that she had thought Hud would want anything to do with her again, but she just couldn't go through with a marriage of convenience. She still loved Hud. Loved him all through her pregnancy, and all the intervening years since. But eventually the crazy burning young love she'd had for him as a young woman had burned itself out. It had transformed into a wonderful deep friendship that it would simply kill her to lose.

"Here we are again, Jo. I'm getting you through another breakup. This too shall pass."

"This is different. I'm done. Done with men. Done with love."

He quirked a brow. "Not you."

"Yes, me. Done, done, done, buddy." She held up her fork, making a proclamation by sweeping it in the air like a wand. "Done."

"You don't give up that easy. You own a bridal boutique, for crying out loud. Love will conquer all and all that crap."

"Not this time, Robert Frost." She made a face. "That's beautiful, by the way."

He grinned. "So I'm not a romantic. I never get any complaints."

"Have you looked in the mirror lately? Who would complain?"

"Right. Because that's me. Just another pretty face."

"Don't forget the hot bod."

He chuckled. "As long as *you* don't forget."

A moment passed between them, a microsecond in which neither one of them spoke. They simply locked gazes over her kitchen counter. The oxygen and tension lay like a coil, thick and heavy between them. It made her skin too tight and she was the first to look away.

He said something under his breath that sounded like, "chicken," but she ignored him and stood to carry her half-eaten plate of food to the sink. When she bumped elbows with him that was different, too. Instead of laughing and calling him a first-class klutz as she normally would, her stomach tightened in some kind of weird anticipation. Of what, she had no idea. But Hud didn't come through with the usual suspects, either. No jokes about how she could quit accidentally rubbing against him and admit she wanted to sleep with him again. Find out if all the rumors about his prowess in the bedroom were true.

But she'd decided long ago that she couldn't be with him again in that sense. Ever. She didn't want to add herself to his long line of women. At least she would always be able to say she'd been his first, if not his last.

"I guess I've got some calls to make."

She hadn't been looking forward to it, but when she looked, there were twenty missed calls. Not one of them from Chuck. The most recent was from poor Nora, who must have crawled out of here this morning.

Hud hung back to give her privacy, she assumed. He started throwing the rest of the food away, food she was happy to see in the trash can.

"Joanne," Nora said as she picked up the phone, obviously recognizing caller ID. "Are you as hungover as I am?"

"Worse." She whispered into the phone. "You couldn't wake me before you left? I was wearing my panties when Hud came over."

"I tried to. You said, 'if you touch me again, I'll kill you.'"

"Oh, no. I did?" She winced. "I'm sorry."

"I never knew you to be so hostile in the morning."

"What's up?" Joanne asked, getting to the point.

"Are you going to take the entire two weeks off anyway?"

"Absolutely not. I'd come in today, but you know…hangover. I'm feeling good otherwise, and I'll be in tomorrow morning first thing."

"I… I wasn't going to say anything, but if the

rumors are true, I thought you should know right away."

Joanne almost stopped Nora from telling her, because she just couldn't take any more bad news. "I should know what?"

"You've probably not been watching much sports TV lately, or ever, but apparently Chuck finally made the next round of the major leagues a few months ago. I think that's what my brother said. He keeps up with that sort of stuff."

"Really. Why wouldn't he *tell* me that?"

Getting to the majors had been Chuck's dream for years. At thirty-four, he was already old for the sport, but he wouldn't give up. His minor-league team had been on the road, but they'd never made it to the play-offs, which made September a safe month to get married.

At one time she'd admired that about him. She'd admired his assurance to know what he wanted and go after it relentlessly. In addition to that, he'd been saving for their future since early in their relationship. He'd been serious about forever.

"And…also," Nora continued, drawing her words out. "He's…um, I heard that—"

"Spit it out!"

"Okay, okay. Now, this one is just a rumor mind you, but he's got a girlfriend. Mandy Jewels, the country music singer."

"Mandy?"

Chuck didn't even like country music. Whenever Joanne had tried to get him out to the Silver Saddle in town, he'd get a migraine. But her first wild guess was that this wasn't about the music at all. He'd stuff cotton in his ears if he had to. Mandy was a beautiful girl.

And young.

"I'm so sorry. I hated to have to tell you this. Remember, it might not even be true. You know how sometimes these industry professionals try to get publicity by dating someone in the public eye."

"Don't worry about it," Joanne said, feeling her throat constrict. "I know I'm better off."

She'd have been better off with a man who had the guts to simply tell her the truth. Honesty. In such short supply when it came to the men in her life. Except for Hud, and she assumed that was simply because they had a different kind of relationship. A real and solid friendship. He wouldn't lie to her because there was no reason to anymore.

"I know you're better off," Nora said. "I didn't want to say anything, but Chuck turned out to be a jerk. A major…a major doodlehead!"

Joanne almost laughed. Almost. Unfortunately she wouldn't be laughing for the next decade. Chuck might soon have money. *Real* money. The kind of money he'd never had while he'd been with her. She didn't care about wealth, having done fine supporting her son and herself all these years. Still, the thought that he'd let her pay for this entire wedding and then not bothered to show up, or cancel in time to get their deposits back… What a dick he was.

"Is there anything else you need right now?"

She'd have thought Nora could wait to deliver this news unless she'd also called for another reason.

"Yes," she said, sounding miserable. "But I want to state right now for the record that I did everything I could."

Great. Now what? "Just tell me."

"It's Tilly Jacobs again. This time she's convinced that you being left—" Nora cleared her throat "—at the altar is bad luck for her wedding day so she wants her deposit back. The dress just needs a little tailoring. Should I give her the deposit back?"

God, no. If they gave back a deposit once she'd already sewn the dress, she'd have been out of business a long time ago. "No. Listen, I'll come down and talk to her."

"You will?"

"Can you ask her to come in and talk to me tomorrow?"

"She's actually here waiting. With her mother."

"Oh."

"I really tried, but I need your help. She wants to see for herself that you're still alive and breathing and not so devastated that you won't show your face in public."

"How ridiculous. I'll show her what a strong woman looks like."

Joanne hung up and turned to Hud. "I'm going over to the shop. Please be here when I get back."

She was for certain going to need another one of his hugs.

Chapter Four

"**Y**ou look beautiful." Joanne studied Tilly's reflection in the oval-shaped mirror inside Joanne's Boutique.

She'd brought out the dress Tilly was afraid might be cursed now, had Tilly try it on, veil and all.

"I *do* look beautiful."

"See? I told you," said Tilly's long-suffering mother, Alice.

"Of course you're going to say that, *Mom*," twenty-year-old Tilly said, sounding fifteen. "But if Joanne says it, I know it must be true."

Now to set the stage.

"Picture yourself almost sashaying down the aisle,

this beautiful train following your every move like it's a part of you. You're poetry in motion. You. This beautiful dress. The veil. Like everything was made for you."

"Oh, I know what you mean." Tilly fluffed her veil. "Just like Keith was made for me. I can just picture him waiting for me at the end of the aisle. He looks so handsome in his black tux. Like a movie star. How did I get so lucky? I can't *wait* to be his wife."

There was a collective sigh from both Nora and Alice.

"Yes, yes. Of course." Joanne fought to recover. She'd lost her touch. How could she forget the groom? "This is a very special day for you and Hud—I mean, Keith!"

Wow, what was that about?

"You're right," Tilly said, turning to Joanne. "Just because you didn't get your happily-ever-after doesn't mean I won't get mine."

"Tilly!" Alice scolded. "Please."

Tilly lowered her head. "I'm sorry, Joanne."

Joanne waved a hand. "It's nothing. I'm fine now."

"Really? But if Keith left me at the altar I'd die."

"Don't be so dramatic," Alice said. "On the other hand, if Keith leaves you at the altar, your father will kill him. That isn't drama, just the facts."

Nora chuckled but Tilly glared at her mother.

"Well, you were the one who brought it up!" Alice said.

"What are you going to do about your dress? The beautiful Valentino. What a waste. Are you going to burn it?" Tilly sounded as though that were the most logical thing to do.

This gave new meaning to a "fire sale." Dang, look at her making a joke. What was *wrong* with her? And why hadn't *she* pictured Chuck at the end of the aisle, waiting?

"Don't burn it," Nora said, wringing her hands.

As if. "I won't. The dress is gorgeous. Someday it will be worn."

Nora embraced Joanne in a hug, squeezing her tight. There was genuine sympathy and compassion in the embrace, and Joanne felt it down to her marrow. Still not as good as one of Hud's. Even when he was tired.

After Tilly and her mother finally left, satisfied, Joanne headed home. As she drove, it occurred to her that she'd face many more years of working with brides, but this time with a kind of jinx over her head. She had to turn this around because she'd already lost her touch with the proper words to set the stage for the bride on her wedding day. Just didn't have it in her anymore. But surely she'd still love dressing brides after this haze finally cleared. One day, one epic fail, certainly couldn't ruin both her life *and* her business.

At home, Hud sat on the couch, arms spread out on either side watching TV, Rachel cuddled next to him on the couch. "Hey. Everything okay?"

"I need a hug," she said, sitting next to him. "On top of everything else, I think I'm going to be a pariah from now on. 'Come see the sad jilted bride, owner of the only bridal boutique in town.'"

Hud didn't say anything, just simply pulled her into a sideways hug and squeezed her tight. She closed her eyes and enjoyed the warmth of his arms as it seeped into her skin, through her clothes and straight to her bones. Straight to her heart.

"I'm still a little hung over." She pulled away. "I'm going to take a nap."

Hudson had half a mind to call the whole thing off.

He'd come up with the idea on the fly. All the guys at the station helped, because every one of them thought of Jo as their little sister, or a daughter for the old-timers. *Couldn't that idiot Chuck see that she was perfect in every way? Beautiful. Smart. A good mother. Devoted to her family.* They'd always been so impressed that he'd carried on a friendship with her all these years without ever wanting more.

It would be even better if that were true.

But what he had planned for today might backfire on him. It could make her sadder. He hoped not.

Besides, he had some apologizing to do and he did

best with actions. Even though he'd done his utmost to avert his gaze, he'd still had an eyeful of Jo's long legs leading up to that delectable heart-shaped butt.

Still, it was wrong.

Sixteen-year-olds were not known for their wisdom and maturity. Upset and angry, Hud had driven too fast and crashed his father's sweet classic Mustang when he'd heard the news that Jo was pregnant with Matt Connor's baby. He'd spent three months in the hospital in traction for a broken leg and arm. Been lucky to be alive, his parents and the doctors all said. The paramedics who had pulled him out of the car had been the reason he'd later become an EMT, then a firefighter and paramedic.

Jo had visited him in the hospital nearly every day, bringing him flowers and cards and holding his hand. Hud had still felt like a first-class idiot. Everything had happened because of his decision. Jo's future had been determined. She'd have Matt's baby and that was the end of it. She'd refused to marry Matt, and refused to marry at all. Then again, she was sixteen and would continue to live with her parents and finish school. Hud didn't even offer to marry her, knowing she'd say no. Knowing he wasn't good enough for her and probably never would be.

While Jo napped, Rachel followed him around as he filled the small rubber wading pool with water and set it in the middle of her living room. He pushed back the couch and set up chaise lounges, bringing in the heat lamps she had outside in the patio area. He hung fairy lights to give the room an atmospheric touch. Then he started the lazy island music he'd downloaded. He changed into his board shorts and started blending drinks. Mojitos. Mai tais.

When Jo came downstairs two hours later wearing her yoga pants and a T-shirt that read I Woke Up Like This, he was ready for her. Lying back on one of the chaise lounges, he held out his Mai Tai. "Join me."

She rubbed her eyes. "What...what's all this?"

"Brought the Bahamas to you." He scanned the room and all he'd done to change it into an island paradise.

She did the same and a tiny hint of a smile curved her lips and sparkled in her emerald eyes.

She wandered to the kitchen and found the blender filled with Mai Tais. "Did you make me a mojito?"

"What do you take me for? There's a pitcher in the fridge."

"This is amazing." She turned back to him, eyes wide. "You got a kiddie pool?"

"Got to have some water nearby and this is the best I could do. Belongs to a two-year-old who knows how to share. Hey, we can dip our feet in at least." He grinned. "Go put on your swimsuit. Might as well."

"I bought four of them, actually."

He took a big gulp of his drink and swallowed, worried he'd be treated to a fashion show from which he'd never recover. She sprinted up the steps with more energy than he'd seen in days.

Hud fist-pumped with Rachel, another trick he'd taught her. "I've got this."

When Jo ran back down in a red two-piece bikini that left little to the imagination, he was surprised she wasn't as self-conscious as she usually was around him. Instead, she allowed her breasts to jiggle as if she didn't realize this was even happening. He wished he could tell her to stop bouncing but he wasn't quite that noble.

"This is so thrilling!" She'd brought a towel with her that she spread on the chaise lounge. "I've always wanted to go to the Bahamas."

I'll take you. To the real place. Just say the word.

Shut up, you idiot. She just got over a very bad breakup and your assignment, which you already accepted long ago, was to put her back together. Remind her how much she's worth. Heal her heart.

For what? So she can go meet some other loser who will break her heart? No one's ever going to take care of her like I do.

True, but not the point. He rose to get her a mojito and brought it to her with a colorful straw and a parasol umbrella. She leaned back on the lounge, sunglasses on. My God, she was so adorable.

"Thank you, cabana boy," she said, accepting the drink. "Would you turn down the sun a little bit?"

Hud adjusted the heat lamp and sat back down.

"I ordered us a pizza. Take it easy with that drink because you don't have a lot in your stomach."

"Pizza delivery to the beach? Awesome."

"You'll eat, right?" He wasn't convinced.

"I'm pretty hungry." She turned to him. "No sausage?"

"Jo, I know how you take your pizza."

She sighed. "Not everyone does."

Yeah, he'd bet Chuck didn't know her favorite flower either, or how she took her coffee. He'd bet he didn't know her favorite movie was *3:10 to Yuma* or that she cried every year on the anniversary of her father's death.

Jo went through that mojito pretty fast and the pizza hadn't yet arrived. He glanced at his wristwatch. They claimed the delivery time was twenty minutes. Thirty minutes ago.

"You know what we didn't do?" Jo straightened. "Suntan lotion. We don't want to get a burn."

"Sure, why not? Let's go all in." But he rose and headed to the kitchen. "I'll make you a sandwich. Damn pizza is late."

"First, another mojito." In the kitchen, she purposely bumped into his hip as she replenished her drink, then giggled. "I'm having so much fun. This is such a great idea."

She danced to the island music as she made her way to the bathroom, presumably for the lotion. He smiled, just watching her move. She often had that effect on him.

He'd finished making the sandwich when she got back. "Eat something before you drink anymore."

"In a minute." She spread lotion on her arms. "After I finish this mojito."

"That drink is going to go right to your head. You have almost nothing in your stomach." Listen to him. Was he her father now?

She stuck her tongue out at him. "I can handle my mojitos."

"Sure." He set the plate on the floor next to her. "But eat this before Rachel does."

Rachel was already sniffing from her perch on the couch he'd pushed several feet away.

"Get my back, would you?" She handed him the lotion.

Was she kidding? "You're enjoying this game."

"I used to play make-believe with Hunter all the time. He was Batman, I was Catwoman. This is so much more fun. I haven't played like this for years."

He hadn't, either. He spread coconut-smelling lotion over Jo's back and if his hands lingered a little too long at the small of her back he could hardly be blamed. Her skin was softer than he'd remembered. Smooth and creamy. Being this close to her, touching her like this, was deeply affecting. For the first time, he gave himself permission for his desire. He didn't try to tamp it down or push it back.

She moved and abruptly stopped his momentum. "Now your back."

When her fingers lightly touched his back, rubbing in a downward motion, it could be said that he hadn't felt as turned on when women had done far more to him. And a lot farther south.

"Wow. You have a nice back. Why did I not know that?"

You haven't seen me naked since I was sixteen? Even then, it was pretty dark in the backseat of my father's car.

She continued, squeezing his lats, "Look at these doohickeys. What do you call them? Glutes and ladders? Or is that chutes and ladders?"

"Lats and traps," he said, thinking that if the pizza guy didn't show up soon, he might have to put his whole head in that kiddie pool to cool off.

Mind over matter. Mind over matter.

Any moment the doorbell would ring with the pizza delivery, or Jo would come to her senses and stop the madness. He wasn't a saint, for the love of God. To demonstrate that to both of them, he removed her hand as it was midway down his back for the fifth time.

He turned to face her. "So, the pizza…"

But she had tears in her eyes. "I'm sorry."

"What? No, don't be sorry." He was the sorry one, because he wanted to bite that plump bottom lip of hers.

"I'm trying to make myself feel better, trying to believe that someone would want me. I know, it's not fair—" Her hand covered her eyes until he brought it down.

"Wait. What?"

"You're so nice to me all the time. You did all this." She waved her hand around the room. "For me. And I'm being so unfair."

"Jo, you're drunk."

"No, I'm not!" she protested. "Is that what you think? Let me show you how un-drunk I am. If I was drunk, could I do this?"

She rose and, God help him, started toeing an imaginary line. He face-palmed. She made it half-way across the room before she slid a little, bumped into the kiddie pool and lost her footing.

"Okay, that's not fair. We both know I'm not very coordinated on a good day. Let me try again." This time she went arms out as if walking a tightrope.

"Why me?" He implored the heavens. "Stop. Come here."

She walked back to him. "Finally. Do you believe me now?"

"I believe you." Because there was a God in heaven, the doorbell rang. "The pizza."

He stood to get his wallet, and that's when Jo suddenly turned ghost white. She covered her mouth and ran for the bathroom.

"If only you'd been here sooner," he said to the kid delivering.

He set the pizza down on the counter, then went to Jo and crouched behind her, holding her hair back. It was so silky it almost slipped through his callused fingers.

"I'm such a mess," she said when she stopped and he handed her a towel. "Why don't you hate me?"

"Because I don't. No one could hate you." He held out his hand to help her stand.

"He cheated on me," she said, eyes watery. "Chuck did. With some young and beautiful girl, Mandy Jewels. The country music star."

The red-hot fire of anger coursed through his veins, quickening his pulse. He spoke through clenched teeth. *"What?"*

"And also he's now going with the major leagues."

"That's…that's really hard to believe." He meant this sincerely. He'd seen Chuck pitch.

"Really, what's wrong with me? Why are men always abandoning me?"

He would swear that his heart had stopped on a dime. That was him. He'd been the first man to leave her. Not long after Hunter was born, her father had died.

"You don't really believe that."

"Don't I? What's wrong with me?"

"Nothing, except you keep picking the wrong

men!" He seemed to be yelling a little bit. He hadn't meant to yell. Shit.

She jerked back. "You never said anything before."

"Well, you never asked."

She seemed to be considering it. "What kind of men *should* I pick? I'm a single mom. You and I both know how hard it is for me to find a decent guy. Someone who has a job and a solid future plan, someone who likes kids and wants to have some, likes pets…you know the drill."

"I have a job. I want kids. I have Rachel."

"You want kids?" Her eyes were narrowed.

"Yes!"

"Hud," she said, a little breathless as understanding dawned on her. "But you…you…"

"Yeah?"

"You like women. A lot of women."

"You're going to hold it against me that I like women?"

He was just a breath away from reminding her that Chuck apparently liked women, too, liked them young, and by the way, Hud had never cheated on *anyone*. But he couldn't do it. He couldn't hurt her by throwing that in her face.

"No," she said, shaking her head, still obviously drunk and confused. "It's just…just…"

Now he hated himself for bringing this up at all. It wasn't the time or place. She didn't have her faculties about her. She couldn't make good decisions. He was an idiot.

"Never mind. Forget I said anything."

"Don't be mad," she said softly, reaching for his arm. "Please."

"I'm not mad."

"Promise?" she said, wiping at her cheeks.

To make his point, he pulled her into his arms. She snuggled into his chest as she always did and he squeezed tighter, as he always did. She snuggled to get comfort, and he squeezed to keep her in his arms.

It just never worked.

Chapter Five

The next morning, Joanne woke up and reached for the bottled water she kept on the nightstand next to her bed. Cradling her head, she noticed she still wore her red swimsuit from last night's um... Festivities. Her incredibly revealing two-piece. She'd chosen this of all her new swimsuits to wear in front of Hud. First the panties. Now this.

"Oh no. What did I do?"

She was alone now. No Hud. Rachel was snuggled at the foot of her bed. Pieces of the evening came back to her. Hud's incredible surprise. So sweet. Oh yes, the mojitos. Too many of those. The lotion she'd spread over Hud's back, while those hard as granite muscles tensed beneath her fingertips. He was sexual desire personified. Torture. Like a dummy, she'd had too much to drink, thrown herself at him, then thrown up and headed straight into feeling sorry for herself territory without passing GO and collecting two hundred bucks.

And Hud… Oh right. He had suggested that he was the perfect man for her, or had she just imagined that? No, he had. And then they'd argued over it. Made up. Or something. She didn't remember much after that, but at some point she'd fallen asleep and vaguely recalled Hud carrying her up to bed where he'd deposited her. Alone.

Which made sense, because Hud would never have taken advantage of her in that condition. And if she hadn't been drunk, what would have happened then? For the first time in years, she was bold enough to let herself imagine it. Hud, kissing her lips, his warm tongue plundering. Taking his clothes off, then hers. Throwing her down to the bed, where he'd…

Stop it! Stop fantasizing about your best friend. This had to be the stress of being jilted at the altar and worrying about the boutique. Well, today she was back to work and showing the world that she'd moved on. Screw Chuck and the train he rode in on. She'd learned her lesson. Never count on a man to provide your happiness. A lesson she'd learned long ago but somehow forgotten. It should be okay to be alone. She'd been happy before Chuck. Dating here and there, nothing serious, but mostly focused on her business, her son, her mother and her friends.

Joanne splashed water on her face and took a look at herself in the mirror. Not great, but she'd looked worse.

Time to get on with her life.

She showered, then threw on a bathrobe and made her way downstairs, Rachel on her heels. On the kitchen counter, she found a note in Hud's writing:

Back to rotation. Dog food is on the counter Take care of Rachel. She's depending on you. This is your mission, and should you choose to accept it, this note will burst into flames to cover my tracks.
No, really. Take care of Rachel.

Joanne smiled. "Your master thinks he's funny."

She set Rachel down, and the little dog wiggled her butt and promptly peed all over her kitchen tile floor.

"Coco!"

She tilted her head as if she didn't know why, and was a little insulted that Joanne would call her by another woman's name.

"I mean, Rachel!"

Joanne opened the sliding glass door to let Rachel outside in her enclosed backyard. She cleaned up the mess, then found Rachel's food bowl and poured a cup of the dog food Hud had clearly brought over for her. From time to time, Jo had Rachel over for an overnight visit. When Hud was going away with a woman for a weekend, for instance. Hunter especially enjoyed the visits. He was still working on convincing Joanne that he'd be responsible enough for his own dog. But he already had Sarah's rescue dog, Shackles, at his father's house so Joanne was in no rush for another dog. Even though Rachel was technically Hud's dog, Joanne had joint custody.

After feeding Rachel, Joanne made coffee. It was all she wanted but even that tasted rancid. She threw half of it down the sink. This wasn't going to work. "Even the coffee sucks right now, Co—Rachel."

She found her cell phone, where she assumed Hud had left it for her the night before. "Hi, Mom. I guess you heard, but listen, I didn't go to the Bahamas with Hud after all."

"What happened?"

"I got jilted but life goes on. I'll be at the shop if you need me."

"Sweetie! It's too soon. You should take some time off."

"But I don't want to." Joanne took a breath. "It's better if I stay busy. Besides, I have a wedding to pay for now."

"You're not paying for the entire wedding!"

"What am I supposed to do? Leave the vendors hanging? That's not going to improve my position in our community. And this is my town, not his. I'll take care of my obligations. Then I'll go after Chuck for his half."

Joanne hung up with her mother, then quickly texted her son that she'd decided not to go to the Bahamas and would be at the shop should he need her. Rummaging through her closet for her brightest dress, Joanne chose a tailored yellow-and-white short-sleeved dress with pockets. One of her favorite work dresses. Plus, it said, "I'm happy and well-adjusted and ready to sell you a wedding dress."

Or at least that's what she hoped it said.

Joanne was the first at the boutique and opened up the shop. She headed to the computer in the back to check the material inventory and had already pulled up some designs she'd been working on when Nora showed up.

"You're really here."

"I said I would be. There's no point in staying home. Better to keep busy. This shop is all I have now."

Nora gave Joanne a quick hug. "No use in dwelling."

"I'd be bored at home."

Not if Hud were to show up every night and pretend they were in the Bahamas. But she'd probably ruined all that by throwing up. Anyway, he was a busy firefighter and they were headed toward the height of wildfire season. She didn't need to take up all his time with her drama.

"I'm not going to be the sad jilted bride of the bad luck boutique. I'm going to be the powerful and exalted jilted bride."

"You don't have to be the jilted bride at all."

Joanne held up her index finger. "Correct! I'm *so* much more than that."

"I wondered because Hud seemed so concerned about you."

"He is. He was. He won't be anymore." Then Joanne described Hud's surprise for her the previous night. The re-creation of the Bahamas.

Nora swooned. "That's like a scene from *It's a Wonderful Life*."

"It was *pretty* wonderful." Joanne gathered up her designs, pushing the image of a shirtless Hud out of her mind. "Well, I better get to work."

A couple of hours later, Joanne stood when she heard the store's door chime. They had no fittings on the books today so this might be a new client. It was rare to have walk-ins but maybe the rumors were making people curious about the jilted bride. She'd simply have to set them straight. When Joanne reached the front of the shop, she found her mother, Ramona, and her dear and oldest friend, Iris. Both were in their mid-seventies and had been friends for decades.

"Hi, honey," her mother said. "We were just headed to lunch and I brought you something."

It appeared to be a book, and when she handed it to Joanne, she read the title: *The 7 Stages of Grieving*.

"Now, I know what you're going to say—nobody died. But a *dream* died, honey, and that's almost the same thing."

"Except that…it's not." Joanne paged through the book. "Mom, really. I'm going to be fine."

"It's horrible, what happened." Iris, a small woman with her heart in her smile, said, "I would cast a spell on him but all I can do is knit. Our friend Diane is the one who uses spells."

"She does not, *Iris*." Ramona shook her head. "She's simply into extreme positive thinking."

"As in I'm positive I'm going to cast a spell on his ass," Iris said.

Joanne actually laughed. "Thanks for coming in, but unless you need a wedding dress… I should get back to my work."

"Don't you worry," Iris said, patting her hand. "I'm going to talk K.R. into renewing our vows. Then I'll come back and have you design a wedding dress."

"Aw, that's sweet. And when that happens, I'll be here. Thanks for the book, Mom."

But she wouldn't be desperate for business if she could maintain the status quo, even given superstitious Tilly. The Taylor wedding might be Joanne's only chance to have one of her dresses appear in a magazine, as the Taylor family was high profile in Fortune. Brenda and her mother, Patricia, had loved the design ideas, calling them original and romantic.

Yes, that was her. She loved romance. Someday maybe she'd get some of it in her real life, too. But for now, she would go with keeping romance alive in her designs. Joanne designed a few dresses each year and sewed each by hand. She had an industrial sewing machine in the back of the shop and kept a second in her spare room at home. Customers loved that each dress was unique and one of a kind. Joanne strived to make it so. It meant many hours, a touch of occasional carpal tunnel and eyestrain, but the finished product was always breathtaking.

When the door chimed again later that afternoon, Joanne was both surprised and pleased to see her son. "Hey, didn't your father pick you up from school today?"

"Yeah, but I asked him if I could skate over here and bring you something." Hunter dug in his backpack.

Matt was so lenient with their son. Joanne would have preferred him not to skate all over town, even with a helmet, but she'd been trying to let go a little bit more and not be such a helicopter parent. Influenced largely by Hud, of course, who had a lot to say about teenage boys.

Hunter brought out a pink box. "To celebrate."

Joanne blinked. "Celebrate?"

"It's a cupcake from Lawson's Bakery. You can celebrate getting rid of Chuck the Douche."

Then Hunter opened the box, displaying a white frosted cupcake with drizzles of caramel sauce. Her favorite. He sang, "Na Na Hey Hey Kiss Him Goodbye." Considering this was a crowd chant at sporting events, she had to wonder how long her son had been dying to sing this to Chuck. Hunter ended the chant with a little jig and spin on his skateboard.

Nora clapped and laughed with Hunter, fistbumping him. "Hey, little man, you're really good."

"Seriously?" Joanne didn't want anyone's pity but this wasn't good, either. "This isn't something to *celebrate*."

As a mother, she wanted to set a good example for her son and celebrating big breakups, especially when one person had been completely humiliated, didn't seem right, either. Besides, was he completely ignoring whatever feelings she might have about this, or sincerely trying to cheer her up? She took in her teenager's sharp intelligent gaze, so like his father's, and decided he meant well.

But later, they'd have a conversation about all this. She should have considered Hunter's feelings about Chuck more than she had. At the time, Hunter had been adjusting to his father separating from the Air Force and wanting more of a relationship with him. He'd gotten in trouble at school, tagging a fence with his friends, and generally been going through an "I hate everyone" stage. It had been a difficult time. She'd blamed it all on Matt re-inserting himself into Hunter's life and failed to take a deeper look at what Hunter might have noticed that she'd somehow missed.

Hunter shrugged. "Every day is a new day, or something like that. That's what you always tell me. Pick yourself up and try again. See? I listen."

Oh right. Busted. "You're right. It's a new day. I'll eat this for dessert tonight."

"Promise you'll break your diet?"

"Yeah." She'd dug into that wedding cake pretty fiercely but that was uncommon for her.

To Hunter, she was the boring parent. If it sometimes felt she'd been on a health food kick her entire life, it had actually only been the past decade. She'd banned junk food from her home because of her son. All the fun had gone out of her life, too. Then Matt had wanted to spend more time with Hunter. Now suddenly Joanne didn't have control over everything Hunter did or ate anymore, but that was simply expected since he was a teenager. Sixteen, and on his way to a driver's license. She shuddered when she thought of how a young person's life could change with one decision made in a weak moment. It was the reason she'd started talking safe sex with her son early on.

Every once in a while, though she loved her son with all her heart, she allowed herself to imagine what her life might have been like had she not been a teenage mother. Maybe she and Hudson would have gotten back together eventually and been one of those "I married my high school sweetheart" stories she loved reading about. But once she'd found out about her pregnancy, she'd had to accept that she and Hud were done forever. Her focus had to be on her son and their life together.

Being a single mom was the hardest thing she'd ever done, and though she wanted more kids, the next time she'd need a partner to rely on daily. Because she'd never want to raise a child on her own again.

"Are you absolutely sure?" Hudson stared at their probie, whose forehead had broken out in a sweat. "Be sure."

"I mean…pretty sure."

"Pretty sure is not good enough," Hudson said. "This is important. Life or death."

One more moment of intense pressure, and J.P., the probie, folded. "I'm out."

He laid his cards down on the poker table.

"Wise decision, son," Alex, the engine driver said, as he revealed his full house.

"Damn you, Alex." Hudson threw his cards. "Guess I'm dead."

Morbidly, their firehouse called their poker game

life or death. But this was nothing to some of the jokes they shared to deal with the high-pressure stakes of actual life or death.

"Let me see your cards." Alex frowned, turning them over.

He saw clearly the big fat nothing that Hud had. Then Alex turned J.P.'s cards over, revealing a better hand than Hud's. He crossed his arms, feeling a smirk coming on.

"Never play poker with LT again, J.P. You're not ready," Alex said. "Guy has the best poker face I've ever seen."

Hudson supposed that was true enough. He'd carefully calibrated his life to reveal nothing. Zero. Zip. He'd also pared life down to the bare essentials, simplifying everything: women, sex, food, sleep. In that order. Never love. Hell no. He'd tried that once, and almost wound up giving her away on her wedding day. That had been a close call. It probably didn't help that he'd never updated Jo on how he felt. How he'd apparently always feel, given that he couldn't seem to shake her no matter how hard he tried.

And he did try.

The great irony was that Hudson Decker, ladykiller and serial dater, was still hung up on his first love. Should any of his men ever find out how long he'd had it bad for her, the ribbing would never end. But damn, seeing her body so exposed shook him. He hadn't expected to feel so turned on. The way she'd looked in that two-piece swimsuit was an image he couldn't un-see. Nor did he want to. Ever. Jo always dressed conservatively in dresses and rarely even in jeans and shorts. Seeing her that close to naked had him pulling every resource he had to stay away. In her drunken state, he wondered how much she'd remember about their conversation.

Because like an idiot, he'd presented himself as an option. Shocked, she'd gazed at him through her tipsy haze. Brought up all the women he'd dated over the years. Apparently not noticed that he'd never been serious about one of them. Or maybe she *had* noticed, and figured he was still the same sixteen-year-old that broke up with her when she'd helped him discover the wonders of sex. Jackass move on his part, sure. Hud had been solidly in the friend zone for years. When Chuck had shown up in her life, Hud had tried to dissuade her from getting serious with him. But Jo claimed she was ready for something permanent, and Chuck was that safety and security she'd looked for. Hud believed that Chuck was the kind of guy who rode under the radar with women, a player who wasn't obvious about it. In other words, an expert.

The station alarm went off, announcing a house fire. Everyone moved lightning fast, Hud nearly kicking the poker table out of his way. It was wildfire season and a simple house fire could mean disaster depending on the location. Using the laptop he used as the LT, Hudson scoped out the address, relieved to see the home was located in town and not near any open fields. Fortune being a town with strict growth guidelines set by the city council years ago, there were still dry, open parcels of land in the strangest of places. Next to a liquor store. Abutted to a block of single-family homes. It made wildfire season particularly dicey around Wildfire Ridge.

Speaking through their headsets, they exchanged information on the closest fire hydrant and prepared the process. Hud would access point of entry. The rest of the crew would fall back and set up hoses and the engine ladder if needed. But when they pulled up to the address, a senior citizen stood on the front lawn appearing in zero distress. She waved at them happily.

Hudson had a bad feeling about this.

"It's Widow Diaz," Alex said.

"Crap." Hudson exited first and met her on the lawn. "Where's the fire?"

"It's Puggy. Poor baby is stuck under the house again. I knew you wouldn't come unless I said I had a fire."

"Mrs. Diaz, you can't keep doing this," Hudson chastised while he waved to the others the all clear. "We've talked about this."

"I know, but I can't stand his pitiful wailing."

"Told you to call *me* next time, and not the entire fire department."

But his warnings wouldn't work when she knew that Hudson wasn't going to report her as wasting the town's valuable resources. Growing up, she'd been like a grandmother to him.

"I would have called you, but I knew you were at work."

Hud pulled off his gear. "This is the last time."

With that, Hudson crawled under the house, calling the ridiculous name. "Puggy." It was worse than Coco. The stupid senseless dog hadn't yet figured out that he could get stuck down here while chasing whatever critter he was after. A terror mix, oh excuse him, *terrier* mix, he had anxiety issues and liked to bite the hand that rescued him. Swearing and cursing, Hud met all of the spiders, using his flashlight to shine the light on their little homes. Thank God he wasn't an arachnophobe. Or claustrophobic.

"C'mere, you SOB." Hud reached the dog and tugged on his collar, hauling him out. "I've told you this before, but I'll say it again. If you get in, you can get out."

Hud emerged with Puggy and handed him over to Mrs. Diaz. "Last time, right?"

She accepted her dog happily. "Oh thank you, Hudson. You're the sweetest boy. I knew that from the time you were six years old. I don't care how big or tall you are, you're still my sweet boy. And if you come over tomorrow, I'll have brownies for you."

Now *that* he would welcome. No one ever baked

for him. His parents had retired to Florida. Jo was a complete health nut and the women he dated weren't interested in domesticity.

A large part of the reason he dated them.

"Look into that chicken wire fence we talked about before," Hudson said as he waved goodbye and joined the guys, who were all checking their phones.

"Back to the station," Hudson said, gathering up the gear he'd taken off and carrying it back to the truck.

"Oh no. Here comes trouble. It's our favorite badge bunny, but she only has eyes for Hud." Alex snorted.

"Wow," J.P. the probie breathed, staring over Hudson's shoulder.

Hudson turned to watch Grace Smoker walking toward them. "Wow" was right. She was gorgeous, long dark straight hair down to her back. Long legs that she had no compunction in displaying often, in short shorts that left little to the imagination. Today she wore a pair of those shorts with a tight tie-dyed tank top. It was the kind she made and regularly sold at the Mushroom Mardi Gras in town every year.

"Hey, guys," she said. "Everything okay here?"

"We're good," Hudson said. "Packing it up now."

"Thanks, whatever you did." She reached up to touch his shoulder.

Funny, he felt… Nothing.

That's because I want Jo. I can't think of anyone but her.

Except he didn't want to be the rebound guy, did he? Did it count when he was also the first guy? Maybe all the others had been the rebound guys. Well, he could tell himself that. Wouldn't necessarily make it true. All this time, Jo had been looking for stability in her life and he'd been waiting, he supposed.

"Do me a favor?" Hud asked Grace now as he heard the engine ladder start up.

"Anything," she breathed.

"Check in on her every once in a while." He nudged his chin in the direction of Mrs. Diaz's home. "She's alone too much."

"Did she call you about Puggy?" Grace went hand on hip and tossed her hair back. "I told her not to bother you. You have real fires to attend to. It's wildfire season."

"Wait. She asked *you* for help first?"

She had the decency to look chastised and stuck out her lower lip. "There are spiders under there."

Hud had a little shiver of the unwelcome kind. She looked ridiculous and sounded even meaner. Not that he'd expect her to crawl under there herself, but how about calling on one of the many men who would love nothing more than to please her? Hudson had heard she was dating the new deputy in town. She could have called him, but then again, maybe she'd wanted Mrs. Diaz to call the fire department out. There were so many problems with that, Hud didn't know where to begin. First, Grace knew better. She wasn't helpless. Far from it.

And she was still standing in front of him, waiting.

He scratched at his chin. "Something I can do for you, Grace?"

"Now that you mention it, how about that date you keep promising me?"

"Yeah, how about it, LT?" Alex yelled. "Let's get going. Ask her out and get it over with."

J.P. was suddenly at Hudson's elbow. "Or if you're not interested…" He cleared his throat. "Sir."

"Aw, aren't you cute?" Grace winked. "But Hudson and I have a little thing going on."

"We do not."

Hudson clapped J.P. on the back and pushed him back to the rig. "We're on the city's dime. Make your dates on your own time, probie."

And with that, Hud hopped on the rig and they drove away.

Chapter Six

A week past the wedding that never was, the phone calls checking to see whether the boutique was still open had dwindled to one per day. Some thought she'd never recover from the shock and might seek a different profession. Otherwise, how could she get through each day surrounded by all the reminders? She assured everyone that no, she wasn't selling the shop, she was fine, working hard on new designs and ready to sew her butt off.

Today she wore her cool navy blue sweater dress with the short fleurette-covered sleeves and ties. It had a figure flattering defined waist. Joanne required all of her fashion mojo today because she'd moved up her appointment with the Taylors. She wanted to talk about fittings. They'd have to select from the designs she'd prepared for them soon and Joanne wanted to get to work right away. She had a feeling the wedding gown would take her months to get perfect for Brenda.

Hud still checked in with her every day via text, but he hadn't dropped by since the night he'd re-created the beach scene. Since the night she'd made a fool out of herself drinking too much and wearing too little.

She planned on calling him soon and suggesting a night bingeing on whatever current action-adventure series he was hooked on.

"Good morning," Nora said, when Joanne waltzed in carrying two cups of coffee from The Drip. "Is that coffee?"

"Just how you like it. Plenty of foam." Joanne handed Nora's over. "Tired?"

"Taking my work home with me," Nora said with a yawn. "I sewed every single pearl on Tilly's sleeves last night."

"I bet it looks wonderful."

They got to work, talking over the Taylor wedding and whether or not they'd also be entrusted with the bridesmaid's dresses, too. Two hours later, the Taylors didn't show for their appointment.

"This doesn't make any sense. They'd wanted to get in earlier, so I rescheduled."

"Maybe there was a mix-up," Nora said with a shrug. "You should call them."

"I will." But neither Brenda nor Patricia answered their phone, so Joanne left them each a message. Maybe they planned on keeping their first appointment after all, but it was rude not to call or show-up.

The rest of the morning progressed easily, with a visit from Eve, who came by to work on their website and back up their system. Just the thought that Joanne could lose any of her designs kept her awake some nights. Eve was a wiz with anything software related. After Eve left, Jill Davis showed up. Joanne had designed and sewed a sweetheart collar satin dress for the bride-to-be, but the alterations weren't quite done. They had it on the schedule, but Jill wasn't in any rush because the wedding had been postponed to after wildfire season. Since she owned the outdoor adventures camp on Wildfire Ridge and wanted to be married there, it made sense to wait a couple more months.

"Don't worry. I don't expect it to be done yet." Jill smiled. "I just…want to see it again."

"I understand." Joanne led her to the back of the boutique and carefully took her dress down. "Still in love with it?"

"I dream about it," Jill said, beaming.

"The day will be here soon."

"Three months. Three long months." She glanced

at Joanne. "I was so sorry to hear about…what happened. Are you okay?"

Joanne dismissed it with a wave. "I'm fine. These things happen."

Although that wasn't exactly true. She racked her brain to come up with the name of a bride, any bride, that she'd ever known to be jilted.

She came up with no one, but this was a small town.

"Oh good. I'm glad you're okay. Because I was going to ask about colors for cummerbunds. The tux is black and Sam will wear anything I tell him to wear."

"Good man." Joanne led her to the color swatches. "Oh my. This green would really bring out Hud's eyes."

"Sam's eyes are blue," Jill said, disregarding the fact Joanne had called her fiancé by another man's name. "The most beautiful dark blue."

Quickly, Joanne paged to the blue colors. What was wrong with her lately? "I forgot Hud has blue eyes."

"Sam," Jill said kindly and a bit dreamily.

Oh. My. God. This had to stop. She had to get Hudson out of her head! Like now.

Jill, caught in her own little world, thank God, went on. "I'm going to be Jill Davis-Hawker. Or maybe just Jill Hawker. I haven't made up my mind yet."

"I say go with Jill Hawker," Nora said, glaring at Joanne. "*Sam* and Jill Hawker. I love it."

Jill sighed.

"Sam," Joanne repeated. *SamSamSamSam*.

Hudson.

After Jill left, Nora turned to Joanne, hands on hips. "Want to tell me what's going on?"

Joanne didn't know where to begin. "I wish I knew. It's just…something happened."

"I'm guessing it has to do with Hud."

"The other night, and the Bahamas re-creation."

"That sounded very sweet but Hud has always done nice things like that for you. Right?"

Yes, he had. But again, this had seemed different. Physical and intense. At least on her part. "I kind of…lingered on his back when I put suntan lotion over it. And he has a pretty amazing back."

Nora wrinkled her nose. "I'm sorry? You put suntan lotion on? Inside?"

"Yes! We really got into our re-creation."

"That's for sure."

"And I wore my red bikini."

The significance of that statement would not be lost on Nora. Joanne had specifically chosen that bikini to seduce her husband. Nora had helped her pick it out. Joanne had others, too, to be worn in *public*. She tended to be conservative and the red suit was not.

"Why would you wear that one unless you…" Nora quirked a brow.

"I know! Why did I? And why do I keep *thinking* about him? This is ridiculous. I was just jilted and the last thing I need is another rocky relationship. And Hud and I… Well, we didn't work before."

"When you were sixteen, you mean?" Nora crossed her arms and smirked. "Shock."

"The thing is, I obviously wanted him to see me in the swimsuit." Joanne closed her eyes. "Maybe I wanted to feel attractive again. Desirable."

"Or maybe you have the hots for your best friend. Because seriously, he's the total package. Looks, personality, rockin' body, charm, everything. And, in case you haven't noticed, Joanne, he's *crazy* about you."

Those words hit her in unexpected quiet and private places she didn't often explore anymore. Now it felt like a thread had been pulled. She was no longer able to ignore that there was still a pull between them. A connection. But there was a good reason they weren't together. Make that a few good reasons.

"No. He isn't. And he might be the total package, but he's never been serious about anyone. That tells me he's still not ready to settle down with one woman. Maybe not even capable of it. At least, that's what I suggested to him when he brought it up."

"When he brought *what* up?"

"Oh, I guess I forgot that part. Did I mention I'd

been drinking on an empty stomach? Hud started in on me on how I pick the wrong men. I reminded him of my reasonable wish list. He told me he fits every item on it." She took a breath. "And he does."

Nora smiled, wider this time. "In-te-res-ting."

"That's when I told him that he's excluded because he's my best friend *and* he likes women. Too many of them. He took great offense to that."

"Look, it sounds like you two need to talk."

"We're avoiding each other, I think. I miss my best friend. But now I have a problem because I just noticed he's superhot."

"Seriously? You *just* noticed this?"

"It's kind of like I wore blinders for years when it came to Hud. I tried not to think about him... sexually."

But ever since those sinewy muscles bunched under her fingertips... Maybe it had been the alcohol, the beach re-creation, or the way he looked in those board shorts.

"He takes care of me," Joanne said. "And it would be too easy to get sucked into thinking that it's more than a friendship. I can't do that to myself. I've been through enough. What I need now is security. Safety. So, I'm going to forget about relationships for a while and focus on business."

"I say go for it!" Nora said. "Whatever it turns into, a fling or forever, you two will get through it. Nothing will ever destroy your friendship."

Joanne wished that were true. But even if this wasn't the "bad luck boutique" it wasn't the "good luck boutique," either.

She'd have to continue to make her own luck.

Hud was in the meeting from hell. Seated across from him in his office was Chief Fire Inspector Richard Ferguson, Battalion Chief Kevin Murphy and Sheriff Ryan Davis. They had just entered the height of wildfire season with brush fires in remote forest areas that were spreading due to high winds and had reason to be concerned. California wildfire season didn't peak in the summertime. It peaked in September and October, following the dry season and before the start of their rainy one.

Wildfire Ridge was known for wildfires, hence the name, but they'd been controlled for years. A few months ago, one of the deputies had caught a kid throwing a lit rag into a Dumpster and they'd arrested their teenage firebug. Since then, it could be said they were all a little skittish. A house fire, even an accidental car fire could be disastrous, but more often than not, all that was required was high winds, hellish heat, open land and dry tinder.

On top of all that, due to budget cuts they had a huge shortage of federal firefighters. So, they were all doing what they could with state and county Cal Fire. Hud was already shorthanded due to a few of his men traveling to volunteer at the latest forest fire outside of Yosemite. To compound matters, the inspector wanted to discuss the latest place not fit to pass his airtight inspection, a local restaurant.

It was not a good day to be Hudson Decker.

A message flashed across his phone and he glanced at it in the middle of Ferguson's diatribe.

Jo: Movie tonight after your shift? I'll let you pick what we watch but I'm picking up fish tacos for dinner.

Yeah, so eventually he'd learned to appreciate *fish* tacos. Jo said fish was good for his heart. The irony wasn't lost on him, since she's the one who had broken it in the first place. But that was years ago. They were both kids.

He hadn't gone to her house in a few days, giving her space. But she'd officially gone back to work full-time, a good sign. She was moving on from "two-buck" Chuck. Now the question was whether or not she would be ready to move on with Hud into brand-new territory. Jo and Hud, the reboot. It wasn't that crazy an idea. He wouldn't screw it up again this time.

Because the night of the beach recreation, something had shifted between them. And he'd made a surprising decision. This time he wasn't putting his best friend back together so some other man could have her. This was his moment.

After the tense meeting, which gave him a thousand action items, Hud got back to his crew and made them go through drills. J.P. needed them more than anyone else, but they could all benefit from the practice.

Later, done with his forty-eight-hour shift, Hud showered and changed at the station. By the time he got to Jo's, the sun had started to ebb. He found her sitting on one of the steps leading to her porch, dressed in a short blue dress, her mood seeming to match the color.

He took a seat on the step next to her. "What's wrong?"

She turned to him and the absolute look of despair in her eyes drop-kicked his stomach. "I think my shop is going to be known as the bad luck boutique."

"That's ridiculous. What does that even mean?"

"It means I'm bad luck to prospective brides. The Taylors didn't show up, and people are calling to ask if I'm okay and still open for business."

"Maybe they thought you'd gone on the honeymoon without him."

She seemed to consider it. "No. It's just in the way they talk to me. The pity. Today at the fish taco place, the waitress hugged me and cried. Cried! I don't want to be known as the jilted bride, owner of the bad luck boutique."

He took her hand and squeezed it. "And you won't be. It may take people a little time. Why would they think one has anything to do with the other? I don't get that."

"That's because you're a man and you don't know how superstitious brides are about their wedding day."

"How superstitious are we talking?"

"Some down to the date they pick to get married. A lucky number." She sighed. "How am I supposed to convince everyone that I've got good luck again?"

"Start dating someone new." Even though that was in his best interest, he didn't see how it could hurt the situation. "Be happy and show it."

"Who should I date?"

"Me."

She pulled back, searching his eyes. "You're not teasing me."

"No. I mean this. I'm putting myself in the running."

"You…and me?"

"Besides the fact that I do make every one of your list requirements, I also know how you take your coffee. Exactly three tablespoons of soy milk. I know that you prefer that your vanilla ice cream and chocolate brownie cake never touch each other, lest they contaminate each other."

"If I'm going to splurge on cake and ice cream, which I only do with you, I need to take my time and enjoy them—"

"Individually."

She laughed, and he didn't miss the fact that she shifted closer to him, so that they now sat hip to hip. "I'm sorry for what I said the other night."

"I get it. I'm sure I don't seem like the most stable guy when it comes to relationships."

"Not with your recent past. But could you... I mean, do you think you can be exclusive? With someone?" She set her hand on his thigh.

Jo's signature move. He recognized it, and his skin hadn't felt this tight in over a decade. Working out as much as he did, his heart never spiked anymore the way it did now.

He swallowed. "With you? Yeah, I could. Definitely."

Exclusivity would not be difficult with Jo. Not when he'd watched her date other men over the years, realizing that she might be with him if only their timing hadn't been so off.

She smiled. Then she leaned toward him, closer, till she was nearly in his lap. He would have taken the lead, but he wanted, he needed this to be her idea. She had to be sure because they weren't going back. Not if he had anything to do with it. He'd make this work. This time he was ready for them. For her. It would be his mission to prove it. One hand in his hair, she tugged his lips to hers and kissed him. Letting her take the lead, he then responded with the fierceness his body felt at having her so close. She opened to him and their tongues tangled in a blazing heat.

She broke the kiss and they simply stared at each other for several seconds.

"Well, that's still there, isn't it?" Jo finally said.

"I didn't have any doubts." He pressed his forehead to hers. "You asked me if I could be exclusive and I gave you the truth. Now let me ask you something. Are you ready to try this again, you and me? Because I won't be your rebound guy."

"I understand how you feel," she whispered. "But you won't be the rebound guy because you were the *first* guy."

"And I screwed that up. It won't happen again."

"Hud, if you felt this way, why didn't you say something sooner?" She pulled back to meet his gaze.

He wasn't sure even he knew the answer to that question. Jo had seemed happy enough without him, focused primarily on her son for years. Easier not to rock the boat, and yeah, fear, large and gripping, that he'd hurt her again or she'd hurt him. That maybe deep down he didn't know *how* to love her.

"Maybe it had to be the right moment." But he wasn't letting her off easy. "What about you?"

"I don't know. It didn't seem possible for so long. We didn't want the same things. You never seemed interested in slowing down...with all of your dating.

And family is important to me. I always have to put my son first."

"Family is important to me, too."

Hud's parents had moved to Florida, but he still visited them every chance he could. He was a late-in-life child with no siblings and had been somewhat spoiled. But he didn't blame his parents for any of that. It had taken Hud a while to grow up and realize how much his actions affected others. That decisions he'd made in the heat of the moment would affect the rest of his life.

Jo had felt like family because she'd been a part of his life for so many years. Hunter felt like his family, too.

Hud loved Jo's son, but he was still sensitive about Matt Conner. Hud understood he was a good guy and had never shirked from his responsibilities toward Jo and their son. But it was still difficult to be around him at times because he'd been the one to permanently alter Jo's life. She'd changed because of him, as their child grew inside her.

And Matt didn't even love Joanne. Never had.

"I loved the way you took care of Hunter like he was the only thing that mattered in your world. You gave everything up for him."

"Maybe I gave up too much. When it was finally time for my own life to begin again, I had an emotional disconnection in my brain. I told myself who

I *should* want. Who was safe. Not necessarily who I really wanted."

She met his gaze, squeezed his thigh.

He kissed her then, to seal it. To set in stone this was their second chance. Neither one of them came to this relationship as a blank slate. Not the way they'd been the first time. To his mind, this would only make them richer. Fuller. As long as they could shut the rest of the world out.

The kiss grew passionate, wild and hot. He tugged her closer, not able to get her close enough. Hud got hard, and he wanted in the house before they became someone's adult entertainment.

"Inside," he said, as he pulled her to her feet.

"Yes."

"Mom?"

They both froze on the top step and turned to the sidewalk.

The annoyed-sounding word had come out of Hunter, who now stood at the bottom of the first step, glaring at Hud. "What's going on?"

Jo pulled out of his arms. "Hud came by to…to…"

"Kiss your mother," Hud finished, not letting go of her hand.

"Gross!"

"Honey, what are you *doing* here?" Jo asked.

"Forgot my History textbook," he said, storming past them. He slammed the screen door shut.

Jo sagged into Hud's open arms. "Oh my God.

He's been at his father's all this time and he just now comes to get his textbook?"

He chuckled. "I think we have a bigger problem."

"Yes, but I'm trying to ignore that."

"He'll get over it." His hand slid down her back, not wanting to give up contact just yet. But he'd have to leave her alone to deal with Hunter. He knew her well enough to know that she'd want it that way.

"I know, I know. Kids are resilient and all that." She met his gaze. "What do I tell him?"

"Tell him he's not scaring me away. No matter how hard he tries. I'm not going anywhere."

"Oh, Hud." She clung to him and he crushed her against his chest. "Is this really happening?"

"Yeah, and it's about time. Now go inside, talk to your son, and I'll see you tomorrow."

And with that he gave her one last kiss, then watched her walk inside before he headed home, happier than he could recall feeling in a decade.

Chapter Seven

"Hunter Matthew Conner!"

Now that Joanne was out of Hud's arms, she could think straight again. Her son had been incredibly rude to a man who'd been like a second father to him. Yes, sure, it had to have been a bit of a surprise to see her and Hud in a passionate embrace. She was a little embarrassed by that, because it had all gone out of control so quickly. But that's how it had once been between them and nothing had changed.

Hunter appeared in the doorway to his bedroom, holding a textbook. "Did he leave?"

"Yes, and did you have to be so rude to him? He's always been good to you. Taught you how to ride a bicycle, all the things your father didn't do because he wasn't around. Hud deserves a little more respect from you."

"Why? Is he going to be your *guy* now that Chuck's finally gone?"

Joanne crossed her arms. "I'm sorry you caught us like that, but I'm not going to discuss my love life with my teenage son. It's none of your business."

"Okay, great. Then it's none of your business that I'm going to enlist in the U.S. Marine Corps as soon as I graduate. I talked to Sam about it and he's going to give me some advice."

Hunter had brought out the heavy ammunition. His unrelenting desire to drive her to an early grave with worry. She'd thought it was just a stage but now she was concerned there was far more to her son's fascination with the military than a few video games. And no wonder. Their small town was filled with returning servicemen, including their sheriff, a Medal of Honor recipient.

"You should talk to Hud. He was a soldier, too." Hud would talk some sense into him. He'd do it for Joanne.

"And my dad was an Airman. But I'm still going to be a Marine."

"No need to rush into anything." Refusing to be intimidated, Joanne held her ground. "You'll apologize to Hud next time you see him."

"Fine!" Hunter threw his textbook on the couch.

"But I don't get why you need anyone. It's always been you and me and we did fine. Then Chuck the Douche came along and ruined everything. Now, you're going to date *Hud*? He's like my uncle, so that means he's…like your brother or something."

Joanne ignored that. Hud was nothing like a brother to Joanne and never had been. But she couldn't fault her son for operating in the dark with the little information he had. He'd been spared from the family drama of their past. The child who turned their three lives upside down didn't have to know the deep and complicated history she'd had with Hud. With Matt. He didn't have to know that in an alternate reality, she would have preferred for Hud to be his father and not Matt.

The words as to why she needed someone special in her life were on the tip of her tongue, but she couldn't say them.

You're leaving me soon. Whether it's the Marines or college, you're no longer a child. Pretty soon you won't need me at all. I need to have my own life. I want to be happy and in love again. Now I finally have a second chance with Hud.

"Let me drive you back to your dad's house." Joanne got her purse and keys.

"Maybe I could drive," Hunter said.

It was a calculated move on his part, made at a time when he thought he might have some leverage with her. He'd gotten his driver's permit, but the driving hours had been limited to rides with his father. Joanne was terrified of being in the car with Hunter at the wheel. She had to get over this fear but letting go was difficult. Her son was nearly a man now, as tall as his father. She'd lost an argument that Hunter shouldn't get his driver's license until he was seventeen, when teenage fatality rates dropped significantly. She'd done the research. But Hunter didn't want to hear about it, and he'd gotten Matt to side with him.

"Um…" Never let it be said that she wasn't any good at stalling.

"I've driven with everybody but you. I even drove with Sarah the other day. Really, Mom, I'm a good driver."

"I'm sure you are." She gnawed at her lower lip, chewing the rest of the lipstick off. Even Hud agreed that Joanne should let her son drive her a few places around town. Said it would ease her fears to see that he knew what he was doing.

Or reinforce her fears.

Still, she was surrounded on all sides by men who wanted her to let Hunter grow up. And she supposed that if she wanted him to respect the choices she made, she would have to start trusting him a little, too.

Like with her life. Gulp.

She tossed him the keys. "You're driving the speed limit and not a mile above it."

He caught the keys midair. "Hells yeah!"

Joanne strapped into her seat belt and made sure that Hunter did the same. She stuck out her hand. "Give me your phone."

"Why? It's in my pocket. Like I'm going to text with you sitting right next to me?" He snorted.

Her hand hadn't moved from its position. "I'll make sure you're not distracted by it buzzing in your pocket."

He pulled it out of his pants pocket and set it in her hand. "Here. Where's the trust?"

The fact he'd made such a big deal out of it told her that Matt and Sarah weren't insisting he do the same. Well, she'd have to address that issue with them at some point. Still, Hunter did drive reasonably well even if she did correct his position, reminding him to keep his hands at ten and two o'clock. Finally, thank you God, they arrived at Matt and Sarah's residence, and Joanne hopped out of the passenger door and came around the side.

"Thanks, Mom. I did okay, yeah?" Hunter climbed out and immediately put his hand out for his phone.

"You did. I'm very impressed at your speed limit consistency." She handed his phone over, bussed his cheek and had to stand on tiptoes and stretch to do so.

Once she was seated in the driver's seat, Hunter leaned in the window. "Sorry I said it was gross for Hud to be kissing you."

"That's okay. I understand this is tough for you.

And I don't know what's going to happen with me and Hud. This is all very new. It's just that you need to know… I *really* like him."

"I like him, too. He's hella better than Chuck for sure, but I still don't think you should date him."

Yeah, she didn't think it would be that easy. She nodded. "And you have a right to your opinion."

"Okay, then." He turned to go. "See ya!"

"Aren't you forgetting something?" She reached back and handed him the textbook.

He looked sheepish, accepting it. "Thanks."

"Study hard!"

Joanne started up the car and took off, wondering if Hunter really needed that textbook or if he'd come over to check up on her.

Here were a few vital facts about Joanne Michelle Brandt:

She loved lists.

She loved order.

Early on, she'd planned how many children she would have: girl, boy, girl. In that order.

College would be somewhere far away, preferably New York City, where she would study fashion design.

She'd wanted to marry Hudson Decker from the moment she laid eyes on him.

And when she was sixteen years old, she blew up her entire life plan.

So much for planning. How did the saying go? Life is what happens when you're busy making all your plans—or something like that. Joanne did not marry Hudson Decker, she did not go away for college, and she had one child, a boy. So far. And if she ever had any more, she now knew they would not be with a weasel-face, loser, no good, useless man like Chuck Ellis! Good riddance.

Yes, she was finally pissed. Beyond pissed. She didn't know which stage of grief she'd entered, but the anger that woke with her every morning was palpable. She felt it wrap around her neck and squeeze. She wanted to find Chuck, and—well, she didn't know what yet, but it was going to hurt him like hell. He was going to pay her back for every last cent she'd spent on the wedding. No, not even his *half* anymore, because it was his fault the wedding hadn't happened. That wasn't unreasonable.

And yet, when she thought that she'd be *married* to him now if he had shown up—that's when she got really spooked. She'd almost made the biggest mistake of her life. Because she didn't want to wind up alone. Now she had Hud again, telling her he wanted to make this thing work between them. He wasn't going anywhere—his words. It was like living her first dream, brought back to life. A dream she was too afraid to believe now because by now she understood plans didn't work out most of the time. But she and Hud, they *had* something. They always had. They had to work this time. Hunter would get over it, and as for everyone else? Of course, they'd be supportive.

When Matt married Sarah, Joanne's mother had finally given up on her hopes that eventually Joanne would do the right thing and marry the father of her son. *Thank you, Matt.*

Joanne had been kneeling for several minutes in the back of the shop working on Jill's wedding dress train and she rose now, rubbing her lower back. Her phone buzzed, and she reached for it to read a text from Hud:

Silver Saddle, tonight.

She smiled. Once, she'd thought of Hud as the love of her life, but for the past several years he'd been the fun of her life. If she was too tired to go out, he'd find an activity too difficult to resist. She hadn't been dancing in a long time.

She responded:

Maybe.

Hud: That wasn't a question.

"Sometimes I can't believe this is really happening," Joanne said to Nora, when she entered their back room, holding a dress wrapped in plastic. "Me and Hud."

Of course, she'd updated her friend and partner on everything: the kiss, the interruption, the talk with her son. Hud's revelation.

"I understand. To hear Hud say he'll be exclusive would shock anyone."

Panic tore through Joanne. "Why? You don't think he can do it?"

Nora held up her palm in the universal Stop sign. "Whoa, calm down. I didn't *say* that."

"But maybe he can't. And maybe it's too soon for me to be out in public kicking up my heels. I might be seen as coldhearted to be over Chuck so soon."

"Excuse me, but I thought the whole idea was to show everyone how over him you are and how happy you are now. The boutique depends on it. You want to set everyone straight. This is a good thing, not a bad thing. You've come to your senses and thank goodness Chuck stood you up. And I might add that just being seen with Hud is sort of a good luck charm."

All of that might be true, and Joanne was definitely over Chuck. Like a veil had been lifted from her eyes she saw why Hud and even Matt hadn't liked him. He was arrogant, told stories about himself in the third person and liked to feel sorry for himself. "Chuck didn't get picked for the first round of the draft." Morose, he'd fish for compliments. She couldn't think of a single redeeming quality about Chuck, other than the fact that he was reasonably good-looking, and he'd been immediately interested in a commitment and settling down. Having kids.

Frankly, she was going to give herself a pass because he was gone so much on the road with his minor league team that every time she saw him she'd forgotten what irritated her about him. He'd always been on his best behavior with her, but he'd never been in Hud's league. It's just that she'd believed for a time she was also out of Hud's league, other than as a best friend.

She'd seen the women he dated. All model types and beauty queens. She'd turned into a boring single mother with a teenage kid and that didn't attract a whole lot of good men. It certainly hadn't attracted Hud, or so she'd thought.

But if she felt the pressure, the importance of making this work, what could that be doing to Hud? "He wants to take me to the Silver Saddle tonight."

"And he's such a good dancer, too."

"He's pretty proud of that." He'd spent much of his time on the dance floor collecting women's phone numbers.

She definitely didn't like thinking of all the women he'd been with, serious or not. There were bound to be comparisons. She'd always found the women nice enough, but Joanne was not in the mood to be compared to anyone.

She changed the subject. "Have the Taylors returned any of our calls?"

"No," Nora said, frowning.

It was official. They were avoiding Joanne. Whether or not it was because they suddenly hated her designs and had found someone else, or they'd bought into unfounded wedding superstitions, there was no way of knowing without first talking to them. If they were going to go with another designer, the least they could do was pull up their big girl panties and tell Joanne.

"I don't understand. They paid for my designs. We just need their final choice and we need to start sewing soon. It's rude not to at least return my calls."

"Agreed. Listen, let's talk about this tomorrow. Tonight, you go dancing." Nora rubbed Joanne's back. "You deserve it."

Nora was right. Joanne picked up her phone and texted back.

See you there, cowboy.

Dancing a little bit never hurt anyone.

Hud had spent his day off doing handyman jobs around his house and looking in on his next-door elderly neighbor, Mrs. Suarez. When he'd been gone, she'd left a note pinned to his door that her thermostat was broken.

She owned the home so there wasn't a landlord to call, and her children didn't live nearby. Hud looked in on her and took care of odd jobs around the house.

"I think I need a new one," Mrs. Suarez said. "I went to turn on the heater and…nothing."

Granted, as they moved toward autumn their nights were cooler but Hud didn't think it was time to turn on the heater. They were still having some 80 plus degree weather during the day. Still, Mrs. Suarez was on a blood thinner, so she got cold easier. He would suggest she put on a sweater, but instead he would fix the thermostat.

She was already digging through her purse when Hud tapped on it and realized she probably just needed a new battery.

Mrs. Suarez handed him a 100-dollar bill. "And keep the change, mijo."

"No need. Think you just need a new battery."

She blinked. "It takes batteries?"

He smiled. "I've got some next door."

"Let me pay you for them." She tried shoving the bill in his direction but he wasn't taking one cent from a widow on social security.

"I'll be right back with some batteries."

"Ay, que Dios te bendiga. Es un angel."

Hud wished he understood Spanish. She seemed

to think he should. He smiled and nodded. He recognized "Dios" in there, meaning "God" so he figured it couldn't be bad.

A few minutes later he'd replaced the batteries, accepted some fresh baked cookies, and moved on to replacing the sheetrock in his laundry room. Rachel had once trapped herself in there for a few hours and tried to gnaw her way out.

Ever since he'd adopted her, it seemed like his house was falling apart. Like Jo, he had a list now. It involved everything he had to replace because Rachel had either chewed it, shit or peed on it. He almost didn't have enough time to fix all the damage.

He took a bite of his cookie and picked up a new piece of cut sheetrock. Rachel belly crawled to him, sniffing, as she always did when she smelled food.

"*My* cookie. Haven't you done enough damage here?"

She sighed as if wounded and lay on the floor beside him.

Lately on his days off he'd been picking up a shift or two as one of the guides at Wildfire Ridge Outdoor Adventures. He'd been a regular on the ridge where it was situated. As part of the team that performed regular controlled burns, he'd made friends with the owner, Jill Davis, and her fiancé, who both ran the place. Jill had opened the business this summer and hired former military men as guides. Hud had been a regular on the zip lines and rock climbing.

When Sam casually asked if Hud would like to take a shift on his days off, he'd jumped at the chance.

Yeah, he usually took it easy on his days off or managed to have fun. Ride his motorcycle, zip line, rock climb. For the most part, he'd enjoyed being solo. Accepted it. He was a free and single man, after all, unencumbered by obligations. By family. He'd had plenty of money, enough to put some away for the future. That's the way he'd enjoyed life for years. And that had been enough until recently.

But today, no matter what he did around the house, sheetrock or stuck sliding glass door, he thought of Joanne. The night before when *she'd* kissed him first. He hadn't expected that. But she'd opened the door and he'd waltzed right in. And he'd been just as gobsmacked by that kiss as the first time he'd ever seen her, convinced at the time that he'd never seen anything more beautiful in his life. She'd had her blond hair longer then and an easy friendly smile. Everyone loved her. She was wicked smart and voted Most Likely to Succeed at Anything.

He'd taken care of her virginity and his in the same night. Not a cross to bear for him, to be sure, but the act had meant a lot more to her. She'd told him she loved him and started to plan their lives together. It freaked him out. Seeking distance, he'd broken up with her. Temporarily, he'd said, trying to be reasonable.

Both were too young. Blah blah blah. Well, he'd

been sixteen, so he no longer blamed himself. Much. And he'd started to date immediately, to show her that he'd meant what he said. Next thing he knew, she'd been on a date with the big man on campus, Matt Conner. He was the male version of Joanne. Successful at everything he attempted. Highly intelligent. Headed straight to the Ivy Leagues.

Then Joanne got pregnant and decided she would keep the baby. Hud was hurt and pissed, though he had no right to be. He hadn't planned on their breakup lasting forever, hadn't planned much of anything at all, actually. Forever, or so it seemed to his teenage brain, happened anyway.

When he realized he'd lost all hope of a future with Joanne, he'd driven too fast one night, lost control, and crashed his father's car. The injuries hadn't killed him, but they'd acquainted him with the fire and rescue department of Fortune Valley. He'd spent two weeks in the hospital and Jo came to visit nearly every day. She hadn't made excuses or blamed him for pushing her away. In classic Jo fashion, she took on all the responsibility and said she'd be having a child earlier than planned. That she didn't love Matt Conner. She wasn't marrying him. But obviously, she was going to be very busy for the next few years.

But she'd forever be Hud's friend.

Finished with the sheetrock, Hud picked up his tools and cleaned up.

Joanne had never mentioned the *L* word to him

again. He hadn't deserved her love anyway. Not after what he'd done. They graduated, Joanne had her son and Hud joined the Army. He went to fight because from that point on and for years, he'd been a pretty angry dude. Angry at himself. Angry at the world. He'd concluded war would give him a good place to channel all that aggression.

Yeah, he was *that* stupid.

Thank God for years and maturity because even though he'd never been in a serious relationship, he was probably healthier emotionally than most people he knew. There were no lies or deceit between him and other women. No false encouragement or games. Every relationship was always aboveboard and neat. Compartmentalized. There were months he'd go without a woman and he was good with that, too.

He'd learned to be the supportive always-single friend to Jo. He learned to push any desire for her out of his mind and heart. Mostly, it hadn't worked. He'd just faked it well because she was too important to him. Too important to cut out of his life. Any other guy in his position he'd call lame for accepting scraps, but Hud took whatever Jo was willing to give him. For years it had been a deep friendship that only made him love her more.

Yeah, he loved her. Still.

It didn't hurt to admit it anymore, which had to mean he'd made some kind of progress.

Chapter Eight

Hud arrived at the Silver Saddle, the only honky-tonk in their small town. Though many of his friends and some of the women he'd previously dated tried to drag him inside, he made excuses and said he'd see them later. He paced outside until Jo showed up and he walked to her car to meet her. This night would be special because he had plans. Plans to show her that he was in 100 percent. With no regrets.

She looked damned sexy wearing her cowgirl boots and a white sleeveless dress with a full skirt that hit above her knees. Already she was killing him, and they weren't even on the dance floor.

"C'mon," he said, taking her hand.

"Big news." She walked beside him. "I let Hunter drive with me the other night."

He stopped. "Finally?"

"It wasn't as bad as I thought it would be. You're right—it's nice to see that he knows what he's doing. But I'm still worried because of the texting and driving thing. Every teenager believes they're invincible."

He didn't particularly like the flow of this conversation, which sounded too much like a rehashing of their past. "Don't worry. He's a smart kid."

"Sure, he's smart. I'm still going to worry. Everyone acts as if I'm being unreasonable and irrational. But you know better than anyone else that I'm *not*."

The words felt like a punch to the gut. They hadn't talked about this in years. He'd calmly tried to ignore the fact that her fears of her son learning to drive were entirely justified. Because of him.

"Jo," he said softly.

"I mean it. Someone I loved very much almost died in a car accident. When he was *sixteen*."

It killed him that he was still influencing her negative thoughts even now, years later. It was as if he'd painted on her youth with bold, broad brush strokes that were not entirely faded. Unfortunately, the picture was ugly. It was one of fear and abandonment. Pain. He'd done that to her.

And he'd never been able to fix it.

He tugged her into his arms. "He's Matt's son. He won't make my mistakes."

"Making Matt's mistakes wouldn't be much better."

"He'll make his own. We all do."

She bumped her head against his chest. "Look at me, with all the impressive small talk. I'm so boring. I'm the mother of a teenage boy who's about to get his driver's license. What am I even doing here?"

"You're here to dance and show everyone you're over that jackass. Now." Holding her hand, he walked her into the saloon.

The Silver Saddle was a classic honky-tonk owned by an Alabama native, Jimmy Hopkins and his wife, Trish. Like so many in their town, they were former military who'd found their second calling. The place was a classic throwback, with an often-broken-down mechanical bull in the corner they'd nicknamed Bertha. There were peanut shells on the floor. A stage was set up in the back where a live band played in front of a large dance floor perfect for line dancing. This was where Hud had discovered he'd actually liked country music. Or maybe what he'd really enjoyed was the challenge of learning the choreography of a line dance.

"Hiya, Hud," Jimmy said from behind the bar. "Hey there, Joanne. Long time."

Hud led them to the bar to fist-bump with Jimmy

and he ordered them both drinks. Jo took a seat on the bar stool next to him and took a pull of her beer.

Not two seconds later, Trish, Jimmy's wife, walked up to Jo and hugged her. "Oh my God, Joanne. I'm so *sorry*. Are you okay?"

"Yes, yes. I'm totally fine." She seemed to awkwardly accept the hug, patting Trish's back.

"Did you know Jimmy and I broke up a few weeks before our wedding day? Obviously, we got back together. Really, it was all my fault... By the way, I never liked Chuck anyway..." She went on and on, and after a bit Hud tuned her out.

He exchanged a look with Jimmy. After Joanne had assured Trish one thousand—or so it seemed—more times that she was doing well, thank you, Trish finally seemed to accept this. At that moment, the band began to play Tim McGraw's "A Real Good Man." The dance floor exploded with couples, and Hud tugged Jo on to the dance floor.

"Let's *show* Trish how well you're doing."

They fell into a natural rhythm on the dance floor as she kept in step with him. Jo smiled up at him, and he hoped her earlier worries were forgotten for now. Her hands came around his neck, announcing to everyone that tonight wasn't exactly business as usual for them.

Her hands were soft and warm. Despite the fact that he took pride in knowing how to two-step, he missed a step while staring at her full bottom lip. He recovered quickly, and pulled her closer, hands settling low on her waist. Then lower still.

Dancing might be mostly about form, but it also involved understanding your partner. It was about leading, but also sensing where she wanted to go and taking her there. Moving in time with the music. Recovering when you missed a step.

Hud had done that for most of his life, just not always on a dance floor.

She met his gaze, never missing her footing. Completely in time with his movements. Satisfaction spiked through him that this beautiful and wonderful woman was in his arms. He didn't deserve her.

The public nature of this night was new territory, but it also felt natural. Easy. Comfortable.

"Are you okay?" he asked, one hand drifting up and down her spine in a gentle caress.

He wanted to know that she was here tonight and in this relationship 100 percent. That there would be no regrets to jumping in full throttle with him. This relationship might seem quick to some but considering they'd been circling each other for over a decade, not so much. Not for him.

She was his. And he was hers, if she'd have him.

"I'm so good." She tilted her head and rose on tiptoes. "I'm claiming you, Hudson Decker. Tonight, you're mine."

"Always have been."

Heart slamming against his ribcage he took his

cue and bent to kiss her full on the lips in the middle of the crowded dance floor. As the song ended, he broke the kiss, conscious of the hush that had come over the room. But unable to break contact completely, he pressed his forehead to hers.

"If anyone has any questions about us now," Jo said, "they just haven't been paying attention."

He would have to agree.

Joanne strutted off the dance floor with Hud, trying to ignore the looks she received from some of the women in the room. They ranged from happily surprised, to envious, and dialed straight into angry ex-girlfriend territory. Well, too bad. They'd all had their chance with him and now it was her turn. Hud looked so good on the dance floor, moving with such practiced ease, holding her with confidence. When he'd swung her around in his capable hands, she'd entirely forgotten that she was the boring mother of a teenager and remembered that first and foremost she was a woman.

And the Tim McGraw song was perfect for Hud. He might be a "bad boy," but he was also a good man. A regular hero firefighter. A leader in the community. He'd come such a long way from the rebellious boy that wanted to drive fast cars and break a lot of hearts. They danced a few more songs, then headed back to the bar for another drink and this time when

Trish approached Joanne and pulled her to the side it was with zero pity in her eyes.

"Oh, girlfriend, way to bounce back! Hang on to that one."

Turning away from Trish, she spied Hud at the bar, casually reaching for his wallet from his back jeans pocket. He caught her eye as if he'd sensed she was looking, smirked and winked.

"Thanks. I better get back."

"Run."

She didn't run, not her, no sir, but she did rather quickly dash to his side. "I'm having so much fun. We should do this more often."

He waggled his eyebrows. "Yeah?"

The band had started another song, "Friends in Low Places," and it had become hard to hear above the music. "I said we should do this more often."

"I know," he said, or she thought he said. She wasn't all that skilled at reading lips.

Her skills lay elsewhere. Over the years she'd acquired a fair amount of skill at reading people and this was Hud, after all. She knew everything about him. Hud's heated looks and touches were telling her that he wanted her. He was almost making love to her on the dance floor with his hands, with his hot gazes. Hud was a red-blooded man who loved sex. Tonight, she was right there with him.

He was mid-pull on a beer when she reached as high as she could on her tiptoes and tugged him down to put her mouth near his ear. "I want to go home and have sex now!"

Hud looked as though he would spit out his beer in surprise, then he swallowed and grinned. "That's a pretty damn good offer."

She hoped so. Tonight, she wanted to show him that she'd learned her way around the bedroom, too. No wallflower, she knew how to please a man. She didn't think she'd ever felt this kind of longing and desire wrap around her. They'd been so close to being together again until they'd been interrupted. She didn't want to wait another day. Another hour.

"Let's go," he said, slammed his beer down and took her hand.

He followed her home in his truck. Jo observed the speed limit, thinking of her son, but found herself pushing it. As soon as she parked, Jo rushed up to the door to unlock it. Hud was right behind her, his arms wrapping around her waist from behind. She wiggled her butt into his crotch, hearing him groan.

"I'll get this door opened." The lock that stuck half the time was stuck again.

"Let me," he said, and took the key from her.

But they were both a little too distracted by each other and as he bent toward the lock, she licked his neck and kissed it, making him groan again. Then he took her in his arms, key and door forgotten, and kissed her, warm and wet and deep. She opened to him, giving him a preview of coming attractions as her tongue tangled with his. He pushed her up against the front door, pinning her there, and continued to shower her with openmouthed kisses. They were both breathing heavily when Hud stopped everything.

"What's wrong?"

"I... I can't believe I'm saying this, but—"

"But *what*?" Fear gripped her hard and wrapped around the back of her knees. He couldn't change his mind about them now. No, no, no. She was taking him to bed to have wild, hedonistic sex with him.

"I want to make you wait."

"Wait for *what*?"

He winced. "For us. To be together again."

"You said that with a straight face. Good job. That's funny. Okay, let's go inside." She turned to work on the lock again, but he whipped her around to face him.

"I mean it. I'm not having sex with you tonight." His words were not agreeing with his gaze, which looked pained.

"Hud, why not? Why are you doing this?" She pulled on his forearm. "This is what we both want."

"Because, Jo, I want to slow us down. I want to court you."

Court? Who even said that word anymore? "What are you talking about?"

"We jumped right in once before and that didn't work out so well. This time I want a change. And I need you to be sure. I keep telling you this is differ-ent for me, well, this is how I *show* you."

That was sweet, she had to admit. She still hated the idea. "Couldn't you find some other way of show-ing me?"

He pressed his forehead to hers. "Believe me, I've racked my brain. You're smarter than me. Come up with something. Anything. I'm begging you."

Damn, Hud was adorable when he begged. On the spot, she couldn't think of a single thing. He was right. Delaying the sex they both wanted to have and actually going out on dates to get to know each other was the opposite of what they'd done before.

"I think you're right," she said, miserably. "Wait-ing is the very opposite of our past. And we've waited this long…"

"What's another week or so?"

"*That* long?"

"Negotiable." He chuckled. "I could be talked out of a week."

"It's going to be my mission to talk you out of waiting that long." She pouted.

"Good night, Jo." He pulled away, almost prying her hand from his waist. "I'm calling you tomorrow."

"What's tomorrow?" She had work in the morn-ing, and no idea what he had in mind.

"I'm calling to ask you out on a date." He took a couple of steps down.

"Yes."

"Yes, what?"

"I'll go out on a date with you. I'm just trying to save time here."

He smiled and her heart gave a powerful tug. "You are so damn cute."

"I think the word you meant is *sexy*." She did a shoulder shimmy.

His gaze darkened with heat. "That goes without saying."

"No, you *have* to say it. Often. I'm sexy."

"Noted."

He walked slowly toward his truck and she loved watching the way it seemed he fought with his own body to move each step. He didn't want to go. She loved that he didn't want to go but he was forcing himself to do it anyway. She stood feet planted on the porch, carefully watching him, hoping he'd have a change of heart. Knowing all the while that he wouldn't. Past history told her that when Hud made up his mind, nothing and no one could shake him.

In his truck, he rolled down the window. "Hey, sexy, I'm going to watch you walk inside."

She struggled with the key a little more and then it finally came unlocked. Opening it, she made a big show of walking in, then watched from the window as he drove away.

Joanne felt much better the following morning. Sexual frustration aside, she understood what Hud was trying to do. It made sense. After all, he knew better than anyone her six-month rule. She never slept with a guy before dating him exclusively for six months. After that, if all went well, another six months before a man was ever introduced to her son. Sue her if she'd done away with "the rules" for Hud. He was the exception, as he'd been around before she *made* the rules. She'd known him for far longer than six months and he'd known Hunter for his entire life.

But if he wanted to "court" her, she supposed she'd let him. He'd been very cute about it, after all.

"Still no word from the Taylors?" Joanne asked Nora later that morning at the shop.

"No, and this is getting rude."

"It passed rude a few days ago. Seems like they've found someone else." She hated the thought but had to consider it.

"They paid for your designs. That would be crazy and wasteful to hire someone else. Plus, they loved them."

"Maybe I'll have to pull out all the stops," Joanne said. "And fight for the business like I did once before. Start over. Pitch them another idea."

"There you go."

Joanne's phone buzzed with a text from Hud.

Picnic this afternoon.

Really? A picnic?

She texted back:

Who are you and what have you done with my best friend?

Hud: Meet me on Wildfire Ridge. I'm picking up a shift here today. Get Rachel from doggy day care and bring her. She'll love it too.

"Hud wants to take me on a picnic," Joanne said out loud.

"Aww," Nora said, clutching her chest.

"What's wrong with me that all I want to do is jump his bones?"

"There's nothing wrong with you. We are talking about Hud Decker, right? Hunk-a-licious."

"Shouldn't I be interested in more than sex, though? That's a little shallow of me."

"Not when you consider that you already know he's right for you in every way. He's your best friend and you know everything there is to know. All you need to know now is if you can move into that other, ahem, area, so who can blame you for wanting to fast-track it?"

Because of the only problem in this new and tenuous situation. Joanne wasn't sure that Hud was perfect for her in every way. Fun and carefree? Yes. Slightly dangerous in that oh-so alluring way? Uh-huh. But she'd been craving stability and security for so long in a relationship. She'd wanted something that would last. More children, without any possibility of being a single mom again.

Then again, she'd thought Chuck could give her that and it had all been a big, fat lie. She wondered why and how she'd convinced herself she could have security and a future with Chuck, of all people. She hated the first answer that came to mind, but she'd never thought that any other woman would want Chuck, so he was a safe bet. He also had a plan for his future and shared it often.

Later that afternoon, Joanne headed to pick up Rachel and drove up the hill to Wildfire Ridge. She loved this area and its stark and rugged beauty. Hud spent a lot of time here now, both as a part-time guide and head architect of the controlled burns. For years, they'd warded off another wildfire and the wildlife had slowly returned. Mountain lions and deer dotted the hill at times and didn't bother anyone as long as they were left alone. Of course, you really didn't want to have a little dog run loose deep in the hills, but Rachel would be on her leash and wouldn't stray up into the farthest parts of the ridge, where the mountain lions tended to roam.

"Okay, we're here."

Joanne still wore her work clothes, a wraparound red dress and matching flats, because she hadn't wanted to take time and go home and change. The September waning sun would set before long. They'd had a long summer, but soon autumn would arrive, her favorite time of the year even if it meant shorter days and longer nights. She'd just bet Hud could keep her warm all fall and winter long. And just like that her mind was in the gutter again. She couldn't wait to be in bed with him, cuddling, sharing heat, sharing… Everything.

Parking in the designated area, she climbed out, clipped the leash on Rachel and began walking up the trail to the hill. The ground was dusty after a long hot and dry summer but the trees, here for longer than the town, stood firm and tall. They'd weathered rain, drought, and fires with their deep roots. Wildflowers sprouted up here and there across the ridge, spreading a splash of color. Yellow and orange. Purple. The sky was a clear blue and the air smelled crisp and clean with hints of impending autumn. No wonder Hud loved it here.

Twigs snapped as she stepped over them. Wildfire Ridge Outdoor Adventures had been started by Jill, with activities for those Silicon Valley types seeking so-called extreme sports. They had guided hikes into mountain lion territory, wakeboarding and waterskiing on Anderson Lake, rock climbing and ziplining. Joanne had been here once, on Family and Friends day right before their opening and not since then.

She spied Hud in the distance dressed in the guides' uniform, tan cargo pants, boots and a matching long-sleeved black tee pushed up to his elbows.

He was speaking with a small group, possibly the one he'd taken on a guided hike. When he turned and caught her eye, he winked and then nudged his chin. And there a few feet in front of her and to the left under a tree was a blanket spread out with a cooler on top.

"Oh my gosh, he really meant a *picnic*."

Joanne set Rachel down on the blanket and snooped inside the cooler. She found cold beers and what appeared to be salad containers and sandwiches from her favorite deli in town. He'd even brought doggie snacks for Rachel.

"You're going to like this," she said, picking one out for Rachel. She'd been so good on the car ride, sitting on her haunches like a real person.

She turned to give it to Rachel, and... No Rachel.

The leash was gone, too, which meant she'd taken off. Cursing herself for not setting the leash under the heavy cooler, she stood and frantically turned in a circle. She couldn't see Rachel anywhere, and then out of the corner of her eye she saw a white blur. *Rachel!* Headed toward certain death, no doubt, if she got anywhere near mountain lion territory. But damn if Joanne would let that happen. Hud would never forgive her. Rachel was a cute dog with a ridiculous name who'd never hurt anyone.

Kicking off her flats, Joanne began to run in the direction she'd seen Rachel go.

Chapter Nine

Hud has just finished up with the group he'd guided through a seven-mile hike when he caught a blur of red flashing in his peripheral vision.

Jo was running—which she swore to him she'd never do unless someone was chasing her—screaming, "Raaaa-chellll!"

For someone who didn't run at all, she was moving quickly. But she didn't look particularly equipped to be running on the hill, dressed in a short red dress.

"Who's that?" One of the hikers asked.

"That's my…girlfriend. If you'll excuse me." He dropped his backpack and took off after Joanne, who he guessed had to be running after Rachel.

Here's what he'd learned recently as a dog owner: dogs are pack animals. The owner is the pack leader. They want nothing more than to please you, so teach them how. And finally, and he'd learned this one the hard way: never, ever, *chase* a dog if your intention is to catch him. They'll think it's a game. But apparently no one had given Jo the 411 and she thought she'd be able to catch Rachel, who not only outran Jo, but became a little airborne at times. Like a gazelle.

He ran after Jo, who ran after Rachel, who ran for the sake of running. Because she was a dog.

"Jo! Don't chase Rachel!" he yelled.

Jo didn't seem to hear him and with a solid lead, she was still several feet away from Hud. Headed toward the lake.

"No, Rachel! Noooooo!" Joanne waved her arms in the air. "Don't go in the laaaaake!"

In other relevant news, Rachel knew how to swim and rather liked it. Hud was gaining on Jo but just when he was almost close enough to touch her, she jumped in the lake after Rachel. Her dress swimming around her neck, she finally registered Hud's presence.

"Don't worry! I'll get her." She then began to swim after Rachel, who, Hud hated very much to tell Jo, was already drying herself off. On him. He picked her up.

"Jo," he said, biting back a laugh. "She's right here, babe."

She turned in a circle, caught him holding Rachel, then swam back to the edge of the lake. He held out his other hand to haul her out. Wet and muddy, she gave him a little smile. "Good. She's okay."

He pulled her into his arms. "C'mere."

She was shivering. "I thought I'd lost her forever."

He didn't think he'd ever loved Jo more than at this moment. She'd probably crawl under Mrs. Diaz's spider infested house for Rachel, too. Fearless. "She knows how to swim."

"I just found that out." She reached to pet Rachel. "Did you enjoy that little dip, princess?"

"More than you did." Hud chuckled.

"Are you *laughing* at me?"

"Not at all. I prefer to keep my family jewels intact, thanks." He continued to rub her back in small circles. "You're freezing."

She fisted her hands in his now-damp tee. "And I ruined our picnic."

"Nah. We'll just be relocating."

With that, he walked holding Jo's hand, carrying Rachel in the other. In his backpack, he found his SOL orange emergency blanket and tore it open to cover Jo with it.

"Thank you." She drew it tighter around her.

He walked her to his truck and went back to get the picnic blanket and cooler, putting everything, including his backpack, in the bed of his truck.

He hopped in the front seat. "We'll come back

for your car later. This way you won't get your car seat damp."

She pulled on his wrist. "I'm really sorry."

"Nothing to be sorry about. You were trying to save Rachel."

"Who didn't need saving." She sighed.

"Let me tell you a few things about dogs…"

He reiterated everything he'd learned since she encouraged him to adopt the rescue pet while he drove them back to his place. Foolishly, he hadn't prepared to have her over for company. But thanks to his time in the Army, he kept a clean house. Mostly. And also had a maid come in twice a week when he was gone on rotation. Besides, Jo had been over here many times before for a movie, or the few times they'd double-dated with other people. But okay, yeah, he usually prepped better than this.

He'd had every intention of taking her back to her home after the picnic and keeping his hands to himself once again. It was killing him, sure, but she was worth it. They were worth waiting for. He just knew it would be explosive between them because those kisses were simply a hint at what was to come. Given the change of plans this afternoon, he'd have his first real challenge. Because seeing her with that dress floating around her neck and the view below through the clear lake water had him nearly swallowing his tongue.

Inside, he encouraged her into a warm shower and gave her a towel and his bathrobe.

"I'll put your dress in the dryer." He stopped, re-thinking. "*Can* it be put in the dryer?"

She gazed at him from under hooded eyes. "Thank you for asking, but yes, it can."

With that, she removed the dress and wiggled out of black lace panties and a matching bra.

She smiled and tossed them to him. "So glad we're doing this whole waiting thing."

He swallowed hard. This idea to wait had seemed like a good one at the time.

While she was in the shower, he fed Rachel, then settled her in the kennel. He got busy arranging for a picnic on the living room floor. Okay, he was offi-cially corny. If the guys at the station could see him now, they'd razz him until the end of time. He'd never been a fool like this over a woman. He didn't feel good about that now because maybe he'd been unfair to the women he'd dated in the past. While he'd tried to be clear about his intentions, he knew there were some ex-girlfriends who'd believed they'd be the one to change him. To get him to finally settle down.

One of them had sat here in this very living room on a double date with him, Jo and some loser she'd dated a couple of years ago. Not Chuck, but still not good enough. Jo had later warned him that Kris-tine had every intention of making herself "the one." Maybe his stance had made him a bit of a challenge to her, but he hadn't intended that. And when she'd kindly told him, after realizing they weren't going anywhere, that he should just go ahead and tell Jo he was madly in love with her, he'd made *Kristine* sound like the paranoid one.

"Don't be ridiculous," he'd said, or something equally inane.

She'd just smiled and told him to think about it, and to call and thank her when he finally figured it out for himself.

But up until now—what he considered his last chance, whenever he'd allowed himself to consider the possibility—he believed he still wasn't ready to give Jo everything she deserved. That he had to earn more money. Had to save more. Buy a bigger house with plenty of room for both Jo and Hunter to move in with him. Get rid of some of his workout equipment in his spare room to make space for her fabrics and dresses she liked to bring home. Those were all excuses, he now realized.

Because deep down he was terrified of losing her all over again. Deeper still in those small tight spaces where he didn't often dare to look, he wondered if he was the problem. Maybe she couldn't ever love him like she had the first time. Maybe gold didn't strike twice.

Jo emerged from the bathroom wearing his bathrobe, which pretty much swam on her, coming down to her ankles. Despite that, she looked like a cover girl model to him. Her blond hair was damp and pushed back behind her ears. She was fresh-faced, all the makeup washed off, making her appear even younger.

"That was just what I needed." She walked to the edge of the blanket he'd now laid in the middle of the living room. "Oh wow."

This time, he'd added a few touches he wouldn't have ever attempted on Wildfire Ridge. Candlelight. Plates and actual flatware instead of the plastic stuff.

"Ready for our picnic?" Crouching, he dished out her favorite salad on a plate.

She sat on the blanket, then opened up the robe so that her legs were showing. "How did I never know that you're this romantic?

"Probably because I'm not."

"Hud, this—" she waved her hand over the area "—is romantic."

"I'm trying."

"And I love that you're trying." She scooted closer to him, giving him a good whiff of his own soap. On her.

That hint of intimacy drove him wild. He tucked her in close. "You deserve it."

"It's funny you should say that, because I gave up on this kind of thing a while ago. Expectations."

He let that statement settle in his bones, realizing that he'd done something for her no other guy had. "Why?"

She shrugged. "When I became a mom, I gave up on romance and shucked it for responsibility. Security."

"You can have both, you know."

"You're reminding me of that."

They ate quietly for a few minutes, he nearly inhaling his sandwich, rethinking this whole "waiting" thing. How long had they known each other, anyway? Even if their relationship had recently changed status, he'd waited long enough for her. She was finally available, and he'd made his move. He'd made it clear she was special, and not one of his many seductions. Sure, it would be better to know that she was truly over the idiot and not just distracting herself with Hud. Because he needed her whole body and mind and wasn't going to accept anything less.

When Jo crawled into his lap, she had unbelted the robe, and beautiful fleshy soft skin brushed up against him.

"Can I talk you out of waiting? I mean, I nearly died trying to save Rachel."

"I have a feeling you could talk me into anything."

Her fingers threaded through his hair, and he began to lose focus on anything other than her mouth. "I want you so much. Tonight."

"And I need you to be sure." Parting the robe, his hand explored under it, tweaking her nipple.

She moaned. "I'm sure. I've never been more certain of anything in my life."

With that assurance, Hud put out the candlelight, drew her into his arms and stood, carrying her toward the bedroom.

Flush with anticipation, Jo held tight to Hud's shoulders as he carried her. The wait was over. She would undress him and get to witness up close and personal all of that gorgeous taut skin and muscle. With Hud, she easily lost any inhibitions because tonight he'd made her feel desired and special. He'd proved something to her, and now it was her turn to do the same. To let him know he wasn't any rebound guy. He was Hud. *Her* Hud. Always had been, and always would be. No matter what.

Did she think this meant forever? No. She was a grown-up now.

After their very first time, she'd made big plans. Plans to get married, since of course they would have had to now they'd had *sex*. But she wasn't that young and idealistic girl anymore. Life didn't go according to plan. And this time she wasn't going to pin Hud down to anything permanent. Better to take it one day at a time and see where it went. Along the way, she was going to enjoy every second because she'd been holding back for too long.

Hud laid her gently on his bed, and she wiggled out of the robe and tossed it aside. She let herself drink in the sight of his heated gaze, taking in the view.

"What are you waiting for?" She stretched her arms out, wiggling her fingers for him to come and join her.

"We're not waiting," he said, slow and rough as he pulled off his shirt with one hand.

Coming up on her knees beside him, she went for his pants, unsnapping and sliding them down his slim hips. Then, finally, his boxer briefs came off and she thought she'd never seen anything more beautiful. Hud was all man, sharp angles and planes. Hard everywhere. She ran the pads of her fingers down his chest to his abs and luxuriated in each sinewy muscle, and the sensations as he tensed beneath her touch.

"I want to touch you everywhere."

"I'm not going to stop you."

His big hand covered her butt while his mouth came down eagerly to her nipple, sucking hard. Her body buzzed with a sweet ache, and warmth spread between her thighs. Still standing beside her on the bed, hand on the nape of her neck, he tugged her mouth to his for a long deep kiss. Then he took them both down to the bed, his hard body covering hers. She wrapped her legs around his back, burying her face in his warm neck. Licking. Tasting.

"I missed this." She'd never felt this physically connected to anyone else. Her body purred and vibrated under his touch. "I missed *you*."

"We're going to take our time." Hud braced himself above her with a slow smile. "You don't have to be anywhere for the next twenty-four hours, do you?"

He didn't wait for her answer, as he slowly crawled down her body, kissing and licking as he went. His tongue played with the shell of her ear and when his teeth sank into her earlobe, a wild and unexpected pull of desire made her thighs throb and pulse. His lips nibbled at her nipples and sucked each one until she bucked under him, opening her legs.

"Patience."

He kissed and licked his way down, playing with her belly button. But when he lowered his head between her thighs, far from patient, Joanne became so aroused her hips gyrated and her legs trembled. She fought the cresting wave and tried to regain control as he pushed her higher. The wave came anyway, and with one more lick from him in just the right spot, she lost all control. She moaned his name, suddenly aware that she had her hands in his hair, clutching him tight.

"Oh, Hud. I'm sorry." Letting go, she smoothed his hair down from the tufts she'd created. Good thing he had a lot of hair. "I hurt you."

He braced above her, looking no worse for the wear. "I didn't feel a thing."

She quirked a brow though she knew exactly what he meant.

"I didn't feel a thing on my head." He gave her a wicked smile. "The big one."

"C'mere." She pushed him until he went flat on his back. Naturally, he went willingly.

She could feel his body tense as she lowered herself over him, licking down his flat abs, and then licking down to the promised land. She licked once, twice, and took him into her mouth. He groaned and his muscles tensed to the consistency of granite as she teased him mercilessly until he was at the edge of where she wanted him.

When he'd finally had enough, he made her stop and rolled on top of her. "Condom."

Yes, finally!

He rustled through his nightstand to where she assumed he kept his stash of condoms. She wouldn't know. And she didn't much want to think about that right now. The stash of ready condoms. She'd prefer he had only a couple in there, specifically for *her*, maybe even with her name on them, were she wishing for a miracle.

"Shit," he said. "I'm out."

While she wondered just how much sex he'd been having lately to be completely out, he added, "I haven't bought any in a while. It's been…a long time."

Joanne tried not to let that bit of information get to her, but damn if it did.

Her playboy best friend, condom-less.

With her.

"And we were going to wait," he added.

This would all be incredibly upsetting if Joanne wasn't prepared. She'd learned her lesson the hard way, after all. *Never* depend on a man to bring the birth control. Hud looked absolutely disgusted with himself, poor baby.

Joanne bent over the bed to reach for her purse and brought out a tiny silver foil packet. "I'm not out."

Hud brightened, even more so when Joanne ripped the package open and slid the condom on his shaft. She stroked him once, then twice, making him groan. Taking over, he braced himself on top of her. He kissed her, warm and deep making her skin tingle all over, and in one deep thrust he was inside her, making them both gasp.

She'd never seen anything as beautiful as Hud's face, a mask of concentration as he moved inside of her, deeper and harder each time. He wasn't the boy she'd loved once beyond all reason, but a man. A grown man, who'd been through so much and yet he'd never left her behind. He'd always come back to her, one way or another. The knowledge of that pierced her, and she let go of a little more control, allowing the sensations to roll and sway through her body.

The pressure built inside her quickly, like nothing she'd experienced before. She and Hud were like fire together, explosive, both urging each other to the pinnacle in soft whispers and ragged breaths. She bucked against him, wanting more, wanting deeper, harder, and he gave it to her. Faster and deeper he went, taking her higher, until she fell apart in a sweet climax. Only then did he let go and had his own release.

"We've gotten a lot better at that," Joanne said on a ragged breath. She was including herself in there, though it was mostly Hud, were she being completely honest.

Hud tucked her to his side. "I didn't have a whole lot to offer you then, other than my enthusiasm."

"You definitely had that in spades. But you were also very sweet."

"Sweet? Me?"

"Yes, *you*. Or I probably wouldn't have fallen in love with you."

They were both too quiet for a moment, as if the raw memory had shattered them both a little.

"Stay with me tonight," he said, brushing a kiss against her knuckles. "Sleep with me."

"Will I actually get any sleep?"

"We can do some of that, if you want."

"Okay," she said, snuggling closer. "But you have to promise me something. It's very important."

"Anything."

"Next time I take a shower, don't leave me in there alone."

Chapter Ten

"Is it a beautiful day, or is it just me?" Joanne set her coffee orders down. "One soy latte for me, one caramel macchiato for you."

Joanne's good mood wouldn't quit. She had Hud to thank for that.

"It's supposed to be in the eighties later today," Nora grumbled. "I wish fall would hurry up and get here already. You know that's when my order will change to pumpkin spice latte, right?"

"Sure, that's when everything changes to pumpkin spice."

Nora wrinkled her nose. "And you hate pumpkin, so why do you sound so happy about that?"

"I'm not happy about that." Joanne took another swallow of her now-lukewarm latte.

"What's got you in such a good mood?" Nora studied her intently for several seconds. "Oh my gosh, you got laid, didn't you?"

Was she *that* obvious? "What makes you say that?"

"You look the most relaxed you've been in weeks. No, wait. Months."

Joanne supposed there was nothing quite like multiple orgasms to put a little spring in her step, but she hadn't imagined it would be written all over her face. Still, she wasn't going to talk about it. In detail. She was old-fashioned that way.

"Okay, me and Hud. No more waiting."

Nora smiled and threw a hand over her mouth in mock surprise. "Oh, color me shocked!"

Joanne snorted. "You are *not*."

"No, I'm not, because I called it."

"I ruined our picnic and we wound up back at his place." Joanne explained the failed picnic, her impromptu swim in the lake, and later the resulting amazing picnic save on the living room floor.

"Holy cow, this dude is so romantic. I had no clue. But when you think about it, suddenly all the sweet things he's done for you over the years take on a different perspective. Like the Bahamas thing. And also, that time Chuck forgot your birthday, and you later found out it was Hud who sent you those red roses and candies."

She'd almost forgotten about that. He was also the only one besides her mother who remembered the anniversary of her father's death and came over to dispense hugs, go with her to the cemetery and listen to her cry. Over the years, there had been so many sweet gestures that she'd attributed solely to their best friend status.

They got to work together on Jill's alterations, on their knees hemming the dress by hand, chatting the entire morning. When the door chimed, Nora went to the front of the shop to see whether it was the UPS guy or the mailman. A few seconds later, she returned, face frozen.

Bad news. Oh no, *bad news*.

Joanne stood. "What is it? Is it Hunter? Is he okay?"

"It's not Hunter and no one is hurt." She hooked her thumb toward the front of the shop. "But you're probably going to have to deal with Chuck."

Chuck. "He's here?"

Why in God's name was he here? She assumed it wasn't to pay for his half of the wedding but speaking of that… Joanne rushed to the front of the shop.

There he stood, hands in his pockets, avoiding eye contact.

"I'm so glad you're here," Joanne said through

gritted teeth. "You ran out on me without paying for your half of the wedding."

"I'm sorry. Chuck was so confused. He didn't know what to do."

And there went the dreaded third person crap again. "Confused? About what? Directions to the venue? Date? Time? Really, what was so confusing, *Chuck*?"

"You. You confused me. We agreed to get married, but I knew you didn't really love me."

"Wow, okay, what a cop-out. And if you didn't think I loved you, could you have possibly mentioned that to me *before* the wedding day?"

"I know my timing sucked. Chuck isn't known for his timing." He shrugged.

Joanne's hands curled into fists. "Stop talking about yourself in the third person! It's not cute. It's just…weird."

"You used to think it was funny."

"I used to think a lot of things. Like what a good husband you'd make. Boy, was I delusional."

"Exactly. Delusional."

"You don't get to call me delusional!" She pointed to her chest. "Only I get to call myself delusional."

"Okay, okay. I'm sorry! But did you ever stop to think what it was like for me to know you'd have preferred Hud over me in a heartbeat? But he wasn't 'husband material.'" He held up air quotes. "He's a playboy. Well maybe I didn't want to be second best.

You're delu—kidding yourself if you don't realize you're in love with Hud."

"Oh, there you go again with all the paranoid jealousy. Hud has just always been there for me, unlike some people."

"And he loves you and you love him. I was always the third wheel when it came to you two. Private jokes, all the playful teasing. C'mon! Get real."

"I'm sure this is all your way of calling attention away from yourself. I'm not the one who was apparently cheating. I heard about your new girlfriend."

He tossed up his hands. "Hey, I didn't start things up with her until I knew it was over between us."

"Great. That must have been, what, on our wedding day or the day before?" She forced some calm into her voice and went to dig in her purse. "Lucky for you, I prepared you a bill for the wedding. I was going to ask you for half, but now I think you had better pay me for the whole thing."

He cleared his throat. "I'm actually here, not just to apologize…but to get my mother's wedding ring back. I want to give it to Mandy."

Damn him. He'd come here for the ring. Not to sincerely apologize. Not because he was remorseful for what he'd done. No. He needed something from her.

The stupid, awful ring.

On the day of her wedding fail, Joanne had tossed that family heirloom into the trash, but Hud had taken it back out, saying it might be worth something. She could pawn it and get some money for Chuck's half of the wedding. It might have been a good idea, but the ring wasn't worth much other than sentimental value. She'd had it appraised before the wedding to see if she should insure it.

"I don't have it," Joanne said, and that was the truth. She'd thrown it in the bottom of her underwear drawer, unwilling to look at it even among the rest of her jewelry.

"Did you *pawn* it?" Chuck had the nerve to look disgusted.

"I should have, but no, I didn't." She crossed her arms, an evil thought forming. "What's it worth to you?"

"It was my *mother's* ring. You know the right thing to do is just give it back to Chuck. Chuck is supposed to give it to his wife and obviously you're not going to be his wife. Anymore."

Ah, how had she never noticed that before? Chuck used the third person whenever he said something awkward. Uncomfortable. To distance himself, maybe.

Like when he'd said: Chuck loves Joanne.

"Well, Chuck is a *crazy* person if he thinks I'm going to give him back the ring without getting him to pay his fair share of the wedding."

"Be reasonable. I just got through two rounds of the draft and I've no idea when or if I'll get officially drafted to the majors and start earning some real money."

"Dive into your savings."

"*What* savings?"

"All the money you said you were slowly putting aside for our future!"

"Oh, that." He shrugged. "I just said that so you'd think I was a better bet than Hud."

Joanne's stomach churned with what had to be volcano lava. She saw a red haze appear in front of Chuck. He was glowing. Yes, yes. She was going to kill him. The bill she'd been holding was crunched up in her fist.

"You liar! You're never getting the ring back! Never!" Joanne flung herself at him, ready to punch him in the throat, but Nora had obviously heard, come running and pulled Joanne back by the waist.

"Don't. He's not worth it."

Recoiling, Chuck headed for the door and then turned one last time. "This isn't over. I need that ring and I'll get it, one way or another."

"Get out of here!" Nora screamed. "I can't hold her back much longer. She's going to blow!"

Chuck left like the coward that he was, and it took everything in Joanne not to chase him down the street screaming, "Liar, liar, pants on fire!"

But that probably wouldn't be good for business.

"Breathe. In and out. In and out," Nora said, finally letting go of Joanne.

Joanne staggered to the couch in front of the pedestal where prospective brides tried on their dresses. Anger coursed through her, making her skin prickly. Chuck had lied to her. He'd pretended to be someone he was not. Why? Then another realization hit her and when it did, hard and fast, she felt gut punched.

"Oh my God, he's right."

Chuck was the consolation prize. She'd never wanted anyone other than Hud.

"About the ring? No. It may be a family heirloom but holding it hostage is how you get to him to pay for the wedding. That's smart and fair."

Joanne's breaths were coming short and sparse. A cold shiver spiked down her spine. She'd wasted years chasing security and stability when she'd really wanted Hud. But he'd been so unavailable, and so... So risky. What kind of a terrible person traded true love for security?

The kind who wants more children but swore she'll never be a single mother again.

The kind who's a bit of a coward when it comes to her heart.

Nora appeared with a glass of cold water. "Here, hon."

"I'm a horrible person," Joanne said, accepting the glass.

"Don't say that. Everybody makes mistakes."

"Not everybody gets engaged to a...a man like Chuck because she wants the security and safety of having someone who she believes will always stick around."

"You're not being fair to yourself. Most women want that in a man."

"Not enough to give up on love."

"*Did* you? Give up on love?"

"I didn't think so," Joanne said. "But the humiliation of being stood up caused me the most pain. Being dumped for someone younger was hurtful, too. But I haven't really missed Chuck...at all."

Whenever she fought with Hud, and they didn't talk for a few days, she was gutted. Lost.

"I guess that tells you something," Nora said.

It told her that she still loved Hud Decker, her polar opposite. A man who'd never been risk averse. He'd driven too fast and crashed his car at sixteen in a horrible accident. He'd enlisted in the Army. He worked in a high-risk profession and loved extreme sports. He rode a motorcycle.

Hud Decker was the opposite of safety and security.

And still, all she wanted to do was text Hud everything that had just happened. But she'd have him come over instead. She wanted a hug from her best friend, the ones that cured everything.

Probie J.P. had a lot to learn. The first twenty-four of Hud's shift had been relatively calm. Only a few medical calls and then some drills he made the crew go through. The next morning their crew had been sitting at the breakfast table enjoying Alex's Belgian waffles, when J.P. said the worst thing a firefighter could ever say:

"I hope it's not quiet today."

"Rookie, never say that again," Hud said through gritted teeth. "Keep in mind when you say that you're wishing harm on others."

Every first responder possessed a strong superstitious streak. Utter those few words and the day was guaranteed to be utter chaos. And it was. Thanks to J.P., they were called out to assist at a two-alarm fire at a warehouse in San Jose. Several hours later that was under control when they were called back to Fortune to a brush fire by the freeway which had spread quickly. They stopped rush hour traffic to put it out and then everyone was miserable.

But beyond J.P.'s ignorance about firehouse superstitions, there was an underlying disregard for orders. And if Hud didn't rein him in quickly, this would not end well. Near the end of the day, Hud called J.P. into his office to have a little chat.

Hud shut the door.

"Am I in trouble?" J.P. asked.

Arms crossed, Hud leaned back against his desk. "I'll put it this way—you're skating. Next time I give you an order, I expect you to obey it to the letter or you're out on your ass. No questions asked. You're on probation and I can't afford you to get hurt out there."

"I'm sorry, I'm just anxious to get out there. Make a difference, you know?"

"I get it, but you can't get ahead of the learning curve for this job."

Hud might take risks but he was now calculated about them. No matter what he attempted, he always had an exit strategy. Always. He'd learned the hard way that not all risks were worth taking. Now, to impart this heady wisdom to a rangy twenty-two-year-old, who reminded Hud of himself at that age. In other words, J.P. believed he had balls of steel and that nothing could touch him. Ten years ago, Hud had been in the Army at twenty-two and stationed in North Carolina. Far from home, he'd learned to depend on himself and his unit. They grew as close as brothers, which was how he felt about the men in his firehouse.

"We're a family here," Hud said. "And that means we look out for each other. Think of me as your older brother. You can count on me to set you straight when you're screwing up."

"Okay, good."

Hud bent until he was nearly nose to nose with J.P. "You're screwing up, J.P."

Close to thirty minutes later, Hud felt that he'd put enough of the fear of God into J.P. and let him go with one last warning. As he got ready to update the LT coming on duty for the next forty-eight, his phone buzzed.

Jo: I need you tonight.

He smiled. Oh *yeah*. Round two. He texted back:

Shift ends at seven. I'll be over with dinner.

After a night like the one they'd had, he'd had a difficult time thinking of anything besides Jo. On his quiet day, when they'd been sitting around making bets on the 49er game, his thoughts had run to Jo. The sweet little sounds she made when he kissed the right spot. Her energy and passion to go all night with him. He just wanted more of the same, over and over.

He'd waited so long for this chance. Biding his time—for what? To be perfect? There was no such thing. But Jo made plans and she liked order in her life. Now more than ever he understood that need. She wanted stability and security and he didn't blame her for that. After what she'd been through, it was only natural. For the first time in his life, Hud thought he could give that to her. He was ready.

He picked Rachel up and then Chinese food from their favorite place in town. When Jo met him at the door wearing a very short halter dress, it took everything in him not to push her up against the wall and forget the food. Instead, he set Rachel down where she went trotting inside like she owned the place.

"Hey," she said, the corners of her sweet mouth pulling down. "I need a hug."

He set the cartons of food down on the kitchen table and tugged her into his arms. His hand slid up and down her back. "What is it? More bad luck boutique?"

"No. *Chuck* came by today."

Hud's heart nearly stopped and everything inside of him went still and cold. He didn't think Chuck would have the balls to show up again. There had to be a damn good reason he would risk the fear of Hud's wrath for that.

"What did he want?"

"Get this. He wants the ring he gave me, so he can give it to his new fiancée."

Good thing he'd fished that out of the trash. Jo hadn't been thinking straight. "Good. Give it back to him."

She pulled out of his arms to look for plates and set them down on the table. "Not until he pays me back what he owes me."

"Right. When will he have it for you?" He opened cartons and they fell into a natural rhythm. After all, they'd had dinners like this many times before.

"He *lied* about the money he was setting aside for our future. He has no savings, or so he claims. No way he can pay me back. That's why I'm holding his ring hostage."

Chuck was becoming a bigger jerk than Hud

thought possible. No savings. Jackass. How had he planned on helping Jo? Contributing? Hud had been saving for years, not that he'd mentioned that to her.

"Just hock it."

"The only value this ring has is sentimental. I had it appraised and it's not worth much."

"You think he'll somehow find the money to pay you back?" Hud doubted this, and he was also beginning to resent the idea of Jo keeping that ring.

It might be stupid, but he considered that holding on to that ring could be a symbol of not moving on.

Jo served each of them some chow mein and broccoli beef on their plates, then sat down across from him. "I don't think he'll be motivated any other way. Do you?"

Hud considered this, but his own desires were getting in the way of Jo's reasoning. He had to put them aside and think logically. "Do you have the money to pay for the wedding yourself?"

"Yes, because I saved, but it's the principle of the thing."

"I think you should give him back the ring."

Jo dropped her fork and it made a shrill clank. "Are you serious? Why? He's never going to pay me a dime otherwise."

"He may never pay you back anyway. In the meantime, you have his mother's ring."

"But it's my only insurance."

"Insurance for the money, or insurance he'll continue to have to deal with you? Maybe you're holding on and not letting go."

"I have moved on, buddy." She stood and pointed in the direction of her bedroom. "You and me, we moved on. Have you forgotten?"

"Never."

"I wouldn't be *with* you if I hadn't moved on."

"Then give him back the ring and make it official."

She made a frustrated sound. "Why are you being so unreasonable about this? I've got something he wants, so he's going to have to give me what I want."

"Okay, Jo. Do it your way. I'd just rather have him out of your life once and for all."

"And so would I," Jo said, coming around to his chair, straddling him. "But I have to do this my way. Don't be mad?"

When her fingers threaded through his hair, he lost focus entirely. Ring or not, *he* had Jo. As far as Hud was concerned, that was the real prize. And if Chuck ever wanted Jo back, he'd have a hell of a fight on his hands.

Hud guaranteed it.

"I can never stay mad at you, babe." When she buried her face in his neck and kissed, then licked, he forgot how hungry he was, too. He stood with her still straddling his hips. "Let's go."

She giggled. "What about dinner?"

"Later."

Chapter Eleven

Three days later, Joanne waited at the boutique for a scheduled appointment with a prospective bride when the phone rang.

"Joanne's, how can I help you?"

"It's Patricia Taylor."

Finally, they'd decided to return her calls. "We never settled on a dress from the designs you paid for and I'd hoped to get started on the dress soon."

"That's the thing. Would you please go ahead and send the designs over to Trudy's Boutique in San Francisco? We've decided to have them make the dress."

Trudy's was by far Joanne's biggest competition,

an exclusive boutique only the most privileged of brides could afford.

She forced her voice into professional mode and out of the whine she heard in her head. "Did we do anything wrong? I thought you had agreed to keep your business in Fortune."

The Taylors were from Fortune, originally from real estate entrepreneurs who were very public about supporting small businesses in Fortune. The deal had started out with such promise a few months ago, their enthusiasm for working with a local bridal boutique and an exclusively designed dress palpable.

Now everything was falling apart.

"I'm sorry, but we've decided to go with Trudy's. Your designs were by far the best ones and we'll go with one of those. You'll get credit for the design, of course."

But she wouldn't be making the dress, and Joanne knew how it would go. Her name might appear in the fine print, but it would essentially be buried. Trudy's would get all the publicity. Trudy's would be there on the day of the wedding for any last-minute alterations.

"Does this have anything to do with what happened recently? Because I can assure you, it's the best thing to have ever happened to me. I'm happier than I've ever been."

"I was so sorry to hear about that. Did the groom leave you hanging with all the expenses?"

"Well, yes. I'm handling it." Best not to go into the gory details with a client. "But the shop is in good standing and I wouldn't have any problems delivering the dress."

She cleared her throat. "I know you wouldn't. But the decision has been made. And Joanne, I would so appreciate it if you wouldn't spread the word that we're going to San Francisco for the dress. You know that our image is so closely tied with supporting local business. And we try to, in every instance possible."

Except this one.

"I'm a professional and not a gossip, but don't expect me to lie for you. We had an agreement and I'm willing and able to hold up my end."

"I just…you have to understand."

"Maybe if you explained." Joanne kept her words measured and even, leaving the emotion out of it.

"It might not be fair, but everything has to go perfect for my daughter's wedding. My husband expects it. He's not footing a six-figure wedding for something to go wrong with the dress."

"Is there some reason you believe I can't do the work?"

"Dear, you were just jilted!"

"It's not contagious, Patricia." Quoting Hud to a prospective client. New territory.

"That's not what I mean. You're normally so detailed oriented. But with everything you've been through, which was so unfair by the way, I don't have the same confidence in you." She took a breath. "I'm sorry."

"I'll put those designs in the mail for you. And best of luck." Joanne spoke sharply and hung up, her stomach churning.

She didn't think she'd ever sold a design without sewing the dress. Nothing like the feeling that a client didn't want Joanne to *touch* her dress to make her feel toxic. Her designs were good enough, apparently her hands were not. More than likely, her shop didn't have the sophisticated cachet of a big city boutique. Plus, there was the whole jilted bride bad luck boutique thing. The feeling of being passed over sank her spirits. Great that they were using her designs, but terrible that they didn't trust her enough to create them.

She wondered if that's how Hud felt about the ring. If he thought that she was keeping it because she didn't trust they would work out, so she had to hang on to some part of Chuck. To keep contact. But nothing could be further from the truth. She wanted Chuck out of her life. Maybe it was time to think about giving him the ring back like Hud wanted her to do. She didn't like the idea of giving Hud any doubts.

She gathered the designs from the back and slipped them into a manila envelope, addressing them to the Taylors of Fortune. They would be taking their business to San Francisco.

The doorbell jingled and a soft voice called out, "Am I too early?"

Joanne dashed to the front to meet her appointment, Leah Jones. "I'm sorry. I was in the back. My colleague has the day off."

Joanne led Leah to the couch and smiled. "Is there anyone else coming?"

Normally a bride brought in a mother or mother-in-law, best friend, or someone with her. Joanne or Nora would serve champagne as they looked at possible designs and talked wedding details, but this girl didn't look old enough to drink.

"No, it's just me. I'm not from the area."

Leah had long dark hair and wore little makeup. She wore faded jeans and a blue sweatshirt and definitely didn't look like Joanne's typical clients. She was slender. *Young.* Joanne decided against offering the champagne. Still, this was her favorite part of her work. Finding the love story that lived in each bride. Encouraging them to share the romance with her so that she could better come up with ideas for the perfect dress. Each bride then had a uniquely designed dress coming out of their own love story.

"Please, let's have a seat and discuss some ideas." Joanne waved her hand toward the couch and sat.

"Right off, I have to tell you that I don't have much money." Leah clutched her purse.

"Okay. I have several wedding budgets I can work with."

"I've saved up for this. It's going to be the most important part of my wedding day. I want a special dress that no one else has."

"Right. Well, that's what we do here." Joanne took out her sketch pad. "How old are you, Leah?"

"I look younger than I am," she said. "I'm twenty-one."

Old enough to drink alcohol. Joanne still wasn't going to break out the champagne. Leah was alone which meant she'd probably driven herself here. "How long have you known your groom?"

"I've known Jake since we were kids."

"And is he around? Will I get to meet him?"

"He'll be here for the wedding. His family is from Fortune. He already has approval for leave."

Another military man. "What branch?"

"Navy." She sat up straighter when she said so.

"Let me explain my process. What I do, initially, is listen to your love story. Then I come up with ideas once I get to know you. Tell me about you and Jake."

Leah relaxed, and her gaze took on that dreamy quality that Joanne loved so much. Too bad she hadn't noticed it had been missing in her. If she had, that might have been a clue that Chuck was all wrong for her. There was no love story there.

"We met when he was visiting his grandparents in Oregon, where I'm from. When he told me he was joining the Navy, I said I'd never speak to him again if he did."

Joanne gaped. "I'm s-sorry?"

"I know that sounds crazy." She giggled.

Joanne shook her head. No, it didn't sound crazy at all. It was almost exactly what she'd said to Hud when he signed up for the Army. He was eighteen, straight out of high school. After his car accident, he'd developed a kinship with first responders and knew it was what he wanted to do. Joanne was also eighteen, raising a one-year-old, still living at home and enrolled at junior college. The war was raging in the Middle East, and though Joanne was as patriotic as the next person, when someone she loved was shipping off it was a different story.

She hadn't wanted to lose him, even then. And she'd given him an ultimatum, as a best friend. If he went, he'd lose her friendship forever. He'd just smiled and said he was going anyway, hoped she'd change her mind, and he'd look her up when he got back.

If he got back.

For the second time in her life, Joanne had determined that loving Hud was too risky. But when he'd returned, they'd taken up as friends again just as if nothing had happened. Friendship had been safer when it came to him.

"Tell me more," Joanne said, ideas already coming.

"Well, of course, I was lying about the never talking to him again thing. I did talk to him again because thank God he came back. And after that we had this long-distance kind of thing. When I came out to visit him where he was stationed in Virginia, we got married."

"Oh, so you're already married?" It happened. Sometimes a bride wanted a second chance at the day of their dreams.

She held up her finger to indicate her story wasn't complete. "Then we got divorced, because living apart when you're married can be a real strain on a relationship."

"No kidding. This is a second wedding kind of thing?" And they were only twenty-one!

"Yes. This is the one where the entire family, both sides, are on board and they realize no one can talk us out of it." She smiled shyly. "He's my person."

"Your love story is very romantic. How do you feel about tulle?" Joanne went on, trying to capture a sense of what would appeal to Leah and would flatter her slender frame, dark hair and eyes.

"I want my dress to be blue," Leah blurted out. "Can you do that?"

"I can do anything you'd like," Joanne said. "Sure, blue isn't traditional but that's why you're here, right? You want something unique."

"Blue is my favorite color and he'll be dressed in his Navy dress blues. I want us to match."

To date, Joanne had only worked with one unconventional bride, Jill Davis. The first designs had involved something much like a swimsuit because Jill thought she and Sam would get married while wakeboarding. But when the mother of the bride had torpedoed that idea, Jill surprisingly went fairly conventional.

"Sweetheart neckline? Plunging back?" Joanne continued to ask questions to get a feel from Leah. "Pearl sequins?"

They continued to chat about possibilities, and Leah's eyes lit up with excitement.

A lot of people had asked Joanne why she hadn't designed her own wedding dress. She hadn't had the answer to that question, as it had once been her dream to design her wedding dress and sew it. She'd had in mind exactly what it would be. A sweetheart collar with a shorter train and a tiara. Individual pearls sewn on the bodice. A mix of traditional with a little whimsy. The short story? She'd settled. Time got away from her between work, readjusting to Matt being back in Hunter's life and Hunter's general "teenage" passage. And the Valentino dress had been such a steal with her discount. She'd chosen it even though Nora had said the long, Princess Diana-like train didn't say "Joanne." And she'd been right, of course.

Instead the dress said, "I'm thirty-two and I need to get on with it." Now the Valentino dress would probably be sold because Joanne would never jinx herself with it again. Or any other bride, for that matter. Maybe Tilly was right, and Joanne should burn it.

Joanne accepted half of the deposit that she normally asked for a design for the bride because Leah didn't have enough. Joanne would make it work. She had to, for a bride that had renewed Joanne's own hopes in love and romance, even at her age.

After her appointment, Joanne closed up the boutique and drove to her mother's home on the outskirts of Fortune. Mom had been bugging her to come by for days and Joanne had a feeling that it was due to the way rumors spread in their little town. By now Mom would have heard about Hud. And who knew what people were saying?

Looks like Hunky Hud is now having a fling with his best friend. In-te-res-ting.

Did you hear? Joanne's on the rebound with the hottest LT in town.

Sorry. Chuck who?

Her mother greeted Joanne at the door. "Sweetheart! Finally. I've been so worried."

"Sorry. I've just been so busy with the shop… and…" Hud. Busy getting busy with Hud. "Everything. You know how it is."

Mom led her into the cozy living room filled with photos and mementos of Joanne's childhood. Ramona Brandt did not believe in redecorating but instead kept a virtual museum of Joanne's past. There were photos of her and Dad everywhere, the man who, for most of her life, had been Joanne's hero. Tall, handsome and larger than life, he'd worked out regularly but still died of a massive stroke at his engineer's desk in Silicon Valley. High blood pressure, undiagnosed. He'd been too busy to see the doctor.

Not for the first time in her life, Joanne had felt abandoned by a man even if it wasn't entirely his fault. However, from that day on, she'd been obsessed with staying healthy. And sure, maybe a little bit preoccupied with safety and security. Who could blame her?

"Want some coffee?" Mom asked.

"You know I can't drink coffee this late or I'll be up all night."

"Decaf?"

"Okay. Sure."

Joanne waited for her mother to come back from the kitchen, scrolling through her phone to avoid the photos of her smiling dad looking down on her. From heaven, if you believed in that sort of thing, and Joanne did. What would he think about the mess she'd made out of her life? He'd always encouraged her to take risks. To try out for the volleyball team even if she was at best an average player. To apply for the school of her dreams. To ask out the boy she was interested in, instead of waiting for him to ask her.

But at some point, Joanne had chosen safety over happiness.

Mom brought in the cups and set them on the table

near the leather couch, which had seen better days. "Have you read the book yet?"

"What book?"

She cocked her head. "The grief book."

Oh yeah. That. No. She hadn't. "I'm not going to read that book."

"Why not?"

"Because nobody died. And if a dream died, it died a long time ago."

"What are you talking about? Is this about your father?"

Yes and no. Maybe it was a little bit about living the life he would have wanted for her. "No, it's about Chuck. I don't think I ever loved him and even he knew that."

Mom clutched her chest. "Really? But you were going to marry him."

"Don't remind me. It's embarrassing." She picked up her cup, the warmth seeping through her fingertips. "He came by the shop and he wants his ring back."

"The nerve!"

At least they were on the same page about that. Because Joanne had a feeling Mom would not agree with the rest of what she had to tell her. If she'd inherited anything from her mother besides her blond hair and fair complexion, it was that longing for everything to remain the same. Mom didn't even want to replace old furniture or rearrange the way it was placed. "If it isn't broken, don't fix it." A common saying from her mother.

Her mother, who had been there for her when Hud broke up with Joanne. When she'd gone out with Matt in retaliation and gotten pregnant with their son. But that was all such a long time ago.

"I have something important to tell you."

"I hope it's not that you've given him the ring back! Not until he pays you back for every last red cent!"

Oh yay! Another thing they agreed on. "That's exactly what I told him."

She shook a finger at Joanne. "Smart."

"But that's not my news. I wanted to tell you, before you heard through the town rumor mill. Hud and I…we're…we're a thing now."

"Hmmm."

So, she'd already heard. "Alright. Who told you?"

"Iris, because remember, she's very good friends with Trish's grandmother. They see each other every week for their knitting circle."

"Oh yeah, that's right." Joanne waited a beat. "Go on. I know you have something to say about me and Hud. Get it off your chest."

"You know how I feel about Hud. I adore him. He's a good friend to you."

"But…?"

"A husband? I don't know. What kind of thirty-two-year old man hasn't ever been married, or even engaged?"

"That's pretty judgy of you. *I've* never been married and I'm thirty-two."

"That's because you wouldn't marry Matt when he gallantly asked you to."

Not this again. "Matt and I never loved each other."

"You should have tried, at least. He was willing to."

But being married as teenagers wouldn't have been the smartest thing to do, either. They'd both been still living with their parents.

"We were teenagers so we would have probably divorced anyway. He was gone all the time."

"I realize that. What you should have done is snatch him up when he came back to town. If you would have, you'd be married to the father of your child now instead of Sarah. Life would be simpler. Safer."

Joanne might have considered it, too, but she and Matt had been angry with each other for so many years. He'd joined the Air Force to help support their son and was gone all the time. She'd appreciated the regular checks but resented doing the tough work herself. For years. Recently, they'd worked hard to coparent and Joanne thought that was about as good as it could get for the two of them. Besides, she really liked Sarah and was happy for them.

"Maybe love can't always be all about security."

"You have a child—of course security comes first. You put Hunter's needs before your own for many years, as you should have. Hud has been available all this time and never found anyone at all?"

"He's dated." She cleared her throat. "Plenty."

"I'm aware." Mom quirked a brow. "And in all those women he couldn't find *one* that was suitable? That tells me that Hud just isn't the settling down type, much as I adore him."

Definitely not what Joanne wanted to hear or believe. "Or maybe he never found the right woman."

"I just don't want you to get hurt again."

"Well, Mom, I'm fresh off a broken engagement with a man who seemed to be perfect for me. He wanted children, he was supposedly saving for our future, he wanted to settle down in Fortune. He played baseball and was afraid to hurt his hands, so he played it safe in every way. And you see how well that worked out."

"Because he was a lying, conniving bastard. You're hurt, and maybe you just need to take some time and consider all your options."

"Funny, that's exactly what I'm doing. And Hud Decker is option number one. I'm tired of playing it safe, and I'm tired of worrying about something that might never happen. I'm still young enough to want sex and passion in my life. And Hud gives me all that. Plus, he takes care of me."

"What do Matt and Hunter have to say about this?"

"Matt is married. Why should I care what he thinks?"

Okay, that sounded a little defensive. But Matt and Sarah were very happy together, and Hunter had eventually become used to the situation. So, maybe he'd get used to Joanne and Hud, too.

"You two have to coparent, after all. And what about Hunter? What does he think?" She paused. "Or does he know?"

"He knows." Joanne finished her coffee, as she fought for time and the right words. "He's not crazy about the idea."

"And he wasn't fond of Chuck, either. Hunter has a good sense about people."

"That's not fair," Joanne protested. "He mentioned that it's always been just the two of us and we don't need anyone else."

Mom nodded. "Maybe for your son, no one is ever going to be good enough."

But Hud was more than good enough for Joanne. She'd made the decision on her own, just by using her mother as a sounding board. The answer was clear, and her heart raced as she clearly understood what she would do going forward. Hopefully everyone was right when they talked about risk equaling reward.

The bigger the risk, the greater the reward.

Chapter Twelve

When Hud arrived for his next rotation a few minutes late, he was in possibly the best mood of his entire life. Because things with Jo were going better than he could have imagined. They'd spent every night that he was off rotation together, either at his place or hers. But even though he was living out many of his fantasies, he wasn't fooling himself. Hunter would be back living with Joanne at the end of the month and their little bubble would burst. They'd both have to deal with a sullen teenager who'd recently had a lot of changes come into his life. Considering that he'd walked in on their first kiss, Hud wanted to make certain *that* didn't happen again.

He kept trying to take them slow, but with their chemistry they were nearly always going from zero to ninety in seconds. He'd be ripping off her clothes or she'd be ripping off his. Jo was enjoying their time together as much as he was, and that was good, but he already wanted much more. And it wasn't going to be easy to get it with both Hunter and Matt still so much a part of Jo's life.

His past preceded him and Hud realized that.

Coldhearted. Detached. Incapable of emotional commitment.

He called bullshit.

Those were just some of the words a few exes had used to describe him. Others, who understood him better, were kinder. Understood. Like Jo. He'd like to believe she understood that he'd been waiting for the right time and the right woman. It finally seemed within his reach and Hud wasn't going to let the damn ring, annoying though it was, ruin this for him. What he'd do was hang in there until Chuck was nothing more than the stink of a memory.

He wasn't going anywhere, and he wouldn't be intimidated. Both Hunter and Matt would have to deal with him.

As he pulled into the station, Hud forced himself to switch gears just as he did when he went home. The pressures and mental stress of the job could be hell on relationships, and he'd seen this firsthand with his friends. Hud was better than most at compartmentalizing, but that didn't mean that it was always easy to leave the stress behind. A forest fire was currently raging out of control in Yuba County and only about 10 percent contained. Wildfire season seemed to be coming earlier every year. The thought of his firefighter brothers, especially the smoke jumpers being dropped into that inferno, was enough to raise his blood pressure.

Hud got out of his truck and did a double take. J.P. was mowing the lawn. While wearing all his protective gear. Turnout pants, boots, tank and breathing apparatus. Hud stopped walking to stare at him. J.P. waved and kept pushing the lawn mower. From time to time, some harmless hazing still happened at the stations. But the directions from the top down had strongly encouraged all hazing to stop. Hud hated to be the killjoy, but damn if he'd let a promotion slip by because of someone's stupid idea of fun.

Hud found Ty, the other lieutenant of Firehouse 57, pouring himself a cup of coffee in the kitchen. Hud hooked his finger toward the window of the house facing outside and the raucous noise of the mower.

"What the hell?"

"We told him he had to get used to carrying around his heavy gear in all kinds of situations. Why not mow the lawn with gear?" Ty shrugged. "He fell for it."

"He's got a tank on, wasting air."

"Gotta learn sometime. Part of this job is thinking for yourself. Why would anyone ask him to mow the lawn wearing full gear? C'mon, he should have known we were joking."

"Go tell him to take off the gear," Hud ordered Alex, who sat quietly at the table.

"Aw, damn." But he got up from the kitchen table and walked outside.

From inside, Hud watched as Alex waved to J.P. until he stopped the mower.

"So. Joanne." Ty continued to sip at his coffee, apparently in no hurry to leave.

"Did you clock out?" Hud pressed.

"Yeah, dude," Ty said. "Never knew you to be such a stickler."

"Things change."

"Yeah? This about Joanne?" Ty asked with a grin.

"What do you mean?"

"Things. Changing. As in you haven't dated in a while. I believe Kristine was the last one, like six months ago? Now Joanne's available. And, if I remember right, I was the one who suggested it could be your moment." Ty thumped his chest with his thumb.

"Proud of yourself?"

"You're the man." Ty fist-bumped with Hud.

"Yeah, yeah." Hud fought a grin. Even these losers could ruin his mood completely.

"Gotta confess, never thought I'd see *you* with a single mom."

"Yeah, but this is Jo. And Hunter. I've known him all his life. He's a great kid."

"But you've never dated his *mother*." Ty set his mug down. "Take it from someone who *has* dated single mothers. Your life is about to change. Radically."

"For me, that's not going to be a bad thing." Hud helped himself to the coffee.

"Yeah?" Ty crossed his arms. "Say goodbye to morning sex. Say goodbye to sex on the kitchen table. Say goodbye to sex in the shower."

Okay, he honestly didn't like the sound of that, but he was a grown-up now. He could wait for privacy, or they could stay over at his place. Except he knew the last thing Jo would want to do is leave a teenager unsupervised for the night with a house all to himself. Even he knew better than to make that rookie mistake.

Hud cleared his throat. "Hunter spends every other weekend with his dad, and some holidays."

"Ah, yes. The baby daddy." Ty held up air quotes. "That's always so much fun, too. You'll be involved, but not really involved."

"Why are you trying to ruin my stellar mood?" He was in a great one, until he saw J.P.

Ty tossed up his hands. "Just trying to be real, bro."

"Just take your 'real' and shove it up your—"

"Yeah, I know where to shove it." Ty put down

his cup and clapped Hud's back. "I'm heading out. Hang in there. Remember she's worth it."

After a few more minutes in which Ty exchanged details on the previous twenty-four shift, blessedly quiet, Ty was off. Hud clocked in and got back to the kitchen with the rest of his crew. J.P. sat at the table in his turnout pants, but without the rest of his heavy gear. He looked no worse for the wear.

"So, whose turn to cook breakfast?" Hud looked at his crew.

They looked back at him, eagerness and expectation in their eyes.

"Yours," they all said at once.

Oh shit.

After a mostly uneventful rotation, Hud worked some overtime, clocked out, showered and headed over to Joanne's because he was taking her to a movie, then she was cooking for him. He figured it wouldn't be anything very exciting. Probably something like roasted chicken and salad. No problem, because he'd brought a dessert, and he would force-feed her if he had to. It was Alex's chocolate mousse cake and it was apparently better than sex—with some people. Alex had sent Hud with a few slices for Hud's "woman." They were all calling Jo that now, and Hud didn't mind. Except for the fact that they probably believed this was business as usual for him. The thrill of the chase. Then the downside that happened when he'd had enough time with a woman and discovered they didn't really connect on anything but a physical level.

At those times, despite what everyone seemed to believe, Hud feared *he* was the unlovable one. This was mixed with the terrible knowledge that he might not ever find anyone who could put up with him. But then he'd assured himself that if he'd really loved Jo, and he had, the possibility of feeling the same for someone else existed. He was capable of loving someone deeply.

It hadn't been until she'd become engaged to Chuck that Hud had an epiphany he'd fought with everything inside him to deny. He'd continued to live in a quagmire of denial as she made wedding preparations. Had agreed that, of course, he'd be *happy* to give her away in the place of her late father. But not until he'd seen Jo in the wedding dress had Hud realized the wedding would actually *happen*. He was too damn late and had missed his window. She'd marry Chuck, and Hud would have to support that.

So, in a way, he should really thank Chuck for backing out. Hell, maybe he would someday. Thanks to him, Hud had a second chance.

Hud pulled his truck up to the curb in front of Joanne's home. The lights were on inside and as he shut off his headlights, he saw her in the kitchen window, head bent over the sink. The light reflected in her pale blond hair, and she tucked a stray behind her ear, biting her lip in the way she did when she was entirely focused.

The scene felt domestic, something he'd always resisted because it felt like a general loss of freedom. But the facts were that he'd been long ago domesticized by Jo without quite realizing it. The only thing that had been missing in their best friend's style of domesticity was the romance. The sex. With that thought, he shut off the truck and hightailed it to her front door. The sooner they got done with the movie, the sooner they'd be back in bed.

At the door, he handed her the cake. "From Alex. Claims it's better than sex."

She made a face, her nose wrinkled. "I'll put this in the fridge and just grab my purse."

They were going to see some kind of romance book made into a movie, and of course, he was fine with that in this new, supportive boyfriend role. At one time he would have voted this one down and they'd have settled on something between a rom-com and science fiction. Usually that meant some kind of foreign film with subtitles.

"This is supposed to be a three-hanky movie," she said, strapping on her seat belt.

"What's that supposed to mean?" He pulled out on to the street leading to The Granada, the only movie theater in town.

"Really, Hud? Three hankies? As in you'll go through three handkerchiefs with all your tears."

He cringed. "I don't want to sit in a movie theater with you crying about fictional characters."

"Why not? That's when you get to hold me and make it all better."

When she put it that way...

But halfway through the movie, Hud was irritated because the hero was a firefighter. Apparently, no one hired consultants anymore because said hero was in a structure fire with the same kind of eyesight and vision as he would have on a gorgeous day at the beach. Yeah. Not going to happen. Smoke was usually so thick you literally couldn't see your hand in front of you. But when the firefighter ripped off his mask, once outside, to give the heroine "oxygen" he wanted to stand up and walk out. He would have, had it not been for Jo's arm linking through his, holding his hand while with the other she held a tissue.

He leaned close to whisper. "Our tanks have air in them, not oxygen. The same air that's all around them now that she's *outside*."

"Shhh."

"It makes no sense." He shook his head.

At last the movie ended and they made their way out of the crowded theater. Outside, he stopped and wiped away a smudge from under her eyes, caused by her tears. Then he tugged Jo into a sideways hug, and they walked together hip to hip. His mind was on a light dinner and then bed.

"Hud!"

He turned at the sound of the female voice calling out his name and cringed. Joanne stopped beside him.

It was Kristine, with a group of her friends.

"Hey, you two." She eyed them, lingering on the tight embrace, a hint of mischief in her eyes. "So good to *see* you."

"Hi, Kristine," Joanne said. "How are you doing?"

"Not as good as you." Kristine grinned at Hud and crossed her arms. "I *really* hate to say I told you so, but…when was I going to get that call?"

"Yeah." Hud knew exactly what she meant. "Soon."

He felt every one of Jo's low back muscles when they tensed under his touch. But even if what Kristine had said sounded suspicious, he didn't want to stand in a public parking lot with her and Jo and have to explain himself. Especially not when the subject would be referring to when he'd grown the balls to admit he'd always been in love with Jo.

"I guess I shouldn't be surprised to run into one of your exes every time we go out," Jo said once they were in the truck. "But I always liked Kristine."

"She liked you, too."

"What did she mean? Why do you have to call her?"

"Jo, I said I'd be exclusive, and I meant it."

"I know, and I trust you. Does this mean you're not going to tell me?"

"Okay, okay." He fought a grin. "Kristine always thought you had a thing for me but couldn't admit it. Told me to call her and let her know when you finally wised up that you're crazy about me."

"Why do I think that's not exactly the way that went down?" She laughed. "I told you, I *like* Kristine."

In front of her house, he shut off the engine and released his tight grip on the steering wheel. Took a breath. "Okay, so maybe it was the reverse."

"Hud." She spoke softly. Sweetly. She unbuckled her seat belt and reached across the console for him. "I'm crazy about you, too."

This was nuts. It was too soon, and yet it wasn't soon enough. Madness, mayhem, and also the most logical thing in his world. He pressed his forehead to hers.

"Look. I can go as slow as you want with us. But I'm also ready to leapfrog over everything in our way. For years, we've had people come between us. First Matt, then Hunter. Your mother."

"My mother?"

"It's no secret that she always wanted you with Matt, after you had Hunter. Thank God for Sarah, so now Matt's no longer even an option."

She threaded her fingers through his hair. "He never was. I love Matt as the father of my child and that's all. I was never in love with him."

"Now we've got *Chuck*. But I'll wait as long as it

takes for you to get over him. For you to be ready to give him back that ring and move forward with me."

Jo pulled back to meet his gaze, her fingers loosening their hold in his hair. "Baby, no. You don't need to even think about *him* anymore. I'm giving back the ring. I decided."

"Yeah? But how will you get the money from him?"

"Maybe I'll sue. I don't know yet, but I'll find another way."

It was on the tip of his tongue to offer to pay for it all, but he knew Jo would hate that. He had the money and could afford to. But so did Jo and that was hardly the point.

"Or, you know, maybe I'll just let it go. It's only money, right? Maybe it's better to have him out of our life for good, like you said."

He didn't miss the "our life" instead of "my life" and it kick-started his heart.

"I hate to say this, but you know that I could pay him a visit. He's afraid of me."

"For good reason. But you shouldn't have to do that." She rubbed her cheek against his jaw. "I will keep it as an option, though."

Because Hud wondered how Chuck could ever be out of her life without paying her back. The irritation would always be in the back of her mind, but with some luck, in time it would fade. Hud could fill her mind and life with many other distractions. Trips. More picnics. Lots and lots of great sex.

Until one day the guy would be nothing more than an unpleasant memory.

Chapter Thirteen

Oh, my heart.

Hud had believed that she wasn't going to get over Chuck anytime soon, and he was willing to wait until she did. Until she was ready to give back the stupid ring even without getting any money back. Knowing how Hud felt about the ring in the first place, she didn't think she'd ever loved him as much as she did in that moment.

She sealed her words and thoughts with a kiss, which he then took over, and they both quickly got wild and out of control, fogging up the windows. Her hand was on his muscular thigh while he got handsy under her bra, tweaking a nipple and making her moan. The console between them was hardly a match for their determination. She pressed against him, her elbow bumping a visor and then the rearview mirror. They still acted like a couple of horny teenagers.

God, she hoped that would never change.

Then, either Hud or she accidentally pressed the horn, and she jumped.

He burst into laughter. "I think we can afford to go inside now. We don't have to do this in a car anymore."

She agreed, but there was also something so memorable about these moments alone. The memories were warm and thrilling. They slid into her heart and plundered deep. He'd always meant excitement to her. Danger. As a teenager she'd been so attracted to that. Now here was this grown man that to her meant safety as much as frenzy. Passion. The combination never failed to enthrall her. Swept away in his kisses, she forgot anything painful had ever happened. He never failed to stoke her desires to fiery levels.

Always, there was a kind of ease between them. Like they'd been together, this way, for years instead of days.

Inside, he led her to the bedroom, where he pulled off his shirt. No one wore a shirt like Hudson Decker did, but shirtless Hud was a sight to behold. She wasn't ever going to get tired of running the pads of her fingers over those hard planes and granite muscles.

She did so now and loved the way they bunched under her touch. "I wish we could always feel this way."

He met her gaze, eyes hot and serious. "Maybe it's possible, with the right person."

She turned, giving him her back and he slowly slid down the zipper of her dress. He nuzzled her neck as it slowly slid to the floor in a puddle at her feet.

"If not with you, then I don't think it's possible for me." She stepped out of her dress and into his arms.

His rough large hands slid up and down her spine, leaving trails of tingles. "It's possible."

They seemed to move slower tonight, his fierceness held just below the surface, or tamed. One finger looped under the strap of her bra and he slipped it down, cupping her breast. He bent low to cover it with his mouth, sucking almost reverently through the silky material. When he uncovered it and took in her nipple, the sensation of his mouth and hot tongue directly on her naked skin made her gasp.

He moved lower and then lower still, falling to his knees as he kissed her belly button and lingered there. His hands cupped her behind, squeezing as his tongue teased around the line of her sheer panties. She could barely hold a moan in as he lowered them, spreading her thighs. He licked and stroked her folds until she was a quivering mess, holding on to his shoulders, barely able to keep herself upright on limp and useless legs.

Holding on to her butt, he lifted her and set her on the bed where she went to her knees and pulled him close by the loop of his pants.

"These need to come off," she said, kissing his pec as she worked his buckle.

"Way ahead of you, baby."

His hands were a lot faster than hers and he stepped out of his pants and boxer briefs, the evidence clear that he was just as ready as she was. He took a condom from the nightstand, quickly ripped it and slipped it on. Then he rolled on top of her, his warm and strong body covering hers.

"Hmm. I won't ever get tired of this. You, naked. Stay that way for me, would you?"

"I'll try." She wrapped her legs around him, feeling his hardness as he pressed against her belly.

In the next moment, he braced above her and thrust inside her. As he went deeper, she reached for him, touching him everywhere her hands could reach, urging him faster. The bed creaked under the force of their weight and lovemaking.

"Jo, baby. So good."

"Yes, yes. Oh, Hud." He swallowed her moan with a deep kiss. In the next moment she crested that powerful and intense wave of pleasure rippling through her, as she trembled and shook with her release.

A few more strokes and Hud groaned his own pleasure.

They were both out of breath and sweaty as they

collapsed in each other's arms, spent. Joanne burrowed her face in his warm neck and threw her leg over his, trying to catch her breath. Trying to make sense out of her feelings.

Because the warmth that seeped into her heart was caused by more than an orgasm. More to do with his taking care of her first, always certain she'd enjoy herself as much as he did. It had to do with something deeper. Rarer. She loved him. Admired the man that he'd become. A man who put his friends first, who even put the welfare of others above his own in his chosen profession.

But far from the reckless kid he'd been, she could now see he only took calculated risks. He'd never walk into a fire unprepared or without an exit plan. He didn't make rash decisions out of anger. His temper was righteous and controlled. And above all she trusted him more than she ever had any other man in her life except her father. The *L* word had scared Hud once before and it might again. She didn't think so, not this time, but she had to know. The sooner the better.

Especially when her body buzzed and pulsed with the desire to tell him how much he meant to her.

She disentangled from his arms and sat, keeping the covers over her breasts. "I want to tell you something, but you have to *promise* me you won't freak out."

"Promise." His brow furrowed in concern. "But

the way you pulled away from me right now is freaking me out."

At one time, he might not have been mature enough to tell her that. She appreciated the way he'd grown into his emotions. He was comfortable in his skin. She let out a deep breath. This time she could say the words and know they didn't have any conditions or expectations attached to them. He didn't have to love her or change her life. He owed her nothing in return.

She was strong without him, but even stronger with him.

"It's because what I have to tell you is serious. And I didn't want you think I'd say this because you have such a great body. Because you do, of course. Or that I'd tell you this because you're such a great lover. Which, of course, you are. But you know that." Now she was rambling.

"Spit it out, Jo." He narrowed his eyes.

She met his eyes. "I love you."

He reached for her, a smile on his lips, his mouth already forming a word, but she stopped him with a finger on his lips. "Shh. Wait. You don't have to say anything, okay? Just sit with it. Know it."

He quirked a brow until she lowered her finger from his mouth. "Whatever you say. But this is me, *not* freaking out."

She had to laugh. "Look at us, all grown-up."

"The second time around is better, or so I hear."

"That's true, I think." She climbed out of bed and sprinted toward the bathroom. "Meet me in the shower and let me see if the second time around tonight is even better."

"Right behind you."

And in fact, he almost got to the shower before she did.

The next morning, Jo rolled and stretched like a cat. Hud was not next to her in bed, but she heard sounds in the kitchen. Smelled the aroma of freshly brewed coffee and practically salivated. Heard the sizzle of butter in a pan. He was banging around in her kitchen, making them breakfast. A man who'd already captured her heart, simply showing off now.

Yes, I love you. When are you going to stop being so perfect?

"Hud? Coffee, please," she moaned in her caffeine-deprived state, wondering if she should bother to get dressed.

Lately, she enjoyed her constant state of nakedness around the house.

"Stay there," he called out. "I'll bring it."

There was not much point in dressing when everything would come off sooner rather than later. When Hud was around—and lately that was every day that he wasn't with his crew—she pretty much lived in her fuzzy bathrobe and nothing else. Soon enough this kind of lifestyle would change. Hunter would be home in another week and life would return to normal. She'd take off her lover hat and put on her boring mother-of-a-teenager hat. She had no doubt that Hud would stick around, but no idea what their new situation would look like. He'd have to be patient and understand that she was a mother and couldn't always drop everything for him.

And Hud probably wasn't used to that in any other of his prior relationships. Why would he be? He hadn't even dated another single mother. "Too complicated," he'd once said, another red flag and reason she thought they would never work. Either he'd apparently changed his mind about "complicated" or he just had no *idea* what he would be walking into. It was one thing to be her son's friend and pseudo uncle, but this new and complicated relationship was going to be tough on everyone.

Joanne rolled on her back, and a moment later heard the front door slam. Then her son's voice. "You're always here!"

Oh. My. God. Code three! Or whatever first responders said when it was an emergency. Joanne leaped out of bed and shut her bedroom door, locked it, then proceeded to put on as many clothes as she could find. Quickly. She could hear only muffled voices now, Hud's deeper more commanding voice, followed by her son's. It was imperative that she get out there, stat, and explain. Fix this. Maybe she could say that Hud slept on the couch and was making them breakfast. She'd slept in. In her clothes, of course. She'd slept in her clothes. That was her story and she was sticking to it.

"Hi, honey," Joanne said, walking into the kitchen. "I heard you come in."

But Hud stood in the middle of the kitchen, shirtless, wearing nothing but his jeans, low on his hips. He gave her a little smirk and shrugged.

Walking past her, he stopped to press a kiss against her temple. "Going to put on a shirt."

"Good idea," she said on a sigh.

Hunter glared at her, looking disgusted. "I came by to have you sign a permission slip." He threw it on the counter.

"Fine," she said, taking out a pen to sign it, and barely looking at it. Some kind of field trip. Matt's signature was already on it. She handed it back. "I'm sorry we shocked you."

He snorted. "I'm not shocked."

"I would have told you about us, but I was waiting until you came back home from your dad's."

"This is how it's going to be now? Hud always over here? Is he moving in?"

She held up a palm. "Okay, slow down. We haven't talked about a lot of these things. No, he's not moving in."

"Because Chuck never even lived here. Our house is too small."

It wasn't much smaller than Matt and Sarah's,

ironically, and that seemed to be just fine with Hunter. Joanne would be upset by the double standard, but she'd set it up this way. She'd never really had a man in the house, wanting Hunter to feel comfortable in their home. Never threatened. Chuck was to have been the first man to live with them. Her husband. Now she wondered why she'd made it so easy for Hunter to accept the fact that she'd always been alone. Yet Matt was already married and even before he had been, Sarah had lived with him.

"I don't want you to get upset, but this is how it's going to be. Hud and I…we're in a relationship. You'll have to get used to that."

"I'm not going to get *used* to it. First Chuck, now Hud. What if Hud leaves you at the altar too?"

"Whoa. You are getting way ahead of yourself."

"Well, I don't want to live here anymore if Hud's *always* going to be around."

"That's not fair. Your dad has Sarah and you don't seem to mind that."

"Yeah, we all get along okay. Maybe I should go live there."

Fear pierced through Joanne at the thought that her only child would leave her home. *Her* home, where she could keep him safe from harm and life altering mistakes.

"No, you shouldn't." Joanne fought to keep her cool. "You belong here. That hasn't changed."

"Yeah? If you want to be with Hud, then maybe I

want to go live with my dad." He turned to go, and it was then that she heard keys jiggling in his pockets.

"Wait. Don't you need a ride back? I'll let you drive."

"No need," he said, holding up car keys. "I got my license two days ago. Dad let me borrow the car."

"You got your license? *Already?*"

Why would Matt do this? It had been six months since Hunter had obtained his permit, but they were supposed to talk over these kinds of huge decisions together. Coparent. As usual, he was the popular parent. She was the uncool, conservative, nutrition-minded, strict parent.

"Why not? I already had the driving hours logged in, and the test was super easy. Sarah took me. Passed on the first try."

Oh, of course he had! Her son was a genius when he wanted to be. Joanne crossed her arms. "I'm going to talk to your father about this. He should have run it by me."

"Great!" Hunter rolled his eyes and then he was out the door, hand held up in a half wave.

Joanne ran to the window to watch him drive off, half expecting him to peal out in anger. But her son didn't do anything of the sort. He drove Matt's SUV slowly down the cul-de-sac. And then Hud's strong arms were around her, pulling her back to him, dipping his head in the crook of her shoulder.

"I'll talk to him."

"I'm sorry. You didn't sign up for this drama."

"Yeah, I did. I signed up for it all." He turned her to face him. "I'm going to make this better. Whatever it takes, I'm going to make us work. He may not like it at first, but he'll get used to me being around here more often."

"Maybe we shouldn't shove it in his face that we're sleeping together."

"Probably a good idea, but too late on that one."

She plunked her forehead to his chest, groaning. "I know."

"Leave it to me, baby. He's not leaving your home. I'll fix this."

Chapter Fourteen

The next day, Joanne made arrangements to meet Chuck in a public place and give him back the ring. She chose the coffee and pastry shop in town, The Drip, and he agreed easily, probably not wanting a scene.

He was already seated when she arrived and gave her a forced smile. "Joanne."

"Hey there. Joanne is glad that Chuck is here on time." Sue her, she couldn't resist.

Chuck simply blinked. Maybe he now realized how stupid he sounded. "Again, I'm sorry."

Oh yes, yes, she'd forgotten. That fixed everything. He was *sorry*.

"You don't have to keep saying that." She fished in her purse for the ring and planted it in front of him. "There."

He picked the ring up and palmed it. "Thanks. What made you change your mind?"

"Hud convinced me."

"I figured he would have something to do with it." Chuck frowned. "He's always there, isn't he?"

Joanne briefly considered telling Chuck that he resembled a sullen teenage boy at the moment, then decided she wouldn't go there. When he and Hunter had been together, she'd dealt with two difficult "boys" making her feel like a mediator half the time. Chuck had claimed to like Hunter and want more children, but he'd hardly even *tried* to get along with Hunter.

I've been such an idiot. Why was I even marrying Chuck?

It hurt to believe she'd been so desperate not to wind up alone. But with a son who had one foot out the door, it was true that she'd made stupid snap decisions. It was time to stop making those. And if this didn't work out again with Hud and she wound up alone for the rest of her life, she'd somehow deal. Because no matter what happened, she wasn't settling for less than everything. Never again.

"Look, I don't care what you think of Hud. The point is, *you* did a lousy thing. Do you have any idea how humiliating this all has been for me?"

"Not really." He shrugged.

"My business has suffered because of you. Brides tend to be a superstitious group. Just like baseball players. The real reason I'm giving you back the ring is that I don't want Hud to believe I haven't moved on, because I have."

Joanne had been in the bridal industry for over a decade, and she'd heard it all through the grapevine. Everything from bridesmaids getting caught making out with the groom before the wedding, to a last-minute hurrah between the bride and her ex. Caught on video. The actual wedding day could get crazy when one mixed drinking with latent desires of the heart.

Not to mention the marriage itself, when the bride forced herself to ignore the man she really wanted, for the only one she thought she could have.

Sometimes taking a risk was the best choice.

"How are you, otherwise?" Chuck asked. "I think about you sometimes."

"Please don't."

"Hate to say I told you so." He scowled. "I heard you're with Hud now."

"Yes, we're together. You were right. Happy now?"

"Not really."

"How's Mandy doing? I keep hearing her song on the radio. 'I'm Sick of You' or something. I'm sure it's not autobiographical."

"Yeah, we broke up."

They'd broken up. Good thing she'd given him back that lousy ring when she couldn't very well bribe him with it to get her money back.

"Well, I guess… I'm sorry?"

"I think she wanted to marry a ballplayer because J.Lo. married a ballplayer. I guess ballplayers were in season but now she's on to a football player."

"I don't know, Chuck, that sounds pretty shallow of her."

"Right?" He reached for her hand. "You were the best thing that ever happened to me."

"No." She removed her hand. "I wasn't. I could have been your worst nightmare. I didn't love you or make room for you in my life. We didn't even live together because I didn't want you crowding Hunter. Crowding me. I have no idea what I was thinking. Maybe I thought you'd slide into my life, I'd give you a drawer, and we'd keep your stuff in the shed or something."

"You wanted to get married. That's *all* you wanted."

"That's the first thing you've said in a long time that I agree with."

Chuck reached in the back of his pants pocket and set a check on the table. It was made out to her, a sum big enough to cover more than his half of the wedding.

She grabbed it. "How did you manage?"

"I sold the BMW that Mandy bought me."

Joanne gaped. "She bought you a BMW?"

"Yeah," he said, looking morose. "When I was her man. But if I hadn't sold it, she would probably be taking it back."

"Good thinking, I guess."

"You deserve it. If I'm being honest here, I think you still would have been a good deal for me. I would have taken the drawer. I would have kept my stuff in the shed."

"Chuck, that's ridiculous. We both deserved better."

"You've got yours now. Maybe someday I'll get mine."

It was probably that kicked puppy-dog look in his brown eyes, but Joanne squeezed his hand. "I was so mad at you, and I still think it was a lousy thing to do. But now I have to thank you for saving me from making the worst mistake of my life."

Later at the boutique, Joanne forced her thoughts away from Hunter's driver's license debacle back to the designs she'd been working on for Leah. It had at least served to distract her from the Taylors.

"Why is the dress blue?" Nora leaned to look over Joanne's shoulder.

"My bride wants blue."

Nora wrinkled her nose. "For real? A second marriage or something?"

"Or something. It's actually a romantic story." Joanne reiterated everything she'd learned from Leah and her fiancé, also known as her ex-husband.

"How sweet," Nora said, carrying a dress to the front. "Jill is coming in today for her dress, so prepare for a lot of gushing and possibly some tears."

"Aw, she's so sweet and in love."

"Right? It should have been a clue to me when you were so matter-of-fact about your dress," Nora said.

Ignoring that, she handed over the sketch pad to Nora. "What do you think?"

"I love the sweetheart collar."

"This blue is going to be a challenge. I have to find just the right type of material to make it work."

"Oh hey, don't want to freak you out or anything, but I got stuck at the light on Barrett this morning and I could have sworn I saw Hunter driving to school. By himself. Just thought you should know. It takes a village and all that."

"He got his license."

Nora froze. "And you're not having a major freak-out?"

"I'm not happy about it. They went behind my back. I mean, I got voted down that he should get his license at sixteen, but I had no idea he'd do it the month he's staying with his father."

"Yeah, that wasn't cool." Nora hung Jill's dress and began unwrapping it. "But look at you, all calm and collected. I know how difficult this is for you."

"Maybe because I have bigger worries."

"Bigger than being jilted, or having your sixteen-year-old let loose on the unsuspecting public roads?"

"I can't even believe I'm saying this but yes. Last night, Hunter showed up to the house unexpectedly and…well, let's just say he now knows Hud and I are sleeping together."

"He caught you in the act?" Nora covered her mouth.

"Okay, thank you for reminding me that it could always be worse. No, but Hud was in the kitchen making me breakfast. Without a shirt on."

"Well, at least he had his pants on." She paused. "Please say he had his pants on."

"He did."

"How did Hud react when you made him leave? Is he pissed off?"

"I didn't make him leave."

"You didn't?" Nora said. "Remember that time Chuck was over and when Hunter showed up you had Chuck leave out the back door?"

"Oh yeah. Well, it hadn't been six months." Joanne cleared her throat. "Hunter didn't stay long anyway. He said he might move in with Matt if Hud and I are going to be together."

"Manipulative little man, isn't he?"

Joanne scoffed. "It's not going to happen. I'm talking to Matt today."

"Pretty sure he doesn't want Hunter living with

him and Sarah and disrupting his privacy. He is a newlywed, after all."

"Yeah, I'm pretty sure Matt now appreciates what I've been through for years. Having a teenager is not all that different from having a toddler when it comes to privacy. But I'm used to it."

"Hud isn't."

"I know."

That worried Joanne. Maybe after a few months of the teenage drama he'd get tired of being put in second place. But she'd have to work on that. Achieve a balance. She deserved a love life and that's why bedroom locks had been invented.

"But he said he'll talk to Hunter."

"Those two used to get along fine. I'm sure that's all it takes. A nice, long talk man to little man."

Joanne snorted. "Hunter hates when you call him 'little man.' He is six feet tall now."

"I've known the rug rat since he was two. He's little man to me, always."

Once Jill came in the store for one last fitting, Nora and Joanne dropped everything else. The boutique was infused with the special magic of a bride one step closer to her wedding date. One of Joanne's favorite moments and Jill did not disappoint. She arrived with her mother, and her good friends Carly and Zoey, who was now her sister-in-law, too.

Nora poured flutes of champagne while Joanne handed out tissues from the box she kept handy.

"You look amazing!" Zoey said, wiping her cheeks.

"Like a fairy tale princess," her mother said, grabbing a tissue and dabbing her eyes. "Doesn't she look like a princess, girls?"

"She does," everyone answered, practically in harmony.

It was time for Joanne to set the stage. This time she got Sam's name right, thank you God, as she described the way that Jill would walk toward her groom during their outdoor wedding. Everyone seemed enthralled by Joanne's description, but a funny thing happened. She didn't get anyone's name wrong, but the bride she pictured wasn't Jill. It was Joanne. And she found herself describing her own perfect wedding day.

The one she'd longed for when she was a young girl but hadn't allowed herself to dream about for years. And this time, the man she walked toward was the one she'd wanted for what felt like half of her life. Hud, looking incredibly handsome in his tux, his green eyes shimmering and matching the cummerbund perfectly. Just as she'd imagined they would.

After everyone had left, and Nora ran off to make dinner for her boyfriend, Joanne was left alone with her thoughts. She should close up the shop and head home, where she expected Hud for dinner. Because she wanted to see him, of course, but first she needed to get a grip. She couldn't do this to him. It wasn't fair to be thinking about marriage again so soon. She'd just fallen in love with him.

They were just getting to know each other again and already finding obstacles. Hunter wasn't ready. Her mother thought Joanne should still be somewhere in the seven-step grieving process. And God only knew what Matt would say about all this. She might just be the only one ready in this scenario. Ready for her life to begin. The one she'd kept on hold for years while she lied to herself about Hud. While she pretended being his friend was enough for her.

So much wasted time!

"Joanne?"

The door to her shop jingled announcing someone had stepped inside, and there stood Matt Conner.

Straight out of her fantasy into cold, harsh reality. Why not? She lived on the corner of Reality and Sensibility and her address still hadn't changed.

"Hey there. I was going to call you, but the day got away from me."

Not for the first time, it made Joanne's heart ache to see how much Hunter resembled his father. Matt was almost as good-looking as Hud. Her son had really lucked out in the gene pool. He had the same tall frame, long legs, dark hair and square jaw. He'd apparently inherited his father's high IQ, as well. But mostly, she was simply grateful that Matt was a good man and someday their son would be, too.

So many times, she wished she could have loved him. Tried. Despite the fact that she and Matt hadn't always been friends, he'd been right about so many things that she was only now starting to realize. She'd kept such control over Hunter's life and put him at the center of her life for so long that when it came time to put herself first, she'd almost forgotten how to make wise, well-thought-out choices. To balance her own needs with those of her family.

Matt stuck his hands in his pockets. "I should have told you about the appointment at the DMV. Don't blame Sarah. I was called to a last-minute chartered flight and Hunter begged us not to reschedule."

"Maybe I overreacted. I knew he'd be getting his license soon."

"We should have given you a heads-up."

"It would have been nice. But honestly, that's not what bothers me the most about our son right now."

"He's a good kid. You did a great job with him."

"But I'm afraid I let Hunter mistakenly believe he could call the shots in my life. I gave him too much control at some point. Then when I took my life back, I made a huge mistake."

"I'm sure that's not true."

"Really? *Chuck* was a huge mistake."

He shrugged. "Well…"

"Yeah." She couldn't help a strained laugh. "*He* was a mistake. But Hud isn't. Now our son has just informed me that if I keep seeing him, he'll move in with you and Sarah."

Matt quirked a brow. "That's not going to happen."

"Miss your privacy already?" she teased.

"It isn't easy, but I also know that's not what you want. So, it's true. You're seeing Hud."

God, she hoped Matt wouldn't be giving her a hard time about this, too. She was tired of people putting themselves between her and Hud. Now that she'd moved herself out of her own way, if she had to bulldoze through every single other person who had doubts, she would. It was her time to be happy. Finally.

She crossed her arms. "Is that a problem?"

"Why would it be? Look. You and I both know that Hunter derailed our lives."

"Don't say that. *We* derailed our lives. By being young and stupid. Irresponsible."

"You're right. But here's the thing. Maybe it's time Hunter heard about our complicated history. Our very weird triangle."

Joanne had decided that she'd never tell Hunter, because that was grown-up stuff that didn't concern him. He already knew enough. Understood that his parents had been young and foolish. That they hadn't planned on him but still wanted and loved him very much. But telling him about Hud…and that Matt was a complete rebound. She didn't want her son to think less of her. Or less of his father.

"I don't know."

"He might understand why Hud has never liked me. If you think he doesn't sense that tension between us, you're kidding yourself."

"What do you mean? Hud likes you fine."

Matt rolled his eyes. "Hunter's growing up fast, and I think it's time we told him the truth."

"I've never wanted to involve him in any of my drama." Yet that had happened anyway thanks to Chuck.

"You don't have to give him all of the details, but if he knew that you and Hud had a prior relationship…that you might have wound up together—"

"Except for him? No, I can't do that to my son."

"I was going to say that he might understand why Hud is so important to you."

"I'll think about it. But I'm glad we can all agree that Hunter *isn't* going to move in with you and Sarah."

Matt nodded. "I agree. That was fairly manipulative of him, and he and I will have a long talk about it."

"Thanks." Joanne blew out a breath. "I'm actually glad you retired from the Air Force. It was hard giving up all the control, but it's something I needed to do. And I understand that now."

"Sometimes you worry too much, but no one can

blame you. I certainly can't." Matt's gaze swept over her with kindness.

She knew he was thinking about her father's untimely death. Her teenage pregnancy. Hud's car accident. His enlistment in the Army. It had all shaped her life in many ways.

"I appreciate that. More than you know."

"You do realize that Hunter is worried about you? Like mother, like son. I mean, you were supposed to be married less than a month ago. He's heard the small-town rumors about the bad luck boutique."

She hadn't thought of it that way. "Did he ask you?"

"He did and I told him the truth. He was worried about you. That's why he's so resistant to Hud," Matt continued. "He's thinking you're going to get hurt all over again."

"But Hud has always been there for us."

"Well, maybe that's part of the problem. It's the newly defined relationships that are bothering him. Because he doesn't understand how it all happened so quickly. But he would, if he had a few more details to see the full picture. If he knew how long this has been going on."

Matt had a point.

"I'll talk to him, too," Joanne said. "Because Hud and I are in a relationship and it's serious. And *no one* is going to change my mind about him."

Matt smiled. "It's about damn time."

Chapter Fifteen

The next night, Joanne couldn't sleep and woke in the middle of the night. A million thoughts swam to the forefront of her mind, disrupting her peace, demanding attention. Hunter. The driver's license. Getting the wedding money from Chuck. The Taylor wedding and that whole debacle. Leah and the perfect dress she wanted but actually couldn't afford. It didn't help that Hud had pulled an extra shift and would be gone all night. She'd already grown so used to sleeping with him that her bed felt huge and empty without him. Her bedroom was covered in his delicious manly scent. Leather and the soap he used. His divine cologne. He had clothes in her drawers and spare uniforms in the closet. Boots under her bed.

For so long, she'd resisted a man taking over her home but now she didn't know how she'd lived all these years without Hud being the one to take up all the empty spaces.

"Come on up, Rachel. It's okay." Joanne patted the foot of her bed, a place Rachel was rarely allowed.

She happily bounced up, wagging her tail and turning in a circle until she found just the right spot. Then she let out a happy dog sigh. Rachel stayed with Joanne all the time now because Hud was over so much. It no longer made sense to spend all that money on doggy day care, so he only sent her when they were both working.

"It's just us girls tonight."

She felt unsettled. Something had been bothering her about the Taylor wedding. The designs she'd created were good, but not her best work. The problem, she now believed, was that she hadn't really known Brenda well enough to design the right dress. She hadn't asked enough questions, or maybe just not the right ones. Her romance with the groom had been nothing inspiring. They'd met at a law firm in Silicon Valley and their first date had been an all-night trial prep session. Not too romantic.

Joanne grabbed her sketch pad from the nightstand and paged through her recent drawings. She found the dress she'd drawn a few days ago thinking it might work for Leah. But Joanne had realized almost immediately the dress was far too avant-garde for her. It had straight, almost severe lines, with a plunging back. A short train and shorter veil. Sophisticated. Daring and unorthodox. Only a chic bride could wear a dress such as this one. Joanne didn't even know how the concept had come out of her, but like so many of her ideas, it had surprised her. She would certainly never make such a bold statement on *her* wedding day.

No. It definitely wouldn't work for sweet Leah, but Brenda Taylor immediately came to mind.

Joanne didn't know which of her designs they'd settled on, but she knew that this one was far superior than the ones they'd purchased. She could keep the design, because sooner or later she'd have a bride it would fit. But the truth was that she wanted Brenda to have it. All the bitterness Joanne felt at being passed over had dissipated. If the Taylors thought she'd bring bad luck to their wedding day, it was simply because they had no idea that she was in a much better place right now. Far from bad luck, the wedding day fail had been one of the best things ever to happen to her.

And maybe it was high time for them to witness that much better, far richer Joanne.

The plan had come to Hud while on a boring shift where the only calls that had come in were medical ones.

Genius idea number one: he would take Hunter rock climbing at Wildfire Ridge Outdoor Adventures. There was no other sport that required more trust between two people than rock climbing. In some cases, the relationship with a partner could mean the difference between life or death. Hud would demonstrate once more that he trusted this rangy sixteen-year-old, who, let's face it, was like a son to him.

Like a son. If this worked out permanently with Jo, and each day and night brought him more hope that it would, he'd have a stepson. A ready-made family. While he'd always been a friend to Hunter, Jo had called the shots with her son. It was how she'd wanted it. She rarely wanted his advice, but he gave it to her anyway: Give him short bursts of freedom so he learns how to handle himself. Respect the fact that he might need some privacy. *Yes, let him get his license when he's sixteen. I actually agree with Matt.* Understand that he's no longer your little boy.

She'd listened, because he'd pulled the best friend card. Hell, there was no one that understood teenage boys better than a former teenage boy. And Hud had been a hell of a teenage boy. He felt sorry for his parents now, who'd done the best they could with him. But he'd been born to parents who hadn't given him *enough* freedom. By the time they did, he went crazy with it. When he'd discovered sex, it had been like being handed the keys to an ice-cream parlor with sixty-five different flavors. How was he supposed to pick just one? How did he even know what he liked? Shouldn't he at least try them all out once?

That kind of idiocy, the inability to appreciate what he had, was how he'd lost Jo.

Determined that Hunter would not be a stupid kid too, he was ready to enlighten him. He was probably worried that Hud would also hurt his mother, and after the recent events, he couldn't blame him.

So, on Saturday after his shift rotation, he picked Hunter up at his father's house.

"Can I drive?" Hunter asked when he came up to the driver's side window. "I need the practice and you've been driving like…forever, right?"

Hud moved to the passenger seat. "Why not?"

Hunter drove to the outskirts of Fortune and the hill leading to Wildfire Ridge. They'd been here together many times. Hunter liked coming along to occasionally bend Sam Hawker's ear, Jill's fiancé, and one of the many guides here. He'd been a former Marine and Hunter was still at the age where that highly impressed him. But he'd also been on several ride-alongs with Hud, and they'd talked Army and all things military. Growing up in a small town that had at some point become a haven for former military, it wasn't surprising that Hunter wanted to serve.

Hud just wanted to know it was for the right reasons, and he knew Matt and Sam agreed with him.

Hud relaxed in the passenger seat, until Hunter

nearly missed stopping at a red light in time. The tires screeched. Hud didn't even blink.

"You know about my accident?"

Hunter snorted. "Only because my mom told me like a hundred zillion times. She said that's when you decided to be a first responder."

"You never heard my side of the story."

"Was it something stupid? Like you ran a red light?" He cleared his throat. "I'm not used to the brakes on your truck."

"No, I lost control of my father's sports car. Going way too fast."

"Your dad had a sports car? Kewl."

"Don't get too excited. It was an old classic Mustang. But a very sweet ride."

"Was the accident your fault or someone else's?"

"I wrapped the car around a tree, so I guess you could say that's my fault."

No one had ever shared the gory details with Hunter and Hud wasn't about to do that now. Sometimes fears could be just as powerful as misguided courage. And just as harmful. Hunter didn't say anything, apparently using all his attention to make a left turn against traffic.

Impressed, Hud didn't continue talking until he'd safely turned. "And it happened over a girl."

Concentration broken, Hunter glanced at him for a second, then back to the road. "Huh."

"She wasn't just *any* girl to me. I loved her. I was

angry because *I'd* done something stupid. So, she went out with another guy. I was jealous. Don't drive when you're jealous."

Hunter snorted. "Or mad."

"Just kidding. Sometimes you have to drive when you're mad or jealous."

"Yeah. Or I might never drive."

"Exactly. Just make sure to separate your emotions when you get behind the wheel."

"I've already heard *all* this from my dad."

"That's good advice in general. Try not to let emotions rule your decisions. Logic matters too. It's a balance."

"You should take your own advice," Hunter said, turning into the parking lot for customers. "You're dating my mom because you like her, but maybe you should think it over. Don't let those emotions make the decision."

One point for Hunter. He'd thrown it back in Hud's face. No one had ever said the kid was slow on the uptake.

"I *have* thought it over," Hud said, catching the keys when Hunter tossed them to him. "The girl I just told you about? That was your mom."

One point for Hud and the save.

Hunter stared at him blankly. "For real?"

Okay, well, Hud hadn't planned on it just coming out like that. He'd never had occasion to talk to Hunter about his history with Jo because why would he? It was all in the past, and while he would have loved it to stay where it belonged, they were still dealing with the repercussions. And it was time for Hunter to understand that this whole idea of being with Jo wasn't something he'd thought up on the spot at the last minute.

He met his gaze and didn't break eye contact. "For real."

Hud rolled back the shell of his truck cab and pulled out his equipment. The camp offered everything one would need to climb for rent, but years ago Hud had bought all his own stuff. He shoved a bag filled with harnesses into Hunter's arms.

He was still staring. "You and my mom."

"It was years ago. And we were both too young."

"But I thought you guys were just good friends. My friends said you had the hots for my mom, and I said no *way*, he's like my uncle." He scoffed. "You made me look stupid."

"It's complicated."

"I hate complicated."

Join the club, kid. Join the club. Come to the meetings. Pay your dues.

"Now I know why you don't like my dad."

The words hit Hud square in the solar plexus and he hadn't expected that. "Matt's a good man."

"But he took your girl."

"No, it's not like that. She's not property so she

can't be taken. And she had every right to go out with your dad. We weren't together at the time."

"But you wanted to be."

Hud grunted. "Yeah."

They hiked up to the entrance and checked in with Julian, one of the guides. With both an annual membership and employee discount, Hud could bring along a friend anytime, free of charge. Farther in, and at the craggy rock that sat at the base of Wildfire Ridge and faced away from the lake, Hud pulled out harnesses, helmets and ropes. He handed Hunter an extra pair of footwear because he was prepared.

Hud set them up, attaching the carabiner clip to the harness Hunter would use.

Hunter had been rock climbing here before, at least once on Friends and Family Day with Matt and his friends. So Hud knew he wasn't dealing with a complete beginner, but this would be the first time with him. And contrary to Matt, Hud had participated in extreme sports. He'd climbed El Capitan in Yosemite and other challenging boulders. But this wasn't a contest, Hud reminded himself, even if Hunter had called it.

He'd always been a little sensitive about Matt.

For the next hour, he and Hunter were locked in the symbiotic relationship between climber and belayer. Fearless, Hunter climbed, taking direction from Hud, always letting his feet lead him. Too many beginners used their hands to pull themselves up and wound up getting tired easily. Hunter was a quick study and when he was ready to switch places and be the belayer, Hud did his thing. The quiet between them wasn't awkward, but a comfortable silence.

The sun was beginning to set when Hud drove them back to Matt's house.

"I guess we won't be doing stuff like this anymore," Hunter said.

"Why not?"

"Think about it. You took me fishing and camping whenever Mom was off seeing one of Chuck's away baseball games. Before that, it was always whenever she went away for a trade show. But now, *you're* going to be the guy."

Holy crap. Hud had not seen that one coming. His chest constricted with the love he had for this kid. There was just no other word for it.

"I'm always going to have time for you, buddy."

Hunter snorted. "Grown-ups always say that. But...you still love my mom? For *real*?"

Hud didn't hesitate. "Yeah. I do. I never stopped."

"Wow, that's *hella* corny."

"Thanks."

"You should be *sure*, because you shouldn't fool around with a single mom."

"Preaching to the choir."

"Huh. Well, it's okay for you to date my mom, I guess. She should be happy. You better not be a jerk-off like Chuck or I'll have to kill you."

"Give me *some* credit."

"I'm serious."

"I am, too."

Hud parked on the sidewalk in front of Matt and Sarah's home. The light was on inside and he got to witness another domestic scene. Matt and Sarah in the window, as he wrapped his arms around her, pulling her in. There were an awful lot of new couples in Hunter's life. It had to be tough.

"They're so embarrassing to be around. Geesh." He climbed out of the car. "Whatever you do, don't get cutesy. It you call my mom honeybuns or sweetie pie, I swear I'll throw up all over you."

Hud smirked. "You got it."

They fist-bumped, and as Hud drove home, he thought this was about as good as life could ever get.

Chapter Sixteen

Joanne paced the living room, waiting for Hud. She'd never paced in her life, but that afternoon Hud had taken her son rock climbing on Wildfire Ridge. Hunter went up there a lot, whether with Matt or tagging along with Hud here and there, but this was the first time they'd been together since... Well, since Joanne and Hud became involved.

Considering Hunter wasn't thrilled with the idea of the two of them, Joanne had cause to be worried. Okay, so she had to stop freaking out. And when she heard Hud's truck pull up outside, she finally did. She ran to her window to see that at least from the outside, he was intact, no worse for the wear of hanging out with a sometimes-pissy teenager.

"You made it!" She threw open the door.

"What? You had doubts?" He rushed her at the door, picking her up and carrying her inside. "I've been through fires and pulled people out of wrecks. I think I can handle a teenager."

"And don't forget crawled under Mrs. Diaz's house for Pooky."

"What can I say? You fell in love with a real-life hero." He smirked as he put her down. "Who just got the green light."

"Oh my gosh, so he's okay with us dating?" She covered her mouth.

"Yep. But I *did* have to promise him a sports car on his seventeenth birthday."

Joanne gasped. "You didn't!"

"No, it's good. I'll take out a loan." He plopped down on the couch and stretched his arms to the side. "Don't worry, I should be done paying it off by the time I retire."

Poor Hud! She should have warned him, prepared him better. He had so much to learn about kids. They shouldn't be bribed, no matter how much you wanted to. The temptations came early. You couldn't do it, no matter how much you wanted to promise a gallon of ice cream, or a million dollars even, if they would just sleep through the night or let you go to the bathroom alone for once.

Then she caught the mischievous gleam in Hud's gaze. "You brat!"

He pulled her down on his lap, laughing. "Baby, if I'm going to mortgage our future over a sports car, it will be mine. Took you long enough."

Our future. She swallowed, her heart full. "You had me going."

His low throaty laugh was terribly sexy when it sounded like it came from a place of such deep contentment. She'd never imagined he would be this happy, dropped into her dull life. She had a mortgage payment and a 529 Education Fund for Hunter. She lived with a teenager and owned a plain Jane sedan good on gas mileage.

"I think now that we're officially together, you can stop all of the teasing." Her fingers grazed over his chin and the light bristle there.

"Hell, no. I was going to ramp it up." His arms came around her waist, and he slid her a slow smile.

That smile promised her a future and she would grab on and hold tight. This was everything she'd ever wanted. She framed his face. "Are you happy, Hud?"

"Why? If I say I'm not, are you going to do something to *get* me happy?"

He was incorrigible. Still, she giggled. "I might."

"Happier than I've ever been."

She waited, expecting him to tack on a teasing comment, like he'd be even happier if she brought him a cold beer. But he didn't make a joke. Hud knew when to be serious and that truth slid into her heart, warm and sweet. She tugged him up from the couch and he came willingly, smiling when he saw her turn toward the bedroom. They each took off their clothes and fell into bed, where he made love to her, slow and delicious.

Afterward, he crushed her against his chest. "I love you. I always have. And don't you ever forget it."

She kissed him and fell asleep with those words on her mind.

It took two more days and late-night talks with Hud, but Joanne made the decision about her new design.

"Where are you off to today?" Hud asked in the morning.

"The fabric store, lunch with my mother and Iris—" She bustled about the kitchen, pouring them each cups of coffee.

"Uh-oh. Does your mother know?"

"About us? Yes, she knows. And she's fine with it."

He held up his coffee mug in a mock salute. "I will accept that lie."

"Hud, you know she adores you," she chided, hugging his neck. "Stop."

"It's okay, baby. She adores me as your best friend, but I broke your heart once and I get that's hard to get past with your only daughter. I'm going to earn her respect back." He bent to kiss her on the lips.

"And what are you doing today?"

"Brought my toolbox and I'm going to fix your leaky sink. This is real hero stuff."

"That's why I love you." She finished her coffee, kissed him again and headed for the door. "I'll be back late because I have after-hours appointments with two different brides."

She'd gone ahead and scheduled an appointment with Brenda Taylor, with the explanation that she understood someone else would make the dress, but she wanted to talk about the designs she'd already bought. She left out talk of the new design, because in the end it might not be something Brenda would want anyway. Still, the meeting itself would go a long way toward clarifying that Joanne was no longer the jilted bride of the bad luck boutique. Someone was bound to see her coming inside the boutique. And as the influential Taylors of Fortune, their opinion would go a long way to getting the word out.

Joanne wore her yellow dress again. The bags were gone from under her eyes because these days she might be losing sleep here and there, but it was for all the right reasons. She was actually well rested, her skin clear and her cheeks rosy pink. And for the first time in a long while, she was happy in that over-the-top way that she figured was reserved for people younger than her.

Brenda showed up at the boutique a few minutes late. "Sorry, there was bad traffic. I had a deposition in Oakland today."

"We could have rescheduled." Joanne led her to the couch where her new design sat in the sketch pad, still not transferred to a graphic design program.

"Absolutely not. I'm really sorry with the way everything happened."

"You're not the first superstitious bride I've met, so don't be too hard on yourself."

"I'm not the superstitious one," Brenda said, settling back into the sofa. "It's my *mother*. Um, do you have some of that champagne around?"

"Of course." In the minifridge, Joanne found the uncorked bottle they hadn't finished when Jill had come in. Noting it still had fizz, she poured some into a flute and handed it to Brenda.

"Thanks. You're a class act. My mom expected you to get really mad and tell everyone in Fortune that we were taking our business elsewhere. And I wouldn't blame you if you did. My mother can be a real hypocrite."

"I'm okay with all that. That's not why I called you."

"Right. You said it was about the designs?"

"I didn't give you my best work. I like to hear the love story between a couple first. Whether they've always been secretly in love, or just discovered each other. Whether it's been on and off for years, or whether suddenly something just clicked. I didn't dig deep enough with you and I'm sorry."

"That's all right. I'm not the most romantic bride."

"Sometimes the dress tells the love story, but other times it's all about the bride. *Her* story." Joanne brought out her design. "What do you think?"

There was no mistaking the shock and longing in Brenda's eyes. Her fingers swept over the dress, as if it was already made. "This is amazing. It's just what I wanted but—"

"Couldn't put into words?"

"Exactly." She blew out a breath. "Or even had the time to find the words."

"That was my job, and I feel like I'm a little late in delivering. But I didn't make this design because I wanted to beg for the job back. It just came to me, and I want you to have it. Free of charge. No hard feelings."

"No," Brenda protested, finally looking up from the sketch. "That won't work. You have a lot of wedding expenses that bast—guy left you with. You were supposed to make the dress, too, which would have been more money for you."

"Don't worry. He's already paid me back in full. And do I *look* like I'm suffering?" She held out her arms to her side.

Brenda finally appraised Joanne, from the tips of her matching yellow flats to the collar of her dress.

"You look great. I guess being a jilted bride agrees with you?"

The confusion in her gaze was palpable. Joanne held back a laugh. "Sometimes things happen to us, and sometimes they happen for us. Other times we make things happen. And I'm happier than I've ever been."

"That's really good to hear. We don't all need to give into the patriarchy and get married. If you're okay, then no one else should care how you got there." She stood. "I want this dress, but I have to pay you for the design. I also want you to sew it for me. I'm not afraid of you touching my dress, or any ridiculous superstitions. I can see right now you're not despondent and incapable of focusing on sewing the dress. I trust you. I'm pulling rank on my mom. This is *my* wedding, after all."

Impressed that she'd been right and Brenda loved the design, Joanne stood. "Just sewing it for you will go a long way to repairing my boutique's image. I still don't want you to pay me for the design, but I do have an idea if you're interested."

A few minutes later, Brenda had gone, and Joanne had secured the first part of her plan. The doorbell chimed, and this time it was her next appointment. Leah, fresh-faced and so young. Joanne envied her in some ways. Leah would marry her first love, and hopefully she had a lifetime of happiness ahead of her. In a perfect world.

"I can't wait to see my dress design."

Joanne had so many ideas for Leah that she hadn't wanted to pare them down to one. The creativity was flowing out of her as if the well had been unplugged. Released. Leah was young, but she deserved choices. And if Joanne could give them to her, she would. Good thing she'd figured out a way to do that, with Brenda's help. She'd agreed to Joanne's plan. Brenda would pay for Leah's extra designs and help out with the differential on the expensive blue material that Joanne had located… In Paris, France.

"Good news," Joanne said as she pulled out the five designs she'd created for Leah. Each one was more romantic that the next. Flowing skirts, long trains, lace and satin.

So many choices, so little time.

"I moved a few things around and was able to put you into our bigger budget plan, so I have five different designs for you."

She gaped. "I thought I couldn't afford that."

Unwilling to make Leah sound like a charity case, Joanne fudged a little. "Well, I'm having a sale."

"Oh wow! That's great." Leah took a seat, accepting the white lie.

"And I found the perfect material for your blue dress. I hope you don't mind but depending on which design you choose, you might look a little like a certain older sister from the Frozen movie." She held up air quotes.

"That's what I was going for."

Joanne sat with Leah and together they went through the designs one after the other.

Chapter Seventeen

Hud wound up running to the hardware store three times. Once to get the part he needed, the second time to return the wrong part he'd been sold and the third time to return a defective one. This was plumbing. Suddenly a simple household fix meant his entire afternoon was gone. Well, plus letting Rachel outside every time she saw a bird through the sliding glass door daring to encroach on her new territory. She'd laid claim to Jo's house as her own before he had.

When his phone buzzed in his pocket, Hud fully expected to see a text from Jo, asking about dinner. Instead, he noticed he'd somehow missed a call from the station. He slid out from under the sink, bumped his head, cursed, and dialed back.

Ty picked up the phone. "We need you here ASAP. Wildfire Ridge is burning."

Hud wasted no time. He broke speed limits getting to the station. They needed all hands on deck before the winds allowed this wildfire to rage out of control. At the station, Hud suited up, knowing he had zero time to call Jo. She understood that because of his profession, from time to time he'd get called up. But he'd bet she never imagined it would be to Wildfire Ridge. It had been many years since there'd been so much as a brush fire up there.

"When did we get the call?" Hud asked Ty, as they rode in the engine truck together.

"A few minutes ago," Ty said. "One of the guides saw flames on the summit of the ridge. We've got Cal Fire units on standby from all over the Bay Area. We'll get this under control."

"We have to. There are people up there."

A few years ago, Wildfire Ridge had been hundreds of acres of open and protected land, but now there were guides that lived in trailers who worked for Wildfire Ridge Outdoor Adventures. Not to mention Jill and Sam, who had built their dream home on leased land. He wanted to believe they could keep the fire from reaching their property. But the important thing was limiting the loss of life. Both his men and those on the ridge.

When they arrived, they got to work immediately setting up a perimeter. Fire trucks pulled in and hoses were pulled out. The flames in the distance licked and rose from the trees like arrows, sending plumes of gray smoke in the sky. Hud quickly assessed just by the wind shift that the fire was moving fast. By tonight, if they didn't control this quickly, the entire hill would be taken.

Hud noticed when Alex kissed the cross on the chain he kept around his neck, like he did before they went into any burning building. Hud didn't have a ritual. His practice was to notice every single thing around him. The wind. Heat. Ground cover. To prepare for anything. This time, they weren't entering a contained structure. They were in open land where fire could move and jump practically unimpeded. Where, in fact, it was assisted by wind and dry tinder and brush. But they'd had controlled burns on the ridge which should have held. Still, the last time he'd been up on the property he'd noticed sagebrush too close to a trailer which needed to be cleared. He'd spoken to a guide about it. One could never be too careful.

Now this.

He moved closer to the fire, the flames making their own eerie crackling sound. The crew immediately moved to post up to the defensible areas: the house, the trailers where the some of the guides lived.

"Is J.P. here?" Hud asked.

"Either here or on his way," Ty said.

"He's not ready for this."

Hud found Sam outside with his hose, defending the home.

Jesus, Mary and Joseph. Save him from these can-do Marines that believed on some level they were invincible. "Sam, I don't advise this. Let us do our job."

"I could use your help," Sam yelled. "Not sending you away."

"You see those flames over there?" Hud pointed in the distance. "That could come up on us in minutes."

"Sam!" Jill screamed from behind them, climbing off an ATV. She'd apparently been on the other side of the ridge when she saw the flames.

"Get out of here, Jill! And take Fubar with you." He opened a gate, and out came their three-legged retriever, running toward Jill.

She picked him up and turned to her fiancé. "Samuel Hawker, I'm not going anywhere without you!"

"I just finished building this house!" he yelled back.

"We'll do everything we can do save it." Hud clapped him on the shoulder. "The good news is you listened, and you have plenty of defensible space between your house and any vegetation. That gives us time. Go with Jill. She needs you and we've got this."

That seemed to reach him a little, and then he caught Jill's eyes. "Please, Sam."

"Listen to her, man."

"Please."

With that last word from his lover, Sam folded. He dropped the hose and walked toward Jill, tugging her into his arms.

The crew advanced and sprayed the gel pretreatment on the house to keep the wood siding from getting hot as quickly. But it was certainly not a complete deterrent to the fire that kept moving. It would consume several acres per hour until they managed to contain it. As the wind shifted again, they kept the hoses aimed on the fire as it got closer, a sort of useless exercise when it came to this beast. He'd never seen this kind of fire behavior before. Both the intensity and speed were alarming.

Cal Fire crews from the Bay Area pulled in and went to work.

Two hours later, the fire had spread. It moved quickly, devouring everything in its path. Trees snapped. Bushes sizzled. The sky grew cloudy, gunmetal gray and ominous. As the sun slipped down the ridge, orange flames created their own kind of light. Beautiful and deadly.

"Where's J.P.?" Hud asked.

"He's here," Alex said. "Had the hose a minute ago but the chief sent him to help defend the trailer, the one closest to the vegetation. He's got another man with him. All the guides and residents have been evacuated."

"Not much of a defensible area there."

Suddenly an explosion lit up the night sky. Hud saw a trailer consumed in flames. No. Not J.P. He was too young. Too inexperienced. Hud ran toward the blaze, taking the hose with him. Two firefighters lay on the ground, obviously having been thrown. Flames were coming off one of them. Hud tackled him, rolling him until the flames were put out.

But it was only when he saw the Probation emblem on his helmet that Hud realized it was J.P.

As she locked up the shop and headed home, Joanne heard the sirens and, as was her habit, immediately thought of Hunter.

He's fine. A siren does not always mean an accident. It certainly doesn't mean it's Hunter who's been hurt. I have to stop being so paranoid.

Still, she checked in with him via text, making up an inane excuse, asking whether or not he was due to come home next week on Monday or Tuesday after school. She knew very well it was Monday but how else would she get him to respond? He was probably playing some video game when he should be doing his homework.

Hunter: D-uh. Monday.

Whew. Next, she thought of Hud, as had also become her habit, but he wasn't on rotation today, so she wasn't too worried. Joanne headed to the super-market, where she picked up ingredients to make dinner tonight. Usually he cooked, and while he was good at it and didn't mind, she was starting to feel like a slacker in that department.

She texted him:

I'm making Chicken Florentine tonight.

She smiled and added a heart emoticon just for kicks. It wasn't until she was in the checkout line along with other customers that she saw fire trucks careening down Monterey Street, one after another, sirens blazing. They weren't Fortune Valley Fire Department trucks. She caught San Jose and… San Francisco?

Dear God.

She pulled out her phone and texted Hud again.

Hey, what's going on? Are you home?

No answer.

A customer talking to the checker said, "I heard there's a wildfire on the ridge."

"What?" Jo interrupted. "Are you *sure* about that?"

"All you have to do is walk outside and you'll see the plume coming off the ridge. Plus, that's an awful lot of fire engines we just saw."

But that didn't mean a wildfire. It could be misinformation, she told herself. Hud had told her a million times not to jump to conclusions. Rumors spread like wildfire in their small town, way more than actual wildfires did. She knew this, and yet her heart wouldn't stop trying to beat out of her chest because Hud still hadn't replied. One text with no reply was no big deal, but two? He never ignored her like this.

She drove home, ignoring the rapidly graying and smoky skies, praying, envisioning Hud's truck parked in her driveway. It wasn't there. She rushed inside, forgetting the groceries. Tools were left on the floor near the sink, which Hud would never do unless he had to leave quickly. Rachel was outside in the yard and the minute she caught sight of Joanne through the patio door she began barking like a fiend to be let in.

Joanne did so, picking up the sweet dog and cuddling her. "Who's a good girl? You're spoiled rotten, you know that? I thought dogs were supposed to love outside."

This was Hud's fault. From the beginning, he'd treated Rachel like a little princess. Even the name he'd given her. He'd coddled her and given her treats and people food when she begged. Once, he'd cooked boiled chicken and rice, because he'd heard it was good for dogs. Let her sleep on the floor in his bedroom instead of in her perfectly good kennel.

That was because, despite the fact that Hudson

Decker was as big and rugged a man as any, he had the most tender heart she'd ever known.

The tears slipped down her cheeks then and she simply held Rachel on her lap, not knowing what to do. He still hadn't responded, and he wouldn't if he were on the ridge fighting a blaze. She was helpless again just when she'd finally taken control of her life. Just when she'd finally realized how much she loved him. It wasn't fair.

When the room finally darkened to the point where she should turn on a light, Joanne continued to sit in the darkness. Rachel eventually hopped off her lap and turned in circles, knowing something was wrong. Maybe smelling it in the air.

Then someone was tapping at the front door and Joanne rushed to open it, realizing she'd left it open. The thick air outside gave the night a hazy film. Joanne nearly choked on the stench of smoke. Zoey Davis, the Sheriff's new wife who owned the pet supply store in town, stood just outside the door. For a moment, Joanne didn't know what to think.

"Ryan asked me if I'd come and get you," Zoey said tentatively. "He thought you'd be scared if he sent one of his deputies."

Oh. God. Maybe if she hadn't said *that*. "Why? What's wrong? Is it Hud?"

"We don't know for sure," Zoey said gently. "But

there was an explosion, caused by one of the trailers on the ridge, and two firefighters were badly injured and taken by ambulance. Hud might be one of them."

Chapter Eighteen

Joanne didn't say a word during the drive to the hospital. Hard to talk, when she wasn't entirely sure that she could breathe. Rachel sat on Joanne's lap, because Zoey said she'd watch her when Joanne was inside the hospital. Joanne hadn't wanted to leave her behind, because Rachel *knew*. She knew something was terribly wrong. And right now, they needed each other. They both loved the same man beyond all reason.

This isn't happening. I've been afraid of all the wrongs things. Financial instability. Winding up alone. Reckless and careless driving. What I should have been afraid of all along was Hud's profession.

When he'd applied for the Fire Department, she'd actually researched firefighter deaths and found that around 45 percent of them were caused by heart attacks. That was nearly half, so she hadn't worried too much. He ate healthy—she helped with that—and was active. She'd been fooled, lulled into a false sense of security, because Hud was so good at his job. He'd never get hurt or killed. He took precautions. Mitigated the risks they all took and was compulsive about safety on the job.

And now he loved her and would never leave her again.

I above all people know that it doesn't work that way.

Fathers died suddenly and unexpectedly. Even when they had a family they adored and even when they tried to stay healthy. Sometimes it was DNA. Family history. The cruel twist of fate. Because of her father, Joanne's mother had become a widow. A single mother. And then Joanne had been a single mother.

Something she vowed never to be again. Yet she loved Hudson Decker with all her heart.

She thought she'd changed, grown, but she still had one major character flaw. The fault of a romantic. She still saw only what she wanted to see. With Chuck, she'd wanted to see a dependable man that she could eventually grow to love. Even if she should have seen the clear signs that was *never* going to happen.

Now she desperately loved a man that she wanted to believe would never leave her. But there were different types of abandonment.

Zoey dropped Joanne at the Emergency Room entrance. "I'll park and stay with Rachel. Don't worry."

Worry? Worry? Was she joking? "I think I'm going to be sick."

Zoey squeezed Joanne's arm. "Ryan's in there somewhere, and he'll help you. He's really good at that."

These were some of the comforts of a small town. A police presence with a sheriff who was also a friend to many. Deputies who went beyond the call of duty. The sheriff's wife, who came to your house to give you news she thought you should have.

Joanne walked slowly on boneless legs, through the swinging doors of the emergency room. What was she going to ask the triage nurse? She wasn't Hud's wife. Not actual *family*. Was she going to have to call the "best friend" card here? A maniacal sound came out of her that was a cross between a giggle and a sob. She overheard someone, perhaps a reporter, say that the firefighter had been taken to the second floor and was being prepped for transfer to the burn unit in Oakland. Joanne moved faster then, running to the elevator and punching the button like her life depended on it. Hud would not leave this hospital without seeing her first. No matter what.

She stepped off the elevator and in the next moment, she saw him. He stood in the hallway wearing his turnout pants and boots, soot all over his handsome face. A small group surrounded him. Ryan Davis and some of the other deputies.

"Hud," she whispered.

Before tonight, Joanne thought she'd understood relief. Comfort. But this moment was different. This was joy and emotion wrapped up so tight in her soul that it wasn't going to be able to stay inside. He turned, and his gaze swept over her in both surprise and worry, his brow creased. In two steps, he was at her side, taking her into his arms.

He smelled like smoke and fire but thank God, by some small miracle, her Hud was alive. Breathing. Now she could breathe.

"Hud, Hud, Hud," she said over and over again, sobbing, every single fear for him slicing through her, cutting her to the quick. With it came a storm of tears she didn't know how she'd ever be able to rein in.

She was vaguely aware of being carried somewhere, and after being set down, noticed that they were in a private waiting room. Alone. A TV was set to the local news, and a reporter broadcasted that several Fortune Valley firefighters had been hurt and in critical condition. They reported the fire was now 90 percent contained after several hours and hundreds of acres lost.

"I'm okay, baby. Listen. I'm okay." Hud just kept saying the words, calmly, like he hoped she'd eventually hear him through her fog. He pulled her down in his lap and rubbed her back until her sobs slowed. "I'm not hurt. It was J.P., our probie. He's badly hurt."

"What h-happened?"

"One of the trailers on the ridge exploded. There may have been gas inside or some other type of accelerant that caught. J.P. was closest when the blast hit. I don't know much about his condition. They won't tell me because I'm not…family." Those last words were said with an edge, as though he disagreed.

"I h-heard someone downstairs say that he's being taken to the closest burn unit."

"Yeah," Hud said. "Airlifted there."

She framed his face. "I was afraid they were talking about you."

"There was a lot of confusion when it all went down. Remember I talked to you about misinformation? The chief sent me in the ambulance with the EMTs to assist. I had firsthand information on his injuries, because I…found him."

There was a note of pain and despair in Hud's voice that she'd never quite heard there before. He was hurting, too, because this man was his friend and Hud hadn't been able to save him from being terribly injured.

She buried her face in his warm neck. "I'm sure there wasn't anything you could do. You always do your best."

"And sometimes it's not good enough."

"No. Don't say that."

"It's true."

"Where's his family?"

"On their way."

Joanne was afraid to ask the next question, but she did anyway. "Do you…have to go back out there?"

He took her hand and rubbed the back of it, looking at the ground. "I might have to. I don't know yet."

When Hud was informed that J.P. had been transported to the burn unit, he finally felt able to leave the hospital. He needed a shower and some rest before he'd have to get back out there again tomorrow. Even if the fire was contained, and he believed now that it just might be, there would be more to be done. There was also some damage control to do at home. He didn't like bringing his work home with him, but this was inevitable. The look on Jo's face, like she'd seen a ghost, might stay with him for a while. She'd worried over him before, of course, but everything had changed. They both now stood to lose much more.

Never before having been in the position where a

woman mattered this much to him, he didn't know how to handle her meltdown. He'd simply comforted. Assured her. Held her while she cried. But though he was okay, J.P. wasn't, and if he realized how easily that might have been him, he could only imagine the thoughts running through Jo's head.

She'd already had enough loss and turmoil in her life. Hud didn't want to add to it, but he was never going to be the one to walk away from her again. It might be selfish, because, sure, she might be better off with an accountant or a lawyer. Theoretically that was true, but one plus one didn't equal two in this scenario. He figured that was how it worked when a man was crazy in love. He was illogical enough to believe that he'd keep himself alive because he loved her.

When he walked outside the hospital, Rachel was waiting for him too, leaping for joy to see him and licking the soot off his face. Zoey dropped them off at Jo's house. He carried Rachel and slung an arm around Jo.

She stopped suddenly in the driveway. "The groceries. I left them in the car."

He took care of that, then he picked up the tools he'd left all over the kitchen floor. Regret spiked through him. She'd walked into this scene, knowing him and realizing something had to be terribly wrong. It struck him that, had he been home instead, he wouldn't have left this evidence everywhere.

"I need a shower." He came up behind Jo and squeezed her shoulders.

"Okay," she said, not moving, not turning like she usually did to kiss him.

"Baby, this doesn't happen very often. J.P. was a rookie. Young and inexperienced." He bent and spoke soft words brushing the shell of her ear.

She seemed to accept that. "I see."

"You've already looked up the statistics of firefighters who die in the line of duty, and I think you know the odds are in my favor. Long as I keep eating plenty of fish." He turned her in his arms and tried a smile, but it fell flat when she didn't return it.

Hud headed for the shower where he soaped up and let the water pound on tired muscles, taking away some of the aches. He waited, but Jo didn't join him as he'd hoped. This was definitely out of character for her lately, when she took every opportunity to be with him.

He dried off and stepped out of the bathroom, wearing only a towel around his hips, and was encouraged when he found Jo sitting on the bed. Her bare legs dangled from the side. She'd changed into one of his tees, the Giants one. He'd bet, as usual, there was nothing underneath.

"Are you hungry? I just threw a bunch of food away because it might have been in the car too long. Can't risk it. But I was going to make Chicken Florentine tonight."

He came to her side. "I'm sorry."

"No, it's not your fault." She stood. "But if you want to eat, I'll find something. You must be so tired."

With a palm, he pushed her gently back down. "I was but I rallied after I saw you."

"You're lying." She pulled on his towel. "But I want to believe you."

He removed his towel with a smile, because apparently, he had something to prove. Then his T-shirt came off, and as he'd suspected, nothing was under it. Nothing but bare sweet smooth breasts, creamy skin and sexy curves. He made love to her, taking his time, exploring every inch of her soft warm body. Just when he'd believed he had memorized the landscape of her body, what she liked and what turned her on, he discovered something new. He sank his teeth into her earlobe and felt her muscles clench around him as she moaned and climaxed.

"Hud, oh, Hud. Baby, I love you," she said into his neck.

And that was all he needed. The rest they could work out.

A while later, Hud rolled over in bed and reached for Joanne. Her side of the bed was empty. Normally after a day like the one he'd had, he would be tossing and turning all night. But he found he never had nightmares sleeping next to Joanne.

He found her in the kitchen, back in his T-shirt, opening cabinet doors and then bending down to write on a slip of paper.

"What are you doing?" he asked groggily.

"I'm writing a grocery list. Hunter comes home Monday and I want to make sure I have everything he likes to eat in stock. Or, everything he will eat, anyway."

"Baby, it's three in the morning."

"Did I wake you? I'll try to be quiet. Go back to bed." She bent to scribble on the paper.

"Can't you do this in the morning?" He came up behind her and nuzzled her jaw.

"No, I *want* to do it now. Anyway, I couldn't sleep."

Great. He'd somehow transferred his nightmares to her. "You should have woken me up."

"Why? You need to rest in case you have to…to go back up there tomorrow." Her voice shook.

"If you're not coming back to bed with me, I'll help." He glanced at her list, picked up the pen and added corn nuts. Hunter loved those things.

"They're bad for his teeth." She crossed it off, then bit her lower lip. "I can't think of the cereal he likes that's good for him. He's been gone a month and I forgot? What's wrong with me?"

Nothing a little sleep won't cure.

He kept quiet, going through her cabinets, not

knowing what to look for, or what could be missing. But he didn't want to leave her.

She threw the pen down. "I can't do this."

"It might be easier in the morning."

But then she was crying, so he doubted she meant the list. His heart felt as though a thousand daggers had struck him at once. He took her into his arms. "Tell me."

"I love you. I don't want to lose you. Ever."

"You won't."

"Tell me the truth. Did what happen to J.P. have anything to do with his inexperience, or was it just bad luck? Being in the wrong place at the wrong time?"

He didn't want to answer the question, but she already knew. Jo was smart. Capable. She was simply waiting for him to confirm the truth so she could make her point. "Mostly…bad luck."

"I thought so. It could have been *you*, Hud."

He pressed his forehead to hers. "But it wasn't me."

"This time." She wrapped her arms around this waist. "It's one thing for *me* to lose you. But it's another for our children to lose their father. I will not raise a child without a father. And I won't do this alone again."

Shit, well, he hadn't seen that coming. He was both flattered and hurt. She was already picturing their family, with him missing. Gone.

"What are you saying?"

"I'm saying that I love you, but I don't know how to do this. I don't know how to live with this fear. I don't know if I can."

"Jo, this is my job. My calling." Frustrated, he squeezed her arms and made her face him. "What you're really saying is you don't love me enough. Isn't that what you're saying?"

"Don't love you *enough*? How much is enough? I have never loved anyone like I love you. I loved you through our break-up, your car accident, through my accidental pregnancy, and you insisting on going to war!"

She looked pissed, like he had no right to live his life the way he wanted to. Not the way she insisted. Safe, when there was no such thing. He'd made a lot of stupid choices in his life, but every one of them had led him to where he was right now.

"Want to know what's enough? I loved you *enough* to give you away at your wedding, because I thought that's what you wanted." He pulled away from her then, angry and crushed beyond words. "I should go."

He found some clothes, grabbed his turnout gear and boots and left without another word. She didn't try and stop him. He couldn't believe they were ending like this. He'd just proven to himself his own sad theory. If Jo couldn't love him enough, maybe no one could.

Some freaking wonderful day this had worked out to be. J.P. was injured and Hud had no idea how badly, or if he'd ever make a full recovery. He was young. Too young for this to happen to him. When he was outside Hud realized suddenly that he didn't have his truck, since he'd been taken by ambulance with J.P.

With nothing but early morning dark and smoky skies for company, Hud walked all the way home.

Chapter Nineteen

The next morning, Joanne woke with swollen eyes. Crying all night could do that to a woman. Hud hadn't come back. She'd fallen asleep with her phone in her hands, expecting a text all night. He didn't even have a way to get home. She'd waited for him to walk back inside once he realized, to talk some more, and... What? Promise he'd never get killed and leave her alone for the rest of her life? He couldn't make that promise and Hud would never lie to her. Promise he'd give up his job for her? She would *never* ask that of him.

He had a friend in the hospital seriously injured, had been through hell himself, and she'd chosen that night to tell him that she couldn't do this anymore. Oh God. *Hud.* She hated herself right now. She'd never *stopped* loving him, but simply taken all that love and tucked it away somewhere deep inside of her, punishing no one but herself. For years. Then she'd taken a huge risk. Told him how she felt. He'd confessed his love for her. Now she'd screwed it all up and not only missed her lover but her best friend. She'd have to call Nora and Eve to cry and bitch over her latest man disaster. Hud was her disaster, because it seemed she couldn't yet figure out how to behave in a grown-up relationship.

She got out of bed and went through her morning routine of shower, brushing teeth, putting on the outfit she'd laid out the night before. Routine. It was important. She'd have to keep busy. Maybe invite Nora and Eve over for dinner. Hunter would be home soon. She had so much to do.

Thankfully, with two dresses to make in the coming months, Joanne would be busy with work, too. Which was good, because she didn't want to feel anything. Numb was all she wanted. She was done with love, done with all this emotion and fear of loss that wrapped around her heart and squeezed tight.

Having given Nora the day off, Joanne opened up the boutique late morning and tried to keep busy until time for Leah's appointment to be measured. When she arrived, she chatted happily about the wedding venue she'd secured, and her excitement over seeing her fiancé in "a short" six months. Joanne didn't know how the young woman did it. She was terrified to love a firefighter, but loving a military man came with its own set of pressures and risks. Leah seemed immune to them.

Either that, or she was just moving forward. One foot in front of the other. Loving him anyway because what else could she do? You couldn't always choose who you loved.

Shame did everything but cloud Joanne's vision, and after Leah left, she started to close up the boutique. She'd go home and work in her sewing room, where if she burst into tears at any moment, there was no risk of being seen by anyone. But then the door to the shop opened and there stood her mother, holding two cups of coffee from The Drip.

She smiled. "It's back! I've got my pumpkin spice, and for you, a mocha latte."

Joanne burst into tears.

"What's wrong?" She set the cups down. "I'll go get you the pumpkin spice instead, but I thought you hated it."

Joanne nodded but couldn't catch her breath.

Mom rubbed her back. "Yes, I should go get you a pumpkin spice, or yes you hate it?"

Joanne shook her head and staggered over to the sofa, grabbing a box of tissues on the way. She plopped down, covering her face.

"No, I shouldn't get you a pumpkin spice, or—?"

"Hud," Joanne managed between sobs, pulling out a handful of tissues.

"Oh God, no! Don't tell me he's been hurt. Someone at The Drip this morning said a firefighter had been killed!" Ramona covered her mouth.

Why wasn't Joanne better at charades? It would come in handy right now. Instead of waving her arms around to indicate a heart being pierced and shattered into a million tiny pieces, Joanne managed to say, "N-no."

"Oh thank God!" Ramona seemed to fall more than sit on the sofa next to Joanne. "What's wrong, then? Oh no! Is it—"

To end twenty questions, the ridiculous version, Joanne held her palm up in the universal sign for Stop. Composing herself, she dabbed at her eyes. "I broke up with H-hud."

"Oh boy. Why? Did you catch him cheating on you?"

"No!" Joanne glared at her mother and clutched the box of tissues on her lap. "But thanks for that image."

"Well, what on earth could it be? You're obviously crazy about him."

"Did you ever think maybe he's not that crazy about me? Huh? Huh?"

"Actually, no. I never considered that. You were busy on your wedding day, but I got to watch Hud pace. Every time he looked at you it was with long-ing in his eyes."

"W-why didn't you say something?"

"On your wedding day?" She went hand to chest. "It was a little too late. Besides, it really was no dif-ferent than the way he's mooned after you since you were both sixteen. I really thought you saw it, too. Just figured you were ignoring it."

"Maybe I did, for a long time. Until I couldn't. And now... I'm too afraid to lose him to even try. I'm such a coward."

Her mother reached into her big hobo bag. "I think I have a book on fear in here. It's my latest bedtime reading."

"Can't you just give me the CliffsNotes version when you're done reading?" Joanne sighed.

"Fine." Ramona crossed her arms. "But is this about your father?"

"Daddy? No," Joanne said. "It's more about you."

"Me?"

"When he died, it nearly destroyed you. You struggled as a single mom, and then I struggled as a single mom. And I refuse to do that again."

"Honey, it wasn't your father's choice to leave us, any more than it was Matt's fault that you wouldn't marry him."

"It would have been a disservice to marry him when I still loved Hud."

But it was true that Joanne had been given a

choice between being a single mother and married to a man she didn't love. She'd chosen to be alone.

"A firefighter did get hurt yesterday, but not killed. He was a friend of Hud's."

"Oh, I'm sorry."

"It could have *been* Hud. And I keep seeing that. After the fire, I keep thinking that I could lose him. It's one thing to lose the man I love but another for his children to lose him. And I want more children. Hunter at least will always have Matt."

"Excuse me, but have you been given access to a crystal ball that I'm not aware of? How do you know Hunter will always have Matt? No one is guaranteed tomorrow."

"That's true, but with a dangerous job like Hud's…"

"Matt is a *pilot*, honey."

"It's true what they say about flying. Safer than driving," Joanne argued.

"And your father was a software engineer. It doesn't get much safer than that. I'm just sorry that your strongest memory is the one of me falling apart. Maybe I did in the beginning, but it didn't take me long before I realized that I'd been given a gift. All the years I had with him. A beautiful daughter with his eyes. His smile. His honor and strength. I chose a man with great character, and I'm proud that I had a child with him. I think that's some pretty choice DNA. Frankly, the genes of a hero might not be so bad, either. Besides, just think how beautiful your children would be."

"I wish I were stronger. I wish I were more like my young bride, Leah. She's not afraid to love a man in a *war* zone."

"Honey, you *are* strong. Indomitable. You need to remember that. Having a child as a teenager could have ruined your life. But you finished school, went on to study more and always put Hunter first. Single mothers are some of the toughest and bravest people in the world. You're just forgetting that because he makes you feel vulnerable."

"I love him so much."

"Then don't cut off your nose to spite your face, sweetie. Just pull up your big girl panties and *let* yourself love him. Risk it. It's always worth it, no question."

As expected, Hunter came home on Monday after school. Joanne was ready for him, and the talk she'd put off for so long. Too long.

"Hey, Mom." Hunter threw his car keys willy-nilly and they landed somewhere on the couch.

He was driving himself to school now, using his father's old truck. Nothing she could do about that. Kids grew up. It started the minute they left the womb and could no longer be protected. Not completely. Sometimes they made bad choices like drugs or smoking. She'd been lucky with her son in that respect.

Other times kids made honorable choices like joining the military. And her job was to support Hunter's choices, not fear them.

"You're going to lose those keys in the couch."

"Huh?" Hunter crunched into a crisp apple he'd picked up from the fruit basket on the coffee table.

"Never mind." He'd learn the hard way, when he couldn't find his keys and was late to class.

She was going to have to let go.

"What's for dinner?" This he asked between crunches, and due to dumb luck and being biologically connected, she was able to decipher it. Somehow.

"I ordered us a pizza."

He cocked his head. "Really? Cool!"

"Once a week we're going to splurge and eat all of the calories."

"Yeah, right." He plopped down on the couch, doubt heavy in his words.

She sat beside him. "I mean it. We should have a little fun here and there. It won't kill us."

"Yeah? Hey, where's Hud?" He looked around the room. It was the first time in a month he'd come over and not seen Hud. No wonder he'd ask about him.

"He's…probably at work." She took a deep breath and wished she could read from her prepared statement. She'd written everything down on paper but she wasn't sure she could trust herself to deliver it well. "Can we talk?"

"About what?" His eyes narrowed.

"You and me. I'm sorry if I didn't seem to care what you thought about Chuck. I should have paid more attention to the fact that you didn't like him. Somehow I thought you wouldn't like anyone I decided to get serious about."

He lifted a shoulder. "I like Hud."

She briefly closed her eyes against the ache just hearing his name caused. "Yes. I should have dated Hud."

How she would ever fix things between them, she still didn't know. But she was working on a plan and had a list started.

"Why *didn't* you?"

"That's kind of complicated. Hud didn't want to settle down for years and that's what I wanted. We also have a difficult past."

"Yeah, I know. Hud told me."

"I should have been the one to tell you, and I'm sorry."

"That's okay." He continued to crunch on his apple.

"I think I was afraid he'd hurt me again. So, I chose the safe way. Pretending I didn't still love him, but I always have. I never stopped."

He made a face. "Geesh. It's getting real sappy in here."

Joanne laughed and patted his knee. "This is the most important part for you to hear. If you still want to be a Marine, I'll support you."

At this, he set down the apple. "For real?"

"I know you can join with or without my approval, but I want you to know that it's your decision. I realize that I can't protect you. Nor is that my job anymore. You're a man and I'm going to treat you that way." She cleared her throat. "Well, at least I'll try."

"Hey, thanks, Mom." Hunter threw an arm around her shoulder.

Joanne pulled her son in the rest of the way for a hug.

She'd probably wear out her knees in another year or so, because her son was going to be a Marine.

Two days later, the fire on Wildfire Ridge had been contained. Only a small section of Sam and Jill's house had been destroyed and repairs would start soon. All the trailers were dust, however, but at least no others had exploded. No civilian had been injured. At a conservative estimate, hundreds of acres were taken. But the idea of destruction didn't really exist in nature. It would all come back given time.

Unlike buildings, some which were destroyed and never rebuilt. Rebuilding took more than the passage of time. It took hard work and money. Determination. Relationships, too, could die for a hundred different reasons, not the least of them being a man's pride. He hadn't spoken to or texted Jo in days and missed her like his right arm. Jo was his best and closest friend, and besides his parents, the only person who had loved him through careless and poor decisions.

What surprised him most was the anger he'd directed at himself. Anger and frustration that after promising himself he would fight to be with her, he'd walked out on their first serious argument. He should have turned around, gone back inside, and washed every fear away with logic. Made his case. But, tired of Jo finding reasons for them not to be together, he gave up. Which said a lot about his state of mind. Or maybe he was simply tired.

"Beer at the Silver Saddle?" Ty asked as they left the station.

"Nah, I'm not up for it."

He'd been a sad sack lately and was quite frankly getting sick of himself.

"Come on, man, I need a wingman tonight." Ty clasped his hands together, prayer-like.

"Not happening."

Ty gave up, hands tossed up. Good. Hud wouldn't need to make conversation with anyone tonight. He was in no mood for small talk.

He didn't need to be reminded that he'd had his first real date with Jo at the Silver Saddle. They'd started over that night. He'd made her wait, though that hadn't lasted long. Her pale blond hair had smelled like coconuts. She'd worn the short white dress he loved. His longing for her hadn't dissipated, and if it hadn't in ten years, he doubted it would in a few days.

What happens if I never get over her? The thought speared him; he didn't want to be alone for the rest of his life. He wanted children. A family. But he only wanted that with Jo.

He drove home, noting that in his quiet family neighborhood the Halloween decorations were already up. Lots of red, burnt orange and yellow. Pumpkins and gourds sat on porches and balconies. Witches and goblins were lawn decorations. The night was cold and crisp.

Mrs. Suarez sat in the rocking chair on her porch.

"Hey." Hud climbed out of his truck, shut the door and used the keyfob to lock it. "Everything okay with the thermostat?"

She sat with a serene smile curving her lips, nodding her head as she rocked. "Everything's fine, mijo. No te preocupa. Ella te amo. Mucho."

Hud nodded and wished once again that he'd had a passing grade in high school Spanish. All he got out of that sentence was "amo" meaning "love." He had to assume she loved the way her new thermostat was working. The magic of batteries.

"Yeah," he said, and went to unlock his front door, which was…already unlocked.

He cocked his head toward Mrs. Suarez, who was

the only one other than Jo who had a spare key to his home.

Mrs. Suarez covered her mouth and giggled.

Hud swung open the door, and that's when he saw her. She sat in the middle of the living room floor, Rachel on her lap. She'd created a picnic similar to the one he'd made for her the day she jumped in the lake after Rachel.

She wore the same short white dress he loved her in. Cowgirl boots with blue inlays. Her hair was down around her shoulders, loose and wild. She looked every bit like the beautiful girl he'd fallen for all those years ago but lost due to his own stupidity. And no matter how many gray hairs and wrinkles she would one day have, he would always see her that way.

"What's going on?" he asked.

"These are some of your favorite things." Her hand swept across the blanket.

There were two bottles of his favorite ale, a basket of oily looking French Fries from his favorite fast food place, and the king-sized cheesesteak sandwich that he loved.

She thought everything there was bad for his health.

"Does this mean…you're trying to kill me slowly?"

"No!" She laughed. "It means that you've always done so many nice gestures for me. The Bahamas re-creation. The picnic. And that's just a couple from over the years. You never forget my birthday. You never forget the anniversary that my father died. From now on, I want you to have everything you want."

"Everything I want?" He grinned.

"Moderation is the key." She stood and set Rachel down to the side.

"Hud, you have to understand. I'm a single mother and I've been stretched thin for years. I'm both strong and scared. Powerful and weak. But I recently discovered I don't really need a man in my life."

"Um, okay."

She fanned her hands. "This is coming out all wrong. What I meant to say is, I don't need a man in my life. Not just any man. I need you, Hud, because I love you. I don't love you because I *need* you. Am I making sense?"

"Yeah," he said, taking a step toward her. "Perfect sense."

"Oh, whew." She made a show of wiping at her brow. "I'm not very good at this."

"Eating crow is usually my job, so I'm going to cut you some slack." Closing the small distance between them, he took her hand, raised it to his lips.

"Actually, Jo, this goes both ways. I shouldn't have walked away that night. I said no one could or would scare me away, and then I let you do it. My mistake."

"I forgive you. Now would you please forgive me

and let me be your girlfriend again? I mean, I know that I'm a handful." She kept talking as if she had to make her case. "I can be neurotic and—"

That's when he shut down the rest of her words with a kiss. "You're all I've ever wanted."

Her eyes were shiny with unshed tears, but he knew enough to know these were the "good tears."

"You're a good man. I love that you were always such a good friend to me, I love how you help others, like Mrs. Suarez. And I love that you're a real life hero." She took a breath.

"Do you want to know how long it took me to get over you?" Her voice broke. "Never. I never got over you."

She'd had his heart long ago. Hud tugged her into his arms. Yeah, it was official. He was never going to let her go again.

Joanne gazed up at him, her green eyes shimmering. "I used to call you the fun in my life. But you're the *love* of my life, Hudson Decker, and I want to spend the rest of my life with you."

Relief flooded through him, knowing he now had everything he'd ever wanted right in his arms. He kissed the woman it seemed he'd always loved.

In his grasp he held both his past and his future rolled into one.

Epilogue

Eight months later

Joanne clutched Hud's hand as he drove them up the hill to Wildfire Ridge. It was the first time she'd been here since the wildfire, but it was for a very good reason. There would be a wedding here today.

A cause for celebration on the ridge.

"Man, it looks almost spooky up here," Hunter said from the back seat. "Bummer."

"Don't worry. It's all coming back," Hud said, and squeezed her hand.

In the distance, parts of the ridge were barren and battered. Desolate. Trees were missing or torn in half, black and charred. But here and there, nature was rallying. Sprigs of fresh green grass pushed through the damp earth. The early spring weather was mild after the blessedly long rainy season they'd desperately needed.

Thankfully, J.P. would make a full recovery. Only later had Joanne found out that Hud would receive a commendation. He'd pulled J.P. away from the blast at great risk to himself. After the initial sharp pull of shock and dismay that Hud would risk his own life to save another, Joanne had moved swiftly to pride in her fiancé. She continued to work hard every day at choosing love over fear. She'd been with Hud to see J.P. several times after the fire and he'd joked about how soon he could get back to work and kick everyone's butt at fireman's poker. Hud told him to take it easy and enjoy the rest because when he got back, he'd be working his ass off.

For now, weddings were in the air. Leah and her husband, David, had been married outside at Fortune Valley Family Ranch only a month ago. The dress had turned out beautifully, if Joanne said so herself. Both bride and groom were beautiful, young, and wearing matching blue. David, soldier rigid, holding his head high, proud to be marrying such a wonderful girl. She'd become very special to Joanne, too. They'd had long talks every time Leah had dropped by just to see how the dress was coming along. She'd started working part-time at The Drip and Joanne would see her there, too, every time she picked up a decaf soy latte.

And even though Joanne had once thought she'd be married outside too, she and Hud would be married in her mother's church. The same place her parents had married forty years ago. Hud's parents were coming out and it was going to be a big wedding. Big enough that they'd booked the hall in town to fit everyone at the reception. She was sewing her dress, too, this time. The "dream" dress. Everything seemed to take her a little longer these days, and even with Nora's help, the dress would take a few months, which was fine.

She wouldn't need it until after the baby was born.

Hud parked and came around the passenger side to open the door. He put down the stool they'd been using lately and offered Joanne his hand.

"Can you make it up the rest of the way?"

She hefted her rather large body out of the truck with Hud's assistance, stepping on the stool and then the solid ground. Good Lord, she was huge this time. Somehow unable to break with tradition, Joanne was again pregnant before marriage. It was a little embarrassing at her age, but on the other hand, good to know all parts were still present and accounted for. Still working. When she'd found out and done the math, she estimated that she'd become pregnant the night she and Hud had reconciled. In their hurry, they'd forgotten about protection. It only took once.

It was a happy surprise.

Hud was ecstatic, especially when the ultrasound had revealed a girl. He'd actually proposed to Joanne before she'd even missed her period. He'd dropped to a knee on a picnic blanket in the middle of his living room. They did love their traditions. He'd given up his house and all three of them were now living together in hers. Both he and Hunter were working on the baby's room, painting the walls pink and putting together the crib. Hunter had adjusted well, too, and was just as excited about the baby as they were. He'd been hoping for a brother, but he might still actually get one. Matt's wife, Sarah, was newly pregnant. Plus, of course, Joanne didn't think she wanted to stop at just one child with Hudson. She wanted at least one more.

Joanne lumbered up the hill toward the row of outdoor seats, Hud holding one arm, Hunter the other one. Between the two of them they nearly carried her up the hill.

"I'm good," she protested, but neither one of them gave up until she was safely seated in a chair.

Hunter went off to find a friend and Hud sat next to her, holding her hand. He carefully brushed a stray hair from her face, making her smile. Her best friend had turned out to be such a romantic. He claimed she brought it out of him, but he was so good at tender words and thoughtful gestures with her that it almost seemed like he'd been planning it all. Once she'd laughingly accused him of that, and he'd simply met her gaze, eyes deep and penetrating.

"For years."

Some days, she also regretted their wasted time. All the years they'd danced around each other but never taken the leap to be together. She might have been able to have five kids with Hud had they started early enough. When she'd told him this, he'd staged a mock heart attack, clutching his chest.

"Five kids? I'd have to work until I'm seventy."

Sure, the pregnancy hormones had made her a little emotional at times, but she was happier than she'd ever been. Determined to look forward and rarely into the past unless absolutely necessary.

The music began to play, and Jill's bridesmaids filed out, one after the other. Among them Zoey Castillo-Davis and Carly Cooper, her two best friends. Joanne had had to alter Zoey's dress when she also learned she would be five months pregnant at the time of the wedding. She walked up the aisle arm in arm with her husband, Sheriff Davis. Carly followed, holding the arm of her husband, Levi. Two more bridesmaids were arm in arm with the guides, Julian and Michael.

Heartfelt vows were exchanged, both Jill and Sam near tears. Joanne reached for the now ever-present tissues in her purse and dabbed at her eyes. Out of the corner of his eye, Hud smiled, winked and squeezed her hand. She knew what he was thinking. That would be the two of them soon enough. Professing their love for each other in front of a crowd of on-lookers. Their baby girl watching from the sidelines. She couldn't wait.

It was a beautiful wedding, Jill and Sam's spacious house on the hill as a backdrop. It stood as a reminder of how close they'd come to losing it all. But they'd rebuilt the structures, and let time and nature heal the rest. Wildfire Ridge would soon bounce back with renewed growth. Wildflowers would bloom again. Trees would grow tall.

And Joanne would be here to witness it all coming back, right next to her handsome firefighter hero.

* * * * *

Don't miss the first two books in the
Wildfire Ridge miniseries:

More than One Night
Reluctant Hometown Hero

Available now from Harlequin Special Edition!

And look for more great second chance romances:

For the Twins' Sake
By Melissa Senate

Daughter on His Doorstep
By Teresa Southwick

Her Homecoming Wish
By Jo McNally

Available wherever Harlequin Special Edition
books and ebooks are sold!

#2755 FORTUNE'S GREATEST RISK
The Fortunes of Texas: Rambling Rose • by Marie Ferrarella
Contractor Dillon Fortune wasn't always so cautious. But as a teenager, impulse led to an unexpected pregnancy and a daughter he was never allowed to know. Now he guards his heart against all advances. If only free-spirited spa manager Hailey Miller wasn't so hard to resist!

#2756 THE TEXAN TRIES AGAIN
Men of the West • by Stella Bagwell
Taggert O'Brien has had a rough few years, so when he gets an offer for the position of foreman at Three Rivers Ranch, he packs up and leaves Texas behind for Arizona. But he was not prepared for the effect Emily-Ann Broadmore—a barista at the local coffee shop—would have on him or his battered heart. Can he set aside his pain for a chance at lasting love?

#2757 WYOMING SPECIAL DELIVERY
Dawson Family Ranch • by Melissa Senate
Daisy Dawson has just been left at the altar. But it's her roadside delivery, assisted by a mysterious guest at her family's ranch, that changes her life. Harrison McCord believes *he* has a claim to the ranch and is determined to take it—but Daisy and her newborn baby boy have thrown a wrench in his plans for revenge.

#2758 HER MOTHERHOOD WISH
The Parent Portal • by Tara Taylor Quinn
After attorney Cassie Thompson finds her baby's health is at risk, she reluctantly contacts the sperm donor—only to find Woodrow Alexander is easily the kindest, most selfless man she's ever met. He's just a biological component, she keeps telling herself. He's *not* her child's real father or the husband of her dreams...right?

#2759 DATE OF A LIFETIME
The Taylor Triplets • by Lynne Marshall
It was just one date for philanthropist and single mom Eva DeLongpre's charity. And a PR opportunity for Mayor Joe Aguirre's reelection. Giving in to their mutual attraction was just a spontaneous, delicious one-off. But as the election turns ugly, Joe is forced to declare his intentions for Eva. When the votes are counted, she's hoping love wins in a landslide.

#2760 SOUTHERN CHARM & SECOND CHANCES
The Savannah Sisters • by Nancy Robards Thompson
Celebrity chef Liam Wright has come to Savannah to rebrand a local restaurant. And pastry chef Jane Clark couldn't be more appalled! The man who impulsively fired her from her New York City dream job—and turned her life upside down—is now on her turf. And if the restaurant is to succeed, Liam needs Jane's help navigating Savannah's quirky culture...and their feelings for each other.

HSECNM0320

Daisy went over to the bassinet and lifted out Tony,
cradling him against her. "Of course. There's lots
more video, but another time. The footage of what the
ranch looked like before Noah started rebuilding to the
day I helped put up the grand reopening banner—it's
amazing."

Harrison wasn't sure he wanted to see any of that. No,
he knew he didn't. This was all too much. "Well, I'll be
in touch about that tour."

*That's it. Keep it nice and impersonal. "Be in touch"
was a sure distance maker.*

She eyed him and lifted her chin. "Oh—I almost
forgot! I have a favor to ask, Harrison."

Gulp. How was he supposed to emotionally distance
himself by doing her a favor?

She smiled that dazzling smile. The one that drew him like nothing else could. "If you're not busy around five o'clock or so, I'd love your help in putting together the rocking cradle my brother Rex ordered for Tony. It arrived yesterday, and I tried to put it together, but it has directions a mile long that I can't make heads or tails of. Don't tell my brother Axel I said this—he's a wizard at GPS, maps and terrain—but give him instructions and he holds the paper upside down."

Ah. This was almost a relief. He'd put together the cradle alone. No chitchat. No old family movies. Just him, a set of instructions and five thousand various pieces of cradle. "I'm actually pretty handy. Sure, I can help you."

"Perfect," she said. "See you at fiveish."

A few minutes later, as he stood on the porch watching her walk back up the path, he had a feeling he was at a serious disadvantage in this deal.

Because the farther away she got, the more he wanted to chase after her and just keep talking. Which sent off serious warning bells. That Harrison might actually more than just like Daisy Dawson already—and it was only day one of the deal.

Don't miss
Wyoming Special Delivery *by Melissa Senate,*
available April 2020 wherever
Harlequin Special Edition books and ebooks are sold.

Harlequin.com